A TOWN
CALLED MALICE

ALSO BY ADAM ABRAMOWITZ

Bosstown

A TOWN
CALLED MALICE

ADAM
ABRAMOWITZ

THOMAS DUNNE BOOKS
ST. MARTIN'S PRESS
NEW YORK

This is a work of fiction. All of the characters, organizations, and events portrayed in this novel are either products of the author's imagination or are used fictitiously.

THOMAS DUNNE BOOKS
An imprint of St. Martin's Press

A TOWN CALLED MALICE. Copyright © 2019 by Adam Abramowitz. All rights reserved. Printed in the United States of America. For information, address St. Martin's Press, 175 Fifth Avenue, New York, N.Y. 10010.

www.thomasdunnebooks.com
www.stmartins.com

Designed by Omar Chapa

Library of Congress Cataloging-in-Publication Data

Names: Abramowitz, Adam, author.
Title: A town called Malice : a novel / Adam Abramowitz.
Description: First Edition. | New York : St. Martin's Press, 2019. | "Thomas Dunne Books."
Identifiers: LCCN 2018037705 | ISBN 9781250076304 (hardcover) | ISBN 9781466887701 (ebook)
Subjects: LCSH: Gangsters—Massachusetts—Boston—Fiction. | Bicycle messengers—Fiction. | GSAFD: Mystery fiction. | Suspense fiction.
Classification: LCC PS3601.B7312 T69 2019 | DDC 813'.6—dc23
LC record available at https://lccn.loc.gov/2018037705

Our books may be purchased in bulk for promotional, educational, or business use. Please contact your local bookseller or the Macmillan Corporate and Premium Sales Department at 1-800-221-7945, extension 5442, or by email at MacmillanSpecialMarkets@macmillan.com.

First Edition: March 2019

10 9 8 7 6 5 4 3 2 1

With love for Sam and Antonia

There is no commandment to be consoled.

—NAHMANIDES

A TOWN
CALLED MALICE

PROLOGUE

The dream plays like clockwork, before the birds collect their sheet music for the day, a high ghost moon steeping toward a weak-tea dawn: June in Boston and the living is sleazy as Gus Molten cruises his black Cannondale through the neon gauntlet of Washington Street. Hot for so early in the season, mirage hot, the sledgehammer of another Boston summer falling early, ushering in a new Season of Living Dangerously.

Two fifty-four in the morning, to be exact; the bars almost an hour empty, the short strip of the Combat Zone still bustling like the floor of some illicit stock exchange, trading heavy.

Watchu need, bro? Watchu lookin' for?

The usual. On each side of the street, thin track stars lope about in two-piece Fila, Adidas, and Gianni Versace running suits, Olympic gold chains looped around their necks, dull dollar signs and the threat of instant violence fixed in glassy predatory eyes. Home Sweet Home as Gus hooks a right onto a deserted LaGrange, the yo-blow-yo-smoke-yo-pussy mantra echoing off the corners, ringing sweet as a lullaby, familiar and warm to his ears.

He glides the Cannondale to the curb, nurses the brakes to a full stop before an outdoor foyer of black iron bars roughly the size of a holding cell; the entrance, as always, reeking of beer and piss, the floor littered with the spill of fast-food containers and shattered green and brown glass, street diamonds glittering in a shaft of sympathetic moonlight. Above the foyer a broken electric sign reads, GO D TIM S, the hours midnight to 2 A.M. shaded on its shattered clock face. A few doors down, the Glass Slipper is quiet except for the schizophrenic wink of its pink neon illuminating the cartoonish figure of a large-breasted blonde clutching the strap of a sparkling stiletto-heeled shoe brick-painted above its entrance.

She looks nothing like Cinderella.

From where he stands, Gus can hear the rumbling of muscle cars—Thunderbirds, Chargers, Camaros—turning the corner off Kneeland, prowling the block for hookers and late-night thrills; watches for a moment as they wheel up Washington; sets his eyes to blank as a two-tone cruiser peels off toward him and passes out the other end onto Tremont, its strobes spinning blue ghouls into the night. He jangles a set of keys from his messenger bag and slips one into the gate's lock, the bolt giving way with a heavy click like the sound of a hammer on a gun being cocked.

The man comes out of a darkened doorway, walking unsteadily with his head down, his right hand nursing a brown paper bag held close at his side. When Gus turns for his bike the man is right behind him, the bag-hand extended high like he's offering him a drink.

Strange.

It's not like Gus to miss someone standing in the doorway like that. Sure, it's late and dark, but he's normally cautious about checking the street for anything out of whack, any dangers beside the usual sharks and bottom feeders the neighborhood—if you could call it that—draws. Maybe his carelessness has something to do with that reading in Harvard Square the other day, all that "moon in Venus and Uranus" shit messing with his head. Maybe all the cash he's pulling making him cocky. Big-Time Hood. Seen too many Scorsese movies. Maybe he's stoned.

Whatever.

Gus opens his mouth to say something when the first bullet takes out his front teeth, pings off the metal stud in his tongue, and exits out the back of his neck, severing the spinal column. The foyer door swings open as Gus buckles backward, but not before two more flashes catch him, the reports muffled like firecrackers set off under a pillow; not even loud enough to stir the rats from their busywork.

The man's hand bursts into flame.

Gus slams against the inside door and slides down, blood mixed with piss and little chunks of his last thoughts dripping onto his shoulders.

The cruiser doesn't stop for a closer look at him until the sun's wedged itself into the sky. Except for the large pool of deep crimson that seeps from under the bars, over the sidewalk, and into the street, he looks like just another drunk sleeping the hard night away.

They have to torch the gate to collect him; it had been locked with his Kryptonite. Of course by then the Cannondale is gone, as is his pack, leaving only the sidewalk stamped with red footprints that read: Nike, Fila, Reebok, and Adidas.

And one long strip of bicycle tread.

ONE

I'm in the middle of my set at Nick's Comedy Stop on Warrenton Street when Homicide Detective Batista Wells walks in with a beautiful woman on his arm. I haven't seen Wells since I'd been subpoenaed to testify in front of the grand jury that eventually brought indictments against Darryl Jenkins on money laundering and tax evasion charges. Detective Wells and his partner, Brill, would have preferred murder charges but the evidence wasn't there for that; there were plenty of bodies, my friend and business partner Gus Molten among them, but none they could rightly pin on Darryl.

I had cleaned myself up for the court date, which took some doing, bought a pair of polished Camper wing tips, donned a suit and a tie—though not nearly as nice as Wells's; he's the Boston Police Department's sartorial torchbearer—and invoked my Fifth Amendment rights, sparing everybody the agreed-upon lies the Boston Police Department and the FBI had concocted in the wake of Devlin McKenna's bloody return to his former killing grounds.

Darryl is nearly halfway through his four-year bid at MCI

Concord, a medium-security prison situated directly across from the Massachusetts State Police barracks on Route 2, within easy driving distance of Boston by way of Cambridge. I'm not sure if this proximity to the city makes it easier or harder for Darryl to do his time, the shimmering downtown and new harbor skyline visible through the bars of his cell working as a tease or inspiration as he counts down the days toward his release; it's not what we talk about when I visit him if we end up talking at all. Sometimes we just sit staring at each other across the chipped and scarred visitation table, elbows down as if holding phantom cards, our collective history piled like chips between us, searching for a tell in the other's eyes.

After the grand jury had its day I gave my suit to a longtime homeless neighbor of mine by the name of Albert who used to camp out in the loading docks of the industrial loft on Thayer Street I'd been evicted from in the months before Darryl's trial, when I was still recuperating from gunshot and stab wounds at Beth Israel hospital. Albert, as is his way, wasn't much on giving thanks, and accepted the handout blank-faced before turning the collar out, peeking at the label for a recognizable brand name. Then he inquired after my shoes.

"What good's a suit without shoes, Zesty?" Albert mumbled through the catacombs of his beard, crumbs tumbling like ashen snow to the sidewalk. To look at Albert you'd never imagine the suit would fit him, but in truth he was a homeless onion: Peel back the layered T-shirts and sweaters, and we were about the same size.

"You going someplace, Albert?" I said.

"Gotta look presentable. Neighborhood done changed." Albert leaned in conspiratorially, his hot breath an open oven of baking compost. "I'm trying to blend in, see, lay low. Where you living now? I don't see you around much no more."

"I'm renting a closet on Union Park," I told him.

"Oh." Albert took a moment to consider the implications of that address. "So you right in the thick of it. How you like it?"

When I had moved onto Thayer Street it had no lighting, the road was dirt, mud when it rained, the loading docks and sidewalks littered with condoms, crack vials, spent needles, and trash from contractors who would dump their waste at all hours of the night. The Pine Street Inn, the city's largest homeless shelter, on Harrison Avenue, was within view of my windows. Now that the Big Dig's been completed, the artists, musicians, and misfits who had inhabited the rough industrial lofts either evicted or bought out, this once neglected outer edge of the South End rebranded as a historic district, Thayer Street has been reborn with art galleries, a cobblestone path, well-lit sidewalks, high-end restaurants, and condominiums with sand-blasted redbrick exteriors that start in the seven figures.

On Union Park it's bumper-to-bumper BMW and Subaru sedans, the sidewalks clogged with eight-hundred-dollar ergonomic carbon-fiber baby strollers and long-limbed mommies tucking yoga mats trailing the ever-present honeysuckle scent of a perfume that might as well be called Eau de'Entitlement.

"It's different," I told Albert and left it at that.

"They gonna let you stay?"

It was a fair question. "Long as I got shoes," I told him.

Detective Wells is wearing dark indigo Levi's and a fitted Harris Tweed blazer over a gray Converse All Star T-shirt. From the stage I can't see his shoes, but it's a safe bet they cost more than box seats in Fenway. The woman with him has long dark hair that spills out over her shoulders and looks like a million dollars in a little black dress that goes well with everything, even Detective Wells.

"So," I say, stumbling into my delivery, thrown off by the detective's presence. "Seems the Russians just started their own

version of the NBA, successfully bypassing the American fran-
chising fee. Their slogan?" Pause. "Nothing but Nyet."

A fat man who has the entire front row of tables to himself
laughs out loud and I feel the sudden urge to jump offstage and
hug him. There are about twenty-five people in the club on this
Sunday night. Nearly half of them are aspiring comics and fellow
comedy workshop classmates participating in tonight's performance hosted by Hank Aroot, a veteran New York City comic
and former Boston transplant. Hank teaches the stand-up class
twice a year under the auspices of Emerson College on Commonwealth Avenue; for a few of us, this is the first time onstage. It's
ludicrous. I'm actually paying money to fail.

"Nothing but Nyet," I repeat as Detective Wells cracks a smile
in the darkness, whispering something to the woman, who laughs
with her eyes and covers her mouth with her hand. "Which co-
incidentally also happens to be the title of Vladimir Putin's auto-
biography."

The workshop students laugh out loud in an exaggerated
show of support but I've lost the fat man in the front row. Could
he not know who Putin is? I take a deep breath, resist the urge to
explain the joke to him, and move on. I can feel my heart hammering inside my chest, a drop of sweat trickling its way down
my temple past my ear. The red light facing the stage blinks on,
signaling that I have about thirty seconds left before Hank will
come bounding onstage to pry the microphone from my cold
clammy hands. Death by Spotlight, Hank calls it. To be avoided
at all costs.

I'm a bike messenger by trade, a job that places me in mortal
danger every time I slip my size-ten Adidas into a set of toe clips,
and two years ago I'd narrowly survived a collision with a gold
Buick, the first link in a chain of events that culminated with me
staring down the barrel of a gun held by Boston's most infamous

crime boss. I was scared then, but I'm terrified now, squinting into the hot stage lights; which probably doesn't speak much for my level of intelligence. Or sanity. McKenna ended up shooting me twice, one bullet narrowly missing my spine, but not getting a laugh on my last joke hurts nearly as much. There's got to be something *very* wrong with me.

Out of the corner of my eye I catch Hank in the wings twirling his hand in a circular motion, telling me to get on with it.

"So, uh, I started taking a pottery class recently, really enjoyed it. It's relaxing. Creative. But after doing it a few times I started getting nervous because everyone knows pottery's a gateway art to, like, some of the harder stuff. Stained glass. Mixed media. Oils . . . And I didn't want to get hooked."

Crickets.

Hank comes bounding onstage and mugs me for the microphone. "Gateway art!" he says in an inexplicable and exaggerated Irish lilt, Riverdancing with his thumbs under his armpits, which cracks everybody up. My joke but Hank kills with it. "Zesty Meyers, everybody. Nice job, Zesty."

There's a smattering of polite applause as I leave the stage and when I pass the fat man he tosses a couple of beer nuts into his mouth and opines around them, "Don't quit your day job, kid."

I back up and plunk myself uninvited into an empty seat beside him. "Putin's the prime minister of Russia," I tell him.

"Yeah, so?"

"That joke's funny."

"Maybe. But your delivery was terrible."

Onstage Hank is saying, "Our next comic is coming to you from . . . her mother's vagina. Well, not *directly*! Please give a warm round of applause for Caitlin—"

"My delivery?"

"It's practice is all, don't get offended." The fat man shrugs into his shirt pocket and hands me a card that reads, Otto Helms:

NICK'S COMEDY STOP, printed in dark black letters. There's no phone number printed below his name. No Web address. It's a card from the Dark Ages; by all rights it should be etched on stone. "When you're ready. What do you do for day work, kid?"

I tell him and dig out a card of my own, a winged Mercury on a bicycle trailing flames from his rear wheels. "You could actually say I specialize in delivery."

"Now that's funny." Otto Helms pockets the card without looking at it, his attention firmly back on the stage. "Will you look at the rack on this broad."

I look up at my classmate Caitlin. Being the observant type, I'd already sussed out that her rack, as Helms referred to it, is largely the product of a miracle push-up bra and I've heard her tepid material before, which centers around her former marriage to a stockbroker and her current penchant for serial dating policemen. Still, she is easy to look at and I have to give her credit, the stage doesn't seem to make her nervous like it does most of us, the spotlight bathing her in an enervating glow, which she uses to full effect.

"Why are you here? Isn't this a little like bird-dogging the minor leagues?" I flick Otto Helms's card loudly with my index finger, momentarily drawing his eyes off Caitlin's chest.

"Just killing time," Helms says. "Like you kill punch lines."

"Ouch."

"Yeah, try being more funny. Do you mind? I wanna listen to this."

The entire class is slated to perform tonight and Caitlin's last up before we take a short break to give people a chance to hit the bathroom, maybe smoke a few cigarettes outside to calm their jangling nerves. I wasn't going to approach Detective Wells—he's as entitled to a night out without heckling as the rest of us—but he waves and kicks out a seat for me to join them. I amble over but stay standing. It's not that I don't like Wells, but his date is even prettier up close, gold flecks in deep brown eyes, and I've been told that I have a problem with staring so I'm inclined to keep this visit short and leer-free.

"Anitra Tehran." Wells pretends not to notice when I slide the chair back in. "I'd like you to meet Zesty Meyers."

"*The* Zesty Meyers?" His date leans back slightly in her chair as if I were growing taller on the spot. She extends her ring-free hand for me to shake; her name is familiar to me for some reason, only I can't place it.

"I suppose," I say. "Depending on what the 'the' stands for. Detective, how are you?"

"I'm good, Zesty. I was just starting to regale Anitra here with how we met, but she already seems to know that story. Among others."

This is usually the point in a conversation where my defenses go up. Most people who think they know something about me or my family usually start by referring to my mother and her role in the 1986 robbery of the Allston branch Bank of Boston, in which a retired police officer and bank manager were killed. After which my mother disappeared into an underground network of disposable aliases and vacant safe houses, the narrative of my family's history written in blood until last year's revision, when I learned a more complicated truth. Not that it turned out to be easier to bear than the fiction.

I look at Wells, who keeps his blue-green eyes neutral but observant. Not much escapes Wells's notice; it's one of the things that makes him a sharp detective and could make him a solid poker player if he ever chose that route.

"I'm sorry." Anitra Tehran swivels from me to Wells. "Did I say something wrong?"

"He's touchy about his family." Wells dispenses an elaborate shrug.

"Why should he be any different?" Anitra Tehran smiles an

apology and I notice a tiny mole at the corner of her left eye, the effect like an exclamation mark on her beauty.

Walk away, Renée, I tell myself. *Pillar of salt.*

"Would you want your family's history plastered on the front pages for a week?"

"Wouldn't sell as many papers," Wells says.

"You're a reporter." I snap my fingers, Anitra Tehran's name finally catching up to my brain.

"I am." Anitra stretches out the words, narrowing her eyes toward Wells.

"Keep me out of this." Wells holds up his hands in mock surrender. "I'm just here for the elusive laughs."

"You write for the *Globe*."

"I do." Ms. Tehran beams me perfect teeth before turning back to Wells with a quizzical look on her face.

"I didn't know he could read." He winks at her. "Plus, didn't I tell you not to dress like Lois Lane?"

"I've seen your byline. I liked that series you ran on the Midnight Basketball League," I tell her.

"I had lots of help, but thanks. Too bad not everybody felt the same way."

That was because the articles were far more than just puff pieces about the citywide league that had originally been formed to keep at-risk youth off the streets during the summer witching hours, when gun violence spikes in the densely populated and ever-shrinking communities of color. Ms. Tehran's reporting exposed something more sinister: rosters infiltrated by the gangs themselves, teams sponsored with drug money, coaches with long criminal histories, and a complicated snake pit of gambling and money laundering that ensnared a rising star in the state senate who had spearheaded the outreach and public funding for the project.

"So, is Detective Wells, like, your department-issued bodyguard?" I say.

"What makes you think I need one?"

"Where do I apply?" Wells extends his glass between his legs to avoid getting dripped on as Anitra Tehran deposits her elbow into his ribs. "Actually, it's beyond bodyguard status already, Zesty. Anitra's just entered the witness protection program. I figured what're the chances of getting spotted *here* on a Sunday night?"

"Pretty high if you introduce her to everyone."

"Good point. I'll work on that."

"This a new direction for you, Zesty?" Anitra indicates the stage with a tilt of her head.

"Not according to Detective Wells and his partner," I say.

"You got that right."

"Batista," Anitra chides Wells playfully, nudging his leg under the table. "Be civil."

"Define 'civil.'" Detective Wells wolf-grins at her; curls his lips to a snarl in my direction as I silently mouth *Ba-tis-ta*.

"Right now stand-up's just a hobby." I turn back to Anitra Tehran's question. "But I'm a glutton for punishment, so who knows. What brings the two of you here to amateur night?"

I know it's not to see me because the only recognizable name featured on the marquee belongs to Hank, who at the moment is standing to the side of the stage chatting with Otto Helms, Hank's default smile sliding off his face as Helms explains something to him with animated hands and an aggressive belly. I can't make out what the fat man is saying but Hank doesn't seem to like it, his face turning red as Helms spins away.

"Blind luck." Wells raises his eyebrows, points to the stage where Hank's resumed his emcee spot.

For a fat man, Otto Helms moves nimbly up the side aisle toward the rear of the club, Hank eyeing him only momentarily as he launches into the second half of the show and the next introduction.

"Ladies and gentlemen," Hank's smile is firmly back in place, the deal with Helms not enough to knock him off his professional perch, "I'd like to introduce to you a really funny and imaginative comic, but unfortunately I'm stuck with this guy. Please give a warm welcome to . . ."

By the time the show wraps up I'm sitting at the back bar sipping a Coke, my classmates buzzing happily, chatting up the bartender and cocktail waitress, their voices a little too loud, throwing back drinks at a hurried clip, washing down the excess energy of their performance, exulting in killer bits while lamenting blown timing and fumbled punch lines. In the corner, Caitlin jots loose lines onto a cocktail napkin, hoping to mine them into comic gold.

As soon as the club empties Hank will gather us to review our performances, provide some feedback on our material and delivery, suggest things to work on if we really want to improve and survive in front of a paying audience.

Anitra Tehran flashes me a wave as she goes out the door, Detective Wells right behind her, his hand momentarily riding the small of her back before grabbing her roughly around the neck and throwing her to the ground as the open front door explodes inside its frame, a waterfall of glass cascading to the sidewalk.

Someone in the club screams and everybody hits the floor as Wells dives on top of the reporter, grabbing for his ankle holster under his Levi's. I hear the outboard throttle of a motorcycle open up, the sound of a broken bottle shattering on the sidewalk, followed by the soft oxygen pop of ignition as bright orange flames illuminate the window and climb up Wells's jacket as, from his knees, he arcs from right to left tracking a moving target with the small black gun he's pried from his calf.

As I reach the door Wells is scrambling to his feet, the flames riding up his sleeve like a lit fuse, the gun, unfired, held rigidly in two hands, shielding the fallen reporter behind him. I catch a glimpse of a lime green motorcycle as it scars the corner onto

Tremont Street and then hurl a pitcher of soda over Wells's shoulder, a hissing balloon of black smoke punching him in his face, causing him to stagger backward.

Anitra Tehran looks shaken: There's glass in her hair, blood from a cut on her sculpted right cheekbone and elbows and knees from being thrown to the sidewalk, one of her stylish high heels broken and lost in the crush of glass. One strap to her dress is off her shoulders but it looks like she'll live to write another day.

Someone inside the club has started to spray the flames with an extinguisher, killing the flames before they spread. On the sidewalk, most of the gasoline from the homemade bomb has already burned off harmlessly, only blackening the curb. Coal-faced, Wells rips at the fabric of his smoldering jacket, muttering curses in my direction.

"Christ, who's your tailor, DuPont Chemical?" I help Tehran to her feet. "You do know wool shouldn't burn like that, right?"

Wells abandons his alterations, sheds the jacket and flings it into the narrow street. "You get a look at them?" He coughs into the crook of his elbow.

"Probably only what you saw."

"Tell me."

"Two black jackets, black helmets. Jeans. Kermit the Frog bike. A Honda, maybe?"

"So, fucking nothing." Wells holsters the gun back at his ankle.

"Nothing but nyet," I try for the third time tonight.

I hear Anitra Tehran chuckle behind me.

"Thank you very much. I'll be here all week." Actually, that's not true. The shows will move to different venues throughout the week before culminating upstairs at the Hong Kong in Harvard Square, where one of us will be chosen for our first paying slot. I'd assist in dusting Tehran off but my hands can't be trusted around that many curves so I let her shake herself out, do my best to avert my eyes.

Detective Wells surveys the scene, pulls his wallet and cell phone from his pants pocket. Shards of glass from Anitra Tehran's dress tinkle like wind chimes as they dance on a square of burnt-toast pavement. As Wells punches numbers, a blue and white cruiser with its siren wailing and blue lights flashing turns sharply off Tremont, its side-mounted lamp finding him in its blinding glare.

"Well, look on the bright side, Zesty." Wells squints through a half grin into the light from the squad car, shouldering the phone and letting the wallet fall open to reveal his gold detective shield. "Least now you can say you're not the only one who bombed tonight."

"For *real*?" I look to Anitra Tehran hoping for a measure of support, but get only a reporter's objective view.

"It must be the spotlight." She uses my shoulder to balance herself, snapping off the heel of her good shoe to match the other flat. "I've noticed it does things to people."

TWO

Sunshine comes grudgingly to the alley off Berkeley Street, a dented box of tepid light tumbling through the open door of my shared office, an overpriced former coal room in a Back Bay brownstone. On the cusp of darkness is the way Martha, our collective's do-all dispatcher, likes it, the better to work her Victorian pale year-round.

"Tan lines," Martha once told me, deep in shade beneath a sun hat that doubled as a landing pad for Black Hawk One, "are for morons and dermatology waiting rooms."

Personally, I liked cultivating a good tan but knew better than to argue the point. As undeniably smooth and unblemished as Martha's skin is, her tongue tends to be sharper than sriracha on an open wound. I've learned the hard way (as I do most things) to pick my battles judiciously.

"A watched phone never rings," I greet her, bobbing and weaving like a middleweight; from memory dodging the severed pipe ends of some ancient heating system that still jut out from various points in the low basement ceiling. When we moved into the space a few years back we'd covered these protrusions with foam rubber and spray-painted them in bright Day-Glo colors, but at some point Martha had removed the padding and filed the ends into spikes, an unspoken message that the sunken lower portion was her domain—enter at your own risk.

I take my chances only because I've come bearing gifts, a bag of chocolate-covered espresso beans, which I drop on her desk, Martha, unlike me, preferring her caffeine in crunchable form. Come to think of it, Martha prefers most things in crunchable form, having long ago perfected the art of talking and chewing at the same time. Where all the calories go, I couldn't tell you. I've yet to see Martha break a sweat, but from one year to the next she stays thinner than my credit score.

"Aren't you a doll." Martha passes the unopened bag under her nose and squeezes me a tight smile. "Wow, and the good stuff, too."

Above her, an overhead tangle of Christmas and chili pepper lights bathe her in a weak but demonic glow. It's only when my eyes adjust to the dimness that I realize the smile had already filtered from her lips.

"Don't start," I warn her, plopping to the couch, unmooring

a black avalanche of overstuffed contractor bags that slide over my lap and onto the floor.

If Martha *were* to start, she'd likely begin with the homily that those who fail to learn from their past are doomed to repeat it, followed by a detailed recitation of all the times I've tasted Boston pavement during the course of my duties. She'd then remind me that the last of these helmet-free crashes has left me with a thick crescent scar cutting through my right brow and a rare neurological condition that sometimes causes white-hot static to build up between my ears, painful prelude to an ever-changing playlist of songs that tumble off the airwaves into the silver fillings of my teeth.

But here's one of many great things about living in the Hub of the Universe: It's an academic, research-happy city always pining for those rarest of lab rats. So despite a health plan consisting of a first-aid kit, an ever-ready joint, and a bottle of Jameson, I've had the good fortune to be poked, prodded, and scanned by some of the world's leading neurologists for my condition, the end result being an official diagnosis of *musicis phantasiae,* which, in the literal sense, translates to musical hallucinations.

For all intents and purposes, I house an old-school jukebox between my ears, my brain, without much warning, prone to dropping needle-scarred 45s on a turntable with the volume cranked to Early Hearing Loss.

It's a pretty rare affliction, generally limited to those who've had the odds-defying misfortune of being struck by lightning or suffering some sort of massive right-brain hemispheric stroke. And the symptoms vary greatly. Through the course of my therapies I've met a plumber who hasn't picked up a wrench in a decade, his days filled with a feverish attempt to complete Bach's unfinished *Art of Fugue* on harpsichord. I've also played countless hours of waiting-room cribbage with a librarian who can't stop singing 1950s-era show tunes, and pulled dozens of bong hits on the roof deck of a Louisburg Square brownstone belonging to a lightning-struck surgeon who's become obsessed with mastering the entire guitar score of Pink Floyd's *Dark Side of the Moon,* though she never previously played an instrument.

In comparison, I've made out like a bandit, my only complaint being a jolt of high-pitched frequency that leads into the auditory equivalent of an upturned hornets' nest between my ears, painful opening act to my ghostly DJ dropping his two-ton needle on the record. The timing of these musical hallucinations are unpredictable, too, but there's no denying my Head-Spin DJ kicks ass, rotating a killer collection of vintage soul, New Wave pop, and home-grown Boston rock and roll between my ears; not a weak track in the mix.

In the last couple of days I've surfed a repaved Harrison Avenue on the cold-wave electronic pop of the November Group's "Shake It Off," scattered a group of Japanese tourists wandering the Freedom Trail to Ministry's "I Wanted to Tell Her," and battled the hurricane crosswinds of Milk and Summer streets to a live version of Joy Division's "Something Else"; not quite fast enough to accommodate pedestrians intent on committing suicide by messenger, but getting there, rounding my way back into shape again after a long recovery.

I'm told there's not enough medical precedent to predict if this soundtrack inside my head will ever go away, but I've grown accustomed to the songs and figure it's a reasonable price to be paid for surviving. At least until Pandora gets wind and sends me a bill.

Unfortunately, the fact that these musical hallucinations resulted from a crash that *wasn't* an accident only bolsters Martha's argument that eschewing a helmet on Boston's twisted streets easily constitutes the most dangerous act of vanity ever recorded. Only my hair's grown out past my shoulders again, my flying locks as much my calling card in this city as anything else, and I'm not about to cover up now.

"All I was *go-ing* to say," Martha, satisfied her point's been delivered, resumes full-on mastication, "is you look like crap. You having those dreams about Gus again?"

"It's that obvious?"

"Only to me, baby." Martha's voice softens. "You still haven't talked about this with anyone?"

"Does the cat count?"

"Only if he's billing by the hour."

"Then no." What he charges me is a daily ration of kibbles and the consistent shredding of my most valuable possessions. If my cat ever got picked for *The Price Is Right,* I swear he'd kill. And then drag his prizes home and claw them to pieces.

"Seriously, Martha, can we drop this?" I spring from the couch, tired of rebuffing the repeated advances of the garbage bags. "Gus wasn't my fault. I get it. I just haven't shaken the dream yet."

What I don't say is that since I've recovered from the crash and my near-death experience with McKenna, I've actually found myself becoming *more* reckless on my bike, taking even greater risks on Boston's nonsensical streets. Almost as if inviting that kiss of the windshield, the stiff caress of the flung-open car door. I don't carry a death wish, but maybe I've subconsciously adopted Neil Young's *better to burn out than fade away* credo, my father's continued decline into Alzheimer's a constant reminder that my genetic road is paved with potholes large enough to swallow my memories whole. Dark thoughts, I know, but after all, it is Monday.

"Fine, then let's talk business." Martha sweeps her arm toward a short wall of boxes beyond the couch. "You told me you were going to take care of Charlie's shit this weekend."

And now instead it's grown. Aside from Martha, whose salary is split three ways in our little messenger collective, Charlie is my only full-time employee, the business in a continued downward spiral since my fifteen minutes of front-page infamy had expired.

"*And* note the sleeping bag and pillow. What does that tell you?"

That Charlie had crashed here again last night. Though it wouldn't be the first time for any of us, the office often doubling as a clubhouse after business hours are over, situated as it is within stumbling distance of a hundred bars on Newbury and Boylston streets. I've had my own share of nights passed out on this couch. Only it's never been with the forethought of a sleeping bag and pillow.

"No." Martha cuts me off before I get a word out. "I'm not listening to you spin this. If Charlie got hammered last night, you know he's not moving until I stick my foot up his ass. Only he wasn't here when I got in this morning and that's, like, *never* happened before."

"You're saying he'd planned on bunking here?"

"I'm saying take care of this. And since when have you known Charlie to *plan* on anything?"

Not to paint the courier ranks with too broad a brush, but Martha could have been talking about the bulk of messengers who populate the trade in this historic landfill, the job not exactly résumè gold. Which is not to say we're total slackers—the work is hard, the hours long—only that at some point we've all answered the siren call of these insane and incoherent streets, drawn to the flexible hours, miniscule dry cleaning bills, and in varying degrees, a heightened addiction to risk and speed.

But if there's one upside to my injuries besides the tough-guy scars I carry on my face, which now mirror my father's—a lightning bolt scar below my bottom lip and shattered, slightly off-color front teeth where the bonding has yet to darken and match the lower portion—it's the realization that I'm more at peace when on the move; more accepting of my station in life, which from the outside looking in probably doesn't look like much, but provides me with exactly what I need.

My point being, the job has less to do with chasing dollars as hunting a certain *feeling*. Only, if I'm being honest with myself, that feeling's been getting harder to catch in this new and ritzier Boston, these reconstituted post–Big Dig streets having lost their edge, out of focus and unfamiliar to me unless I'm attacking them at warp speed; God help the pedestrian whose head doesn't swivel both ways.

When I'd first met Charlie, he'd been working as a somnambulant doorman on Newbury Street. He'd done two tours in Iraq and lost his leg to an IED while on patrol outside of a town most Americans will never hear of. But he discovered he could still ride a bike with the prosthetic he wore, the city streets reawakening him from the depressive, near-comatose slumber he'd been in.

Like most couriers, Charlie gets paid by the run. The busier he is, the more money he makes. Only lately it's been hard not to notice the shrinking direct deposits into my account, technology killing me softly; a glut of competition driving down prices and forcing some of the other smaller services to either fold or merge. I hadn't realized business was so slow that Charlie couldn't afford to keep a roof over his head.

"And if that's not enough." Martha, exhibiting the caution of a vegan forced to handle a pissed-off lobster, reaches into the top drawer of her filing cabinet and gently places an oil-stained paper bag into my hands.

"What the hell," I say. From its metallic smell and unbalanced weight I recognize what I'm holding without having to look inside.

"It fell out of one of the bags when I started to move them."

Martha starts gnawing the inside of her cheek, a stress habit I'm pretty sure she is unaware of. "That's why I left the rest where they are. I want that thing out of here, Zesty. I'm serious. Is it loaded?"

I unfurl the bag to pull out a smoky blue-black 9mm Beretta, holding the short, almost rectangular barrel facing down and away from Martha. I turn my back to her, engage the safety, which is off, slide the chamber, and pop a full fifteen-round clip out of the butt end above the waffled grip, a little more familiar with guns than I'd like to be. The barrel and slide are freshly oiled, my smudged prints visible where I've touched it. The light in the room is poor, but I can see where the serial numbers have been scraped off, the rough indentations darker where oil has pooled and attracted dust and dirt.

"What am I supposed to do with this, Martha?"

"I don't know, Zesty. And I don't really care. It's his service gun, right?"

"I suppose." Considering that my brother, Zero, could walk into a couple corner markets in Mattapan or Dorchester and come out lugging an expired gallon of milk and a freshly loaded Stinger rocket launcher, I know enough not to believe all the weapons manufactured for our recent wars are accurately accounted for.

"Are they even allowed to bring that home after they serve?"

"I doubt it. Not with PTSD and the suicide rate what it is." There's also the scraping of the serial numbers to consider, which I don't mention to Martha, preferring not to freak her out any more than she already seems to be. With most people who are on the verge of hyperventilating, you tell them to *breathe, just breathe.* With Martha I'm about to tell her to gnaw on something when she tosses some of the espresso beans into her mouth, reading my mind again.

"You think Charlie has PTSD?"

It's hard to imagine Charlie *wouldn't* have PTSD, considering he was one of only three survivors from his unit when his M2 Bradley rolled over an IED so packed with explosives it blew a six-foot doughnut hole through the personnel carrier's protective under-armor and lifted the vehicle airborne. Charlie and I have spoken a few times about his experiences in Iraq, but I could tell we only scratched the surface of his time there, much the same way I don't open up much about my upbringing: my radical mother, who's been in the wind for over twenty years, and my father, who's now suffering in silence through the late stages of Alzheimer's, but whose checkered past has already caught up to me once and nearly killed me.

In the handful of times Charlie has crashed at my place in Union Park, I've witnessed him twitching violently in his sleep, heard him crying out names and warnings, the endless loop of that day in Iraq replaying under sealed lids. But I've never brought attention to this, never spoken at length with him about his loss or injury, that side of his life reserved for a veterans group I know he attends every couple of weeks or so, the meetings sometimes followed by a night of heavy drinking and brawling among his jarhead buddies, who light it up in some of the darker watering holes in town.

Honestly, it's an invitation I'm thankful not to have received, having once witnessed the intensity of their displaced rage during a show at the Paradise, the bouncers having to rely on Boston's Finest to restore some semblance of order as they got into it with half a dozen BU chuckleheads who thought it was a good idea to thank them for their service with a political lecture on the nature of American imperialism.

Has Charlie ever watched me sleep? Has he seen me replaying the dream of Gus that I can't seem to shake, felt some form of kinship—the Damaged Goods Club?

I doubt I'll ever ask him, preferring to keep my internal battles to myself; Martha pried it out of me only because somehow, to her, my head is transparent. Maybe I really should wear a helmet. Or at the very least, a pair of sunglasses to hide my tell-all eyes. Still, the question: What to do with the gun?

"I'll lock it up in one of the lockers," I say.

"No. You will fucking not. I want that thing out of here. And I'm not trying to be harsh, but that goes for Charlie, too. This is an office, Zesty, not a home."

"One thing at a time, Martha. I'll talk to him, see what's going on. He's still got a job; things can't be *that* bad, right?"

"No?" Martha tosses another handful of beans into her mouth. "What do you hear?"

"Only your bicuspid blenders," I say.

"Exactly. The phones have been dead, if you hadn't noticed."

"My wallet's noticed. When I sit down I can hear it scream." I shoot her a grin. "But the summer's over. People get lazy soon as the first frost hits the air. It'll start picking up."

"And if it doesn't? There's not enough work for the two of you if you're planning on coming back full-time. How long you think you can keep Charlie on?"

"You tell me. I just deliver shit; you're the one who knows my real numbers."

"Well, they're not good. And I don't know what Charlie was paying for rent in Medford, but it couldn't have been close to what you're shelling out for your Union Park digs."

Charlie had grown up in Medford, a working-class suburb roughly five miles from Boston, his commute by bike no more than a thirty-minute ride across Somerville and Cambridge to our Berkeley Street side-alley address. But the reverberations of the Big Dig have been felt in every town within hailing distance of the city's borders, skyrocketing rents and property taxes pricing long-time residents out of neighborhoods they'd lived in their entire lives.

"So?" I say. Charlie's predicament isn't an isolated one, but what could I do about it?

"Zesty, I'm not sure you're even making your *own* rent this month. And didn't Zero have to co-sign your lease for you?"

"Your point being?"

"That alone you can't even get a roof over your head in this town. Zesty, I know I sound like a cold-ass bitch, but you're going to have to cut Charlie loose. You can't afford to keep him."

"I can't do that, Martha," I say, shaking my head. Charlie, like Martha, gets paid entirely off the books. If I let him go he won't even qualify for unemployment. And while he probably has access to health care through the VA and maybe some form of pension, I'm pretty damn sure the benefits won't amount to much in this gilded city. Is Charlie my responsibility? He's a grown man and makes his own choices. But he's also my friend and that's got to count for something.

"Okay, a discussion for another day then," Martha concedes, digging a finger deep into a molar to wedge the remnant of a bean free.

Good to the last crunch.

"But get rid of that fucking gun; I don't care if you have to bury it."

"I'll take care of it." I drop the gun back in the paper bag, place the bag in the main hold of my pack, and store the clip in a separate front pocket lest they get tempted to mate. Zero has the Magilla of all safes in his office. I can stash the Beretta there until I get a chance to speak to Charlie and hopefully before he notices it's gone missing.

"Well then, to end on a high note . . ." Martha riffles Post-its stuck to the side of her computer and peels one off. "I got a call this morning from an outfit named . . ."

"Solarte Associates." I read the Post-it, squinting at the chicken scratching of a Kenmore Square address.

"Lady I spoke with sounded eager but wants to meet first."

"Never heard of them," I say. "You?"

"No. From what I can tell it's some kind of corporate security firm, consultants maybe, I don't know. Their website looked like it was designed by a ten-year-old."

"Perfect. Send Charlie to ink them. Win-win."

"Nice try. She asked for you personally. Seriously, Zesty, I don't have to tell you how hard new clients are to come by. Make time to go over there. Like *now*."

"All right."

"And act professional. You wearing deodorant?"

"I *got* it."

"Fine. So . . ." Martha, recognizing the point of diminishing returns, shifts gears to rattle my gift bag of espresso beans. "To what exactly do I owe *this* honor?"

"Consider it a bonus for a job well done." I snap my messenger bag closed, but don't hear it, a wave of hot static washing over me, causing me to wince.

"You're paying me in coffee beans now?" Martha, a witness to this show on my face before, lays down the beans and hits a couple of keys on her computer.

"It's called the barter economy." I dig my thumb into the raised scar over my right brow, trying to disperse the electric shock of guitar feedback that follows the static. "Everybody's doing it."

"In that case, take it to Verizon. They're about to cut us off."

On the computer, a file titled *Radio Zesty* pops on-screen and when Martha opens it, a running account of my internal playlist appears, a veritable who's who of mostly obscure and generally forgotten Boston bands, some slightly better known Motown-era soul outfits, and a slew of New Wave and ska acts like XTC, The Jam, The Clash, English Beat, and Squeeze. Only a handful of the Boston bands listed so far had risen beyond local fame—The Cars, Morphine, the Pixies—the majority having only reached big-fish-in-a-small-pond status; maybe for a short time popular enough to eke out a living doing what they loved, which was possibly payment enough.

There are dates noted beside each song along with a number indicating how many times my internal DJ's repeated the record; Martha is fond of searching for patterns where none exists, trying to make some sense of my auditory mix. I'm not organized enough to maintain Martha's level of record keeping and honestly, I don't really see the point. I'm just thankful not to be punished by a daily dose of New Kids on the Block.

Martha, her fingers hovering expectantly over the keyboard, waits for me to identify the band and I do.

"It's The Neighborhoods," I tell her, the frying pan sizzle lifting for a heavy thunder of drums, Dave Minehan coming in over the top belting:

> *This year I'm gonna get it right*
> *Up from the bottom*
> *I will find a light*

It's the title track from their album *Fire Is Coming,* Martha adding it next to "The Prettiest Girl," a song that came damn close to making The Neighborhoods a household name beyond Boston.

"And hey, look at that," I point out, probably too loudly, as a phone begins to ring. "The power of positive thought."

Only problem, it's Detective Wells calling.

THREE

Solarte Associates occupies a second-story high-ceilinged suite in an old building with all the attendant details and wear: thickly painted crown molding and baseboards framing the outer room, a little chipped and worn in spots, revealing a kaleidoscope of previous color schemes beneath. The floors are hardwood, wide planks, badly gouged in places, beautiful. Cheaply framed R. B. Kitaj and Frida Kahlo prints hang on the walls, mismatched chairs tilting insolently beneath each one, front legs lifted off the floor, like juvenile delinquents. A battered oak desk, solid as a thirty-year mortgage, faces bow front windows looking out over Kenmore Square and a thin side slice of the iconic Citgo sign above the BU Barnes & Noble.

Whatever Solarte Associates is selling, it must sell itself because according to Martha, their website isn't exactly an oracle of information, the desk is littered with glossy pamphlets advertising a cleaning service bearing a Roxbury address, and the shiny silver Solarte Associates door plaque tells me nothing new beyond the fact that they can afford a shiny silver door plaque. One thing for sure: They didn't plow their money into security. The downstairs door was ajar when I arrived and I didn't have to buzz to get in.

There's nobody manning the desk now, no chair there to suggest anybody does, but it's easy to imagine someone perched there through the years watching Kenmore Square morph from the enticingly seedy, slightly dangerous hub of the Boston music scene to the generic shopping plaza it's now become. Boston's a city populated by ghosts. In Kenmore Square they rattle pocket chains and sport leather, Levi's, and Doc Martens. Where the Rathskeller once stood, they howl loudest.

My father had been part of that local music scene. Before he'd begun to carve out his living at the poker table, he'd managed a number of Boston rock bands, none larger than Mass, whose self-titled debut LP immediately garnered the attention of Peter Grant, Led Zeppelin's manager, who'd caught a show at the Living Room in Providence, Rhode Island.

Zeppelin's *Physical Graffiti* had just been released and was already sitting at the top of the charts when Grant tapped Mass to open for them at the Boston Garden and then continue on as the opener for the remainder of the tour. It was the sort of break every band dreams of and Mass had the talent to capitalize on it. Only when tickets went on sale during a brutal February cold snap, Garden security made the mistake of letting fans inside the normally restricted advance ticketing areas and all fucking hell broke loose. The mob rushed the turnstiles, went all Spider Man on the catwalks to snatch the Celtics and Bruins championship banners, brawled and bloodied the Bruins ice rink in their best imitations of Derek Sanderson and Gordie Clark, and stole every souvenir they could pry out of the old building.

Zeppelin, not even on the East Coast at the time, was banned from the Garden for five years; even my father's deep connections in the mayor's office were unable to sway the city council to vacate their hamfisted ruling. In a fit of rage, Grant cut Mass off the tour and it was Game Over after that. Mass took the fall for the Zeppelin ban, and fan backlash had them booed off of every stage in the 617 area code. And shortly after that cruel twist of fate, Mass's golden-piped lead singer and songwriter, Karl Klaussen, stumbled out the door after a show at New York's famed CBGB and has never been seen or heard from again.

Of all the bars that have come and gone in Boston, and there have been many—the Channel, Chet's, Bunratty's, just to name a few—it's the Rat I miss most. On nights my father couldn't find someone to watch over Zero and me, he would rouse us from our sleep and haul us to the roving poker games he hosted, on the rare occasion playing, but on most nights just dealing the cards and taking a cut—usually 10 percent—of the initial buy-in.

By the late 1970s, poker was how my father carved out his living, walking that razor's edge of legality in a racially and ethnically divided city that couldn't seem to make up its mind as to which direction it was headed—the provincial and segregated East Coast backwater that the bussing issue exposed on the national level or the modern liberal metropolis it's become.

My father's game was hardly the only place in town where you could risk your money over cards—Chinatown had pai gow and blackjack in its numerous backroom gambling dens, the North End carrying their own social club versions—the city awash in illegal book and gambling joints. But what set my father's game apart was its neighborhood neutrality, the multiple locations he'd rotate through, mostly music clubs and restaurants after-hours, purposely staying out of the ethnic strongholds that would have required tribute payments to the powers that be, a slice of the action my father couldn't afford to give.

It was an invitation-only affair. They played poker, but often the game was more Camp David than Las Vegas, the green felt docket of his octagonal table a place where business deals were struck, arrangements made or reparations paid, alliances forged or severed without the fear of imminent reprisal. Which is to say, nobody got shot at my father's poker games or suffered a blackjack to the back of the neck, pockets turned out and emptied after a winning night.

My father garnered citywide respect for his poker skills and twice that for his silence, his eyes never betraying judgment of the powerful men who would look into those impenetrable eyes, dark as a sealed vault, and unburden themselves of their sins.

I've often wondered how my father was able to manage this weight, to listen to the venal acts and impulsive misdeeds of men who were beyond the reach of the law but felt the overwhelming need of confession. Wondered how he didn't let the darkness that spilled out of these men corrupt his own heart; unbalance the ethical scales he always taught Zero and me to be mindful of, though never blinded to the opportunity to lay a finger and tip those scales when the right time presented itself.

There will come a time, my father always preached to Zero and me, *there will always come a time. You just have to recognize the moment and act.*

Maybe it was my father's seeming neutrality that empowered him because nobody truly knew where his loyalties lay, how he was able to operate freely in a city where the boundaries were so clearly drawn, where nobody operated without tribute or consent from city hall or the various Mob bosses who controlled their slices of the city pie.

My former landlord, in the days before he evicted me from my Thayer Street loft, told me this story: His father, he claimed, had gambled in my father's game. And lost. As he also lost on the greyhounds at Wonderland, the ponies at Suffolk Downs, the NFL betting cards available in just about every neighborhood bar and corner grocery, and probably anything else he could wager on—two squirrels crossing the fucking Boston Common, for all I know.

His father was a loser. My landlord's words, not mine, but his tale illustrates one of the things that makes Boston so special and potentially dangerous: It's a small town, karma lurking around every corner and often firing with both barrels to make up for her lousy aim.

What's my point? That maybe in light of Devlin McKenna's return, the way I continue to view my father is naive, a self-deluding narrative that enables me to see him in only the most positive light, like choosing to focus solely on the brightest of colors refracted through a dark tinted prism. At the very least, I've come to understand that my father was many things. And as his Alzheimer's has worsened, a deepening silence settling in, I make little effort to unravel the secrets that used to spill from his lips, separate fact from fiction, and parse his conversations with the spirit world, my mother chiefly, her ghost-love last to fade.

The irony of my father's new, more permanent silence doesn't escape me. My father's always been fluent in silence, valued experience over words, even if it came with a few lumps. Here's what was important to him: Loyalty. Music. The languid rhythm of a baseball game, the brutal honesty of a boxing match. Awareness: *Know who you are.*

Zero and I grew up at the poker table, where we sat behind our father—always behind—and watched him work the turn of the cards, the pressurized silences and muttered curses that followed. But he also exposed us to other places where we were less welcome and had to weather the hostile stares of Baby Doc–scarred Haitians, or the snarl of the old Irish guard holding up the bar at the local VFW, the open condescension of the silver-haired patricians snacking on shrimp cocktails in the marbled dining rooms of the Parker House Hotel. High and low. Watch and listen. Keep your mouth shut until I tell you otherwise. Pay attention. Who are the dinosaurs? Who will be here in twenty years? Who will adapt? Tell me now. Tell me why. What's that riff? Who's blowing that horn? What song did that sample? Why did Lady Day die penniless? How come Evan Dando broke out of the pack?

The Rat was just one of the many bars and clubs my father operated out of after-hours, the games lining the pockets of the club managers and owners, who were happy to keep the lights on as the rest of the city snoozed, content with the knowledge that they could count on him if they needed a favor down the line, an ear at city hall, a beef smoothed over.

Sometimes we would arrive well before closing, greeted at the door like royalty by Mitch Cerullo, the club's longtime doorman who always sported a gray Wolf Man beard and matching three-piece suit regardless of the weather or how rough the crowd was. That suit was always a mystery to me as it was never wrinkled or torn as he "escorted" sporadic trouble out the door, though the rumor that he was wired into the Boston Mob probably tempered much resistance to his rough embrace on the rare occasions he had to employ it.

A stained soul and a clean suit was how my father described him years later without elaboration, as was his way.

The greeting between my father and Cerullo took the form of ritual, a brief hug followed by a warm handshake with a discreet exchange of bills and a detailed account of the evening's highlights, which always included an assessment of the energy in the room, for my father believed strongly in such things where poker was involved. Poker is foremost a game of skill and nerve, but sometimes that slim margin between winning and losing comes in the ability to tune in to something less tangible, the karmic vibrations of the night itself, not only the players, camouflaging themselves in thickening smoke while lobbing up false signals like hand grenades, trying in every conceivable way to separate you from your money.

"Tonight's a special night," Cerullo would broadcast through the metallic voice box he required and would sometimes let me hold to his throat, the robotic vibrations thrilling me, "as we were treated to the musical styling of Willie Alexander followed by the always energetic Nervous Eaters, who opened with 'Loretta' to great aplomb."

"Energetic, huh?" My dad's sly grin lit up the jagged barb-wire scar under his bottom lip. "Willie manage to keep his shirt on tonight?"

"He didn't even make it through 'Mass Ave.'" Cerullo chuckled without the box, a silent pantomime of laughter. "Paid the price for it, too. Some chickadees jumped onstage and burned him good with their cigs."

"Wouldn't be the first time," my father said. "Least his shirt's in one piece." Which in itself was an accomplishment at some shows at the Rat, where you could come out looking like you'd been fed headfirst through a wood chipper.

"Ah, but what fun he had." Cerullo shrugged up his sleeve to glance at his watch. My father's game would start after the club closed at 2 A.M., the staff diligently cleaning around him as he prepared the octagonal table that was stored above the bar, sorting and stacking the heavy clay chips he'd had custom-made for his games while Zero and I broke the seal on two brand-new decks of Bicycle playing cards, removed the Jokers, and shuffled.

After an hour of cleaning the staff would depart, though from the results of their labor you'd never guess they'd even made the effort. The walls wept beer. The air held the perpetual tang of sweat and smoke. The carpeted stairs to the basement were petri dishes of sweat-glopped hair gel, spilled alcohol, wads of gum. If a pandemic ever broke out in Boston, the first place the CDC would have quarantined was the Rat.

"They rowdy down there?" my father would inquire even though we would be playing upstairs.

"No more than usual, but The Real Kids haven't gone on yet. Your boys will like them, especially that one." Cerullo pointed at Zero. "He's got that hellion look in his eyes, I'm telling you. Well, if he's itching to brawl, this would be the place and the band for it. He can just say he's slam dancing. All will be forgiven."

To understand why the Rathskeller was my father's most frequent location for his cash-heavy games, you would have to understand how divided Boston was in the early nineties, a city of closed neighborhoods and fiercely protected fiefdoms. I suspect that the Rat benefitted from its proximity to Fenway Park, one of the few Boston institutions that could be claimed by all its residents, no matter where they rested their heads at night. Kenmore Square was therefore something of an island, not out and out claimed by the DeMasi crime family, who controlled the Italian North End and most of downtown and were making inroads to the rapidly gentrifying South End. Neither was it territory ruled by Devlin McKenna, who had garnered a vise grip on South Boston, Charlestown, and Somerville, or Jerry Dapolito, who ran Revere, Chelsea, and an all-black Roxbury, the Big Dig yet to carve up the city and change its borders forever.

For whatever reason, the black box of the Rat was a safe haven and proving ground for my father, where he could sharpen his skills at the green felt docket of the poker table, practice stilling the blood coursing through his veins, erase any trace of light from his midnight eyes. As it was, too, for the hundreds of local bands who tore it up nightly, sometimes in front of only a dozen fans, which was no less than acts like Metallica, The Police, or the Beastie Boys drew to that basement stage as they were starting out. Some of these acts—Human Sexual Response, The Bosstones, just to name a couple—went on to long careers and gained national recognition while others equally talented—La Peste, The Titanics, The Blackjacks—rose not much further than local fame and notoriety before imploding or just disbanding, done in by shady record deals, bad timing, drug addictions, and ego; the music business, like poker, chalked a thin line between busting loose or busting out.

Today, sometimes still, when the stars are aligned just right, you can hear the echo of that Bosstown Sound in places like the Paradise, the Middle East, and T.T. the Bear's Place, though technically, the latter two clubs reside on the Cambridge side of the Charles River.

What's sacred anymore in Boston? Nothing. Especially when prime real estate is involved: The hallowed Boston Garden replaced by an arena with all the charm of an ATM. The Charles Street Jail converted into a luxury hotel where bars on the windows will set you back a few extra dollars. Fenway's Green Monster topped by seating for people who must be made out of money.

The Rat was demolished over a decade ago. In fact, practically the entire block had been torn down to accommodate construction of the Hotel Commonwealth, where, if you ignore the ghosts of rock and roll past, you can snag a seat at the Standard, groove to piped-in music with an algorithm beat designed to stimulate spending, and sip a fourteen-dollar ethically sourced cocktail served up by a bartender—excuse me, *mixologist*—who couldn't even fake you a solid Boston accent. Who the fuck lives in this city anymore? Where do they all come from?

I'd ask the mocha-skinned, chardonnay-eyed woman who opens the door to the adjoining office, but she's on me too fast.

"Hey, I appreciate you coming in. It's Zesty, right? Alianna Solarte." She walks our handshake all the way to her desk, the door to the outer room left open behind us. "It's good of you to come in so quick. I know I was insistent. Please, have a seat. Can I get you something to drink? Coffee? I hear you messengers drink a lot of coffee."

"I'm all set, thanks."

Alianna Solarte's dark eyebrows jump in astonishment, revealing she knows something about bike messengers.

The Tao of Zesty goes something like this: high-quality coffee, any quality marijuana, just about any woman foolish enough to roll the dice. I explain to Solarte that I'd already had my defibrillating two mugs this morning. What I leave unsaid is that I would have accepted a third if the machine on the windowsill weren't one of those instant-cup contraptions that I consider to be to coffee what Keanu Reeves is to acting.

"That's for me? Thanks." Alianna Solarte accepts the offer of my standard courier contract and list of fees, which she then drops onto the keyboard of her open laptop without a second glance.

"I hope your dispatcher didn't think I was being pushy, asking you to come in personally, but I'm, like, sort of a people person. You?" Ms. Solarte's People Person smile is bright and wide, an open invitation to share. She's a compact woman yet sitting doesn't seem to make her any smaller; she sits as she stood, tilted minutely forward with a therapist's posture.

Outside the windows I can hear the gentle ebb of the city, a staccato of beeps as cars and trucks move through the square, foot traffic picking up as fans head toward Fenway Park for early batting practice. There's a rare late-September day game left on the Red Sox schedule due to a rainout, a trickle of bobbing heads that will soon turn into a swarm of unwavering loyalists, of which I am one.

Go Sawx!

"Me what?" I say.

"A people person."

"I charm the living hell out of receptionists and front office staff," I boast. Only it's probably on account my visits last only a few minutes at a clip. Ask anyone else, especially some of the women I've dated, and they'd pitch you an entirely different story.

"I imagine that's a requisite skill in your line of work." Solarte troubles herself for a brief smile that doesn't transfer to the rest of her body.

"Integral." I dust off my big-boy words. "Only you should know up front if we end up working together I won't be the only messenger you see." I point to the contract and list of fees drooping off the side of the keyboard. There's a sizable oil stain on the bottom of the front page that must have come from the bag with Charlie's gun in it, only Alianna Solarte doesn't make note of it when she picks it up from her keyboard and sets it even further aside.

"So tell me about yourself, Zesty. Why should I hire Mercury Couriers?"

"This is an interview?" I sit up straighter. "Had I known I would have worn fancier shorts." As it is, I'm dressed in my standard outfit of black Lycra racing tights under paint-spattered cut-off black jean shorts, white Trefoil Adidas T-shirt under a gray and white Trefoil hoodie sweatshirt, and a pair of black high-top Adidas basketball sneakers. If I had an agent, Adidas would be covering my expenses. As it is, I'm Boston's cheapest billboard.

"I mean, I looked online." Solarte forms a steeple with her hands. "There are plenty of courier outfits out there, pretty much all of them bigger. And cheaper . . ."

Two years ago I would have told Alianna Solarte that hiring me guaranteed her Boston's fastest bike messenger—one-way streets, squirrel crossing pedestrians, and bike patrol cops be damned—only I still wasn't back up to full speed, opting to spend as much time as I could handle with my father, the job of caregiving draining me even though I have more help than most.

"So why didn't you call them instead?" The words come out sharper than I'd intended.

"Because they're not nearly as intriguing as you are." Solarte squints me a forgiving smile, accentuating the crow's feet at the corners of her eyes. Her brown hair pulled tight in a ponytail has the hard shine of lacquered wood and makes it seem as if her whole face is being pulled back, the skin smooth over high rounded cheekbones, those light wine eyes almost with an Asian slant; pretty in the way older women who don't fight aging age, a dab of makeup meant to accentuate, not conceal.

"You mean you've read my press clippings." I'm paying more attention now, not enjoying the direction this conversation is going.

"Sure. You got the touch of celebrity about you. Come on, Zesty. I can't be the only star fucker in this town."

No, I decide after a moment, I couldn't have heard right. She wouldn't have said that.

"Excuse my French."

Or not.

I need to start focusing. Only it's hard as another 45 drops between my ears, my head-wax DJ deciding there's no better time to spin The Outlets' "Knock Me Down" just loud enough to startle everyone meditating on Walden Pond.

Solarte's on-point, though. After my highly publicized run-in with McKenna I did record a temporary uptick in my love life, bullets and beatings working as some strange aphrodisiac on a select type of girl. Only lately I've been back to spending nights alone with my cat, still trying to figure out how to put a positive spin on *broke, college dropout,* and according to Martha, the forthcoming *behind in my rent.*

"Hey, Zesty." Solarte snaps her fingers in my direction. "You still here?"

"I'm with you." Only not to talk about my suitability as a mate or of my past. And according to the clock on the filing cabinet, I am due to meet Detective Wells in the South End in less than an hour. "What can I do for you, Ms. Solarte?" I'm on high alert now, the song receding as quickly as it came, leaving only the empty-groove hiss of needle on wax. "I don't mean to be rude but I have another appointment I have to get to."

"Call me Alianna."

"That's okay." I rise from my seat, Solarte watching me carefully from under lifted brows, not budging an inch as I reach over her computer, lifting the contract I'd given her before folding it back into my pack next to Charlie service revolver. "I'm getting the sense you don't really need a messenger, Ms. Solarte."

"Not exactly. But please stay a few minutes, Zesty. I'll pay you for your time if that's the issue."

"That's not necessary. It's always good to meet new people." I look around the office, no longer distracted by the song or my desire to hook a new client, paying more attention to what I was looking at but not really seeing: Alianna Solarte's body language, the framed photographs hung behind her, a local celebrity in each one, the elaborately carved ornamental base centered on the cracked ceiling overhead, which would be the room's only pristine reminder of old-world charm had it not been desecrated by a tiny camera pointing toward the door.

"Are you some sort of PI, Alianna?" I sit back down.

"Now what makes you say that?" Alianna turns up the wattage of her grin, unduly pleased about something.

"Well, because if you've done your homework on me as I think you have, then you know I've had my share of law enforcement in my life."

"You mean on account of your mother's role in Bank of Boston? Or your brother—"

"Take your pick." I fight the urge to bolt out the door, picturing Martha's wrath if I came back to the office empty-handed.

"Timing really is everything in life, isn't it?"

"What do you mean?"

"Well, I'm talking about your father now. Imagine where he'd be today considering his skill set. Probably on TV, selling baseball caps, mirrored sunglasses, and subscriptions to Internet poker sites. Why do you ask if I'm an investigator?"

"Because I think you used to be a cop."

"Okay."

"And a lot of cops go into security, consulting work, after they retire. Only you're a little young to be retired. . . ."

"Aren't you sweet." Solarte's voice is playful, only I've already noted the shift in her energy, as if she's joined me in doubling down on her focus. "What gave me away? Or are you inclined not to tell?"

"I'm not a magician." I shrug. "Two things, mainly. I didn't pay it any mind at first, but when you sat down at your desk you cleared your jacket like most detectives do. At least those who are right-handed and are used to carrying their service revolver on their left hip. Only you're not carrying, so it must be a habit you haven't shaken or didn't even notice you have."

Solarte frowns. "And the second?"

"Those pictures behind you. Most people look into the camera for those types of celebrity photos, but even though you're smiling, it never makes it to your eyes. And it doesn't matter who you're with, Ortiz, Wahlberg. You did some work for Aerosmith?"

"Yep. You can't see it, but at that very moment there, Steven Tyler was grabbing my ass."

"Well then, all the more power to you. It doesn't make it into the picture." In every photo Solarte was looking beyond the lens, scoping her surroundings, clocking people outside the frame. "I'm assuming you were working."

"I was. And let it be noted, the concert that night, Tyler only handled the mic with his left hand." Solarte winks at me.

"Is that what you do now, security work?"

"Occasionally. For people who actually want real protection."

"As opposed to . . ."

"The clowns who like having a couple of bookends three steps slow for the NFL beside them to attract attention, let everyone around know how important they are." Solarte reaches inside her jacket, removes her wallet, and opens it to flash me what looks like a bona-fide private investigator's license issued by the state of Massachusetts. I'm impressed. It has a state seal and everything and looks about as official as a badge from the now defunct Jack's Joke Shop.

"Why am I here, Ms. Solarte?"

"Because I *would* like to hire you, Zesty."

"Only not as a messenger."

"Not exactly."

"So what, then?"

"It's not often I can say this, but basically I'm overbooked and need an extra set of eyes for something I took on. Short-term surveillance while I wrap up another case."

"You don't have someone on staff or someone you normally farm this sort of thing out to?"

"You're looking at my staff. And as for farming it out to a pro, well, I'd lose money on the deal."

"Why me?"

"Come on, Zesty. Don't be modest. For all the reasons you showed me already. You pay attention even when it seems you're not. You see things others don't."

Which is true, my years attending my father's poker games tuning my senses to the little tells that everybody eventually gives off, allowing me to weed out the false signals and manufactured tics from the unintended obfuscations that complicate the read of every player.

Ignore the words. I can still hear my father's voice bouncing around inside my brain. *How are they sitting? Breathing? The eyes alone are unreliable because too many people believe their own lies, construct their own truth. But it's the rare man who can simultaneously keep the lie off the pulse in his throat, ears, hands, the slump and rise of his shoulders. And in return, show them nothing. The stillness of a corpse.*

Only how would Solarte even know to audition these attendant details unless she'd been talking to someone on the short list of people who know me that well? There's Zero, of course, but he's a closed book when it comes to sharing and would have reached out to let me know someone was asking questions. Homicide Detectives Wells and Brill also cross my mind, but they're unlikely candidates for a job referral, considering I totally fucked their homicide investigation when McKenna hijacked Bad Santa's sleigh back to town. Same goes for FBI Agent Wellington Lee, though he did eventually parlay the mayhem he'd jump-started into a promotion to Boston's FBI regional director. Only Lee's as tight-lipped as they come. So who does that leave?

Darryl Jenkins.

"Big deal," I say. "So you've got friends in low places."

"Like you." Solarte beams.

"Those are the best kind," I admit.

"And see, there you go proving my point again. Come on, Zesty, you telling me you can't use the money? I can afford you, if that's what you're worried about. You don't need the work?"

"What do you know about it?" I say, ruminating on my predicament with Charlie. And though Martha was too selfless to mention it, her employment status is also hanging in the balance, as she is just as dependent on the volume of work coming in, taking a percentage of each run made on top of a salary that belongs to an earlier decade. If I can't drum up business fast, there's about to be some serious trickle-down poverty around these parts.

"You really want me to answer that, Zesty? I've seen your tax returns. Don't look so shocked, they're not so hard to get."

"It's not that," I say. "I'm just surprised I file taxes."

"Yeah?" Solarte laughs. "Give your office girl a raise."

I just did, albeit with coffee beans.

"What exactly is it you're asking me to do, Ms. Solarte? I'll admit I've got a touch of the voyeur in me, but snooping on cheating spouses, working for a bunch of crooks masquerading as insurance companies, doesn't really appeal to me."

"Perfect, then. It's not a divorce case or an insurance scam.

I just need you to follow this man." Solarte slides a couple of pic-tures from under the blotter on her desk toward me, two differ-ent angles on the same man, tan-dark in the first, almost clay red in the second, with a sharp V hairline and shoulder-length black hair tucked behind his ears. I'm guessing probably somewhere in his late fifties or early sixties, unusually tall for someone with such pronounced Aztec-like features, his head only clearing the door-way by a couple of inches. Black jeans. Dark turtleneck curled under his chin.

"His name's Martine Andino." Solarte pauses, looks like she's going to add something but doesn't.

"Is that supposed to mean something to me?"

Ms. Solarte shrugs *no clue*. "I'd be shocked if it did. Only I don't think that's his real name."

"Why's that?"

"Would you believe woman's intuition?"

"No offense, but no. Not on its own. There must've been something else. Hold on." I pick up the pictures and look at them more closely. Behind Andino's right shoulder is a corner of a framed print on a wall. Above him, thickly painted crown mold-ing with different colors showing through chips and cracks.

"These pictures were taken here," I say. "You've also got a camera set up where, over the door in the waiting room?" I point up at the ceiling without looking. "To go along with the one above me in the center chandelier thingy? Feeds into your laptop?"

"God, I'm such a solid judge of talent." With her right hand Solarte reaches over her left shoulder and pats herself on the back.

"Did this guy threaten you or something?"

"No." Solarte rears back in her seat. "And if he did, I wouldn't involve you in the situation. Mr. Andino is tangentially involved in a pending case, but it's nothing to be concerned about."

"So what's with the pictures?"

"Nothing. I take them of everybody. Facial recognition software's come a long way lately, saves me the trouble of asking for IDs. Mr. Andino's Arizona license was real enough, his Social Security number checked out, and he's had no arrests or convictions attached to him. He's not a danger to me or to you."

"But . . . ," I say.

"He's had some surgical procedures on his face. Really well done around the eyes, his mouth, expensive and skilled. Most people probably wouldn't have picked it up."

Solarte is as polished at reading people as I am, developing those same skills for however long she was a cop. Probably a necessity if you didn't get the answers you were looking for while beating suspects with a rubber hose.

"You worried I'm asking you to do something dangerous, Zesty?" Solarte's eyes twinkle in delight.

"You're joking, right? I make my living riding a bike in Boston." Where signaling is a sign of weakness and red lights are poetry, meaning: open to interpretation. Helen Keller could get her license in Boston. Stevie Wonder could drive a bus for the T.

"Do you do this often, Ms. Solarte?"

"What's that?"

"Invite others to share in your invasion of their privacy. Offer work and money to unreliable people with violent and ethically questionable bloodlines?"

Alianna Solarte stiffens, a spark of feral anger lighting her eyes, a small, almost blue scar on her cheek pulsing with a beat of its own, inadvertently revealing herself to me for the first time, like an accidental turn of a down card. My slight was intentional. Sometimes you have to poke at people's core to get a real look.

"I know this office doesn't look like much, Zesty, but the location can't be beat and, like you, I've got bills to pay. It's work, plain and simple. If you don't like what I do, if your conscience is somehow offended, there's the door. I'll watch you leave on my laptop, make sure you don't steal a painting on the way out."

"Basic surveillance," I say, smiling. I don't know why, but it feels good to be dressed down by someone other than Martha for a change. I definitely need more women in my life.

"Just surveillance." Solarte's anger drains as quickly as it arrived; maybe she's even a little embarrassed she showed me that much of herself. "I'm just looking for eyes, take a few pictures, make a few dollars. . . ."

"Why not," I say, before it occurs to me I should probably ask what the case involves.

"Now that, Zesty," Alianna Solarte points at me, "I'm not at liberty to discuss in detail, seeing as you're not officially an employee nor are you licensed by the fine state of Massachusetts. But like I said already, no cheating spouses, no insurance; your ethics intact at least for another day. What I'm asking you to do is pretty simple, just some straight-up surveillance while I close out this other thing I've got going. Listen, you don't like what you see, get bored, spooked, I'll pay you for your time and you can wash your hands of it. All you have to do is let me know where Mr. Andino goes, what he does, take a few pictures, pocket a few bucks. Hell, maybe you'll enjoy the work, learn some new skills. Come on, Zesty. What do you say? I mean, what have you got to lose?"

FOUR

"Come to headquarters," Wells had said when I'd spoken to him from my office, the detective multitasking poorly, the phone scraping hard on his perfectly manicured beard, an off-kilter tapping at a computer in the background. I've witnessed Wells typing before: all his fingers in motion brushing the keyboard, a diversionary cover for the fact that he uses only the two middle fingers of each hand to actually punch the keys.

"I don't think so," I said. I could feel the added heft of the gun in my pack and shifted it lightly to the side. I've been described as reckless, but even I wasn't dumb enough to walk into the shiny new Boston Police headquarters strapped.

"Why not?" Wells inquired, the phone thumping to the desk before being picked up again. "The coffee's free."

"I've had your coffee before," I reminded the detective.

"True, but you were a suspect then. We poured it from a different pot."

"Why doesn't that surprise me? Meet me at the Buttery in the South End. Corner of Shawmut and Union Park."

"I know where it is." Wells sounded annoyed. "You buying? That place is so expensive, instead of an ATM they got a guy named Vinny in residence offering loans from a corner table."

"Cry me a river. Don't they give you expense accounts for these types of meets?"

"You mean like for CIs? Why, you got somebody you want to snitch on?" Wells banking subtlety for a rainy day, angling toward Zero, who owns Zen Movers, a company staffed by a wide array of ex-cons Wells had once noted carried rap sheets so long they could double as packing paper.

He wasn't wrong, but Zero was a believer in second chances—he'd been given one himself when my parents adopted him off the streets—and there weren't many places that would hire somebody with a criminal record even if they were ready to turn the page on their past. And anyhow, if a man *did* happen to slip up, unable to resist his recidivist nature—the Safe Whisperer, the Mario Andretti of getaway drivers—well, Zero found a use for him as well. And for this, Zero engendered loyalty in his crew, a diamond-rare quality among thieves and hard cases.

In the past when I've been strapped for cash or fell behind in my bills I would jump in on one of Zero's bandit moving crews for some extra work. Only it's been a while, my body not quite ready for the awkward rigors of moving, too many twisting stairs in the older Boston buildings and triple-deckers, far too many un-balanced weights and impossible turns in narrow hallways built to accommodate smaller, less-well-fed populations.

"Buttery or nothing," I held firm. "I've got other things to do."

"As do I. So let's make it in a couple of hours, then. It'll give me time to hock my watch so I can afford you."

FIVE

South End Buttery in Union Park still sports its original pressed-tin ceiling with the world's tiniest tables and most uncomfortable chairs outside, but if you can withstand the discomfort, it offers a pleasant view of Union Square Park, turn-of-the-century brown-stones with wide stoops and flowering vines, and a parade of beautiful people sauntering by like they'd cornered the market on all the leisure time in the world.

Wells has added a real fedora to his outfit today, looking every bit the modern Philip Marlowe if Marlowe had sported a two-hundred-dollar haircut, a suit cut by laser beams, and dark cherry boots polished on the wings of an angel. There *is* a guy sitting at a corner table wearing a leather jacket with slicked-back hair, but he doesn't seem to be doling out money or negotiating terms of the vig.

"I guess you're buying," I say to Wells, who gets a lot of at-tention at the counter, furtive glances and direct come-on smiles from the entire afternoon shift. Though I live near the bakery, my budget doesn't afford frequent visits, so I order a chocolate croissant and the largest coffee they have. If I'd spotted a more expensive pastry, I would have ordered that instead.

"Is it my imagination," I say, sniffing at Wells as we seat ourselves in the sunshine, "or do you still smell like ashes?"

Wells sips his black coffee and looks at me over the rim of his ceramic mug. I took my coffee to go in a paper cup. That about sums up the difference between us.

"It's always such a pleasure to see you, Zesty."

"Hey, you called me."

"Remind me why."

"You didn't say. Only I've got nothing to add to last night if that's why we're here. Honestly, I just came for the free food. Where's Brill? You guys have a falling-out or something?"

"Every day. Keeps us sharp."

That, they were. Cutting into each other the wrong way, the yin to the other's yang, one detective always finishing the other's sentences. Only never with the right words.

Detective Wells is the Theo Epstein of the Homicide Division, the poster child of a newer, shinier Boston. Gold shield by thirty. Fine threads, analytics, and instinct, working angles nobody else sees. Brill is his opposite: an aspiring cynic and grouchy old-school, old-dog detective, one foot squarely planted in the Smithsonian display case. If opposites attract, then Brill and Wells collide.

"So really." Wells sets his cup down, smiles at next year's runway sensation as she sashays by. *Returns* her smile, I should say. "You've got nothing to add to last night?"

"Nada. And you know I was inside when they shot up the door."

"The door wasn't shot up. A rock broke the glass."

Some men, like Wells, are born for what they do, their calling probably having come to them at an early age. Which makes him the polar opposite of most everybody I spend time with in the messenger and moving worlds, jobs populated by people who have stumbled along the path of least resistance with little planning for what the future might hold. It isn't just the clothes and the hair that make Wells unique, it's his commitment to the mission, to speak for those who can no longer speak for themselves, and it wouldn't surprise me if Wells had run CSI Roadkill as a kid.

"I misspoke. Also when the Molotov cocktail exploded. I'd say you and your date were pretty lucky not to get burned."

Wells nods but says, "It wasn't a date."

"Really? You tell that to her little black dress and high heels?"

"And anyhow," Wells ignores my words. He's good at that, which only comes from practice. "It wasn't luck, either, not really. According to Boston Fire, based on how long the sidewalk burned, that bottle bomb was practically empty."

"You were targeted by the city's stingiest hitmen?" I say, screwing up my face. "Saved by OPEC?"

"Possibly. Or it could just be a matter of coincidence, wrong place, wrong time."

"Could it have been a warning?"

"Now what makes you say that?" Wells feigns indifference, making a show of clocking the steady traffic of well-dressed men and women shuffling in and out of the Buttery, half of them commuting all the way to their phones to move money around, buy low, sell high; what the fuck do these people do that affords them this lifestyle?

"Those articles your nondate wrote must have made some heavy hitters pretty unhappy," I say, even though it's been nearly six months since those stories ran. And anyhow, I'd think Boston crews know better than to go after reporters, bring that type of heat down. And that goes double for targeting cops. "What about one of her more recent pieces?"

"You have one in mind?"

I do.

Tehran had written a series of articles that brought to light the volume of foreign nationals, mostly Eastern Europeans, purchasing astronomically priced real estate in the city: entire floors of luxury buildings still under construction on the new seaport and downtown and a number of high-end condos in Beacon Hill and the Back Bay. While the purchases themselves were legal, the creation of shell companies that moved the money and paid for the condos—always in cash—obscured the true ownership of these properties and the source of the money. Tehran had managed to chip away through the layers of some of these shell companies and named names—many of them claiming dubious sources of income from overseas, a number with ties to corrupt foreign regimes or Eastern European organized crime figures.

Essentially, what Anitra Tehran had exposed was a perfect way to launder money: Funnel it into a safe investment that was likely to turn a profit down the line as it rode the wave of a Boston real estate boom that looked to have no end.

Wells laughs when I run my theory by him.

"What, you think the Boston Realty Association took a hit out on Ms. Tehran because she wrote a few pieces about shady real estate deals?"

"Molotov cocktail," I remind Wells.

"And Nick's Comedy serves Stoli. How did I miss that connection?" Wells bops himself with the heel of his hand and rolls his eyes before something sharper comes into them.

"What?"

"Nah, no way, Zesty." Wells metronomes his finger before me. "All the weed you smoke, your short-term memory's not that good. Maybe Tehran's 'Midnight League' series you'd remember because you're a hoops junkie and that was your man Darryl's crowd. You went home last night and paged through Tehran's bylines."

"So what if I did?" And I did.

The story had kicked up some dirt for a bit, but from what I could tell, nobody in the DA's office was particularly keen on rattling sabers with the chamber of commerce or the real estate board or whoever was making money on these multimillion-dollar deals, some of which, no doubt, ended up in some politician's reelection coffers and kept Boston's wheels spinning.

"Maybe it was your Vladimir Putin joke that set them off?" Wells swings for the fences.

"All right. *No más.* You've made your point. What's Ms. Tehran working on now?"

"That's a pretty astute question, Zesty. Only what makes you think I would know?"

"Well, if it wasn't a date, either she was working you for something or . . ." I hold out my hands.

"Or what?" Wells leads with a pugnacious chin.

"Nah, fuck it. I can see you're pissed already. I'm not putting it into words."

But if Tehran *wasn't* working Wells, then the inverse applied: which would qualify as an unusual arrangement, for a reporter to be so compromised. But then again, the same could be said for Wells. A cop who leaks without approval from the bosses risks working in blue until time immemorial. Though Wells had likely looked pretty sharp in uniform, too. Probably took the waist in a couple of inches to sit just right on his narrow hips.

"Why can't Tehran and I just be friends?" Wells dials down the resistance but holds my gaze, those liquid eyes impenetrable, like a gravity pool with a plexiglass cover.

"I don't know, Detective. But work with me here a minute: Who would you rather listen to, Barry Manilow or Barry White?"

Wells allows the fissure of a grin to cross his face, blinks once, and the lid to the pool is gone. At the corner a dark van pulls halfway onto the curb and parks, the engine idling. The man sitting on the passenger side looks at us for a beat, reaches into the glove compartment, and screws something together on his lap and out of our sight line. Wells, who had picked up his coffee, sets it back gently on the saucer, his other hand slipping idly inside his unbuttoned jacket. There's an audible metallic *clink* that comes from inside the van followed by a soft pillow of marijuana smoke drifting out the window, which mingles with the aromas of fresh-ground coffee and hot baking bread.

It's the Zesty Meyers holy trinity of desire: weed, coffee, warm pastries. I do my best not to drool. Wells picks up his cup again, shoots his cuff, and glances at his expensive watch.

"You got somewhere you gotta be?" I ask.

"No." He smiles. "And no Barrys."

"Okay then." Game on. "Prada or Louis Vuitton?" I rub my hands vigorously.

"Really, Zesty? Prada. By a mile."

"The Y on Huntington or Equinox Back Bay?"

"I'm flattered you think I work out." Wells flexes, throws a kiss toward his biceps.

"Skip it. What suit is that guy wearing?" I tilt my head to a slim blond man being walked by his fox terrier down Shawmut Ave.

"Mmm, that's hard. From the cut and fabric I'd have to say John Rocha."

"You made that up. I don't even know who that is."

"I pity you." He looks like he means it.

"All right, onward: Bette Midler or Barbra Streisand?"

"Bette Midler." No hesitation.

"Cocteau Twins or Ministry?" Wells's face draws a blank. "Skip it."

"Judy Garland or Marlene Dietrich?"

Wells laughs loudly. "What, is your gaydar down or something?"

"Not usually." I shrug.

"It matters to you? One way or the other?"

"Not in the least."

"So why ask?"

"I dunno." I shrug indifferently. "Styling tips?"

"At this point you're beyond help."

"Harsh." I mug a face. "Perspective, then."

"How so?"

"You'd know better than most. People seeing different things even when they're looking at the same thing."

"Are we looking at the same thing, Zesty?"

"I'm just looking at you and Anitra Tehran. Am I off-base saying maybe there's a little quid pro quo going on?"

"That what you and Darryl call it?"

"Excuse me?"

"Come on, Zesty, why is it we always have to do this dance? You had to get clearance to get on Darryl Jenkins's visitation list and you sign a logbook every time you check in. Darryl might be inside but we know he's still got sway, Cedrick and Otis keeping it warm for him until he gets out."

"Keeping what warm? Darryl lost his corners when he went down. By the time he gets out, he won't even recognize his own neighborhood." Darryl's Roxbury like Charlie's Medford, too close to the city to ward off what people with deep pockets always refer to as "progress."

Darryl had seen it coming, too. He fears no man, but it's hard to fend off Starbucks and Whole Foods when they're attacking on all fronts.

"Darryl didn't *lose* anything. You know damn well that play he made was to get out of the corner game. He just rode the wrong horse. You don't think I know your old pal Sam Budoff sold his little franchise to Darryl before he got locked up? . . . What's with the face? You still got those records spinning in your head?"

"Yeah."

Wells knows the drill and contents himself with his coffee, waiting for the song to settle into a less painful groove, a new local single for Martha's list coming in loud and clear: Tribe's "Joyride (I Saw The Film)." Another Boston band that at one time looked poised to hit the big-time.

> *I saw the film said that's the life for me*
> *Forsake the mundane for some instability*
> *So sue me*
> *Now you're hiding upstairs*
> *And now I'm not so sure*
> *What is all this for?*

"You good?" Wells breaks the silence when he sees me dancing in my seat. "So, Sam Budoff . . . ?"

Sam Budoff was a veritable one-man wrecking crew to the misguided notion that MIT was solely a nerd paradise, having achieved near-legendary status for brewing up small-batch recreational hallucinogens out of his Charles Street apartment. He wasn't a drug dealer per se, seeing as he never made money on his product except to recoup costs, but he had turned a nifty profit when he sold his formulas to Darryl's lieutenants, Otis Byrd and Cedrick Overstreet, a deal I'd brokered for a little goodwill among lunatics.

> *Oh you've done it now haven't you haven't you*
> *How many times I didn't unfold you*
> *Look at your face I hardly know you*
> *Oh I'm in it now up to eyebrow*
> *Oh I've done it now haven't I*
> *Oh me thinking you'd be my joyride*
> *I'll be lucky just to survive*

Had Otis and Cedrick started cooking? Was Sam helping them? Rarely have I had the opportunity to tell Wells the truth, so I roll it around on my tongue for a moment to see what it tastes like.

Bland. "I don't know anything about it." It tastes bland. But it's all I have to offer. "Is *that* what this is about? Last I talked to Sam he'd moved back to campus to finish his dissertation."

"Why would he do that?"

"I don't know," I say. "Bulimic coeds and toga parties?" More likely because MIT had a ten-year limit on completing doctorates and he figured a move back to the dorms would be torturous enough to motivate him to complete the work before the university cut the cord.

"Zero move him?" Wells has his pad out now. *Focus,* I tell myself, but it's hard as the song blasts and fades, blasts and fades, the volume knob like it's come under the control of a two-year-old spinning dials.

"Sure." I force myself to sit still and stare at Wells, a look he returns in spades. "I hooked him up."

"Everything he had went into a single dorm room?"

"I have no idea. I wasn't on the crew."

"He take out a storage unit?"

"Same answer." The song evaporates. "For all I know he had a killer yard sale. What's with all the Sam questions?"

"Nothing, really," Wells says, but the pad stays out, says something different. "Due diligence. I'm just crossing names off a list."

"What list? You're working a body?"

"What I do."

"Who?"

Wells, no doubt remembering all the good times we've shared, mulls his options before answering, "Rambir Roshan."

I shake my head. The name means nothing to me.

"Really?" Wells doesn't buy it. "Mass Ave. Bridge a couple of weeks ago? Roshan went to MIT."

And Anitra Tehran had covered the story. It was one of the other articles I'd paged through last night. But Roshan's name still doesn't mean anything to me on a personal level; the day he was killed is memorable only because the Boston and Cambridge police departments had sealed the Harvard Bridge (as it was formally named but never called) at both ends, the only vehicles on scene the mobile lab tech units and squad cars from each department. Essentially, the entire bridge became a 364-smoot-long crime scene, uniforms and detectives walking up and down the span collecting evidence, while a police boat tacked below redirecting kayaks and scull crews from Harvard, BU, and MIT, which all kept boathouses on the Charles River.

The Mass Ave. Bridge was a major thoroughfare between Boston and Cambridge and closing it created gridlock that reverberated through both cities for the entire day; Charlie and I ran off the chain with package deliveries that would have normally fallen to DHL or FedEx. Beyond that, I hadn't followed the case, but the *Globe* gave Anitra Tehran a front-page byline, which wasn't surprising considering the central location of the crime and the victim coming from a prominent university. Anitra Tehran had then followed up with a profile of Rambir Roshan, an economics major on scholarship at MIT from Mumbai, India, but that looked to be the extent of her coverage up to this point.

"What's Rambir Roshan got to do with Sam?"

"Probably nothing. His name came up cross-referencing class rosters. Roshan was the TA in a class Sam had taken." Wells consults his pad. "Poker Analytics and Theory. Sounds like something you might be interested in."

"It's MIT," I say. "It sounds like math."

"I'm told it's the hottest class on campus, taught by a professor named Yuki Fuji. There's even a lottery to get in. I guess blackjack's fallen out of style." Wells is referring to the MIT card-counting crews that had formed years ago, their exploits glamorized in a best-selling book and popular film. "If Budoff reaches out to you, tell him to give me a call, pronto."

"What, now I'm your messaging service? You can't get ahold of him?"

"Apparently he doesn't own a cell phone." Wells pockets the pad. "But you could have told me that, right?"

True.

Sam always carried a touch of justified paranoia from his chemistry days.

"I've also left messages at his dorm, but if he's picked them up, he's not returning my call. MIT police knocked on his door, but he hasn't been around."

"Since when?"

"Why, you worried?"

"You're the one asking about him." I pause to think for a moment before speaking again, something I rarely do. "You telling me MIT doesn't have cameras in the dorm lobbies?"

"They do."

"So . . ."

"Private sandbox." Wells shakes his head. "They're not sharing and they get to make up the rules. Student privacy and all that jazz."

"Their chief's not some former Boston cop you can back-channel, pull some strings on?" Sitting on a bloated pension and padding it with another fat salary to watch the kids play Ultimate Frisbee and break up heated arguments over the merits of the *Star Wars* prequels.

"No, she's not." And therefore he couldn't compel MIT to cooperate because while his inquiry might be part of a murder investigation, Sam probably falls short of a person of interest and

I'm guessing nobody's come forward to file a missing person's report.

In the past, it wasn't unusual for Sam to go off the grid for a few weeks at a time. Only why now? And with his dissertation deadline looming.

"*Should* I be worried?" I ask Wells. "Actually, scratch that. I don't care. It's none of my business."

"That's an unusual attitude for you, Zesty. You got something you want to tell me, or am I going to have to find out the hard way?"

"Are you serious?" I throw up my hands defensively. "I've only talked to Sam a couple of times since he found his way back to the womb and he never mentioned this Roshan kid to me or even that he was back taking classes. And as far as last night goes, in the handful of times I've visited Darryl he's never mentioned Ms. Tehran and I don't know a thing beyond what I saw, or more accurately, didn't see last night."

"I've heard you say something like that before, Zesty."

"Yeah, well, I had my reasons then, but this is totally out of my wheelhouse." I pick up my cup to finish my coffee, a mess of grounds sloshing around the bottom. I lean over and peer into Wells's ceramic mug. It's as clean as his conscience.

Fucking typical.

"You talked to everyone inside Nick's already?" I mumble through the grinds.

"Getting there. And running background checks, but it'll take some time. Only you keep forgetting, I'm not on that thing."

"So then why am I here?"

Wells takes a deep breath, lifts the fedora off the empty seat where he'd set it down, runs his fingers along the inside band, and twirls the hat in his hands. He parts his lips as if he's about to say something and then seals them again in a frown. All this while watching me with baleful eyes, but also taking in a gay couple holding hands, a long-limbed brunette going all sex Gumby to pick up her fallen yoga mat, a couple of black guys unloading boxes from the back of a truck parked on Shawmut Ave. Wells's leg shakes beneath the table. He tugs on one earlobe, his face pinched as if a bitter pill is lodged halfway down his throat. This is a new Wells, one I've never seen before; maybe human after all.

"I need a favor," he finally says.

SIX

I pick up the second shift watching Martine Andino, stationing myself at the corner of Clarendon and Stuart streets, kitty-corner from the Loews Hotel, where Andino had registered. The Loews has the distinction of being the last Italianate Renaissance build-ing built in Boston, meaning there was granite involved and plenty of it. It also happens to be the previous Boston Police headquarters and though it had undergone a major reinvention it still main-tained vestiges of its colorful past—a set of blue globes flanking the long perp walkway out front and a pair of thirteen-foot-tall brass exterior doors kept as shiny and polished as Zdeno Chára's Norris trophy.

The big changes came on the inside, where the interior had been gutted and renovated: a restaurant with strung lights and sunken outdoor seating where the holding cells had been; two floors added to the original seven. On the second floor, four mu-nicipal seals were set within ornate box balconies guarded by a set of flinty-eyed stone eagles. And just in case you didn't pick up on the context clues, the words "Boston Police Headquarters" were still carved into the space between the first and second floors.

Welcome to today's Boston. Blink once and the Freedom Trail will have sold the naming rights to New Balance, the JFK Federal Building will be converted into a Pottery Barn, the John Adams Courthouse into an Apple store.

And maybe aside from the occasional murder of someone like poor Rambir Roshan, major crime in Boston is going out of style. This trend keeps up, Wells and Brill will soon be sharing a soup line with Charlie.

They sure won't be sharing it with anybody who can afford the Loews. Which tells me either Andino has money to burn or scored one hell of a Groupon. Not that I'm complaining. The hotel's only a few blocks from my office and just a quick cut down Public Alley 32, where there's a Flour Bakery where I can coffee-up regularly and use the bathroom.

"Wow, on time and everything." Solarte spooks me, materializing out of the foot traffic and looking every bit the tourist, a Nikon camera hanging around her neck and holding a question mark of pink cotton candy drooping off a paper cone. A matching pink *Cheers* cap is pulled low on her head, shading her eyes. She'd warned me I wouldn't see her coming. Either I was off my game or she was just that good.

"Listen, it should be pretty straightforward." Solarte tilts a sideways bite off the cone, editing the punctuation. "Andino doesn't have any reason to think he's being followed and certainly not by someone who looks like you. Nice bike." Solarte makes a face toward my Trek hybrid locked to one of Boston's four billion No Parking signs. It actually is a nice bike, but I'd purposely grimed it up some so as not to attract a thief's discerning eye. There are entire crews in Boston who do nothing but city-rove with blunt tools separating bikes from poles before reselling them on the cheap or shipping them out of town. It's practically a rite of passage to have your bike stolen in this town. Just as it is to crash it; not so much a matter of whether, but *when*; a carelessly flippered car door or personalized front bumper out there waiting for everyone.

Welcome to Boston. Get yourself a T pass.

"Are you fast enough on that thing to follow a car in case he grabs a cab?"

"Do pigs fly?"

"No." Solarte looks at me blankly.

"Then I'm bad at metaphors. But if you look closely you'll see I took the training wheels off."

"You bring another shirt like I told you?"

I did. It was one of Zero's Zen Moving Company shirts and I'd placed it in a plastic bag to protect it from Charlie's oily Beretta. I'd briefly considered tossing the gun into the Charles River but didn't want to pollute the water, seeing how they'd cleaned it up to the degree that some people actually chose to swim in it. When I was a kid, if you fell into the Charles, they'd administer last rites and name a disease after you.

I'd also considered burying it, but if there's one thing I've learned in the last couple of years it's that nothing stays buried in Boston for long.

"If you think Andino's seen you more than once, change your shirt. Little things help."

"Like a cotton candy beard?" I point to Solarte's pink chin.

"Exactly." Solarte lifts the camera from around her neck. "I don't need you to go all Annie Leibovitz on me. Just take one or two wherever he goes. If he meets with anyone snap them, too. You don't have to bring me the chip, just upload the pictures and send them to me. You know how to work this?"

"Yes."

"Any questions?"

"Yeah. How come you don't have a frosted glass door and a really hot secretary I can trade quips with?"

"Wow." Alianna Solarte puffs out her cheeks. "Darryl really wasn't exaggerating. I actually did have a secretary for a while."

"Hot?"

"It was my daughter."

"So that's a yes." I smile.

"Nice try," Solarte deadpans. "Keep it in your shorts."

"No, really, you have a daughter?" I try not to sound too interested, but I'm riding a cold streak to end all cold streaks and you can't do much better than an intro from Mom.

"A couple, in fact." Solarte opens her wallet, flips past her PI license to a picture of two girls who look to be in their twenties and have the same dark hair and serious eyes of their mother. They also share the same small nose and high cheekbones. One of them has a tattoo that starts somewhere behind her ear, snakes around the side of her neck and down toward the cleavage of her open shirt: dragons, flames, and other amusement park staples.

"Is that one single?" I point to the girl with tattoos.

"You like 'em like that?" Solarte arches her brows.

"I was just kidding. I'm sure they're both great."

"They're both a pain in the ass. Marinette, with the tattoos? Runs around with fools and fuck-ups. Couldn't even hold down the job I gave her. And her baby sister, Marisol? She's at John Jay, criminal justice major. Go figure."

"I've got a brother," I say. "We're pretty different, too." But then I realize Solarte probably already knows that.

"Andino's in there right now, but I doubt he'll make an appearance tonight. The man wore me out. You'll see when you look through the pictures. If anything about them jumps out at you, let me know. If he shows himself, stay with him until he returns and you think he's hit the sack. See that eagle statue? His room is three windows right above it. He doesn't have a car. At least not parked with the hotel. You got this?"

"I was *born* to waste time," I boast.

"Find something else to be proud of. Call me when you knock off. I won't answer, but it'll give me an idea of when I should pick him up again tomorrow."

"What about the camera?"

"Hold on to it. In the morning, upload the pictures and email them to me. I already emailed the ones I took. You'll have to watch both entrances, he could come out either one."

I do as I'm told, clicking through the pictures Solarte had taken, Andino getting around like she'd said—Newbury Street, the Fenway, Harvard Square, Porter Square, Broad Street downtown—but seemingly without much purpose, always alone, and insulated, I get the feeling somehow, or at least well versed in the art of selective attention as crowds surge and pass around him.

I catch him stepping out of the hotel at around eight thirty and watch him smoke a cigarette and chat amiably with the valet. After which he descends the stairs and sits on the sunken patio beneath the strung lights and eats something. Once he's finished with that, he walks once around the block as I circle counterclockwise on my bike and I see him reenter the hotel through the Berkeley Street entrance. I forget to take any pictures, but then again he didn't really go anywhere.

As far as I can tell, nobody comes to visit him. The light in his room goes on five minutes after he returns and off around midnight and I cruise the few blocks into the South End.

Finally, easy money.

SEVEN

I cruise Berkeley all the way to Washington, hang a right and meander past the Gothic Cathedral of the Holy Cross, an anchor of this South End neighborhood for over a hundred years. Without purpose I loop around to Harrison Ave. and before I know it, drift onto Thayer Street, something that feels like unfinished business always drawing me back to my former street.

Why is it, I ask myself, bumping over the cobblestones, that every time I return to Thayer, I expect it to be as I remember it, as if the Art Deco streetlights hadn't been installed, the high-priced galleries and million-dollar condos hadn't replaced the rough industrial loft I used to live in and the illegal after-hours clubs I used to frequent? Why do I keep stalking my past as if expecting to come across something different, as if the city hadn't changed from someplace I called home to where I'm now just a barely tolerated visitor who can't afford the views? What can't I see that everybody else sees clear as day?

My former homeless neighbor, Albert, isn't in his loading dock. But to my surprise, as I cruise back through the neighborhood and up Worcester Street, Detective Brill is sitting on the stoop of number 34, bright construction lights shining in the first-floor brownstone apartment, the windows propped open and a heavy toxic smell like turpentine mixed with crack cocaine drifting through, nearly overpowering Brill's trademark cigar, which smokes between his thick fingers like a sixth appendage.

"Well, I'll be damned. Look who it be." Brill screws the cigar into his mouth, makes it glow, and looks at his watch. I've only seen Brill in a suit, the kind that comes out of the cleaner's pre-wrinkled, so it's jarring to see him in a pair of blue jean overalls with the clasps undone, the front folded down and hanging like a Labrador's panting tongue. A fine white dust covers his three-day beard and thinning hair, giving him a look that falls somewhere between Old Man Time and a powdered cruller. A filthy surgeon's mask hangs around his neck.

"I'm here with a request from the neighborhood board," I say. "Either close those windows so they can't smell the bodies under your floorboards or douse the cigar. You're lowering property values."

"In this Shangri-La? Now you know *that's* some bullshit, Zesty. Hell, black people could move here and prices still goin' up. To what do I owe this pleasure?" Brill glances at his watch again. "At this time of night?"

"Young and carefree," I say. "I don't expect you to understand. What's with the reno? Isn't this your cousin's building?"

When I'd first met Brill, it had been established that he'd grown up here on Worcester Street, taken in by an uncle who used to run a popular blues club on Mass Ave. that my parents had frequented. For a time my father had lived across the street and there was a picture in his rented Brookline home now, my dad seated with a trio of tuxedo-clad, long-haired, wild-eyed white guys mixed in with a dozen or so black men in suits and fedoras, a group of neighborhood children squatting at the bottom of the stairs. Brill was one of them.

It was just the first of many crossed paths between them, a closer acquaintance formed when Brill started working at his uncle's bar, even as my mother was wanted by the FBI for a bomb she'd set off on the Harvard campus. The explosive was rigged to go off well before the scheduled start of class. My mother's compatriots had wanted to send a bloodier message, but she consid-

ered herself an activist, not a killer, and wasn't down for that. At
least it looked that way until shit got real with Bank of Boston.

"It's my building now," Brill says.

"You moved out of Newton?" I'm surprised. It seems like only
yesterday Brill was extolling the virtues of a fenced-in yard, grass
between his toes, and a morgue-like silence after 8 P.M.

Brill glows the cigar and releases a slow curling wave of smoke
that drifts out the side of his mouth. From inside his windows I
can hear Ella Fitzgerald scatting *shing-dinga-biddly-boom-boom-ah*
(or something close to that) on a cheap boom box. I look up to the
second floor, two windows covered with grime and one of them
broken, through which I can see boxes and construction materials piled high to the ceiling. Same deal on the third floor, but with
sheets hung poorly for window shades, the building otherwise
obviously vacant.

shing-bada-biddly-boom-boom-dip-diddly-ah, Ella sings.

The outside bricks are in dire need of repointing, some of
them sticking out like hand grips on a rock climbing wall, the
window frames rotting from the outside in like junkie teeth.

"Cut the bullshit, Zesty. I know Wells sent you here to check
on me. So here I am. You still a messenger, right? Deliver this:
Tell him to go fuck himself."

"Wow," I say. "Glad to know you guys have maintained an
equilibrium. Only now I'm just plain curious: What's the deal?"

"With *what*?"

"Everything, I guess. The move. Wells asking me of all people
to check on you."

Brill huffs and spits to the curb. "He didn't tell you?" He's got
his detective face on now, his hound dog eyes running me over,
taking in every detail.

I throw out my hands palms up.

Brill actually grunts a *hu-rumph* and says, "Turns out suburbs
wasn't my thing."

"What part of it?" Uninvited, I lean my bike against his scrolled iron fence, which also needs sanding and repainting. "The lines at Cumberland Farms? Or not enough black people for you?"

"Funny thing, it wasn't even racial."

"No?" Probably because Newton and the other nearby suburbs are liberal hotbeds where the only color that matters is green: fat annual checks cut to the United Negro College Fund to help assuage the guilt of de facto segregation.

"So what was it, then?" I point to the stoop and Brill nods acquiescence, letting me take a seat. Ella has been replaced by someone I don't recognize but she's damn fine. "Who's that singing?"

"You don't know?" I shake my head. "New girl named Adele."

"She's good."

"White girl, too. Not as raw as Amy Winehouse, though."

"Not many are."

Brill nods solemnly. "Lotta things went into the move, actually. First being, it was classic dog out of the pound. It's hard to explain. Almost like it was *too* nice out there. Like I kept looking around feeling like I was living in some Pleasantville-type shit. That make any sense to you?"

"It does." And it had the familiar ring to what Zero often preaches: When things are going well, it's just the cosmos delaying the punch line. Arguably not the healthiest worldview, but maybe some people really are better suited to living with a keen skepticism, sleeping with one eye open. "Only I think the analogy's 'fish out of water.'"

"It's what I said it was. Bull in a Chinaman's shop." Brill mangles another idiom but I don't correct him. Wells had told me that Brill had been acting strangely lately and he'd wanted my take on it.

I try to recall my father's first sign of slippage but it's hard to pinpoint because he'd long practiced his form of benign stoicism, his ink-black liar's eyes concealing every tell. But I have little doubt that my father's first response when he recognized something wrong within himself was to try and reason with the disease, negotiate the narrative of his loss. *Here's what you can have,* he'd tell the plaque building up on his brain: *I'll give you my entire West End childhood, throw in Scollay Square, the Gershwin catalog, and the '75 World Series on top of that. The wife stays. Zero and Zesty.* Did he believe enough in a higher power to pray? Or to curse the heavens? Of that I have no idea.

But Wells confiding in me and not another cop makes perfect sense. If Brill was coming loose at the screws, there's no telling what the BPD response might be. Desk duty followed by an early retirement? A hustle out to pasture? I've been through the Alzheimer's wringer and contrary to my mouth always in motion, I know how to keep secrets. After all, I'd learned from the best.

"The worst part was," Brill's voice drags me back to the block, "I'd get invited to these dinner parties, all neighborly, I have to go, right? And what do white people talk about?"

White people talk about their jobs, *What do you do?* the opening line in that world. On the other side of the tracks it's usually *Who you with?* And you'll find out pretty quick if you're at the wrong party.

"So let me guess, you'd tell them you're a homicide cop and the room would go all cold on you?"

"See, that's the thing. Total opposite. They'd be all hot and bothered wanting to know the grimy details. What the blood smelled like, how many holes did the vic have in him. Some of the divorced gals? They were rubbing their legs like crickets they were so excited having me up in their plush living rooms, all blood and no stain."

"You mean they were too far removed from it?"

"Bingo. From the *real* shit of it. People crying so hard they're puking in the street. You know what I'm talking about, you been there. The hood closing up right quick, everyone all *I din't see nut-hin', I don't know nuthin', Detective,* knowing damn well they're just going to take care of shit themselves."

"You didn't tell them that part?"

Brill sucks his teeth hard. "Let's just say they weren't moved."

"So how many holes did Rambir Roshan have in him?"

Brill screws the cigar back into his mouth, pulls it to a Chernobyl glow, and releases a massive cloud of smoke that obscures his face. "Now why in hell you want to know something like that?"

"Sam Budoff," I say.

"What about him?"

I wave at the smoke between us. Not because it bothers me, but to get a better look at Brill's face. Detectives, in general, are pretty decent poker players and the men and women who played in my father's games—always at the invitation of someone higher up the food chain—had the requisite skills to do well. The vice cops were particularly skilled, though openly despised for their hit-and-run tactics, maybe winning a few dollars before calling it quits, disrupting the flow and evading the long-game traps and feints the real sharks were setting.

The homicide cops didn't fare as well. Even as their large amateur stacks were erected—maybe the result of a good run of cards, some righteous moves, even—they were always targeted for a methodical dismantling because as a group, if there was one massive hole in their game, it lay in their obsessive pursuit of a hand that needed to be released. The homicide players, almost to a man, were keen observers of others but could hardly recognize their own faults and weaknesses; they stuck around too long and often got burned.

Detective Brill isn't a natural liar, he'd just picked up the skill later in life. Only he isn't lying now. Budoff's name didn't figure into the Roshan murder as far as Brill knew. Or perhaps Wells's concern for his partner isn't unfounded, things slipping his mind.

Or am I missing something here, a rift grown between the two men, Wells using me to draw Brill's ire, prick him like a thorn?

I let him in on Wells's Sam inquiry, which draws a laugh at my expense. "So he called *you*? And *I'm* supposed to be the one that's lost his damn mind? What else he lay on you?"

"Nothing."

"So he didn't tell you I was suspended?"

"No." But that at least partially explains why he's up at one in the morning working on the building. And didn't know Wells was on the hunt for Sam. "Congratulations. What for?" I could just as easily have said, *Who did you piss off now?*

"Nah, I'm not getting into it with you. You so interested, read the papers."

But I had. At least the stories Anitra Tehran had written and there was nothing regarding Brill's suspension. And I'd seen the photographs, the overhead shots of a fedora and a cigar-chomping detective on the Mass Ave. Bridge. Brill *had* been on the Roshan case, or at least on the scene, and now he wasn't. What had he done?

That, I didn't know, but I can tell he realizes he screwed up with the mention of the papers and tries changing the subject. "I heard about the bombing at Nick's."

"I wasn't *that* bad."

"Double bombing," he follows up without cracking a smile and I hit the imaginary snare for him. "Hell of a coincidence he found you there, don't you think?"

"He wasn't looking for me," I correct him. "He was on a date of some sort."

"Who with?"

"You know Anitra Tehran, the *Globe* reporter?"

"She was there?" Brill narrows his eyes and begins to chew the corner of his lip, the flavor apparently not to his liking. "Yeah, that was no date, that fucking idiot."

"You got suspended over something related to the Rambir Roshan case." I leave the question mark out of my voice.

"They tell you that?"

They. As if the two of them were working together. I hadn't been sure, but I figure it for gospel now. So what had compelled Tehran *not* to write about a veteran homicide detective removed from duty on a high-profile case? Why sit on it?

Which brings me back to the Nick's bombing. If it was meant as a warning for either Wells or Tehran to back off the Roshan murder, it was way too early in the game; Wells was still knocking on doors and pursuing low-return leads like Sam Budoff. Maybe even desperate, considering he'd called on me to point him in the right direction. Wells didn't have shit. Which means Tehran had the same. And Brill was sidelined, at least officially. So who was brazen or stupid enough to go after a cop *and* a reporter?

"Hard to discount the Eastern European angle." I throw a line into the night and let it sink in. A silvery cloud slides across the moon like a slow wink as Adele gives way to Irma Thomas singing "Anyone Who Knows What Love Is (Will Understand)." It's hard to disagree with her.

Brill finds it hard to disagree with me. "Be foolish not to." He swallows the hook.

EIGHT

Detectives Wells and Brill might run a Tom and Jerry routine in public but the men are close as brothers.

"And you think Roshan's connected to Eastern Europeans, Russians? How?" I ask.

"Poker."

"The MIT poker analytics class?" I don't get it.

"That's the angle we were working. The Nick's bombing last night was the tactical error that confirmed it. Even the street gangs, the Mob—what's left of it—know better than to go after a cop and a reporter. Whatever Tehran dug up, this level of response is something new." Rare emotion, something close to fatherly concern, shows on Brill's face. "The Roshan kid for sure was involved in something."

"And you know that because?"

"He was shot at close range, for one." Brill taps me low on the sternum, leaving a white plaster dust mark like a bullet hole on my shirt. "But at an upward angle. Burn marks and fiber analysis indicated three different types of threads and only one of them belonging to Roshan."

"So Roshan maybe knew the shooter," I say. "It would explain the closeness?"

"Possibly."

"So the other two fibers came from the shooter?"

"Right. Liner, coat thread. Right through the pocket."

"How do you know that?"

"What, you forgot already? World's greatest Homicide."

"No, really, how?"

"Fuck you, Zesty," Brill says, but his eyes are smiling. "Coat was tossed off the bridge into the Charles. At first a Northeastern crew thought they got a floater. When they saw all the activity on the bridge, they pulled it out and handed it over."

"Okay, so not a random shooting. Still don't see Russians, though."

"Neither did we. Until we get Mr. Roshan to the ME's office and they find a couple of poker chips inside his Reebok socks, Reebok kicks."

Buy local, die local, I think, a cold chill running up my spine.

It's not the usual trigger for my cranium-dwelling DJ to spin another record, but I already hear the opening notes of the New Models' "Permanent Vacation" dropping loud and clear.

"The chips were from the poker analytics class? That's really why Wells was grilling me about Sam."

"That's a negative." Brill's smile has all the wattage of a Steven Wright joke. "The MIT class is all theory, probability, risk management. Whatever you get when pi sticks his dick in the theory of relativity. They don't actually *play* the game."

"So from a casino? Foxwoods?" I pick the nearest legalized den of bad carpeting.

"Not casino chips, but professional grade."

"So Paulson's, then." Paulson has been the supplier of choice to most of the Vegas casinos for decades, their manufacturing process an expensive and highly guarded secret to prevent counterfeiting. What look like painted strips at the edges and sides of the chips are actually compression-molded color embedded *into* the chip. Did Sam find a way to re-create these chips? Did Rambir Roshan?

Brill sucks his teeth hard. "Maybe I *am* slipping. Of course you know something about poker chips." Brill looks at me too long and too hard. "So go ahead, Zesty, you've come this far. Those chips on Roshan, who do you figure they belong to?"

Zero, what have you done now? I think, but don't say. In fact, I say nothing at all, a rarity that blesses Brill with a rare laugh.

"See, that's what we thought, too. We catch a body, poker chips, shades of the Meyers clan, right? Only Zero's not running anything except his moving company, far as we can tell. He's not in this. Which is good for you, looks like it might be bad for Budoff, and just got even worse for Anitra Tehran."

"How's that?"

"Those chips on Roshan are house chips from a poker club across from the Stockyard, that longtime joint by the Mass Pike."

"I know it." The original Boston Food Co-op my mother had co-founded was just a couple blocks away. "Who runs it?"

"Ukrainian mob."

"That still Russia?" Geography and geopolitics were never my strong points.

"Close enough. Same tactics. The place is managed by a guy name of Oleg Katanya, sometimes goes by Mikhail Sergachev."

"You learn this before or after your suspension?"

"Common knowledge if you in the game." Brill wasn't talking about poker now. "Katanya runs the day-to-day operations, worked his way up from drug dealer to pimp, possibly a hitter. He's got ties to Russian organized crime in Brighton Beach, considered something of a psychopath even by New York standards."

I ask Brill what someone has to do to earn that distinction.

"Word was one of his whores had been holding out on him. A hundred here, a hundred there, nothing major, but he found out about it. One night he pulled all his girls off the street, put them in a van, drove them out to the Brooklyn railyards."

"Do I have to hear the rest of this?" I ask Brill.

"Yeah. Because knowing how you like to stick your nose in places it doesn't belong, I want you to understand what you're dealing with here. Katanya doused this girl—and by the way, she had a kid, that's why she was setting money aside—in gasoline and put a match to her. Made the others watch while he kept peeling off fifties and throwing them into the flames."

"Scary."

"Jewish." Brill widens his eyes.

"That fuckin' supposed to mean something to me?"

"Whoa, take it easy, Zesty." Brill uncharacteristically retreats a step. "I hit a nerve?"

I suppose he did. I've never been a particularly devout Jew, haven't practiced any of the customs or traditions since childhood, but I'd retained a finely tuned ear for the anti-Semitic aside, which has always drawn a sharp Pavlovian reaction that I've never quite gotten a handle on. My father would have been disappointed in my shop-window transparency.

"This Oleg Katanya, he's moved to Boston full-time?"

"Looks that way."

"Poker club's his?"

"No. Katanya answers to a guy by the name of Jakub Namestnikov. Higher up the chain."

"How high?"

"Think like the equivalent of a capo. Runs his own crew, pays tribute to the Boston boss, Antti Voracek."

"Never heard of him," I say. "Is Namestnikov or Voracek someone who Tehran might have pissed off with her real estate articles?"

"Not in any way we could connect. The Ukrainians are just starting to fill the vacuum now that the Italians and Irish have been neutered. It's still mostly entry-level shit: narcotics, prostitution, protection rackets. These penthouses and condos that Tehran wrote about are top-shelf multimillion-dollar deals. The poker club and all that other stuff pales in comparison."

"You're saying it might be a coincidence?"

"What I'm saying is Roshan doesn't make sense in the scheme of things. Only those poker chips didn't get into his socks by accident."

Hiding them there as if he wanted to leave a message behind for someone to follow. But who? And why? Did Rambir Roshan know he was in danger? And if he did, why did he take the meeting on the Mass Ave. Bridge, assuming he wasn't just flat-out ambushed?

"You know for sure Roshan was playing in Namestnikov's club?"

"Not really. The chips were all we got. By the time we came knocking, the place had shut down. And it looked like in a hurry, too. Poker tables, the bar, the liquor, everything was still there. Custom-made stuff, expensive."

"Sounds like they're running. But why? You guys don't have shit or you wouldn't even be talking to me."

"Too true. And besides the chips there was no Roshan/ Ukraine connection. And like I said earlier, the way he was killed doesn't have the familiar markings of their type of hit. Russians would have put one in his grill and probably just disappeared him."

"Public spot, though, smack dab in the middle of the bridge. That's pretty Russian, isn't it? Makes a bolder statement."

"Debatable."

"Cameras on the bridge?"

"Boston end only. Big Brother's not welcome in the People's Republic of Cambridge."

And I am with them 100 percent. Next thing you know Boston will rig cameras onto every street corner and my mailbox will start blooming radioactive-colored moving violations for riding on sidewalks and cutting up one-way streets.

"We looked through the Boston tape and there wasn't anything there. As for Namestnikov, from what we can tell, he doesn't own any property here. Doesn't appear to be on that level yet or he's done a good job concealing it. Anyhow, now we can't find him or Katanya. It's like they were never here."

So who threw the Molotov cocktail last night?

"Is Tehran considered a legitimate target?"

"You're talking to the wrong guy, Zesty. All I know is after last night Wells requested a uniform to park out front of her place, make their presence known."

"Where's she live?"

"Thacher Street."

"That's the North End," I say. "How's the cruiser going to find a parking spot?"

"It must be a disease." Brill shakes his head.

"It's timing," I say. "I'm still working on it."

"It's more than that," Brill counters. Maybe he's right.

"So what's Wells doing now?" I ask.

"How the hell should I know?"

"He's not keeping you in the loop? And what was that suspension about again? When'd it kick in?" I take one last stab at it.

"Nah, I'm not getting into it with you. You so interested, ask the Dynamic Duo. But I'll tell you, the pair of them together, that's some bullshit, though."

"Okay." I let it drop. "So what's with all this?" I throw a thumb behind me to the brownstone.

"Timing." Brill shrugs off his cop armor, takes a seat beside me. "The siren song of home. Whatever you want to call it. My uncle passed a while back and left the building to my cousin, Charles. Only, last couple of years he's been taking equity out of the place, supposed to be fixing it up. . . ."

I look at the building, peer up and down the street. It's the only sore spot on the block. "What he do with the money?"

"What do you think?" Brill looks at me sideways.

"I was giving him the benefit of the doubt," I say, but from well-kept brownstone to derelict in just a couple years suggests drugs or gambling.

"Tenants started complaining, stopped paying rent after a

while and he had a mess of violations, fines piling up. These buildings are solid but they need to be maintained. Roof was leaking.
Wiring was old. Tenants had enough, finally moved out. 'Course,
then he turned around and rented to people he shouldn't have and
it was all downhill after that. People squatted, started stripping it to
its roots, copper wiring, fixtures. I only found out about it because
the Precinct Fourteen blues kept getting called by the neighbors.
Long story short, those crooks disguised as a bank, Wells Fargo,
was about to foreclose and I stepped in. Sold the Newton house in,
like, five minutes and here I am. Didn't Zero tell you?"

"Tell me *what*? Nobody tells me shit, obviously." Brill just sits
there grinning at me. "Aw no, you can't be fucking serious," I
groan.

"Why not? Friends and family discount." Brill twitches me a
wink. "Your man Sid and the Rabbi there are a trip."

"Who?"

"Did a fine job, too, for a bunch of ex-felons. Anyhow, I don't
have much in the way of value to steal so I figured it was winner-
winner-chicken-dinner for me either way. If they ripped me off
I'd finally have something on Zero that stuck."

"Brilliant," I say. "You tip them?"

"I was supposed to tip them?" Brill leans back a little and releases some smoke to hide behind, but I can still see him. And
while his mouth isn't moving, something behind his eyes is. He'd
tipped the movers. I'd bet my life on it.

"Place doesn't look habitable." I gaze up at the building. "You
actually staying here?"

"Making do. Joined the Y for showers. Walking that tiny
hamster track over the basketball court. Even saw your sorry ass
clanking jumpers couple weeks ago."

"Must have been an off day," I say. "Happens about once every
leap year."

"Right." Brill looks at his watch again, grumbles an anatomic impossibility under his breath.

"You expecting someone?"

"Supposed to have a work crew come in do a couple things."

"At *this* hour?" I say incredulously.

"Shee-it. The way this city's going, people working practically round the clock to make it happen."

"So what, your crew, they're on black time?" I say.

"Zesty, you are one racist motherfucker." Brill laughs, using the rail to pull himself to his feet. "Though I gotta respect you for being so up-front with it."

"I was just kidding." I smile.

"I know. So was I. I don't respect you at all."

"Oof."

"And anyhow, my guys are Guatemalan. You speak Spanish?"

"I know *trabaja* means 'work,'" I say. "That's about it."

"Yeah, my crew, we talk in hand signals. They're probably just stuck at their main job up Beacon Hill or maybe found deeper pockets. Either way . . ." Brill extinguishes his cigar by smudging it into the granite stoop, the ugly mark joining a dozen other stains where he'd obviously done it before, which would necessitate a power wash later. Only I don't say anything about it. If Brill's foray into construction is anything like what I experienced trying to fix up my old loft on Thayer Street and make it livable, his project will cost twice as much as he thinks it will and take three times as long to complete.

"What about it?"

"What about *what*?"

"You don't look to be in a hurry to go anywhere. In the mood for some *trabaja*?"

"For you? Hell no!"

"Come on, boy. I'm paying cash money under the table. You ever take lead paint off of bricks?"

"Nope."

"I find that hard to believe. I've heard your material before." Brill uses two fingers to form a gun and shoots me dead. "Come on, Zesty. Don't be so hardheaded. I'll shine a couple lights, set you up in front of a wall and let's see what happens."

NINE

Zero's Zen Moving Company is on Beach Avenue in Somerville, a thin side street in a commercial zone with auto body shops, warehouses, and scrap-metal yards whose footprint keeps shrinking as MIT, Tufts, and Harvard keep buying up property nobody else can afford. There's an industrial laundry at the northern end of Beach that perpetually kicks out massive clouds of steam that smell like a dog's peed-on blanket and when the wind blows just right, cotton-thick shrouds drift about the warehouse bricks, transforming the narrow avenue into a spooky film set replete with beggar extras—homeless men and women rattling their scrap-metal-laden shopping carts into and out of the mist.

The Zen Moving Company garage door is rolled open, the parking bays empty—a good sign—meaning all of Zero's pirate crews are on the job and out of trouble, at least for the time being. Along the southern wall, Erector Set shelves are stocked with enormous pallets of flattened Zen-logoed cardboard boxes, giant containers filled with straps, bands, blankets, and tools. Portable metal storage bins form the wall directly across, stacked and secured until the owners request delivery to their new digs. Or not. Sometimes people just stop paying the storage fees, choosing a clean break over their old possessions, and are never heard from again.

Sam Budoff still had his bin with Zero, marked with his name, the roll-top door sporting a fist-size padlock like all the others. Zero provides the locks. The renter receives the only key. They lose it—and they tend to lose it—Zero charges them an exorbitant fee to clip the lock though he employs a half-dozen guys who could pick the thing in their sleep.

There's a weight bench set up in the large room that leads to the back stairs up to Zero's office, reject couches, chairs, and love seats horseshoed around it as if watching someone lift heavy objects after working all day lifting heavy objects were somehow spectator-worthy. Maybe it is, considering the bar's stacked with enough iron to suggest the last person who'd been lifting was either Zero, Sid, or King Kong.

Make no mistake, raw strength in the moving business is crucial, but the sought-after skills are endurance and the patience to manage the stress of the people relocating, having the insight to gauge where the customer is emotionally during this major transition—good times or bad. Nobody moves for nothing; it's just too much trouble.

Zero is particularly adept at this, another poker skill spun into positive action, though he rarely jumps in on moves anymore. Same goes for Sid, though most of his time these days is devoted to looking after my father and coordinating the other men who rotate in and out of my dad's rented Brookline home, providing him with the twenty-four-hour care and supervision he now requires, his Alzheimer's long ago obliterating his circadian rhythms and rendering sleep mostly obsolete.

Sid is gentle and infinitely patient with my dad, probably on account of his own experiences with a father who suffered from dementia, though it wasn't diagnosed as such thirty years ago.

"It was a race between booze and a fucked-up brain," Sid once confided in me. "And the booze lost. He would have done us all a favor if he'd chugalugged Drano instead."

I remove seventy-five pounds of iron from each side of the bar and lie flat on the bench. I can still smell the diesel exhaust hovering just under the ceiling thirty feet above me, but it doesn't seem to bother the pigeon that hops along one of the steel beams and swells with a cooing chuckle as it sees what I'm up to.

"Fuck you, you're a pigeon," I say, take a deep breath, and grunt into the lift. Maybe somewhere in China a bee pollinates a flower, which triggers an earthquake in Bolivia, but the bar doesn't budge, it only laughs at me. At least until I realize it's Jhochelle laughing.

"Zesty, what a pleasant surprise and a happy coincidence. I was about to call you." Jhochelle is Zero's Israeli wife and mother of my nephew, Eli, who must be napping in his crib upstairs in Zero's office. Prior to her pregnancy, Jhochelle was dark and lean, retaining the body honed in the mandatory two years of service in the Israeli Defense Forces. She looks no different now, a little more than a year into motherhood, except around the eyes, which are the same color as my father's, ocean-bottom black and impenetrable, now stamped with the tired half-moon imprint of every new parent's.

"Do you think you could lift this?" I ask her.

"Why on earth would I try?"

"I dunno, to impress yourself?"

"I could use a little of that," Jhochelle admits. "There's nothing quite like having a child to make you question your self-worth. Or sanity, for that matter."

"The kid didn't come with instructions? What kind of baby factory did you get him from?"

"Considering his lineage, a shady one."

I grunt into the lift once more. This time the bar vibrates. Progress.

"Anyhow, I don't rely on brute strength, you know that."

It's true. Jhochelle, in addition to being a general badass, was

trained as a sniper and could assemble an Uzi with her eyes closed.
But barring firearms, she's also one of those women who prides
herself on the well-placed knee or chop to the larynx, moves I've
seen deftly employed in crowded bars on men with grabby
hands.

"Come." Jhochelle leads the way upstairs and I follow into
Zero's cluttered office, where feng shui must have crawled up and
died. Aside from the tidy crib with a mini Calder mobile suspended above it, the office is populated by a dizzying array of
rejected knickknacks, cast-off furniture, and incomprehensibly
bad original art.

"What's with *this* crap?" I sidestep a pair of rust-streaked
oxygen tanks and a palette-size rack of caged lighting, like the
type you'd see illuminating a ballpark. Over the tanks, on a bicycle hook screwed into the ceiling, hangs a bulky yellow suit that
looks more hazmat than diving, the helmet, nearly box-shaped
with a large plexiglass shield riveted along the seams and attached
by a bungee cord, giving the appearance of someone who's nod-
ded off standing up.

"Those?" Jhochelle dismisses the mess with a backward wave
of her hand. "They've been there for weeks. I keep waiting for
Zero to add a captain's wheel, some plastic lobsters, and fishing
nets to complete the scene."

"Who'd the boys move, Jacques Cousteau?"

"Possibly." Jhochelle peeks in on Eli, who's asleep, before
seating herself behind my brother's desk. "So."

"Is it safe, keeping the tanks in the office? They look pretty
rusted out."

"I'll have Zero or one of the guys move them if you're concerned."

"What kind of suit is that? Not warm-weather, it looks—"

"Zesty, enough about the gear already. I haven't seen you in
months. What's prompted this visit?"

"You go first," I say. "I need a favor but you said you were about to call me."

"Yes. Perfect. So it'll be a trade, then."

Only I'm uncomfortable with Eli in the room and keep the stained paper bag with Charlie's gun in my pack. "Is there somewhere you can put Eli for a minute?"

"Why?"

I tell her.

"Really?" Jhochelle's eyes widen.

"It's not loaded," I add hastily. "Don't ask me where I got it but I need to put it in the safe, at least temporarily."

"I'm afraid I can't do that." Jhochelle reads something in my reaction and then adds, "Allow me to clarify. I *literally* can't do that. I don't have the combination."

"Since when?"

"Since Zero changed it last week."

"Why?"

"Why did he change it or why doesn't he give me the combination?"

"Both." Though I know better to expect transparency in regards to my brother's relationship with his mercurial wife. My relationships with women have never lasted long enough to confirm this, but I've long held the view that the daily lives of every married couple are governed by a communicative series of hieroglyphics rendered in smoke signals, forever changing in the breeze. In simpler terms: Who the fuck really knows what goes through the minds of two people who've conjoined their lives to such a degree that they've created another human being?

"It's not a matter of trust, Zesty, if that's what you're thinking. But the alternative, if you ask me, is actually worse."

"Which is what?"

"Obviously there's something he'd rather I not see. He's protecting me from something."

"From what?"

"If I knew—"

"Come on, Jhochelle. You married the fucker, I thought you had him figured out."

"As if."

"So are you worried or just pissed?"

"Considering the last couple of years . . ." Jhochelle contemplates the question, swaying lightly from side to side like a scale adjusting to an unbalanced weight, a movement that conveys neither anger nor pressing concern. "Let's just say I'm wary. Zero is not impulsive, your father had trained that out of him at an early age. You must have been sleeping during those lessons. I'm assuming he's decided to lock the safe to protect me from something. Making this not the first time he's chosen to shield his family, would it?" Jhochelle referring to *both* my parents' role in the Bank of Boston robbery, knowledge Zero had kept to himself until things began to spiral beyond his control.

"I won't lie and say it doesn't bother me, but now is not the time to press the issue. Is the gun you have registered?"

"The serial numbers have been filed off."

"Has it been fired recently?"

"How would I know?"

"Wonderful." Jhochelle shakes her head. "That's why I love you, Zesty, you're a paragon of responsibility."

"Hey," I say. "Since when did you master sarcasm?"

"When I married your brother. And irony as well, you'll soon see. I need you to go pick up Zero."

"From where?"

"The Lounge in Charlestown. Do you know it?"

"I know *of* it." Only I preferred to frequent bars where women with teeth might show up. And then stay long enough for me to show off my tough guy scars. "What's he doing at the Lounge in the middle of the day?" Zero's not a boozer; aside from occasional beers with his work crews after a job I've rarely seen him drink in daylight hours.

"Last I was informed, he was tearing the place apart." Jhochelle smiles bitterly. "I'd have called Sid but he's covering your father right now and as you saw from the empty garage, all the men are out. Which leaves you."

"Has he done this before, Jo?"

"Done what?"

"Gotten plastered in the middle of the afternoon."

"I never said he was drunk, Zesty, I just told you where he is. But I do think perhaps the combination of fatherhood and your father's steady decline have brought up issues for him which I don't think he can rampage his way through. Try as he might. Talk to him, Zesty, he'll listen to you. And get him out of that fucking bar before the authorities have to. The last thing we need is the Boston Police Department all over our business again; god only knows what Zero is really up to."

"Will do," I say. "But quick question. You still keep up the logbook for the storage bins downstairs?"

"Of course. It's part of the rental contract." With a two-signature itemized list so Zero is held accountable for the belongings while simultaneously the renter can't take something out and claim the movers stole it.

"Can I see it?"

Jhochelle starts studying me anew, like she missed something in the first read; as if asking her to stash a stolen gun wasn't troubling enough. "Why?"

"It's probably nothing, but . . ." I fill Jhochelle in, her eyes darkening, recalculating at the mention of Brill and Wells; like Zero is wont to do, weighing the opportunity against the risk as I report Sam's prolonged absence and his tenuous connection to Rambir Roshan.

"So Wells hasn't been able to get ahold of Sam since this

young man was murdered and this was how long ago, two weeks?"

"To the day. But I'm not sure how long after he was killed that Wells established the connection to Sam."

"Well, personally, I didn't see your friend, but as you know I'm not here full-time. . . ." Jhochelle selects a binder from a shelf and flips pages, running her eyes down each one until she comes to a stop. "He was here." She spins the book so I can see. "And if it's been two weeks precisely since Mr. Roshan was killed, it was the day after." She pins the date with her finger, Sam's signature and an item marked *box/miscellaneous* added to the storage bin.

"There a backup of this in the computer?" I close the binder.

Jhochelle smiles at me without meaning. Record keeping at Zen Movers is a nebulous matter, cash payments encouraged and generous discounts offered to customers who are willing to forgo any formal bill of service.

"Can I get into the bin?" I ask Jhochelle.

"You're concerned?"

"Too many coincidences, considering the timing of Sam's visit and ghost act."

"Zesty, I sympathize but you know damn well going into a bin runs counter to policy and violates the renter's bill of rights," Jhochelle admonishes me with a mother's tone. "It also happens to be against the law."

Which is probably why the hard snap of the bolt cutters feels so satisfying to her. I kick the lock aside, roll up the door to the unit. The cardboard box is at the front on the floor, marked *textbooks* in black Sharpie ink.

I pick it up and can tell immediately it's not full of textbooks. Any experienced mover would have come to the same conclusion, especially if the contents are purported to be made of paper. Porn is especially easy to gauge—though sometimes we're fooled by *National Geographic*—gay porn heavier than hetero, don't ask me why, it's something about the paper stock. Imported Swedish gay porn is even heavier, they might as well just print it on the tree trunk.

Jhochelle opens the box with three quick slashes of a box cutter. At the top is a rough draft of Sam's dissertation, the exact opposite of porn. Buried under the papers is an aluminum poker chip case with a little bit of heft to it. I bring it over to the weight bench where there's a fresh de Kooning swirl of white and green pigeon dropping hardening on the bar. I open the case, run my fingers over the full rows of chips, and look up. The pigeon inches a few steps to the right, trying to line me up.

"Don't even fuckin' think about it," I say, pulling out a random handful of chips, and show Jhochelle the markings.

"They're real?" she asks.

"I think so. They're all Vegas casino chips." Caesar's. Mandalay Bay. The Venetian. No chip has a valuation under a thousand dollars. With space now between the rows, I run my fingers down them again. Not a single chip matches the chips Brill had described Oleg Katanya using for the poker game he ran for Jakub Namestnikov and which Rambir Roshan had hidden in his shoes when he was killed.

"You'll take care of the box and the lock?" I return the chips to the case, slide the case into my bag.

"Of course. And perhaps it's best you keep the gun," Jhochelle says, pragmatically.

"Like I've got a choice." I hear the pigeon cooing directly above me now and step swiftly beyond its target range before noticing it'd already scored a hit; something green and slimy on my sneaker. "Fuckin' bird," I mutter aloud before recognizing what it really is: seaweed.

And it's wet.

TEN

There are some places, entire blocks in Boston's older, traditionally ethnic neighborhoods—Southie, Dorchester, Charlestown, Roxbury, even—that seem to exist in a parallel dimension, entered only through some time-bending portal where you'd swear you've stepped into a land preserved in soot-stained amber circa 1980.

Somehow, these streets have remained invisible to the deep-pocketed developers who prowl the city like hyenas and you can thank places like the Lounge for scaring them off. It's a squat dark bar sandwiched halfway down a block of three-deckers that lean in above it like shoulders reflexively bracing for a direct body blow. It's a drinking bar that attracts no new customers, welcomes no new blood, but every once in a while someone stumbles in and their life changes forever

Here's how it happens: You've gone to Notre Dame, maybe even local BC or BU, played a little varsity lacrosse or some D-1 football, showed some measure of controlled aggression on the field that got you a pat on the ass, a chest-thumping ovation from teammates. Hell, maybe there was even more savage in there; knocked some skulls in that drunken frat rumble that spilled out of Mary Ann's in Cleveland Circle or was it Bill's Bar on Lansdowne?

And now, look at you, pulling down that white-collar bread, got your first big-city apartment, worked hard and followed that righteous path your parents laid out in front of you. You're out drinking with your buddies, your broken-in Levi's and BoSox T-shirt betrayed by your four-hundred-dollar Aldens; you might as well have a neon sign blinking above your head that reads, SLUMMING.

You've heard of this neighborhood before, of course, read up on the depravity of Devlin McKenna, Jerry Dapolito, and any number of psychopaths who'd somehow escaped the classification of serial killer because the mask was always off. And for damn sure you've watched *Good Will Hunting,* seen the interior of a bar like this in *The Departed,* and you've had a few too many and to be honest, you're not entirely sure how you got here—this dark street, this darker bar.

But by the time you realize you've been left alone, recognize that the mick who's been staring at you with eyes that have the warmth of icicles, the one with the strange S-shaped part in that permafrost hair, which is actually a massive pink wormed scar running from his forehead down behind his ear like some crazy Boston street, it's way too late. You make a move to leave but your legs are filled with sand just as the guys playing pool start to move with the measured precision of wolves eyeing fresh meat, the last break on the cue ball sounding like someone's neck snapping.

Your head starts to pound and the smell from your armpits is one you don't recognize, because it's straight-up fear, and it's too late, you know it's too late, and when you wake up from this with tubes in your arms, your eyes reduced to maraschino slits, your head screwed into a mobilizing halo—you'll never look at the world the same way again. Your hair will grow back to cover where they shaved to drill a hole into your skull to relieve the swelling on your brain, but in a weaker shade, thinning to a premature gray. Your friends will become uncomfortable with your prolonged silences, with how you probe their soft layers with your faraway sleep-deprived eyes; what now passes for Morpheus' thin blanket always bringing you back to that place where they didn't even bother to wipe up your blood before reopening the door to the public and downing their next drink.

The Lounge in Charlestown is one of those places and Zero preferred to do his casual drinking in these types of bars where a brawl is tolerated, if not expected, and I push through the door with my eyes closed so they'll adjust quicker to the darkness, in case I have to start ducking haymakers and beer bottles. Only my precaution is unnecessary. Aside from someone who has the dimensions of an oil tanker pressing an ice-filled rag to his bloodied face, the place is calm, back to its midday rhythms. On the bar, in front of the large man, sits a short stack of twenty-dollar bills, likely Zero's monetary apology.

Zero has blood streaked across his swollen knuckles, a large red welt at the side of his neck, someone getting in a good one that was repaid in spades. His throwback Yastrzemski jersey is ripped at the sleeves revealing an alternative color scheme of tattoos printed on coiled muscles built through years of hard labor and supplemented by the weights.

Two guys are out cold in the corner, one in a smear of vomit, another scrabbling the floor on his hands and knees either looking for lost contacts or missing teeth. For a place where all hell broke loose, it looks relatively in order and it takes me a moment to figure out why. The bar stools are deflated red pads atop swivel stools screwed into the floor. Same goes for the linoleum-topped tables, the chairs tethered by heavy chains to D-rings covered by small metal plates. Aside from the bottles of liquor themselves, there's not a glass in the joint, all the beers on tap, the drinks served in lightweight plastic cups. In fact, on the whole, the bar is the drunken equivalent of childproof, a high scissor gate fronting stairs to the basement, the swinging door to the back kitchen sporting stained pillows duct-taped to the tops and bottoms; the bar itself is protected by worn leather padding riveted along its length.

Zero doesn't say anything or turn to look at me as I plunk myself down next to him. There's no doubt he tracked me in the dark bar mirror as soon as I opened the door, the lessons imparted by our father at the poker table still in full effect, the feints and jabs ignored to watch for the damaging haymakers.

"Jhochelle called me." I waste an explanation, point to a bottle of Jack Daniel's behind the bar figuring, when in Gomorrah.

The bartender stands impassively with his arms pretzeled in front of him. He shakes his head. I take a deep breath and place money on the bar. The bartender shakes his head again.

"He won't serve you," Zero says. "I've been officially eighty-sixed from the worst fucking bar in Boston."

"That's a bad thing?" Growing up, Zero and I had been kicked out of countless clubs and bars, unwelcome until my father's influence kicked in or a changing of the guard was at the door. Meaning someone who Zero hadn't punched in the face, which sometimes took a while. I swear, Zero's rung more bells in Boston than Anita Ward.

"I'll miss these guys." Zero looks around nostalgically.

"Fuck you," the bouncer says, reaching across the bar to twist fresh ice into the rag.

"Shut up and count your money," Zero tells him.

"You do all this yourself?" I look around more closely. The guys on the floor aren't much but they still have numbers and the bouncer looks capable of folding an iceberg.

"Hey, give me a little credit," the bouncer says. "Nah, it ain't even that. I had it under control. It was the Rabbi did most of the damage."

"The Rabbi?" I say.

"Rabbi. Hell's Angel, fuckin' big bearded fuck, what's the difference?"

I don't tackle that question, though I'm tempted to say, *Knowledge of the Talmud.*

"I'm telling you." The bouncer scoops the money from the bar, tips his head in gratitude. "The guy was a savage."

"And you don't got manners anymore?" Zero swivels to me. "That's Andrew Wolf on the floor there. Ain'tcha gonna say hi?"

"Hi Andrew. Long time," I say over my shoulder before doing a double-take. "Hold on, what the hell's Wolfy doing in Dorchester? Isn't this a little far from his turf?"

"Turf?" Zero barks a laugh. "What turf? Since the Dig it's like free-range townies out there, guys wandering around like they cut a hole through the wire. You haven't noticed these losers walking around gazin' at the sky as if the stars look different from one neighborhood over?"

I'd noticed. By dismantling the rusted green behemoth of the elevated expressway and replacing it with the giant four-lane Ted Williams Tunnel—at twenty billion dollars, by far the most expensive highway mile anywhere in the world—the city had reconfigured entire city neighborhoods; a two mile patch of greenway was now the only border between the formerly all-Italian North End and Faneuil Hall, Southie linked to downtown via a burgeoning waterfront, new money flowing freely, the borders washed out by a sea of green.

Only a few years ago wandering into these neighborhoods was an open invitation to rumble, people tending to stick to their own neighborhoods, temporary passes issued for weekday working stiffs and for special events like a championship celebration or St. Patrick's Day parade. But once it was dark, you best consult your street map; just setting foot in an unfamiliar street was enough to get you punched in the neck.

Still, new Boston or old, it doesn't explain why Andrew Wolf thought it was a good idea to mix it up with Zero in a bar that hadn't stamped his neighborhood passport.

"Hell, it's gotten so's you can't hardly even get mugged in this city anymore," Zero laments. "Ain't that right, Andrew?"

Andrew grunts quietly and sits upright with his back to us,

adjusting something at his waist, his head lolling from side to side trying to shake out the cobwebs.

"So what's the problem, Zero, all this?" I place my messenger bag on my lap, adjust the strap that had been digging into my shoulder, pulled down by the combined weight of the gun and the poker chips.

"You wouldn't understand."

"Try me."

"All right." Zero takes his time, glances at my bag. "In the park by Dad's house, I saw a blind man crying his fuckin' eyes out. They were still good for that."

In the filthy bar mirror Andrew does a Rocky Balboa, rising unsteadily on the nine-count, his nose bleeding onto the front of his Dropkick Murphys T-shirt. He has a purple braised-onion bruise swelling on the side of his face. His sneakers are unlaced green Converse high-tops with shamrocks on the tongues. The knife in his hand is one of those survivalist throat slitters with a knuckle grip and curved handle.

"You're right, I don't understand." I swivel on my stool with the Beretta pointed languidly toward Andy's crotch.

"Go home, Andrew," I say, but I don't think he hears me over the bark of Zero's laugh and the bartender yelling "Hey!" And the bouncer dropping for cover off his stool with a loud *thud*.

"What?" Andrew looks stupidly from my gun to his hand, like he can't figure out how the knife got there. "I'm sorry. This ain't the proper response."

"Like wrong hat, wrong rabbit?" Pure amusement alights Zero's face. "And say thank you to Zesty."

"Huh? For what?" Andy drops the knife and backs away with both hands raised, angling for the door.

Zero's hard to understand because he's laughing so hard but I think he says, "For saving you from a second ass whipping, you fuckin' numbskull. If I ever catch you with so much as a butter knife in your hand again, I'm gonna make you swallow it."

"I'm sorry," Andrew yells, stumbling out the door.

Zero's still chuckling as I put the gun back in my bag, but he's also shaking his head, telling me I'd made a careless mistake, revealed a card too soon.

"You gotta go," the bartender says. "I got my limits. Bobby, toss them the fuck out." He jerks a thumb at the bouncer, perching himself back on his stool.

"You're kidding, right?" he says.

"No worries. Just give us a minute." Zero warns him off with a look and invites an explanation from me with an entirely less patient face. I explain the gun quickly along the lines of: *It's not mine. The serial numbers have been scraped off. I need you to stash it for me.*

"Let me get this straight." Zero's always big on paraphrasing when he hears something that annoys him because it gives him adequate time to work up a lather. "You want me to hold a hot gun in my safe, like I don't got enough to worry about, half my guys with their POs coming around checking up on them, and after what we went through with Dad? You're a bigger knucklehead than Wolfy."

It's hard to disagree. I hadn't thought out the implications of an unregistered gun in his safe, I just knew it would be beyond Charlie's reach.

"And you being here means you've already been to the office, asked Jhochelle to stash it, and she tells you she's got no access and sends you here to pull me out. The safe, by the way, is none of your fucking business. Got that?"

"I got that. But this," I wave my hand at the mayhem, "I don't get at all. Playing house with Jhochelle, it's too much pressure for you now?"

"I told you already, you wouldn't understand."

"Try again," I say, but I know how difficult it is for Zero to express himself with words, too much time spent choking down the traffic of his inner demons; a one-way street when it comes to introspection, self-reflection, whatever the fuck you want to call it. The hard shell is what Zero gives most everybody, the hard knuckles if you rub him the wrong way.

"Pressure." Zero snorts. "You *really* don't fucking get it, Zesty. What pressure? I'm happy is what it is, I gotta spell it out for you?"

"You're *happy*?" I hadn't seen that coming. "So then what's with all this shit?"

"Collateral damage?" Zero winces.

"Of happiness."

"I dunno. Call it what the fuck you want. I'm having a hard time getting used to it, is all. You understand what I'm saying?"

"Maybe."

"Nah, no maybe. You do, that's why you ride your tricycle like you got a fucking death wish, why your head's always in a weed cloud. Because you don't want to think about tomorrow, about what's gonna happen next. You think you can avoid shit forever, but you can't."

"You're one to talk."

Zero concedes the point. "Having Eli's changed all that. Only not the way you think. You have a kid, you're supposed to gain some perspective, right? Be less selfish?"

"How should I know?"

"Yeah, well, here's a little secret for you. I'm still a muthafucka. It runs too deep. Nothing's changed and words don't matter. Mom's still been gone forever, Pops has his ticket punched, riding the third rail into never-never land. Life ain't fair." Zero throws up his hands and out of the corner of my eye I see the bouncer flinch. "I guess I'm just not equipped to handle it, happiness. But it's what I got."

Meaning now Zero has more to lose. His philosophical

musings are deeply rooted in our father's poker training perspective, that when things are going well, you can't lose sight of the probability your luck will turn; that no matter how well you play, how efficiently you manage your chips, Lady Luck will cast her eye elsewhere, spurn your advances, and bring your house tumbling down.

Some people might consider this outlook blatant pessimism, but it's more nuanced than that. Zero and I were raised on the hustle, uncertainty the only true constant. Happiness? What the fuck's that look like? Was my father ever happy? My mother? Were they happy together or was it just an illusory time; did they know the clock was running down on them and just held on to each other for as long as they could?

"Happy." Zero eyes me with rare empathy. "How fucked up is that. Pops hasn't said a word in months and the doctors don't think he ever will again, he's that far gone. Shits himself, can't even feed . . ." Zero turns himself away from me. "That why you've been avoiding the house last couple of months?"

"I'll make it a point to get over there soon."

"That's not what I fuckin' asked you." Zero's voice is barely above a whisper, a sure sign he's crossed into anger, misdirection a staple of his personality: quiet when angry, joking when serious, offer you coffee, serve you tea.

"I guess."

"Yeah, well, I don't blame you. It takes a toll." He turns back to me, his eyes dry as desert sand. "I hired on some new help to give Sid and Van Gogh a breather, but you need to get yourself ready."

"For what?"

"Don't be an idiot. You weren't old enough to remember when Mom left, but I'm telling you, you need to have your head together to get through this, Zesty, it's gonna fuck you up bad. That's *really* why Jhochelle called you. She sees something in me she don't rec-

ognize since Eli was born. I don't know how to explain . . .
it's . . ."

"A paradigm shift." We both swivel to the bouncer, who
shrugs sheepishly. "I went back to night school."

"You're fired," the bartender says. He looks serious.

"So fuck it, if I can't handle it I'll just make sure you come
around more often. Now you gonna tell me what else is in your
bag?" Zero says warily.

I take the case out and show him. He eyes the chips for a moment, slips a few out at random and lines them up on the bar,
slides off his stool and picks up Andy's dropped knife. He looks
at the bartender, looks at the bouncer, who both turn away, and
with a quick violent motion stabs the chips hard, breaking off a
chunk of each one. He inspects each piece and holds up each shattered chip to show me.

"Congratulations," I say. "You just stabbed three thousand
dollars to death."

"Where'd you get these?" Zero pulls a few more chips out,
his eyes widening at each valuation, his Rube Goldberg brain
already running risk/reward calculations that would have earned
Liberty Mutual a billion dollars if Zero had a single straight bone
in his body.

"Sam Budoff's storage unit." I give Zero a condensed version
of Sam's cross-pollination with Rambir Roshan and everything
I'd learned from Brill and Wells. He's pissed, but having well over
half a million dollars in poker chips sitting in front of him keeps
him focused.

"You clipped the lock?"

"Jhochelle did the honors."

"Pretty smart playing the hunch with the unit." He bestows
a rare compliment on me.

"I wouldn't have thought to look if Wells hadn't asked me
about it."

He nods. "I'm surprised he didn't come see me first like last time."

"Why would he?"

"Because I've been to that club across from the Stockyard." Zero surprises me. Aside from the occasional games at the moving company, where Jhochelle usually does most of the damage, I didn't realize Zero still took an interest in poker.

"Any Russians or Ukrainians there?"

"Sure. And Greeks and Poles and Indians and Armenians. Fuck the Olympics, poker's the only thing anybody can agree on."

"You win or lose?"

"What do you think?"

"What kind of stakes we talking?"

"It varied, but you're not getting through the door without at least a couple grand in your pocket. But I'll tell you something, Zesty, I went maybe three, four times before I realized I didn't need the action anymore, wasn't catching that high. So barring that, what's the point?"

"Money," I say.

Zero shrugs with the nonchalance of someone who has some. "Maybe it's another example of what Night School here says. Anyhow, I'll take care of the case until your buddy resurfaces, but that gun I'm not fuckin' touching, you don't know where it's been. Also, I gotta tell you, I'm a little sore Budoff stashed these chips in the warehouse, put us at risk like that. Nobody walks out of a casino with this kind of haul. What's the point? These chips are real, but they ain't kosher."

Only what's done is done and as we exit the bar into the bright afternoon sunshine, it's hard not to feel like we've stepped out into heaven's blinding light. Or is it the train rumbling down the tunnel track?

Sometimes it's hard to tell.

ELEVEN

The Atlantics, one of my all-time favorite local bands, is already blasting their hit "Lonelyhearts" inside my head when Martine Andino steps out of the Loews holding a black guitar case, tips the doorman, and folds himself into a cab.

> *I see fear and despair*
> *Written all over your face*
> *But it's no disgrace*
> *A life that's lived alone*

Andino had changed into a suit and from the corner I catch a glimpse of what his turtleneck had concealed, a colorful explosion of inky flames sprouting from the open collar of his shirt and running up his neck. I toss the remains of my lukewarm coffee and follow as the cab swings a right onto Columbus Ave., fake-brakes and guns it through a red light. The mark of a professional. If Grandma were crossing the street, he would've swerved to take her out, too, burnish his reputation.

It's a little past nine, traffic light, which forces me into a sprint until we hit the glass cubes of the new Boston Police headquarters and take a right up Ruggles.

> *Take a crowbar to your heart*
> *And pry it loose*
> *Just don't blow a fuse*
> *While everyone's throwing stones*

On Huntington, the cab turns left and then about a half mile later left again, crossing the MBTA tracks where they wind up North Broadway toward Jamaica Plain, the terrain getting hilly, forcing me to stand up on my pedals and dream of a cure for gravity.

Lonely,
lonely, lonely hearts
There's nobody like lonely
lonely lonely hearts
You know that I can hear your heart beat
I know what's going on—

The static comes in hard then, a hot-skillet explosion that blinds me for a moment and sends me careening against the line of parked cars, my toe clips shaving paint off a minivan before I clip the mirror and swerve back into the street. I lose sight of the cab cresting the wide curve of Centre but there are multiple traffic lights ahead and I catch up when the driver hits a red light and concedes a full stop.

The cab passes me again in front of the giant plaster cow's head sticking out of the J.P. Licks building, business brisk even at this time of night, and we cruise the next quarter mile past funky soft-glow restaurants and coffee shops before turning onto Lafayette, which winds through the Hispanic hold-steady section of JP, a formerly Irish borough that had ceded to a Mexican and Dominican wave in the 1980s and sunk just enough roots not to be easily supplanted as the new money poured in.

When the cab pulls over in front of the Hacienda restaurant on the corner of Lee Street and Mayfair, I zip by and circle the block past two large plate glass windows with heavy red curtains drawn across, blocking the interior views, maybe meant to dissuade the neighborhood hipsters from checking out the vibe in case the young men smoking and jostling at the curb weren't enough of a deterrent.

Posters and handbills are taped to the windows to the right of the door. I roll past too quickly to read them, with the exception of a large Spanish Budweiser poster that has olive- and dark-skinned Latinas posed provocatively in red and white bikinis. Beach balls. Sand and surf. Foaming bottles of Bud. It's not subtle, but it is effective. All of a sudden I crave a Budweiser. And a Latina girlfriend.

Andino steps out of the cab leading with his guitar case, his appearance setting off a near-choreographed flicking of cigarettes to the curb, one man peeling off back into the club. The shortest of the crew unburdens Andino of his guitar case just as another group of young men exit the restaurant, each one giving him a deferential nod before Shorty leads him into the L-shaped alley that runs behind the restaurant and exits out the other side on Lee Street.

I lock my bike about forty yards away, a wave of mariachi accordion music spilling out as another man, older, with a full head of dark hair and matching mustache, steps to the curb, surveys the street, and rounds back to the alley.

I take Solarte's camera out of my pack, step into a doorway, and unscrew the exposed lightbulb with a quick twist. After a few minutes and a half dozen pictures, the original batch of young men regroups and fresh cigarettes are lit. Andino and the dark-haired man aren't with them. Which means either I'd lost him as they'd strolled out the other end of the alley or there's a back door and they've entered the club.

I watch the bar for about a half hour, cooling down quickly as my sweat dries in a chill breeze, and slip on the Zen Moving Company T-shirt over what I'm wearing.

All the smokers are young and wearing golfing outfits in colors I've only seen in tub-size sherbets produced by Monsanto. Radioactive lime green pants. Pornographic pink shirts with orange stripes tight on their biceps and flat chests. Identical neck tattoos and Mexican national *fútbol* club haircuts, buzzed above the ears, long, chisel-stiff, and swept to one side across the top.

Fifteen more minutes pass and I realize why cops prefer their stakeouts from cars. Heat. And the ability to pee into their empty coffee cups. It also dawns on me that maybe I'm not cut out for this type of work. It's the lack of movement, I think. The act of not acting.

"So move," I say aloud, confirming what my father had often told me, that I liked the sound of my own voice too much.

Nonetheless, move I do.

TWELVE

I'm relieved to see there isn't a sign above the doorway that reads, NO GRINGOS WELCOME, and the group steps aside as I turn in toward the door, one even reaching out quickly and pulling it open for me.

"Gracias," I say, showing off those two years of UMass Spanish. Hell, I might even be able to order something off the menu.

"Sure thing, dude," he replies, bringing laughter to his friends and reminding me I have another open mike scheduled for tomorrow night.

The restaurant is warm and busy, one large room with a full bar along the right-hand wall, small round tables covered in wine-

colored cloth arranged in front of a small stage elevated about a
foot off the floor. There's a tall partition to the left of the stage
with a built-in alcove where the waiters and waitresses enter their
orders and beyond that, a swinging door that must lead to the
kitchen.

Martine Andino is already onstage when I walk in, lifting a
sunburst acoustic Gibson from his case. On the wall behind him
is a mounted canvas ad for Modelo Especial beer. Much more dig-
nified than the Budweiser poster. No sizzling semi-nude Latinas
with impossible cleavage. I take the only open seat at the bar and
I'm about to order when the woman behind the bar greets me
with *"Estas perdido?"* which brings laughter from the patrons
closest to me. I don't know what it is about me, but apparently I
bring joy to the Latin community just by showing up.

"Uno Budweiser, por favor," I manage. What can I tell you, I'm
advertising's easiest mark.

The bartender leans both her elbows on the bar in front of
me. Her black eyebrows are a symmetrical masterpiece, her full
lips shiny like pink tin. Andino spins the Gibson deftly, the move
like a seasoned gunfighter spinning his revolver and coming up
with his finger on the trigger.

"I didn't ask you what you wanted to drink," the bartender
says. "I asked if you were lost."

"He's not lost." The man with dark hair from outside fills the
newly vacated seat beside me. "He's just taking in the neighborhood. Perhaps a little advance scouting for Google? Maybe Starbucks? How are you, my friend?"

"I'm good. You?"

"No complaints. Am I right?"

"About what?"

"You new to the neighborhood? Looking for a spot for a nice
coffee shop, maybe? A Chipotle." The man purposely mispro-
nouncing Chipotle to sound like *Chip-Otle.*

"I grew up two miles from here," I say.

"Brookline?"

"Other way. And I used to work at the Hi-Lo on Centre."

"In which case you might have carried groceries for my abuela." The man smiles warmly. "Xiomara. Where are your manners, the man ordered a drink."

Xiomara doesn't look happy with my change of fortune but brings me a frosty Budweiser and sets it down on a matching coaster. It doesn't come with a side order of hot Latina, though there are plenty in the restaurant, a lot of dark hair colored in various shades of pink and copper. In the last seat of the bar a young woman with bright red hair and a haltertop that barely halts anything stares at us openly with a slightly bemused smile on her face. She's not quite Cleopatra, but in this neighborhood, she's sure to launch a thousand Camaros.

Onstage, Andino makes a couple of twangy adjustments, his fingers adorned with heavy silver rings, turquoise and amethyst, skulls and saints. There's a tall glass near his weathered snakeskin cowboy boots and he picks it up and tilts it our way in greeting before taking a sip.

I've either been made or Andino knows my host. "This your place?" I say.

"Yes." The man extends his hand and we shake, exchanging names. Andino watches me and Arturo Moreno closely over his drink, sets it down, and unrolls his sleeves to expose a burst of tattoos that rival Zero's, but with a more Latin/Christian/Death theme. "Is it to your liking?" Moreno asks.

"It's cozy," I say. "And live music is always good."

I'm about to say something else when Xiomara clicks something on a black electronic board behind the bar, the stage lights rotating and bathing Andino in color. In response, Andino sits upright, tilts his hat down as if he's about to take a nap, and opens with an elaborate rasgueado, a finger-strumming technique commonly associated with flamenco guitar music. It also happens to be where my knowledge of flamenco music ends.

There's no microphone, but instantly the room quiets, the clinking of silverware ceasing, the busboys no longer collecting plates off the tables. In the beam of colored light wisps of smoke drift onstage from the outside smokers, the only sound now Andino tapping his foot to establish a beat and then singing in Spanish, his head tilted down, not looking at the crowd.

"Holy shit," I say, too loudly, which makes Moreno laugh and Andino smile as he continues in a smoke-sonorous voice that fills the room and sets it back in motion—no conversations, but the waitresses and busboys hustling around, dishes being collected, drinks served.

Andino sings:

"La droga inunda sus calles,
y el congreso lo sabe,
Pero como es buen negocio,
a los güeritos les vale."

His fingers move effortlessly along the neck of the guitar, causing the muscles in his snake-inked forearms to shift and stir, and now I notice thick braided scars, like rope on the back of one hand, shiny skin like melted wax, the type you see on burn victims. Under the lights it's hard to tell how old Andino is, but at least hard into his fifties with lacquer black hair and thundercloud eyes that lighten or darken depending on how the stage lights hit him.

Moreno leans into me so he doesn't have to raise his voice. "Do you understand the song?"

"No. But I get the vibe. It's some kind of ode."

"Yes, exactly. You know narcocorrido?"

"They're songs that glorify the Mexican drug bosses."

"Yes." Moreno seems impressed.

"Is that what he's playing?"

"Of a sort. It's quite an honor to have someone so well known play here."

"Unscheduled." I point my beer to the playbill of the week's acts taped behind the bar. Andino isn't on it. But if I come back tomorrow night it looks like I'd be treated to a dueling death match between accordion players.

"Yes. What's the word in English . . . preempted? He has pre-empted our scheduled performer tonight. But there are no hard feelings. Señor Andino is quite well known in Mexico. It is a great coup to have him in my humble establishment."

I can see why. Andino continues to play, singing in a haunted voice, his hat tilted to shade his eyes, totally immersed in his music. I don't know much about narcocorrido music beyond being able to identify it when I hear it, but I do know that narco bosses in Mexico commissioned songs to be written about them as lasting tributes, aware that their exploits would probably be short-lived. Who was Andino paying tribute to? Arturo Moreno?

Definitely *not* the young striker who comes in behind the bar and leans across to whisper in Moreno's ear. Up close I notice that his elaborate pompadour also includes the modern twist of shaved sides with lightning bolts and arrows pointing skyward like instructions for the barber as to which way the tornado should flow. I also notice just how short Elvis really is, the hair and the boots adding five inches at least. And yet still not enough to reach Moreno's ear without standing on his toes.

Andino brings the song to a close, the guitar fading until there's only the echo of his voice lingering past the last note before being lost to applause and shout-outs I don't have to be bilingual to understand.

"Did you like it?" Moreno waves Elvis away as Andino tips his hat and sips from his drink.

"It was beautiful. Maybe even more because I didn't understand the words; it just frees me up to catch the tone."

"Yes, exactly." He taps his heart with his fist. "You only absorb the feeling."

"Hey, this might sound like a strange question, but you ever do anything here besides music?"

"Such as . . . ?"

"I don't know, comedy? Stand-up." I try to think of a funny Mexican comic for reference but can only come up with George Lopez, and I'm pretty sure Freddie Prinze was Puerto Rican.

"You tell jokes?" Moreno laughs even though I hadn't told a joke yet.

"Just starting out," I say. "Practicing."

"Okay, so practice. Tell me a joke."

This is not an uncommon occurrence when I tell people what I'm working toward. As if every comic is some kind of joke vending machine they could slide a quarter in and get a funny line out. "What kind?" I say.

"Oh, I don't know. Like a gringo walks into a Mexican bar after taking pictures outside."

Moreno and I smile at each other for too long, neither of us meaning it. I finally go with: "What can I tell you, from outside your place has a glow. I was trying to capture it."

"And did you?"

I shrug, knowing any more words would be wasted, having felt, a few moments after Young Elvis had left the building, that the room had already tightened on me, a subtle shift I would have picked up sooner if I hadn't been distracted by Andino's talent and now by the static building again between my ears.

"If it's really that much of a problem I'll delete them."

I wince into the lightning reverb, a Letters to Cleo song already in my rotation starting to come in clearer: "Here and Now," Kay Hanley filling me in on how she's spending her Sunday morning.

I drop a five on the bar and lean for my bag, which I'd stashed under my seat, but Moreno places his foot on it. "Don't," he says. "Come. We'll discuss this outside. Do you smoke weed, Zesty, or is that a foolish question?"

I look around the bar. Onstage Andino eyes me placidly, tuning his guitar for another song; Elvis is planted at the front door, no doubt the crew of smokers out front in case I hurdle him.

"Twist my arm," I reply, hoping nothing's lost in translation.

THIRTEEN

We walk behind the partitioned wait station and through the swinging door to the kitchen, not a single member of the kitchen staff looking up as we tread our way on slick black rubber mats and out the side door into the crook of the alley.

Moreno chirps a quick whistle and two men posted on each side of the bend draw in closer, forming a small huddle. Elvis to my right strikes a flame to a joint that smells like a skunk bathing in Chanel No. 5, takes a hit to get it going, and passes it clockwise to one of his crew members as I whistle the chorus from "Pass the Dutchie (on the left hand side)" by Musical Youth.

"You're a fuckin' clown," Elvis informs me, recognizing the tune.

"Thanks. I prefer the term 'jester.'"

When a fifth member of the golf club exits the kitchen, he has my open bag with him and shows Moreno the contents.

"So it seems we have a problem." Moreno nods solemnly.

"If it's the gun," the half-smoked joint reaches me, "I can totally explain." I take a hit, drawing in deeply. "I want you to note it's not loaded."

Moreno lifts his eyes to the bag holder, who confirms it with a nod. "He's got a clip, but it's in another hold."

"Exactly." I exhale.

"So explain. Are you, A, the world's dumbest assassin—"

"Whoa, hold on a—"

"Or B, a racist who believes he needs to bring a gun into every neighborhood of color for protection?"

I smoke weed because I like how it makes me feel, not as a salve or to relieve stress, though it does that for me sometimes. Only I don't rely on it for that, or anything really. In fact, I've noted that pot sometimes gives me a clean-window clarity that *brings on* stress because it forces me to see things the way that they really are, stripping away my layers of deniability, the minutia of minor distractions that allow me to justify shelving the issues I should be confronting head-on. It's not an overwhelming sensation like paranoia. I'm just more open to the flow, even if it exposes that golden nugget of truth, which hurts sometimes.

"What's C?" I take another hit when Elvis stings me with a right cross, sparks exploding from my mouth and behind my eyes, the roach spinning smoke to the ground.

Wasteful.

When my eyes clear, it looks as if nothing had happened, Moreno and his men rendered to still-life models, Elvis contemplating the moon. But my lip is cut and I can taste blood with the smoke, the thick scar I carry on my inside lip from the last time I caught a beating opened up and leaking.

"Listen." I spit blood into the alley. "This is embarrassing. I mean for me, but I've never seen *West Side Story* before. Are you supposed to be the Sharks or the Jets?"

"*Maricon.*" Elvis tries doubling me over with a punch to the stomach that I knife away from.

"See, *that* I understand." I straighten up. "So Sharks it is."

"Enough." Moreno reaches into the bag and lifts the camera, his face and chest lit by the readout, clicking through all the pictures of Martine Andino that Solarte and I had taken. "Who sent you?"

"Nobody. I told you, I can explain. And Elvis, if you hit me again, I swear you're gonna wish you died on a fuckin' toilet."

Moreno turns the camera around to the group, who collectively wince as they see the pictures. Striker mumbles something in Spanish until Moreno cuts him off.

"English," he snarls. "I want our friend Zesty to understand."

"We didn't see him, *patron*. When we followed on Newbury, Harvard Square. Nada." Only I hadn't taken those pictures, Solarte did. And obviously she was good at what she did as I'd learned firsthand when she'd spooked me across from the Loews. The question is why were they following Andino, especially if he was coming to them tonight?

"Believe me, boss, this clown we would have spotted."

"Fuck you," I say. "And Moreno, I gotta tell you, this is now like officially the worst high ever."

"So explain, then." Moreno's tone is diplomatic as he pops the chip out of the camera and pockets it. "Why have you been following my musical guest?"

I could ask Moreno the same question but I doubt he'd answer and I'm suddenly and acutely aware that therein lies the problem. I don't even know the answer to his question, my don't-ask-don't-tell messenger ethos not serving me well here.

"No?" Moreno mugs a sad face and it brings to mind a mover who occasionally works for Zero, a quiet, bespectacled fire hydrant of a man with gentle eyes behind John Lennon glasses. I'd nicknamed him Johnny Thunder because he rarely spoke and when he did, it was in a hushed tone reminiscent of what a grief counselor might employ to comfort a struggling mourner. And if you so much as uttered a cross word or looked at him the wrong way, Johnny Thunder would punch you square in the face without warning, which probably explains why he's never lost a bar fight in his life.

I kick Elvis square in the balls, feel a crunch of bone as I back-elbow Striker in the eye before a staccato of punches and a sharp echo of pain send me up against the brick wall, where I turtle into my rope-a-dope defense, letting my arms eat as many of the punches as I can, nearly sitting on Elvis writhing on the ground beneath my feet.

A punch that lands flush on my ear brings a ringing, tuning fork whistle and I wonder if something's wrong with my eardrum. It hurts like hell, but fists I can deal with. The trick is to stay off the ground and away from their soccer skills.

"Let's try this once more." Moreno's voice cuts off the punches. "Because perhaps we are having but a cultural misunderstanding, Zesty. I want you to see things from my vantage point. You've come to my establishment having followed my guest, obviously for days. You carry a gun, yet it's not loaded, which for an assassin, I grant you, makes little sense. And you have no identification besides your business card, which would take five minutes to produce though it matches your shirt. Is Zesty Meyers really your name?"

"Yes." I spit more blood to the ground, hear the still-lit roach sizzle at my feet.

"Would you by any chance be related to Zero Meyers?"

"Guilty as charged," I say. "Brothers."

"An interesting wrinkle."

Really interesting, considering the slideshow of thoughts passing through Moreno's eyes, a subtle movement of his jaw that I've been trained to notice. It's the emotional decisions that get you in trouble. I can't tell what Moreno's thinking, but at least he's thinking.

"Nonetheless," Moreno arrives at a conclusion, a dark light I'd seen pass through, returning. "Why are you following Señor Andino?"

"Honestly, I don't know." I look at one of the Sharks, who holds his bloody knuckle that might have come from a blow to my jagged front incisor.

"Somebody has sent you. But you're not going to tell me who."

"Correct," I say.

"Because that is how you operate in your family, a code of silence, yes? Your stock in trade?"

"We work with what we got." Elvis finally gets to his feet, walks gingerly toward a Dumpster, and vomits against the side.

"So further beatings are unnecessary?"

"Totally." I point at him emphatically. "See, that's why you're the boss."

"So then." Moreno reaches into my pack and pulls out Charlie's gun, my reflexive flinch stiffened by the grip of two of Moreno's men who hold me in place. I bang the back of my head against the brick wall as Moreno screws the gun past my teeth, forcing my mouth wide, my tongue cut on the sharp indentations of the scraped serial numbers.

"There is no point in carrying around an empty gun, Zesty. It shows either a lack of nerve or the ability to bluff with no hand at all. Did you check the chamber, Tito?"

"No, *patron*." Tito looks at me like he wants to eat my entrails. *Did I?*

And before I can think to remember, I hear the *snick* of Moreno pulling the trigger, see a bright explosion of fire as something connects to the side of my temple, the L-shaped alley swirling above me like a black tornado lifting toward the sky. I hear a metallic *clink* as I slip toward darkness, the last light across my field of vision a smudge of blue-orange flame, followed by the fuse

glow of a lit cigarette, the deep crackle of tobacco, and the cere-
monial incense of a Saturday night havdalah candle from deep in
my memory. Clove smoke, the chanting of ghosts, and then darkness, blessed darkness.

FOURTEEN

I fall in love too easily, there's no sense in denying it. It's become
a reflex of sorts, like your knee jumping to the tap of a rubber-
tipped hammer. It doesn't take much, really: a glance or a curve
(too often a curve) and off I stumble. Arguably, it's my most consistent trait, this lack of emotional discipline. My Cupid long ago
ditched his bow and arrow and now hunts with a net.

   I come-to half sitting, half slumped in the darkened doorway
where I'd unscrewed the vestibule light. Cleopatra from the bar
is sitting beside me, smoke languidly drifting from her mouth
forming a wispy heart-shaped valentine above her.

   I want to say something witty but there's still that tuning fork
vibrato in my ears overlaid now with a wobbling hiss like someone's left the needle on a warped and badly scratched record. I
turn to the side and vomit onto the pavement.

   "Ay yo!" Cleopatra springs to her feet, smudging the smoke-
heart. She's covered up her haltertop with a black satin jacket and
towers over me in skintight black leather pants and high heels
that tap out the annoyance of someone who's got somewhere else
they'd rather be.

   "Here." She stops the Savion Glover routine long enough to
hand me a bottle of water and shoot me a withering glance. I spit,

gargle, and spit again, using my tongue to count my teeth, starting to take inventory. Not too bad considering, except for the ringing headache, maybe a little swelling around the eye that might
be purple, half closed, half sexy, by tomorrow.

Accentuate the positive.

"Can you stand up?"

"Not yet. The record's still skipping."

"What?"

"Nothing. Just give me a minute." I extend the bottle back to
Cleopatra.

"You're joking, right?" She takes a monster drag off her cigarette, flicks the butt off my spokes.

I stand up slowly, glancing toward the Hacienda, a wave of
music spilling into the street every time the door opens. The smoking crew isn't out front anymore, nobody coming in or out of the
alley. My empty bag is dangling off the handlebars of my Trek
still locked to the pole. I look back to the bar.

"What are you, fucking crazy?" Cleopatra says, following my
eyes. "They're not there anymore and you ain't getting shit back
anyway."

"What do you know about it?"

"Just that." She rears back. "Can you maybe try not to stare
at my chest?" She zips the satin jacket to her neck, shakes out her
hair.

"I apologize. Bad habit; I didn't even realize I was doing it."

"You weren't." She laughs. "I was just fucking with you.
You're still loopy. Why don't you sit back down?"

"I'm all right," I say. Now I *am* looking at her chest, but really
only to gauge my recovery. In love? Check.

"What's your name?" I make my move.

"I don't think so." Cleopatra shakes her head slowly, rolling
her eyes.

"Strange name," I say.

"Funny. Listen up, Romeo. Likely, you got a concussion. I've seen a few in my day. If you keep vomiting, go to a hospital. And if you won't do that, at the very least try not to go to sleep tonight. Think you can handle that?"

"I might need a little help with that last one." I try to wink at her, but I'm pretty sure it comes off as a grimace.

"Wow, you're just relentless, aren't you? And either dumb as rocks or you got a fuckin' set on you, waltzing into the lion's den like that. I don't know what kind of business you got with Moreno and his people, but you sure know how to step in it. Want some unsolicited advice?"

"Not really." I rub my temples gently.

"Rhetorical question," Cleopatra says. "Stay in Whiteyville. Which at this point is like ninety-nine percent of the fucking city anyhow. How come you got to come around here to make trouble?"

"I don't even know what to say to that," I admit. "Except what the hell did I ever do to you?"

"Nothing. I got housing issues." She lights another cigarette, doesn't offer me one. "Don't take it personal."

"So why *are* you still here?"

"Moreno gave me two hundred bucks to stay with you until your friend showed, make sure you were okay."

"What friend?"

"Fucked if I know. I just started dialing the contacts in your phone. You know, getting a volunteer to come pick your ass up was like trying to sell Ebola. Someone's on the way, though. And damn, if that girl ain't got a mouth on her. And if I'm not mistaken, here she is now. Hope your bike comes apart, Romeo. Ain't no way it's fitting into that clown car."

FIFTEEN

"Can we drive around a little?" I've got one arm out the window holding my bike in place on the domed roof of Martha's Volkswagen Bug, Zero's Zen Moving T-shirt wrapped around the toe clip so it doesn't scratch the paint. "I need to clear my head."

We cruise Centre Street back the way I'd come, the copper bracelets stacked from Martha's wrists to her forearms jangling with all the subtlety of advancing heavy artillery every time she hits a pothole. The street's newly paved, but I know for a fact that every night while Boston sleeps the DPW sends out work crews to pickax potholes halfway to China—two guys doing the heavy work while three supervisors hone their Win for Life ticket-scratch lottery form.

We swing a right onto Huntington riding in silence, configuring our ears to the city's late-night rhythms, the audible popwink of streetlights as they change from red to green, cruise past the flickering of fluorescents inside the new Northeastern buildings as maintenance crews go about their business clicking office switches, opening windows, running vacuums and floor polishers that mimic the sound of distant traffic, steady as waves breaking ashore.

We cross Mass Ave. gliding parallel to the *Christian Science Monitor* reflecting pool before hanging a right on West Newton, taking it deep into the South End, the flat streets deserted now, the neighborhood folded in on itself like a box with its flaps pulled closed. We pass handsome turn-of-the-century townhouses on streets lined with trees not yet ready to give up their leaves;

meander until we hit Blackstone Square, where we exit the Bug and sit on a bench facing Washington Street. There's a smattering of silver clouds but they give way to a paper moon hanging high above us, our bodies backlit like Kabuki theater, shadows stretching like ghost taffy over the curb.

"Ho, shit." Martha winces, catching better sight of the bruise and swelling I can feel coming in under my eye. Down-breeze I catch her familiar scent—white chocolate, cocoa butter.

"You should see the other guy" is all I manage.

"Really? What'd you do, beat him with your face? Don't answer that. Tell me what you've gotten yourself into this time. All of it."

I do as I'm told, starting with Alianna Solarte and ending with my beating at the hands of Los Fuckwads.

"It's not Charlie's gun," Martha says when I run out of words. "But really, Zesty? After what you went through with your dad and Gus, you're stepping into someone else's shit *again*? What the hell's wrong with you?"

"All I did was take a job, Martha."

"You're a messenger, Zesty, not a fucking detective."

"We need the money, don't we?"

"Not that bad we don't."

"Yeah? Tell that to Charlie. What do you mean it's not his gun?"

"Just that. Not." Martha enunciates at a glacial pace. "His."

"So who—"

"One of his vet buddies who he managed to talk off the proverbial ledge."

"Well, that's a relief. Only I don't know what to tell you, it's gone now."

"You know, Zesty." Martha shimmies a shrug, dips her head between her legs, and fluffs out her straight blond hair. "Honestly? I think you did them both a solid getting it off their hands. It's not like Charlie's in such a good place himself. Talk about the blind leading the blind."

More like the wounded leading the shell-shocked. Only problem was, now the gun's in Moreno's hands and who the hell knows what he might do with it? Could it be traced back to Charlie's buddy? Or me and Charlie if our prints are still somewhere on it?

"Charlie tell you he lost his apartment in Medford?"

"He did. Landlord raised the rent and told him he should be thankful, that he'd put it off as long as he did. You know, on account of his veteran status. Then he offered him a hundred bucks for his Purple Heart. How fucked up is that?"

I shake my head slowly, a touch of static drifting in and out on a weak signal.

"Do you ever get the feeling that maybe this city's moving along without us, Martha? Like maybe we're some kind of dinosaur who's just too stupid to adapt to change?"

"More and more every fucking day, Zesty."

"So how long do you think you'll keep doing this?"

"I don't know." Martha offers me a rare sweet smile. "How long you planning on staying in business?"

"Long as I can."

"Well then, there you have it. But what's on your mind, Zesty? What aren't you telling me?"

Like I said, to Martha my head might as well be made of glass: "I had this conversation with Zero earlier . . . about my dad. It wasn't the type of talk we've ever had before."

"How so?"

I try to think of the right word to explain it to Martha, to myself. "Zero was conceding," I say. "To the Alzheimer's. To the disease. Not giving in, just, I dunno, facing the reality of it, seeing everything for what it really is. He told me I needed to start preparing myself. For the end."

"How do you do that?"

"That," I point at Martha, muster a weak smile, "he didn't say."

"What's *he* doing to prepare himself?"

"I'm not sure. But I think he's right, though, that I've been avoiding thinking about it, putting it on the back burner, which I guess is how I handle most of my shit. Only now, with everything that's happened with my dad the last couple of years, it's sped up the timetable on him. He's gotten real old too fast. This isn't the way I want to remember him, Martha."

"Is that why you've come back to work?"

"I guess. I have a hard time seeing him like this. The more time I spend at his place, this image of him, weak and dependent . . . the way he is now feels more permanent inside me. Like it's pushing out all the other memories I have of him. All the good times, how strong he was to push through all the heartbreak and disappointment he had to overcome to raise Zero and me. Does that make any sense to you?"

"It does. It makes perfect sense. But don't sell yourself short, Zesty. You've been a good son. You and Zero. *Present.* Loyal. Resilient. These are things your father taught you, it didn't come from nowhere. You want to remember your dad as he was, you just need to keep being you. Live the way you want to live and don't let others define you, tell you where you belong. You understand what I'm saying, Zesty?"

"I think so."

"Good. So hey, I got a little sideways question for you, then: Did your dad ever host any of his poker games at the Western Front, that old club in Cambridgeport?"

I can't help but smile. The Western Front was long gone, but at one time it was the hub of the Boston reggae scene, what little there was of it. And though my father never did host his game there—it was a resolutely black Jamaican club in what was once a rough patch of working-class Cambridge—he'd sometimes bring me and Zero there whenever someone like Sugar Minott or Beres Hammond was in town, headliners that could fill stadiums in Europe but only a small club in a racially charged Boston.

"The Western Front? Nah. But it might be the first place I ever got high, all the smoke up in there. Why do you ask?"

"I was looking through those pictures Solarte emailed us. I grew up just a couple blocks from there and recognized the corner. And Zero?"

"And Zero what?"

"He liked the Western Front?"

"Not so much." If Zero had to smell that much weed he'd prefer it in the bleachers, where a cloud of pot smoke would hang over the pitcher's bullpen and a misplaced punch of a beach ball in the cheap-ticket crowd would incite a small riot.

"But speaking of those pictures, I've got about an hour to kill, can we hit the office and take a look at the rest of them?"

"What for?"

"I'm not sure, but there's something about Andino that feels like I should know already but just can't get at."

"It can't wait?"

"No. There's somewhere I gotta be soon."

"At this hour?"

I'd promised Brill I'd return to keep scraping paint off his bricks if he kept paying me in cold hard cash. It was hard dirty work, but there was something gratifying about it, maybe because as I chipped away I could get a sense of what it would look like when it was done, a more visible progress in the work than I was accustomed to. I also had the odd sensation that stripping the layers would free the ghosts trapped inside those walls to let them sleep in their own rooms again.

My own sleep will have to wait. I have bills to pay, too many jobs to do, and between my ears still the hiss of a needle spinning on an empty groove, only now accompanied by the echo of Martine Andino working the strings of his acoustic Gibson, laying down tracks for the Angel of Death singing softly in my ear. It's a voice I've heard calling to me before, but she sounds so much sweeter now.

Soon, she sings. *Soon.*

SIXTEEN

"So, what exactly am I looking at?" We'd already shuffled through the three pictures of Martine Andino standing at the corner where the Western Front had been and now we're looking at him killing time on Green Street just off Central Square, smoking a cigarette and doing a whole lot of nada. And then more of the same nothing, only in front of the entranceway of a shop on Newbury Street, NEWBURY COMICS visible in the reflection of the storefront window. Diddly in the Fens at 88 Queensbury Street with a confused look on his dark face. Andino in the same clothes Alianna had photographed in her office—faded jeans, a worn pair of cowboy boots, black turtleneck—loitering downtown on Broad Street.

In none of the pictures is Andino meeting with anyone, exchanging envelopes, or leaving a newspaper on a park bench to be picked up by a jittery Matt Damon. Lunch in the Middle East café, window seat, far corner table with his back to the wall. Coffee at Au Bon Pain in Harvard Square, same spot: window, corner, so he can see the entire restaurant, the sidewalk, and the door. Nobody gets behind this guy. Careful. Possibly paranoid. World Beating People Watcher. Had Solarte noticed the trend?

"What are you looking for?"

"I don't know." But whatever it is, I don't see it in the next series where Solarte had captured Andino buying what looks like clove cigarettes from Leavitt & Peirce. Andino smoking those cigarettes while watching the next Tracy Chapman play guitar. Andino dropping a handful of bills into the open case before her.

Generous.

"Well, to me he looks like a tourist wandering around town maybe a little lost, a little lonely." Martha chews through the last of the pictures. "Solarte didn't tell you why she's tailing him?"

"Nope."

"Didn't tell you how dangerous it might be? What you were supposed to be looking for?"

"Nope. Just follow and—Hold on. Scroll back to that shot on Green Street."

"Why?" Martha clicks back until she gets to the right one.

"I'm not sure," I say, but then I see the pattern. "Look at the way he's looking up at the building. All the buildings. And doesn't go into any of them. Now click the previous one." Martha does. This one of Andino in the Fens on the corner of Kilmarnock and Queensbury and then again Andino downtown on Broad Street. Two of the buildings residential, Broad Street strictly commercial.

"Look how he's just standing there staring at the buildings or with his back to them, scoping the neighborhood."

"I see. But so what? And why these spots? There's not much there."

The only common denominator I can see, beyond the somewhat vague and disappointed look on Andino's face, is the fact that most of the buildings are of relatively new construction, which from an architectural standpoint is a disappointment, but to a mover likely means a working elevator and wider staircases.

Without my having to ask, Martha Googles the address in the Fens and reads aloud, "Eighty-eight Queensbury Street. Built on the former site of Jumpin' Jack Flash, an iconic Boston bar named after the Rolling Stones song . . . You remember that place?"

"Before my time, but I've seen pictures of my father there, back when he was part of that scene. The marquee had those giant red lips."

"Was *that* one of his poker places?"

"I don't think so."

Martha replicates the search for Green Street in Cambridge and Broad Street downtown and comes up with two other former music clubs, Green Street Station and Cantone's, both once popular venues that had closed years ago.

"So all three spots were former nightclubs," Martha muses aloud. "And the Western Front makes four. You think he's what, like taking a tour down memory lane? The All the Places I Got Laid in My Youth tour?"

"Maybe." I could do the same thing now in our glorious New Boston except it would be called All the Places I've Struck Out tour. And the list would be too long to fit onto one shirt.

The remaining locations aside from Leavitt & Peirce were all connected in some way to the Boston music scene of the early eighties, the address on Newbury Street the former site of Syncro Sound, a recording studio owned by The Cars and where a number of Boston bands recorded albums. Between them and Rick Harte, who ran Ace of Hearts Records just a couple blocks away, it became the epicenter of the Boston recording scene.

So what did it all add up to? Our man Martine Andino was taking a musical stroll down memory lane, lamenting the passing of time and the sea change that had come to Boston? Conducting a one-man reunion tour, walking himself back in time like my father did on the daily without even having to leave his couch.

Was Andino communing with ghosts, looking for something he'd lost along the way? I don't have those answers, but I'll let Solarte know what a fabulous job of sleuthing I've done and maybe she'll make more sense of Andino's movements and his connection to Arturo Moreno, since she's the one who knows what all this is really about.

Am I curious? Sure, but chasing after the past isn't a luxury I have right now. The temperature's dropped precipitously since yesterday's high of sixty-five. The Sox have left town to play out the string on a disappointing season, the highly anticipated Rauschenberg Retrospective at the Museum of Fine Arts has been canceled, and word on the street is Seiji Ozawa had just been by-passed for a Grammy by the New York Phil again, the Beacon Hill muckety-mucks wicked pissed about that and ready to lay someone the fuck out.

And as I'd predicted yesterday, the phones had started ringing, business picking up as the chill set in, Martha having spent most of her day barking addresses into the Motorola and sending Charlie out to terrorize pedestrians and make tiny talk with receptionists from Back Bay to Faneuil Hall.

And as I wheel toward Brill's apartment on Worcester, the midnight streets blurring in my speed-induced periphery, the song I didn't realize I'd been waiting for drops onto the turntable of my brain and everything becomes crystal clear.

I hadn't heard a Mass song in years, but I was hearing one now, Karl Klaussen's wounded howl on the opening notes of their local hit "Never Again," his anguish as stark and real as that of those blues singers my dad loved so much.

It was a voice that could have been the voice of a generation, the kind that only took one note to etch into your memory where you'd been and who you were with when you first heard *that* song. And it was the voice I'd heard singing Spanish odes to Mexican cartel kingpins tonight at the Hacienda in Jamaica Plain; not a fucking doubt in my concussion-scrambled mind.

Karl Klaussen, the dark prince of Boston rock and roll, was alive and kicking. And that lying motherfucker was back in town.

SEVENTEEN

Brill had kept himself busy in the last twenty-four hours. There's a large Dumpster brimming with debris parked directly in front of his stoop and he'd taken down walls to the studs and widened a doorway between the large high-ceilinged living room and what could be a formal dining room. Same deal in the kitchen, where he'd torn out all the cabinets and trashed the old dishwasher and fridge, their grime-chalked outlines still visible on the hardwood floor like the markings of a double appliance homicide.

"Goddamn," I say, peering in from the front entrance foyer, the canvas-tarped staircase leading to the second floor littered with antique copper and glass doorknobs, carved hardwood moldings, light fixtures, and balusters. "What'd you do, rob Restoration Hardware at gunpoint?"

Brill knows I live at pace, looks at me, taking in my black eye and bruises, and asks me no questions.

"That big barn door there and the rigging I got from a salvage place in Dorchester called Olde Bostonian. Rest of this stuff I've been collecting piecemeal for years. There's more upstairs on the second floor."

"How much more? Like enough to rig the whole building?"

"At least."

"You kept all this shit in Newton?"

Brill shakes his head. "Storage."

"From where?"

"Crime scenes mostly." Brill removes a fleck of tobacco from the tip of his tongue, challenges me with a look.

"Murder scenes?" I try to keep any judgment out of my voice, but my mind conjures images of blood spatter on marble, hardwood floors, crystal doorknobs.

"Some." Brill dials it back. "But I started collecting when I was still in uniform. Kept adding to it over the years."

"I'm surprised the department let you," I say. Unless they didn't know about it until now. Was this what had finally caught up to Brill and kicked him to the sidelines?

"Wasn't a secret." Brill shrugs noncommittally. "None of it was evidence or like part of a case. It was just . . . *there*."

"What neighborhoods we talking about?" As a mover and messenger I've been inside of some of the swankiest houses and apartments this city has to offer, and in terms of quality, craftsmanship, and materials the items lining Brill's stairs—now that they've been repaired, polished, stripped, and sanded to their original beauty—are in every way their equal.

"Come on, Zesty, don't play stupid. You grew up around these parts. What neighborhoods historically carry the bulk of violent crimes in this town?"

Brill was talking mainly about the neighborhoods of Roxbury, Dorchester, and Mattapan, places that at the turn of the twentieth century were still considered the suburbs and became home to a large Jewish community who had settled there after moving out of Boston proper when the inner-city population swelled with immigrants from other distant shores. As in places like Brookline and Newton, the Jews of Boston built stately Victorian homes and synagogues in thriving neighborhoods, only by the early sixties changes in transportation, politics, and social unrest prompted a panicked exodus into the true suburbs far beyond Boston's borders and turned these neighborhoods into its revolving door. First came the Irish followed by an influx of southern blacks and then a wave of immigrants from Caribbean nations into an aging housing stock that was too expensive to repair, and neglected by land-lords, except to subdivide into smaller spaces that housed far too many people.

"I'd see these places all boarded up or abandoned or I'd be called to clear squatters out of them, junkies," Brill tells me. "And I'd be looking at carved balustrades with five coats of paint, marble fireplaces, pressed-tin ceilings, stained glass. Beautiful craftsmanship camouflaged in filth. Sometimes in blood. A lot of these houses were crime scenes, a lot of them burned down. That's why they got so many empty lots getting built on in the Berry today."

"If you got the coin," I say.

"Sure. But twenty years ago? Shit, you take an overhead shot, some of those streets looked like Leon Spinks's grill when he smiled, gaps everywhere. So whenever the city was about to step in, tear a place down, I'd chalk my name and the demo crews knew to call me. I'd throw them a few dollars, load up the cruiser. Same goes for the firebugs, the cats getting paid by absentee land-lords to go in and torch the places. They'd double up and give me a call, too, because word got around. I mean, what was I supposed to do, call the Arson Squad, arrest them? They hadn't done anything yet. And if it wasn't them, it would be someone else. Didn't know what I was going to do with all the stuff at the time, but it felt wrong, all that history just disappearing. It's cost me some money storing it all these years, but here we are, full circle. Maybe we got something in common after all, Zesty."

"Yeah, what's that?"

"Sometimes the sky just falls and we gotta move out from under. But hey, doesn't mean we have to turn our backs on where we came from, right? After all, what's that saying? The past is a terrible thing to waste?"

We work for a while and then we get the barn door out of the hall and lean it against the exposed brick wall where I'd chipped off most of the paint. Here and there were still some dirty white or gray patches that the wire brush seemed to only tattoo further into the brick.

"I actually like it." Brill runs his fingers over a couple of the spots. "It's got a nice vibe to it, like you sealed in some history. Leave it. Whatever rich-ass motherfuckers I rent this place to don't like it, they can live somewhere else."

"I thought you were taking this floor."

"I'm talking about upstairs. Gonna hit the same layout for each space."

"You sure you want people above you? Why don't you take the third floor?"

"I'm not getting any younger. Anyhow, Boston Ballet School's just down a ways, I'll rent it to a couple of dancers. They don't eat nothing, move like angels. I won't hear a damn thing. Tonight's goal is to get that barn door hung on its rail. How are you with power tools?"

"I'm Jewish," I remind Brill.

"And here I thought I'd hired one of the original day laborers. Didn't your people build the Pyramids?"

"Move away from the brick wall," I tell Brill. "I don't need the competition."

"That what your eye and bruises are all about, competition? I saw your bike's in one piece. Who you pissing off now?"

"I'm not sure you'd believe me if I told you."

"Go ahead, try me."

I do. And when I'm done, Brill says, "You're right, I don't believe you."

"Why's that?"

"Well, for starters, Klaussen being alive is like a thousand-to-one shot."

"I *heard* him," I say, shaking my head. "Granted, he doesn't look like the pictures I've seen of him but it's been over thirty years and Solarte said he'd had some expensive surgery done too."

"Yeah, well, that's the other reason I don't believe it. You do any background on Alianna Solarte before she roped you in?"

"No. You know her?"

"She tell you she used to be a cop?"

"I figured it out."

"She tell you she worked Internal Affairs?"

"No. Why's it matter?"

"Doesn't to me." Brill shrugs. "But she took down a lot of dirty cops about six, seven years back. Worked undercover with some Vice guys wired into some of the construction crews that had contracts with the Big Dig. Some state police, some local."

"So?" I didn't see Brill's point. "She did her job?"

"Yeah. Some thought maybe too well."

"What's that mean?"

"It got messy. Supposedly this crew was stockpiling cash, drugs from raids, skimming seizures. They knew they couldn't spend; they were looking ahead. To get access, each one held some kind of key, like a piece to a puzzle so they could only get at it together. Well, she took a bullet during a raid that had all the markings of a setup, like the crew had been tipped she was IAD. Her Kevlar had been messed with, only she'd swapped it out with one of her own and lived to tell the tale. Barely. Only when the hammer came down and these guys started turning on each other, most of the stash was gone. Someone had figured out a way in without the others."

"They think she took it? How?"

"Not something I know. But those cops were tight, even lived on the same street, some of them. Funny thing is, with the stash raided the thing that sealed the case against most of them wasn't even Solarte's testimony. It was the swimming pools done them in."

"I don't get it."

"Shit used to go missing off the Big Dig sites on the regular, you ought to know something about that."

It's true. When the Dig was just getting ramped up and the residents of the lofts on Albany, Thayer Street, Harrison Avenue—mostly artists, musicians, messengers—realized they were going to get forced out soon, they would sometimes vandalize the heavy digging equipment or hot-wire a digger and deposit it in the Bay. Sometimes brawls even erupted between the construction crews and residents. But all of it backfired and actually sped up the inevitable evictions, the police called in to bring the peace, the fire marshals on their heels to ring up violations and board up lofts that weren't zoned for residential living. City hall got in the mix and if they weren't all the way in the developers' pockets, they were at least somewhere in the linings, and worked their way up the creases.

"Still don't get the pools," I say.

"One of the big-ticket items that went ghost were these imported Italian aqua blue tiles they were going to inlay the Ted Williams Tunnel with. Artisan-level-type shit, about a million dollars' worth. Never solved. Well, traffic reporter's up in the copter one day, notices a string of pools in Swampscott, just like a side comment." Brill poorly mimics a white announcer's voice: *"Gorgeous sunshine up here, perfect day to sit by these amazing blue pools that I'm looking at, over so-and-so street in Swampscott."*

"The tiles from Teddy Ballgame Tunnel." I put together Brill's story. "All the pools belonged to the cops?"

"Not all. They off-loaded some of the tile to their neighbors."

"At discount, no doubt. All the cops went to prison?"

"No. Some turned and got Wit-Proed out. Only the marshals know where they're at now. One ate his gun. A couple were smart enough to plan an exit ticket in case shit went south."

"Solarte?" I say.

"Disabled out, I guess. She sure as shit didn't make any friends. I'm actually surprised to hear she put a shingle out in these parts. She's from New York originally. And people around here got long memories."

"So what is it you remember about Klaussen makes you so sure it's not him back from the dead?"

"You mean, what do I remember about your dad back then, don't you? You're a cagey motherfucker, Zesty, always talking between the lines. Well, all right, but you're not gonna like what I got to tell you."

"Take your best shot. After McKenna, what the fuck could be worse?"

Brill stops what he's doing, and gives me the full measure of his detective hound dog face, and takes his time doing it. "Klaussen wasn't the first," he says finally.

"Wasn't the first what?"

"To disappear."

EIGHTEEN

Brill changes the CD to Marcus Roberts's *Gershwin for Lovers,* the opening piano notes like drops of rain from a heavy predawn sky.

"I was just coming into my second year as a patrolman. Your dad used to bring Klaussen into my uncle's joint on Mass Ave., give him a little blues education, taste of the other side of the tracks. Klaussen had a steady girl then. I don't remember her name. But she had a drug problem, I remember that."

"Why's that stand out to you?"

"Well, you know the rules my uncle had. Heavy hitters checked hardware at the door, didn't tolerate nothing but weed. I caught her shooting up in the bathroom and had to kick her out. Messy. Blood-on-the-walls-type shit. Your dad didn't argue the point. I think he was embarrassed, even."

I ask Brill how he came to that conclusion.

"Was a while before I saw him again after that. Could've just been busy, managing Klaussen and the band, riding the wave of that song, looking like they were going to hit it big. Then the girl disappears."

"What do you mean disappears?"

"Just that. *Poof.*" Brill brings his hands together, a white cloud of dust exploding into the air. "Gone. Parents filed a missing-persons report. Camilla Islas." Brill snaps his fingers. "That was her name. Parents lived just outside Davis Square."

"They think something happened to her? They know she was a drug addict?"

"They knew. And they pointed fingers, too."

"Klaussen."

"Of course. It usually *is* the boyfriend. And he was an addict, too, at this point."

"Was the album out yet?"

"It was. But it was the single that was eating up the local airwaves. You telling me you don't know all this?"

"The music part only. Nothing about the girl. What kind of name is Islas?"

"Mexican. Spanish. Klaussen himself was at least part Mexican or Native American or something."

"You're full of shit," I say.

"What are you talking about?"

"There's no fucking way you'd remember all these details from so long ago."

"Is that what Wells told you, that I'm slipping? Anyhow, who said from so long ago? When that whole McKenna shit went down me and Wells pulled up everything we had on your family, especially since our local Feds weren't so eager to share. I'm just remembering shit from two years ago."

"And Klaussen's name was in my dad's file?"

"See, that's where things got mighty *interesante*. Klaussen's name is in there but most everything else was redacted. Someone had blacklined the shit out of that file."

"Meaning what?"

"Come on, Zesty, don't play coy. You know the FBI was protecting McKenna as long as he was ratting out the Italians. Your dad was so tangled up with McKenna, that shit with your mom, they were protecting him, too."

"From what?"

"What do you think? He covered Klaussen like a blanket. Anything Klaussen did, your dad knew about or was there. If Klaussen killed his—"

"Why would Klaussen kill his girlfriend?"

"Why does anyone?"

"So you're telling me Klaussen was a suspect and that automatically made my *dad* a suspect?"

"I don't blame you for being upset, Zesty, but it's not that farfetched."

"Nah, fuck that!" I'm heated now. "My dad wouldn't have any motive to want her gone. What, because she embarrassed him at your uncle's joint? That's fuckin' bullshit."

"No, you're just spitting lightning because you're emotional. Your dad had plenty of motive. The single was on fire and the album was about to drop heavy. Everybody knew how big Mass was going to be. Your dad had his golden goose to protect and Camilla Islas was like a cancer firing on the lymph nodes. Your dad had every reason to get rid of her."

"So how come he was never picked up for it?" I try to punch

a hole through Brill's reasoning but the logic is hard to argue with; for a hot minute there Mass did look like my father's ticket to another life.

"He *was* questioned."

Until the FBI stepped in and declared him off-limits and then redacted whatever was in the file. My mom was also on the FBI's radar at this point for the Harvard bombing and her Central American political work, but not yet topping their chart for the Bank of Boston, which would come nearly a decade later. My dad was a credible suspect with something to lose. With a lot to lose.

And as expected, Mass's album dropped like a nuke on the Boston airwaves and Grant signed them as the opener for the Zeppelin tour. And then Lady Luck kicked Klaussen and my dad square in the balls.

"Was my dad ever a suspect in Klaussen's disappearance?"

"For like a hot minute. But see, on that there was no angle, no profit motive."

Like, say, with Tupac, who cut a shitload of songs that were never published and who's sold more music dead than alive, breathing life into all those conspiracy theorists who think Tupac is still kicking, lounging on some remote island and drinking coconut juice out the crack of some Tahitian model's ass. Not something I'd believe for a second if Klaussen hadn't made his own return out of history's dustbin.

"You really think that's Klaussen you heard at the Hacienda earlier?"

"I'm telling you. I know it was."

"Well, if that's the case, Zesty, then you're getting played like a motherfucker. Because there's no way Alianna Solarte brought your ass in on this without knowing who Klaussen was. That lady's twisting your spokes for real. So the question you got to ask yourself is what the fuck is she really after? And one other thing. Aside from the redacted file on your dad that wasn't worth shit, everything else tied into Camilla Islas was gone and that includes the murder book."

"What murder book? You said it was a missing person's case."

"It was. But after seven years, Camilla's parents had her declared dead, as was their right under Massachusetts law. So it became a homicide."

"Why would they do that?" For an older person who might have a life insurance policy to collect on, it would make sense, but I doubted someone as young as Camilla Islas had anything like that and her parents had nothing to gain except funeral costs.

"Closure, maybe," Brill surmises. "Though I don't know how a piece of paper would give that. Somewhere in their hearts they've probably still got that gnawing pain not really knowing brings."

"Or maybe to kick-start a murder investigation," I say. "I'm assuming it went into a cold case file?"

"Sure. But that's what I'm telling you, Zesty. There is no cold case file on Camilla Islas. No evidence box, no murder book, not that there'd be much in it considering she just Houdinied out. And as you already know from experience, when BPD moved from Berkeley Street, they also digitized all the old files, but there's nothing in those files, either. As far as BPD is concerned, Camilla Islas never existed and anything that connected her to Klaussen or your dad is a Popsicle on a summer's day. You want to memorialize Camilla Islas, you might as well just write her name and 'RIP' on the stick and hammer it into the ground. Fuck Karl Klaussen. That girl is gone. Ain't no second acts in American life once you're buried in an unmarked grave."

NINETEEN

Brill and I knocked off at about five in the morning and he paid me a hundred dollars, bringing my three-day total to six hundred bucks, nontaxable, which in Massachusetts is like forty thousand gross. I was awash in cash and bruises I didn't even know I had until I got home and showered, collapsing onto the bed and the exploded marshmallow stuffing of my pillow. The cat had been at it again. Like I said, he's got a nose. Probably dug the Marshalls receipt out of the trash and went to town.

By the time I lock my bike up outside Buttery it's two in the afternoon, the kind of crisp New England fall day that convinces you to start boxing up the summer gear, the college girls hustling around the streets wrapped tight in their *Law & Order* sweaters, shiny as Honeycrisp apples.

I bring my coffee outside even though it's chilly, but in a ceramic mug this time to get a taste of how the other half lives. The coffee tastes the same. What had been a Laundromat for as long as I can remember across the street is undergoing a major reinvention, a giant plate glass window being crane-fitted into the frame, allowing me to see my reflection among the lounging class. I look good in dark plate glass windows. Always have. In fact, much better than the reflection of one of Moreno's men, who I catch clocking me from a stoop about thirty yards away.

Interesting. Maybe a little worrisome. But not enough to stop drinking my coffee and dipping a scone so dense you could drop anchor with it. From a safety standpoint I'm not particularly worried about him, but I don't really know why he's following me. I don't have anything that belongs to these people, they have *my* stuff. Obviously, they know where I live, but they aren't sending me a direct warning or he'd make himself more conspicuous.

Losing him certainly won't be a problem when the time comes, especially if the tricked-out Honda double-parked in front of the stoop is his. All it'll take is one quick wrong-way cut up a one-way street and then it's sayonara, sucker.

Not yet, though. Somebody has left a copy of the *Globe* on a nearby table and I pick it up and leaf through it. My coffee seems hotter than normal, a small cloud of steam rising off of it. Maybe it's the ceramic mug. Moreno's man looks a little cold, possibly a little envious. Once in a while I pick up the mug with both hands, take an extended joyous sip, and scrunch my shoulders like they do in the commercials right before reaching climax.

The Sox have lost their last game of the season, kicking off the long wait for spring and Hope Eternal, all eyes now turning to the Patriots, Celtics, and Bruins, pretty much in that order. One day, the stars will align, all the pro clubs will win a championship in the same calendar year, and the entire city of Boston will drop dead with a smile on their face.

Rambir Roshan, who was killed two weeks ago, didn't bring a smile to anybody's face, according to Anitra Tehran's reporting in her Metro Region follow-up piece that offers up no mention of a Russian/Ukranian connection to poker clubs or real estate, of a pimp and drug dealer named Oleg Katanya or his boss Jakub Namestnikov. And though I can't make out the faces of the plain-clothes detectives inside the yellow-taped cordoned-off crime scene photo, one's wearing a fedora and the other looks grumpy, even from a distance.

But I do learn that Rambir Roshan was discovered by a jogger at a little past four in the morning and that by five eighteen, the twenty-two-year-old second-year MIT graduate student from Mumbai, India, was moved off of the 182nd smoot point, where he'd died, exactly halfway between Cambridge and Boston across the Charles River, give or take an ear.

The story was essentially a rehash of Tehran's original reporting with the added official response from MIT and coverage of the joint Cambridge/Boston mayoral news conference that was held to reassure citizens of the safety of the two respective cities. They had numbers to back it up, too. And though initially it was unclear who would take jurisdiction over the case, I know that it fell to Brill and Wells, though Brill was now forced to the sidelines.

I put the paper back where I found it and adjust my seat so I can keep Moreno's man in my periphery, the plate glass window now flush in its frame. When I ditch him, I feel pretty crafty about it until I'm locking up my bike outside Solarte's office and spot Elvis loitering across the street, making himself about as inconspicuous as a traffic cone in a garden of tulips.

When I whistle at him, he gives me the finger. I don't think he's telling me I'm number one. I'm sure he would have much preferred to grab his crotch, but considering the shot I gave him yesterday, it was probably out of commission. Was it only yesterday? Time sure flies when you're getting the shit kicked out of you and working three jobs.

TWENTY

I have to be buzzed in downstairs this time, but the door between the waiting room and office is already open. Karl Klaussen sits in a chair beside Alianna Solarte's desk, almost facing the windows to Kenmore Square. Solarte sits where she'd sat a couple of days ago, her face neutral but unworried. Her camera is on her desk. Charlie's gun is nowhere in sight.

"Fuck you." I point at Solarte. "And fuck you, Andino. You both got some 'splaining to do."

Screw political correctness.

"Have a seat." Solarte sighs heavily and I have to remind myself that I own today's indignation, tired of being lied to.

"No. I don't need a seat. I need some straight answers. You know who this is, don't you?" I point a finger toward Klaussen, who's dressed himself up for this meeting, a chocolate brown suit, white shirt, and lemon yellow tie. Up close I realize how red and dark he really is, almost like burnt ochre. And Solarte's right about the facial surgery, his skin pulled tight against high narrow cheekbones, shiny, like armor. I can smell the clove cigarette smoke embedded in the suit and a fresher version, likely an open pack somewhere in his pockets.

"Initially, no, I didn't," Solarte says, looking at me full-faced. "But I suspected as much. Considering what he'd asked me to do."

"I'm not following you."

"What Ms. Solarte is saying, Zesty, is that I'd hired her. Essentially, you've been working on my behalf."

"Following you around?" I shake my head. "No, that doesn't sound right."

"Well, deception breeds mistrust. I should have been more forthcoming with Ms. Solarte about what I was trying to accomplish."

"You mean, like telling her who you really are?"

"That would have been a start. But it's complicated. I had to be cautious coming back to Boston."

"Yeah, why's that?"

"Ms. Solarte can explain. At least why you've been pulled into this. I hadn't asked for you to be included, though I have to admit it was a shrewd move on her part. And it is good to see you, Zesty.

Obviously we've never met; I was long gone before you were born but your father and I were close once."

"What Klaussen's saying," Solarte cuts in, "is that I brought you in because your father is involved. How come you don't look surprised?"

"You know who Lady Gaga is?"

"Of course."

"Poker face," I say.

And because at one time it was taken for granted that my father was the place where secrets went to die, never to see the light of day. Until Alzheimer's set in and the Big Dig followed and the bodies and lies everyone thought would stay buried forever started churning toward the surface like weeds cracking through cement. Devlin McKenna might have been my father's biggest and most dangerous secret, but it doesn't mean it was his only one.

"So get to it," I say to Solarte. "You brought me in because you suspected Andino was Klaussen, but you weren't sure. If you were right, you figured I'd flush him out and be able to connect you to my dad?"

"Pretty much. Had I been able to go directly to your father, I would have kept you out of it and just gone straight to him," Solarte continues. "But the advanced stage of his Alzheimer's makes that a no-go, correct?"

"My father's all out of words," I say.

"And Zero presents his own complications, no?"

"Sure," I say.

"I'm assuming you're familiar with the story surrounding my disappearance, Zesty?" Klaussen offers me a sad little smile.

"It's a Boston rock and roll legend."

"Yes. If you believe such things."

"You're telling me there was more to it?"

"Isn't there always?"

"And it involves my dad."

"Yes."

"Let me guess." I take a measured pause to work on my timing. According to Hank, a lot of comedy boils down to tragedy plus time. Your girlfriend dumping you is painful when it happens. Funny when you hear the guy she left you for gave her an STD. "He helped you disappear."

Both Solarte's and Klaussen's eyebrows jump in synchronized revelation to what was essentially a guess, but one that makes perfect sense. When the time had come for my mother and Rachel Evans, one of her accomplices in the Bank of Boston robbery, to disappear years later, my father pulled it off without a hitch. Like he'd done it before. Like he'd had practice.

"Yes, exactly." Klaussen appraises me with something that looks like renewed interest and grudging respect. I've had this happen before. It's that Siddhartha moment when somebody realizes I might be more than just the stuff of romance novel covers.

"And now you're back," I say. "Looking for what? To do what?"

"Like I said, it's complicated. But essentially I'm looking for a woman."

"You mean Camilla Islas," I say, shock registering in both their eyes but something more wary coming into Solarte's, like she'd just realized she'd been misreading my cards all along and was about to pay for the mistake.

"How do you know that?" Klaussen's first to find words.

"Nah, I'm the one asking questions here. You think Camilla Islas is in Boston?"

"I *know* she's in Boston."

"Yeah, how's that?"

"Because I killed her," Klaussen says, looking for some sort of tell in my eyes. "And your father helped me cover it up and get rid of her body."

TWENTY-ONE

We've left Solarte's office and walk up the spine of Commonwealth Avenue under the canopy of elms and past the life-size bronze statue of the former Argentinian president Domingo Sarmiento, who looks serious, but no more so than Klaussen, who's wrapped a black scarf around his neck against the chill.

"Let me start with this, Zesty, to put your father into perspective for you because I'm not sure how much you really know of your dad's early years and what he did prior to your mother coming onto the scene."

The wind picks up and the leaves become like birds scattering around us and it occurs to me that this part of Boston, the part that has always had money, is the rare Boston avenue mostly unchanged since Klaussen had been here last and that with every faltering step he is moving backward in time into a city that has stood still in his mind and songs.

The old Boston, the part that has the generational coin—Back Bay, Beacon Hill—exists as fortresses that, for the most part, have rebuffed change, their leafy Charles River views protected by a phalanx of high-powered lawyers or the timely designation of historic districts, their boundaries preserved with cold hard cash.

In these rarified buildings, change happens behind closed doors and most people who occupy the middle rungs never really get to see the opulence inside. It's the people at the bottom who know: the maids and cleaning crews, the invisible army of underpaid concierges and doormen, the two-minute visits by messengers, or the one-day assaults by white-gloved moving crews, minor actors who move about the hardwood floors, the gleaming stainless steel appliances, and the Italian marble countertops like barely tolerated intrusions.

The only intrusion we have now is Elvis walking gingerly about twenty yards behind us, where I feel his eyes boring into me and keep getting this sensation that he's coming up fast to stab me in the back.

"Is something bothering you, Zesty?" Klaussen picks up on my discomfort.

"Yeah, can you get rid of Elvis or at least have him walk in front so I can see him?" I'd offer him my bike but I doubt the seat would be comfortable.

"Nestor makes you nervous?"

"Very."

"Then your instincts are good. Only I can't tell him to leave, he's been told to watch for me."

"Care to explain that?" Solarte says.

"Only if I must."

"You must if you want me and Zesty to keep working for you. Obviously what you're trying to get at is something a little more delicate than what Moreno's people can handle, maybe something you don't even want them to know about."

"This is true. They watch, but they don't know exactly. I'll clarify over lunch, but first I'd like to explain to you, Zesty, how far back I go with your father."

"Why?"

"Because context matters. April fourth, 1968. That date mean anything to you?"

"Yeah." It means that if Mr. Callahan, my old history teacher, were around, I could prove I was paying attention even while trying to sneak a peek down Sue Woodward's shirt. "It's when MLK was assassinated," I say. "Is this going to be on the quiz?"

"Sure," Klaussen says, and in that one word I hear his Boston accent return to him in spades, either a sign his guard has slipped or he's allowing Solarte and me to see behind the curtain of his tanned and tattooed Aztec façade. "Obviously a major day in history, but it's also the very day your father became a player in city hall. Really, he's never told you any of this?"

"No." The admission stings. Does Zero know this story?

"James Brown was scheduled to play the Garden the night King was killed and tickets had already been sold. It was getting on to early evening and word had spread about the assassination and right away some of the neighborhoods started heating up."

"You mean the black neighborhoods." Solarte probably doesn't need the clarification, but if Klaussen is intent on painting us a picture, I wanted to make sure he followed the numbers.

"Black, mixed." He shrugs the admission. "Roxbury, Mattapan, the South End. People were angry, buildings were already burning in Newark; soon they'd be burning in Watts. Back here things were getting dicey, too many spots for the police to cover, and the way Boston was built, all the old buildings, carved up even more at this point into rooming houses, all jammed together, it wasn't going to take much for this city to end up in flames. Kevin White was the mayor then and Barney Frank, who'd later become Congressman Frank, was his right-hand man.

"Your dad had done some outreach work for White, knew the Boston ward bosses and how the city ran, had already started to frequent the black jazz and blues clubs, so he was known in the neighborhoods where you wouldn't see a lot of gringos. Orchard Park projects, Robert Gould Shaw House. Anyhow, a call came in that a bus carrying about a dozen white people was surrounded by a mob on Blue Hill Avenue and Barney Frank asked your dad to go with Dan Richardson, Chuck Turner, neighborhood activists I'm sure you don't know, to try and defuse the situation. Which they did.

"But the pattern was basically repeating itself all over the city and worst of all, you had thousands of young blacks streaming toward the Boston Garden for the James Brown show, only the Godfather of Soul was holed up in his hotel room refusing to play. He wanted the show canceled."

"Can you blame him?" Solarte says.

"No, of course not. But try to picture thousands of angry, heartbroken young black men locked out of the Garden, their tickets not being honored, the city already a tinderbox on the verge of exploding. It was the perfect storm to reduce this city to ashes."

Like had happened a hundred years before that, only minus the racial component, when over seven hundred buildings burned downtown in a raging blaze that could be seen lighting up the sky by ships as far away as the coast of Maine.

"Mayor White dispatched Frank to convince Brown to perform and try to create some kind of Kumbaya miracle, but he flat-out refused until your dad was brought in to talk to him. William never told me what he said to Brown to convince him, but Brown agreed to go on, with one caveat."

"Which was what?"

"The man wanted to be paid in advance." This kernel produces a giant grin on Klaussen's face. "I mean, the music business back then was a racket. And Brown? He was the highest paid act in the game. Highest paid colored act, anyway. The man wanted his money up front, but that's not how the Garden operated and they had their own legitimate worries about a riot starting *inside* if they let people in. So now White's got James willing, but no money to pay the man."

"Really?" Solarte says, incredulously. "Boston back then and there's no slush fund they could pull it out of?"

"Of course there was," Klaussen responds. "But again, it's all about timing. The slush fund had just been tapped out. This was the cash that Zesty's dad and I would run into the neighborhoods and distribute to all the mayor's outreach programs. A cut for the ward bosses, a cut for the activist groups, a cut for the street players. This was old-school politics and it happened in every neighborhood, Southie, Charlestown. . . ."

Though I had no doubt those bags were a little heavier, the denominations higher, for the all-white neighborhoods.

"So what does my dad do?" Had he threatened James Brown in some way or made him some kind of promise that went beyond money?

"Well, things get a little fuzzy here because as you know, your dad plays it pretty tight. But the public story, what little there is of it, goes something like this: Back in the late 1950s when Boston was headed toward municipal bankruptcy and was really turning into a shithole, a group of bankers and industrialists got together and formed a semi-secret consortium called the Vault. At least that's what the press called it when they got wind of it.

"And don't misunderstand, this group didn't get together to *save* the city. Their goal was to put a mechanism in place for them to administer the wreckage *after* it failed and profit from it. But by the time of the MLK assassination, the Vault had taken on a few new, more liberal members, the founders of Filene's, Jordan Marsh, CVS. Hell, if you wanted to wipe out the ruling classes of Boston, one bomb under the table at Locke-Ober, where they sometimes convened, would have done the trick."

Only nobody had taken the shot, and the old-money roots just grew stronger, the neighborhoods became more insular and segregated, the white flight that had prompted Brill's foray into salvage and restoration creating another level of class divide that the Boston Mob, in all its iterations, feasted on for decades. This was the city my father cut his teeth on and became a player in.

Does he remember any of it?

We cross Commonwealth at Gloucester Street and walk north

toward Newbury, Nestor still behind us but far enough away to be out of earshot.

"Your dad accompanied the mayor to the Vault and made the pitch. He was quite a persuasive man; that I know firsthand. The Vault coughs up thirty thousand dollars, which wasn't even half of what Brown's going rate was, and remember, back then, that was a shitload of money. But it was enough up front to convince him to perform with the rest of the cash promised for later."

"And the city survived," Solarte says. "Finally, a happy ending."

"Not if you're James Brown." Klaussen laughs bitterly.

"Let me guess," I say. "The Vault stiffed him for the remainder."

"You got it. Only that's not the end of the story. Your dad had promised Brown his money, probably looked the man square in the eyes and swore he'd come through. And what's your dad's reputation been all these years . . . ?"

He was a man of his word. Someone who could be trusted with secrets, take the weight and keep his lips sealed. That was the public view, though the truth, of course, was far more complicated. Neither Solarte nor I have to say aloud what my father's reputation was built on for Klaussen to continue.

"I don't know how, but your dad got Brown the rest of his money a couple of days later. He kept his word. And the black community knew about it, too. Knew the Man had stiffed the Godfather of Soul and William Meyers had come through. Why do you think your dad was so welcome in all those neighborhood joints, that jazz club he loved on Mass Ave., Slade's on Washington, where the whitest thing that walked through the door was the newspaper?"

"I just thought it was his threads," I say, wondering if Klaussen's version of my dad's all-access pass had been passed down to Darryl and his men, who all grew up in Roxbury.

We turn off Gloucester down Public Alley 431 and through

the blue-and-white-tiled side door of Casa Romero, Boston's old-est and most expensive Mexican restaurant. The restaurant is empty, that sweet spot in between dining hours, but a few Span-ish words from both Solarte and Klaussen bring smiles from the staff and a table.

We order and as a round of Cokes is delivered, my phone rings and I see it's Detective Wells calling. "Hold on," I answer it, stepping out the door, Nestor resolutely guarding the alley at the corner on Gloucester Street. I don't offer to order him any food. He doesn't offer to watch my bike.

"What?" I say.

"Sam Budoff." Wells dives right in. "Does he have any tat-toos?" I could hear car doors shutting behind Wells, the busy chat-ter and squawk of walkie-talkies, the sound of something like crime scene tape blowing and flapping in the wind, and metal pinging against a pole.

"Where are you?" I say, a cold chill running through me.

"Never mind that. Just answer the question."

"Sam's got a tree, a pine tree on his forearm, a bunch of birds on his wrist. You're on the waterfront," I say.

Wells curses under his breath.

"What do you have?" I say.

"Listen, Zesty—"

"What do you have?" I grind through my teeth.

"A body." The wind in his phone sounds like a gale. "With tattoos."

"You pulled it out of the water?"

"Yes."

"And there's not enough face to make an ID?"

"Might be," Wells answers. "If I had a face. So far I only have parts. Torso. Legs. A hand without fingers. Sam have any tattoos on his chest?"

"No."

"Well, if the legs go with the torso, then it's not Sam Budoff. I'm no Mr. Potato Head expert but I think they go together."

"Sam still hasn't gotten ahold of you?" I briefly contemplate telling Wells about the nearly million dollars in poker chips I took out of Sam's storage unit, but hold on to that play, seeing how I'd just brought Zero into the mix.

"No."

"Did *you* know he got himself a job at a place called Kirilenko Labs?"

"No. But they sound familiar. What do they do?"

"Cyber-security firm. They're a big deal, I guess. Did you know Sam had those kind of skills?"

"Wells, he's a fucking genius. He probably even knows how to put one of those little ships inside a bottle. So?"

"He's been a no-show for two weeks with the flu. They even sent him chicken soup."

There's a long pause on the line but that's okay because another song's coming in between my ears and it's a good one, "Shoulda Woulda Coulda" by Beverley Knight.

"You know what your problem is, Zesty?"

"Speak up," I say, probably too loudly, Nestor looking up suddenly from his reverie at the corner. "Beverley Knight's killing it!"

"You think you're slick, but you're not."

"Now you've really lost me."

"I served Zero up with a search warrant this morning."

"For what?"

"Sam Budoff's storage unit. Office records. Zero's safe. Funny how there's no security cameras in Zero's warehouse. I wonder why."

"No, you don't. Zero open the safe for you?" Exposing whatever it was he didn't want Jhochelle to see? Where he might have stashed Sam's nearly million dollars in poker chips?

"Funny you asked that. Your brother's wife says Zero's out of town on business. You wouldn't know anything about that, would you?"

"Cain and Abel," I answer.

"Which one are you again?"

"You get in the safe?" If he did, it wasn't through Jhochelle.

"As if. I forgot to bring a big enough can opener, if one even exists. Meanwhile, your sister-in-law sicced her celebrity lawyer Andrew Tetter on us, challenging the access to the safe, so we're waiting on a judge's ruling."

Wells surprises me with a genuine laugh.

"What's so funny?"

"Well, we can't get in, but we *can* hold the safe to make sure the contents aren't tampered with."

"You mean move it? Are you out of your mind? That thing weighs, like, three thousand pounds. You notice that section of the floor is reinforced concrete?"

"I got that. And supported by a metal girder from the garage level below. That's why I'm laughing. Obviously the thing has to go through the window, right? Out back where that lumberyard is. I called Brill and told him to check them out, actually. They have some wide-plank flooring there that's unbelievable. Expensive as hell, too."

"You know why that is?"

"What the market will bear, I'm assuming."

"It's more than that. Most of the wood's salvaged from underwater, rivers in Pennsylvania, Carolina, even as far as Oregon. It's the logs that sank as they used to float them down to the mills. These trees are a couple hundred years old, perfectly preserved. These guys dive and attach these massive fucking balloons to surface them, dry them out, and then cut them. It's expensive as a motherfuck but they set the rate, the stuff's so rare."

"That's pretty interesting," Wells admits. "The moving business so slow that Zero's moonlighting for them?"

"What?" I don't get what he's saying, but then I do. The diving equipment in Zero's office that Jhochelle kept deflecting. But Zero wasn't working for anyone; he made plenty of money with the moving company and whatever other irons he kept in the fire that I wasn't keen on knowing about.

More likely, one of the lumberyard divers was working for Zero. If so, doing what? Something recent; that seaweed on my sneaker had been fresh. "Zero wouldn't work for them," I dispel Wells's notion. "They're always at each other's throats about parking and noise and whose garbage belongs to who."

"That's also the impression I got. But what I was laughing about before is those ZZ Top–looking dudes who we called to come move the safe."

"You called Death Wish Movers?" Death Wish are specialists of the heavy lift, things that need to be hoisted by crane through windows or skylights dismantled to the frame—pianos, safes, giant sculptures. Their T-shirts are like Willy Wonka's Golden Ticket, a rare and prized item you can only acquire if you work for them or hire them out, and they are damn expensive since the work is so specialized.

"Honestly," I say, "I'm surprised they took the job. Those cats and Zero are pretty tight."

"*Yeah* they are. They showed, only with two cases of Sam Adams and no crane. They just wanted to see what was going down and what we'd do about it. Good times."

There's another long pause before Wells says, "Brill told you about Oleg Katanya, Namestnikov, and the poker chips on Roshan." It isn't a question. "He tell you about the suspension, too?"

"Yep," I half lie. He'd told me he was suspended. He didn't tell me why. And I don't bother asking Wells because he'd no sooner give me details than show me his down cards if we were heads-up in a poker game with all the chips stacked in the middle.

"Fuck me," Wells castigates himself sharply. "I knew this was a shitty idea. I literally looked at myself in the mirror and said to myself, Batista, this is a shitty idea. What else he tell you?"

"I'm having lunch," I say. "What do you *want*?"

"Like I said, Budoff's still off the reservation."

"And he took the same class as Roshan, we already established this."

"Yeah, well, there's another connection. Roshan interned at Kirilenko. Sam got him the in."

"So what. That's how shit works in this city. Sam's in trouble for this?"

"No, but *you* are for removing whatever was in that box in his storage unit."

"I don't know what you're talking about." My lie to Wells comes easily because I've had the practice.

"That's pretty good, Zesty. Are you looking at the cue card or did you memorize that? Whatever. Least I know it's not Sam fillets we fished out of the harbor. So what's your take on Brill?"

"Grumpy as ever," I say. But what he's really asking is whether I'd noticed any of those miscues Zero and I had seen with my father and chalked up to late nights and sketchy company, a mind full of secrets that started leaking through the fissures of his brain.

"I just think he's suffering from a case of nostalgia," I offer up my diagnosis. "Heeding the siren song of the old neighborhood. You ever hear that calling?"

"No."

"Maybe it's a Boston thing." Wells isn't from Boston. Actually, and as far as I can tell, he isn't from anywhere. Doesn't seem to affect his work, though. He is a fine homicide detective in a city that sometimes naps and if the dead speak to him, the Boston accents don't seem to throw him off. "If I hear from Sam I'll let you know right away." I lay it on thick.

"Will you really?"

"Sure," I lie again. "But only if you tell me why Brill was suspended."

"I'm assuming you read Anitra Tehran's follow-up piece today, seen the pictures."

"Uh huh."

"Well, if you looked real close at that overhead shot, you see how the body was, like, smack dab in the middle of the bridge, prompting the question of whose jurisdiction the crime scene fell under. It was literally halfway between Boston and Cambridge. A couple of Homicides from Cambridge accused Brill of salting the crime scene, moving the body a couple smoots to the Boston side."

"Did he?"

"You'll have to ask him, he got there before me. Anyhow, he ends up getting into it with these guys, Powers and McGowan, punches McGowan in the face and breaks his nose. The brass worked it out between them, Brill gets suspended, but I keep the body, catch the case."

And none of that ends up in any of the stories Anitra Tehran wrote for the *Globe*. So that seals it; likely the two of them worked something out. Maybe he keeps her in the loop with the investigation and she holds on to the story about Brill contaminating a crime scene, which would get him tossed from the force if it went public.

Wells took a big chance, sticking his neck out there for his partner and compromising himself like that. And if I'm right, Tehran is also compromised because she's sitting on what would be a major story and keeping it from her editors.

Welcome to Big City Poker, everybody in the game holding cards and checking on the first round, waiting to see who'll make the first move to risk some chips into the pot.

Actually, that's not right. Somebody had made moves: the firebombing at Nick's Comedy Stop. Rambir Roshan's murder. I believe in coincidences but not in the form of bullets and Molotov cocktails. Not with a reporter and homicide investigator looking into the same things; Russian and Ukrainian names popping up everywhere so soon after Tehran's real estate exposé.

"This stays between us," Wells says, unnecessarily. "And I still want you to keep an eye on Brill. I need him in my corner, but if he's going to come out of this with his job and pension intact, he needs to steer clear until I put this thing to bed. You hearing me, Zesty? I'm bouncing things off the old man only because I know that if I don't, he's going to go after Katanya and Namestnikov himself. Not only is he not authorized to do it, but these people will kill him in a heartbeat. Keep an eye on the old crank. By now you should be good at this kind of thing."

TWENTY-TWO

The food is on the table when I return, Klaussen and Solarte already digging in.

"Did I miss grace?" I say.

"By a mile." Solarte winks at me as I slide into a chair beside her. I could have sat next to Klaussen but his guitar case occupies the seat beside him and anyhow, Solarte's much smaller, giving me plenty of elbow room. I can tell she's not happy with the seating arrangement, her back to the door, which would force her to crane her neck every time someone came into the restaurant. Only nobody comes into the restaurant. Maybe it's the off hour. Possibly it's Nestor and his violent pompadour.

"So what's the word?" I say.

"What do you know about Mexican culture, Zesty?"

"Really? First it's MLK and now this? Okay, it'll be short: I know Cinco de Mayo, Quinceañera, that the Aztecs used to put gold flakes into their coffee because they believed it ensured sexual potency." Something I'd be willing to try but can't afford. "And Día de los Muertos is a holiday that honors the dead and loved ones pray to speed the dead's journey into the afterlife. How'd I do?"

"Sadly, better than most. But you're spot on about Día, which is really why we're here. Día starts on October thirty-first, which leaves us less than a month."

"To do what?"

Solarte reaches into her jacket and lays down three photographs, two black-and-white, one color, of a pretty woman, maybe late teens, early twenties; it's hard to tell with the heavy black and purplish makeup on her face, the eyelashes painted long, maybe fake, possibly not. Cherry lips in the color photograph. Dark eyes with charcoal stripes underlining them in that one, like what a ball player wears to fight the glare or just look tough. It doesn't make Camilla Islas look tough, though, just sexy. If you could ignore her junkie thinness and the faraway look in her eyes.

"Cool jacket." I point out the leather coat that could have been stolen from Chrissie Hynde of The Pretenders. Spikes on the shoulder to dissuade pigeons from roosting. Red stripes on the sleeves.

I look long and hard at the photographs and then up to see Klaussen's eyes, deep and dark and brimming with tears that flow quietly down his angular cheekbones like water over stone, a level of pain in them that surprises me, probably similar to the fresh grief Rambir Roshan's loved ones are experiencing right about now. Only this girl in the pictures has been dead for over thirty years. And Klaussen killed her and then disappeared her body with my father. What right does he have to cry?

The second photo is crowded with people, Klaussen and Islas together in a graffiti-covered equivalent of what was once the green room of a Boston club, both of them looking thoroughly wasted but happy, a snapshot of the high-octane Boston rock and roll scene of the time.

"That one," he points out, "was backstage at the Channel, long gone now, right?" He uses the back of his hand to swipe the tears from his face. "When this picture was taken we'd been together for close to two years and if you can't tell, we were both hard-core junkies then."

"The album was out at this point?"

"Yes. Locally, we were as big as anybody. It was us, J. Geils, Aerosmith, you can actually see Peter Wolf in the background there. . . ." He trails off. "Your father was probably prowling around somewhere, but he's not in any pictures I still have. Camilla and I, we were both using but I'd gotten her pregnant and she was trying to kick, to get clean. This was just a few months before we were supposed to open for Zeppelin and, well, you know the rest of that story. We were sharpening our set, playing out a lot, and somebody gave me something, somebody was always giving me something, and I pressured Cam into shooting, one last time, always just one last time." The tears had stopped falling, but they'd left behind a shine in Klaussen's eyes that made them glint like hard dark marbles in his face.

"We had a show on the Cape and when we got back into Boston I woke up and Camilla's beside me, a needle sticking out of her arm, and your dad's trying to revive her. I was so fucked up, Zesty; I didn't, couldn't do anything. I don't remember where we were, but your dad had wrapped her body in a sheet and we drove, not too far, might have been Southie; I remember seeing oil tanks and smelling the marshy waters, industrial waste. . . . And we buried her. Your father made me shovel, we both shoveled. . . ."

Klaussen's wide shoulders shake and silence settles in at the table, a waiter approaching but waved off by Solarte with a discreet wag of her finger.

"We all know McKenna had buried bodies at Tenean and Wollaston, and that Ritter, McKenna's hatchet man, led the state police there when he cut his deal," Solarte fills the void after some time has passed. "But Camilla Islas wasn't one of the bodies recovered so we've ruled those places out."

"But you think she's buried at—"

"I don't know where she's buried. I'm just telling you what I remember. She's somewhere in the city, that's all I know."

"And why's this suddenly so important?" I don't bother trying to hide the anger in my voice, but who am I angry at? Klaussen for forcing his girl into an overdose during her pregnancy? Or my father, who let it happen and covered it all up and was now unable to answer for his sins, his ever-growing laundry list of fucking sins? "Why the fuck are you back now trying to fix something you can't make right?"

"You ask me a question that, regardless of what answer I give you, won't satisfy you, Zesty. You realize that, don't you?"

"Deal with it. She's been dead for over thirty years, for fuck's sake. Why now?"

"I don't know what I can tell you beyond the fact that this has weighed on my conscience for those thirty-plus years, and to be absolutely truthful, this is the first time I've felt strong enough to confront the guilt. She's been calling to me, you know."

"Fuck you." I slam the table, the silverware jumping.

"I don't blame you for being upset, Zesty. I get it. But I'm curious, do you believe in such things, the voices of the dead? In spirits and ghosts?"

I'm not sure what I believe. Did the dead speak? Not according to Brill, who claims that the dead are silent, which is why he works so hard to speak *for* them, to give them the last word.

"What I believe," I say, finally, "is that you're a fucking ass-hole and probably a liar."

"Yes, I am." My words sting Klaussen about as much as a butterfly's kiss. "But what reason do I have to lie now? I don't want anything from your dad. I don't need money. Camilla was of Mexican heritage. I only want to give her a proper burial so she doesn't suffer any more than she already has."

"Yeah? So while you're at it, why don't you go turn yourself in to the police and get them to help find her?"

"And what would that gain? Tell me. You think I haven't suf-fered for my sins, is that it?"

"Yeah, pretty much," I admit.

"Well, you don't know me." Klaussen shrugs dismissively and it takes every ounce of restraint I have not to jump across the table and punch him in his smug and bronzed fucking face. "And do you really want to drag your father's name into this? I understand he's beyond the reach of the courts, but do you want them pok-ing around, dragging your family's already infamous past through the papers again? Looking into Zero's business and affairs?"

Thanks to Sam Budoff it's a little late for that but I don't want Zero to have to battle on two fronts at once.

"Here's the thing," I address Alianna Solarte. "Him I get not going directly to the police, but I need you to be straight with me. Coming into this, did you know that Camilla Islas's case was non-existent as far as BPD is concerned, that it's all gone, the files, the murder book? That except for a tombstone and an empty grave, Camilla Islas never existed."

"No." Solarte doesn't try to hide the surprise in her face. "I just knew that they'd never let me take a look at it. I think you know why."

Klaussen interjects, "Which is why we need to be the ones to find her. It's not right what they've done, rendered her invisible.

Any more than what I have. Camilla deserves to be remembered. Isn't that what your people believe, Zesty?"

"My people?"

"You're Jewish, are you not? As long as somebody remembers the dead, speaks their name, keeps them in their hearts, they're alive."

"Something like that." My ignorance is like a cold slap across my face.

"Well, I remember Camilla. But after me . . . ? I know I don't have the right to be the one entrusted to carry her, but there's nobody else who knew her like I did. Alianna says Camilla's parents are gone. She had no siblings, no other relatives that I know of. Her spirit needs release, Zesty. Whether you believe in these things or not, I know it to be true. . . . There's no other reason I've been left alive but to make things right and aid in her safe passage. I know you don't want Camilla to be forgotten, Zesty."

"No." I think of Zero and his locked safe and newfound happiness. Of my father's locked mind and newfound silence. Of my mother, who's been gone so long she hardly even qualifies as a memory anymore.

"Then help me, Zesty. Help Alianna find Camilla and make this as right as I possibly can."

"I'm not really sure what I can do for you, Karl," I say.

"Well, for starters," Klaussen says, "you can take me to see your father."

"Why the hell would I do that?"

"Because what's the harm?" Klaussen pleads. "It's been too long and I miss him terribly and owe him my life. But if all that's unconvincing to you," Klaussen raises his glass, takes a sip and pats the guitar case beside him, "despite my many shortcomings, your father always thought highly of my musical abilities. Perhaps he'd enjoy listening to some live music again."

TWENTY-THREE

There's a Brookline Police cruiser parked in front of my father's house on Beals Street, a defibrillating shock of panic spiking my heart until Sid sees me out of the corner of his eye and twitches a wink in my direction. I'd left Casa Romero a few minutes before Klaussen and Solarte and caught rocket fuel in the form of the Modern Lovers' 1972 Boston classic "Roadrunner," which powered me through Kenmore Square and up the gradual incline of Beacon Street until I turned into Coolidge Corner and coasted until I hit Beals.

The cruiser's flashers are off and two uniformed policemen are standing at the foot of the three stairs that lead to the open front porch of my father's house. One of the blues has his foot on the second stair, writing on an open notepad balanced across his thigh.

Sid's not so much blocking their entrance as forming a tandem wall with the man who pretty much fits the description the bouncer at the Lounge had given for the guy he called the Rabbi, the mountain of a man wearing a large black overcoat that could conceal a bazooka, an unruly nest of a black beard blanketing his face, and an unusually low hairline that makes his forehead seem small. At least from a short distance, he looks only a shtreimel short of walking out of a Polish shtetl at the turn of the century.

"This is what I told the officer at the scene last night." His voice emanates as a rumble, but with a strange off-kilter pitch that makes it sound like he's whining. If a boulder could whine. The Rabbi strokes his beard and cocks his head defiantly. An awning of scar tissue hangs over his brow, shading his eyes. "Perhaps you should compare notes."

"What he means," Sid cuts in, "is no disrespect, Officers, but we thought we had this cleared up last night."

"That was before Rabbi Bloomberg noticed that the padlock on the side door was broken and there were two empty bottles of Manischewitz under the lectern."

"Of this, I know nothing." The Rabbi takes offense. "A little sweet for my taste."

"What's going on, Sid?"

"A little misunderstanding. Officers, Mr. Meyers's son, Zesty."

"What can I do for you officers?" I say.

"You have any identification?"

I produce an ID that's not a driver's license and the officer with the pad records whatever he's supposed to record. Later they'll run my name and I'll come up clean as a whistle, proving that miracles still happen.

"Are you aware your father and Rabbi Day here almost got arrested last night?"

"For what?"

"They broke into Temple Israel." The officer cocks his head toward Harvard Street, the temple out of sight, but just around the corner.

"'Broke in' is a little harsh," the Rabbi rumbles, spreading his hands placatingly. There are large red scars on his knuckles, a bandage that needs changing on his left hand, dark red blood seeping through.

"You broke a padlock on the side door with what, a crowbar?" No-Pad says.

The Rabbi shrugs, half confession, half apology.

I look at Sid, who shrugs the other half of each one. "Your pops wanted to take a walk. Rabbi Day offered to go. What's the big deal?"

"The big deal is they broke into a temple."

"Watch your tone." Sid points at me.

"We'll take care of any damage," I say. "The two bottles of holy juice." This is an unusual role for me, I realize, playing the grown-up. Zero might be sketchy, but I'm usually the one getting pulled out of shit shows. "What else do I need to do to make this right, Officers?"

"We're aware your father has Alzheimer's, that he's a wandering risk. But that doesn't give him or whoever's watching him the right to break into places."

"Understood," I say at exactly the same time the Rabbi says, "A man wants to go to shul, he should be allowed to go to shul."

"Excuse me?" The officer with the pad looks up sharply.

A couple houses down Alianna Solarte and Karl Klaussen unfold themselves from a cab and I hold my finger up to them to stay back a minute, the porch crowded enough as it is.

"No, I agree with you wholeheartedly, Officer." The Rabbi softens his stance. "My issue is with the locking of the temple itself. I understand the security concerns, the political climate being what it is, but if a man wishes to pray, should he not be allowed to enter a house of the holy and commune with his God?"

"At three in the morning?" The officer goes back to writing on the pad. It looks like a lot of paperwork for a lot of nothing.

"My dad's internal clock isn't working anymore," I say by way of apology. "There's not a lot of sleeping going on around here. I'm sure they were both pretty loopy at that point."

"I understand that," No-Pad says.

"My dad asked to go into the temple?" I look to the Rabbi.

"He led and I assisted."

With a crowbar? I thought but managed not to say.

"Nobody's looking to press charges. We just want to reach an understanding here, gentlemen, for future reference. Rabbi, do you have a temple you're affiliated with?"

"I'm, at the moment, as they say, between congregations."

"Who's 'they'?" I say.

The Rabbi shoots me a withering look from deep behind his beard and brow. I'm sure it's a look that's frightened many a recalcitrant bar mitzvah boy to death, only I'm not particularly religious.

"Is there a problem here?" No-Pad picks up on the vibe.

"No," I say. "Again, probably just a lack of sleep."

"What's with the hand, Rabbi?" Pad doesn't look up from his scribbling. A future detective, this one. He has the languid demeanor of a card shark, not even his fin sticking out of the water. But he's seen the blood seeping through the Rabbi's bandage, knows there's more to this story than what the Rabbi's divulging.

"The joys of learning a new trade," the Rabbi says.

"Oh yeah, what's that?"

"I work at the Zen Moving Company," he responds cheerily. "Coming hard to the realization that it's a job for graceful apes who have the ability to dance backwards like Gene Kelly in high heels. I skinned my hand."

"Okay," Pad says, not buying any of it, but moving on. "You also understand how maybe you wouldn't want *your* temple broken into in the middle of the night?"

The Rabbi throws up a Talmudic shrug. It seems to be enough.

"Perfect. So the next time Mr. Meyers feels the urge to pray, you'll attend during regular temple hours, agreed?"

We watch as the squad car pulls away. "Brookline's Finest. How much luckier can a cop get than to have Coolidge Corner as your beat? The finest of coffees, fresh bagels, and hello, who do we got here?"

I make the introductions all around, Sid extra-attentive to Alianna Solarte as he is with all women, a fool for love, or at least a tire-kicking roll in the hay. But he does a double take as Karl

Klaussen's name registers with him, Sid only a handful of years younger than Klaussen and a music lover in his own right. Hell, he'd probably seen Mass play out in the clubs and undoubtedly knew the legend of Klaussen's disappearance. Did he know more? Sid has spent a lot of time with my father the past few years, been privy to my father's one-way conversations. Had my dad spoken of Klaussen? Of Camilla Islas?

"No fuckin' way! Zesty, you're always full of surprises. Where the fuck did you find this guy?"

"Long story," I say.

"Man, I used to see you guys all over town: the Rat, Chet's. I think I even got my first blow—"

"Sid!"

"Oh shit." He reddens. "I apologize."

Alianna Solarte winks at Sid, distracting him from his fan-boy moment, and we step into the house leaving behind a sky the color of dried roses, a line of softer pink and blue at the tail end of the street as dusk settles in. But it's already dark under the canopy of oak where we are, the motion sensor lights on the porch flicking on as I shut the door behind me.

My father sits motionless at the large octagonal poker table we'd bought for him a couple years ago and where he prefers to sit and seems most at ease. His eyes remain vacant as we trundle through the front hall like the starting five to some misfit basketball team. Two giant forwards in Sid and the Rabbi; Klaussen the thin, wiry center ducking his head, probably out of habit, as he comes through the front door; Solarte looking like she could run around forever; and me running point, though everybody'd probably complain I don't dish enough, always looking to squeeze off my own shots.

There are chips stacked in each well of the eight-seat poker table, two decks of cards at the ready on the green felt, my father

watching *The Cincinnati Kid* from across the small living room.
His eyes rarely blink. His pupils, onyx stones. *The Cincinnati Kid*
is one in a rotation of poker films my father seems to enjoy along
with *Rounders* and *A Big Hand for the Little Lady,* the poker scenes
igniting some neural connections deep inside his brain, something
returning to him in the narrowing of his eyes and twitching of
his fingers, as if they were attached to electrodes.

Klaussen gestures to a seat next to my father and I nod, watching as he leans his guitar against the wall between them, my
father momentarily glancing at the case before looking at Klaussen
as if seeing him for the first time. And then back to the television.

"It's good to see you, William," Klaussen says softly.

My father doesn't respond. I kiss him on the crown of his head
and sit on his opposite side. He lets me take his hand between
mine, his palms worn smooth and dry, slippery as talc. His lips
move but no sound emanates.

"What did he just say?" Klaussen asks, having seen my father's
lips.

"Fucked if I know," I say.

"I'm sorry." Klaussen looks away. I don't know if he's being
polite or the sight of my father is too much for him to bear.

Sid takes the opportunity to guide Alianna Solarte gently by
the elbow, giving her the grand house tour, which in Sid's fan-
tasy would be cut short in one of the two bedrooms upstairs.

"And here," Sid narrates pictures unnecessarily, "is Zesty and
Zero when they were kids. . . ." All the pictures have masking tape
affixed to the frames, yellowed captions detailing who appears in
the photos, the locations and dates; at this point the notes have lost
all meaning to my dad, as far as I could tell.

At one point, on the stairs, I catch Sid leaning in close to smell
Solarte's hair, balloon hearts practically popping out of his chest.

I shake my head at him, eyes wide to warn him off, but really, she might be the perfect lady for him: Sid likes them dangerous. Which is probably why he's so tight with Jhochelle.

"So, skinned your knuckles?" I chin-point to an open seat, but the Rabbi ignores the hint.

"It's been an active few days." The Rabbi's smile reveals a cracked front tooth. He's the largest man in the room but has the unease of the smallest fish in a packed aquarium. "And just to impart some knowledge so you don't judge me too harshly, the Torah says that sometimes it is permissible to lie."

"Yeah? When's that?"

The Rabbi clears his throat. "There are certain exigencies."

"Such as?"

"To keep the peace." The Rabbi unconsciously rubs his knuckles. "To practice humility."

"So you were double dipping?" I say.

"I don't understand."

"Doing both. You didn't want to take credit, 'fess up for bringing my dad to temple."

"That was not the lie. Your father steered me towards the temple on his own accord. I just opened the door. Why do you find this hard to believe?"

"My father wasn't religious. I'm not even sure he was bar-mitzvahed."

"Were you?"

"No," I say, a sharp sting of regret hitting me. *What the fuck?* I think.

"And your mother?"

"Next subject," I say. Temple Israel is a building my father had probably seen a thousand times since we'd moved him into this house six years ago. It's a large domed temple with far too many stairs for my father to climb at the Harvard Street entrance.

Of course there must also be a ramp that I'd never bothered to notice. But the police had said that they'd entered the temple after breaking a lock on the side door, the Rabbi most likely using a crowbar, which he conveniently had on his person. So perhaps this wasn't my father's first foray to the temple with him. Had he gone before to attend services? Not to my knowledge. Had he truly led the Rabbi to the side door himself, accustomed as he was from his after-hours games to use alternate exits and entrances, the Rathskeller a rare front door exception?

"So not religious," the Rabbi says. "But you practiced other customs, no?"

Yes, we had customs. Poker, music, baseball, time we spent together. Was the Rabbi saying customs were a form of religion? I ask him.

"Well." He warms to the question, but not enough to take a seat. "They exist for a reason. Like prayers we don't necessarily understand, but repeat time after time until the words are but a blur. We say them but we no longer remember why. Perhaps the beauty is in the blurring, the smudging; what's lost in clarity is gained in devotion?"

The Rabbi poses his statement as a question, but I have no answers for him. If the reason for praying is forgotten, aren't the prayers themselves meaningless?

Klaussen has kept Camilla Islas alive in his memory and now he wants to secure her passage to the other side in time for this year's Day of the Dead. Does that mean that the difference between the living and the dead is only the difference between the forgotten and the remembered? When the last person who remembers my father dies, is that when he'll truly be gone?

"What did my father do inside the temple?"

"He sat. We drank some wine. The walk tired him."

"Did he pray?" I'm thankful for the straight answer, return the gift with a straight question.

"I've yet to hear your father's voice," the Rabbi says. "Would he know how to pray?"

"I don't know," I say, but a memory floods back to me, perhaps the only discussion my father and I ever had concerning prayer. I was young, maybe eight or nine years old, and had asked how we ever knew our prayers were being heard and what happens if you couldn't remember the words or recited them wrong. His response to all those questions was simply: *Just say the alphabet, Zesty. That's all you have to do if you feel the need to pray. God will sort out the letters.*

I don't remember if I understood him then. I'm not sure I believe it now.

"His lips were moving." The Rabbi nods. "In shul. So I took the Torah from the ark and let him hold it. It seemed to mean something to him."

"Where did you come from again?" I say.

"Perhaps your father is preparing himself." The Rabbi skirts the inquiry.

"For what?" I say, angrily, unfairly. I know what the Rabbi is alluding to. The question really is, why am I so angry about it? My father won't live forever and he's declining fast. It's just that Zero and I don't talk about the end, utter not a word about that possibility. Until yesterday. Something's shifted beyond just living and trying our best to take care of our obligations.

And now all conversations have ceased, the only sound coming from the clacking of the poker chips, like bone on bone, in my father's badly shaking hands.

"This is something you and Zero should speak about." The Rabbi recuses himself to the kitchen.

"My father's not going anywhere, Rabbi," I say loudly to his back, his large frame bringing the illusion of midnight to the short hallway that separates the rooms. "What the fuck are you saying?"

"I did not mean to intrude." The Rabbi stops, but doesn't turn around. "But there comes a time for all of us. Zero speaks of this often."

"Not to me he fuckin' doesn't." I'm enraged and swallow hard.

"I apologize. Obviously this is a family matter. If you'll excuse me." The Rabbi continues into the kitchen and I can hear the back stairs creaking under his weight just as Sid and Solarte descend via the front and seat themselves at the poker table.

"The Rabbi's staying here?" I say to Sid. My face feels flushed.

"Zero's call," Sid says.

"For how long?"

"Who's to say? Talk to Zero. He's been good for your dad, though."

"Oh yeah, how's that?"

"Breaking into the temple's pretty funny." He shrugs. "They were *both* pretty fuckin' hammered."

"Wonderful."

"Hey, listen." Sid maintains the placid gaze of a New Age Buddha. Bedroom eyes. Basement fists. "He got Pops out and walking around and I was able to get some shut-eye. What's the harm?"

"The harm is I couldn't get a straight answer out of him. Where'd he turn up from?"

"Where do any of them turn up from? He showed up at the warehouse a couple months ago looking for work. You know Zero's always looking for reliable guys. He checked out." Which means Zero ran an extensive background check that included somebody also hitting the bricks for a little peekaboo coverage. "Even did a stint in the Israeli Army like Jhochelle. Fuckin' huge for a rabbi, right?"

"I don't know, Sid, what sizes do they usually come in?"

"Nebbishy?" Sid grins. "Jewy. Extra-Jewy?" Sid grabs me cat-quick and plants a rough kiss on my cheek. "Don't get your beanie in a twist. It's all good."

But is it? Only a couple of months in and he's brawling in bars with Zero, looking after my father, and sleeping shifts at his house. Where the hell have I been? Why am I so bothered by this? Is it because this is really my role and I've been avoiding doing these things, shirking my duties as his only blood-related son? I suppose I should be thankful Zero has the resources to provide the care our dad requires, but I'm embittered, ungrateful.

Klaussen seems at home, though, apparently content to sit and look at my father, perhaps familiar with some version of him from the past; this silent iteration doubtful to be his lasting memory of him.

Never trust anyone who is uncomfortable in silence, I can still hear my father say to me, and the memory drains my heat and makes me smile. I remember long periods of silence growing up, but it never bothered me as much as it did Zero because I knew, without a doubt, my father *saw* me. Silence has been the coin of my family's realm for a long time, which made me the outlier because I always seemed to have something to say. Maybe this is my true rebellion: It's not the job, the hair, the weed. It's my mouth, a constant distraction from the lies I try to convince myself are true.

I watch Klaussen, looking for his lie, and see nothing. *The Cincinnati Kid* starts rolling credits and I turn off the TV and we all sit around the poker table, Sid absently dealing out hands of seven stud, all the cards up, everyone, including my father with his badly shaking hands, reaching into their wells and throwing chips into the center, the winner raking the pot. My father wins the third hand with a Broadway straight, catching the inside queen on the river card, a statistical improbability that's roughly forty to one, and as poker strategy goes, a quick way to go broke. It was probably a hand he would have folded in one of his high stakes games, but who knows? Every situation is different. And sometimes you're left with no option but to chase that inside straight, pray for Lady Luck's mercy, for some love sprinkled in your direction.

"All yours, Pops," Sid says, but my father makes no move to rake the pot, the cards laid out in front of him not registering in his eyes; the value of his hand might as well be written in Sanskrit.

It's a moment that makes me swallow hard, a sharp sadness hollowing me out and rendering me weightless, like I could float off into oblivion if there weren't a roof over my head. But that moment passes quickly because Karl Klaussen's lifted his guitar from its battered case, his chair scraping the floor as he shifts to give himself some room, his fingers sliding over the frets of the sunburst Gibson, which, from the light above the table, reflects an orange and yellow dawn on the bare white wall. In a strong high voice he begins to sing the song that should have catapulted him to fame, the toll of his age and hard living only adding a layer of pathos missing from the sound captured on vinyl. Klaussen sings:

No sense howling for the moon
No sense worshiping the sun
If we live to see tomorrow
I'll be done
I'll be done

My father's lips begin to move. And though faint and barely above a whisper, once again I hear his voice.

TWENTY-FOUR

We sit outside on my father's front porch, Klaussen handing out clove cigarettes all around.

"I want my gun back," I say, once my cigarette is lit. "It's not mine, but I'm responsible for it." The smoke tastes better than I remember it, my lips sweet to my tongue. Now if I could only get somebody to confirm that.

Sid looks in my direction and winks. He's sitting close to Solarte, their thighs practically touching on the swing, separated only by the space of the Glock on her hip, Solarte carrying again. Is there something she's not telling me? Sid whispers something in Solarte's ear and she giggles like a little girl.

Unreal.

"I'll see what I can do," Klaussen says. "It's not as simple as just asking for its return."

"Why's that? Obviously Moreno and his crew are working as a protection detail for you."

"Not *for* me, but yes, on my behalf."

"And why is it you need protection, Karl? Somebody maybe not happy to see you around?"

"I can't really say. I view it as an unnecessary precaution, but it's not up to me."

"So who is it up to?" Solarte quits flirting long enough to join the conversation.

"Like I said, it's complicated, but I'll do my best to explain. After Camilla overdosed and your dad and I did what we did . . . ," Klaussen sputters out, maybe due to Sid's presence, but more likely, I think, because he's finding it hard to give voice to what he'd done, something faraway coming into his eyes.

I have no idea if Klaussen has ever spoken about his crime, has ever tried to unburden himself of the guilt he claims to have been lugging around for more than thirty years, talk therapy not everybody's panacea.

"After the whole Zeppelin debacle . . ." Klaussen takes a deep breath, gathering himself again. "Everything started going to shit. And why not? Somebody had to pay for not giving her family a chance to say goodbye, hold a *velorio* for her. This is important in Mexican culture and I'd failed her. Failed everybody.

"Of course, I wasn't seeing it so clearly then, I was so fucked up on alcohol and heroin. You know that saying, Zesty, that at the core, the best definition of an addict is an egomaniac with low self-esteem?"

I nod, smoke.

"Well, then, you have a good picture of what I was. And then throw in the local attention we were getting, the headliner status." Klaussen takes a heavy drag off his clove cigarette, the glow flaring in his eyes. "I didn't hold up well. None of us in the band did. You know Lorin Reese, my bassist, committed suicide after things fell apart. Chip Dwyer, our drummer, drank himself to death. Fuckin' sad. We were so close, Zesty, so fucking close."

"To what? Some rock and roll wet dream?"

"To *matter*." Klaussen's answer surprises me because I understand it core-deep. "Even on a local level, in this town, there's nothing like it. And that was even before the real money hit. I'm talking like WBCN, local-top-ten-type fame, everyone in town glued to the radio or spinning your record. Shit, we still lived like kids. Our apartments were dives, even after the album dropped, but we didn't care. It was all about the music. About making something that says we're here. We exist."

"And the drugs," Solarte reminds him.

"Yeah, it caught up to almost everybody. Even to some of the guys that made it. Anyway, your dad was the only one who was holding his shit together as we were getting booed off every stage, brawling with the same cats who just months before treated us like gods. I was spiraling and your dad just got me out. Made arrangements, told me he could pull it off, but it would have to be permanent. Like forever, because the cops were all over us, these two homicide detectives. . . ."

"Polishuk and Nichols," Solarte says, obviously having done her homework.

"If you say so. I honestly don't remember, but I was going to go down for Camilla; they just didn't have a body yet. But who knew how long she'd stay gone, and I didn't know if there was anything there to connect me."

"So you took my dad's ticket out."

"Through New York. Played that show at CBGB, walked out, and didn't see daylight again until I was across the Mexico border."

"And then what?"

"From there I was on my own and I just went and did what I do. I knew Spanish, started playing on the streets, in bars. I was a full-blown alcoholic and junkie, it was just a matter of time before I took a hot shot or crossed somebody and ended up with my neck cut in some alley."

"Only . . ." It isn't my intention to be rude, but I have somewhere to be and hope Klaussen will get to the point already.

"My dying yet just wasn't in the cards. I was approached by somebody who took a liking to my music. He took me in, got me clean."

"A narco trafficker." Solarte sees it before I do, disdain chalking her voice. "You started composing songs for a Mexican cartel boss. Narcocorrido music." Like the ones Klaussen played at the Hacienda.

"Of a sort."

"What the fuck does that mean?" Solarte's lost that loving feeling and now has Sid glaring at him, too, from the porch swing. "You wrote songs glorifying a Mexican drug kingpin. Which one? Is he still alive?"

"Not a drug boss." Klaussen only addresses part of the question.

"What other kind of cartel kingpin is there?" Alianna Solarte spits, shooting him a poisonous glare.

"Oil," Sid says, all heads turning to him. "PetroNarco. Gasoline. Pipeline siphoning and distribution, but on a massive scale."

"And how the hell do you know that?" Solarte is practically bug-eyed, reassessing her porch swing suitor.

"I read the papers." He winks at her salaciously. "I'm not just a pretty face. And crime interests me." Now Sid winks at me, but absent the lust.

"Is Sid right?"

"Spot on." Klaussen clears his throat.

"And Moreno?" Solarte asks.

"Is an outpost of sorts."

"You mean he also owns gas stations?"

"Not quite, Zesty."

"Then what? He washes money through the Hacienda?"

That gives Klaussen a laugh at my expense. "You're not grasping the scope of the fortune my boss—who shall remain nameless—maintains, Zesty. I'm talking about the one percent of the one percent."

"Meaning," Sid interjects, "that the money's already clean. So then what's with the visit and this security detail I hear you have? And I'm assuming this is where Zesty picked up that shiner and lost the gun that ain't his. You didn't just come back to Boston to find this dead girl. That's why you hired Alianna here, to try and keep whatever else you're doing separate, only it looks like that blew up in your face."

"Sadly so," Klaussen agrees. "But it's really just a hiccup. If Ms. Solarte agrees to stay on the case with Zesty, they can keep working and be paid well for it and I can accomplish what I've been sent here to do for my boss. Nothing's really changed."

Alianna had started shaking her head before Klaussen had even finished his pitch. "I don't think so."

"Why? Because you won't take tainted money, is that it?"

"Basically, yes."

"That's a naive view of money, then. My boss is a business-man, internationally known, respected."

"But his fortune came from stealing."

"As the Bronfmans' came from bootlegging during Prohibi-tion and the Rockefellers' from union busting. Don't propose to lecture me on ethics if it doesn't have anything to do with Camilla Islas. I've done the worst kind of wrong and I'm trying to fix that with your help if you'll give it to me. The rest is just business. His business happens to steal gas from the pipelines, distributes it, pro-vides protection for gas stations that sell his petrol, creates thou-sands of jobs along the pipeline routes from Guadalajara and Chiapas all the way into Texas and Arizona, where the focus is on stopping illegal immigrants, not money and gas. You don't think the big data companies are manipulating your information, siphoning your data, and selling it to the highest bidder? Are you really that blind to the way the world works, Ms. Solarte, Zesty?"

Alianna Solarte and I look at each other to see who's more stung by Klaussen's rebuke. It looks pretty much like a tie. And we could both obviously use the money.

"So what will *you* be doing as Zesty and I resume our search for Camilla Islas?" Solarte speaks for us both.

"I'll stay out of your way, make sure Moreno and his men do the same while I work to accomplish what I was sent here for orig-inally."

"Which is what?" Inquiring minds want to know.

"Nothing illegal, I can assure you of that. Boston has certainly changed since I was here last; those towers going up in South Boston Waterfront have some magnificent views."

"They fuckin' suck," Sid says.

"Yes, well, more business for your moving company once they are completed, no?"

"They still fuckin' suck." Sid shrugs, but can't deny the point. "So you're doing what, looking at real estate?"

"Yes."

"To invest in," Solarte says.

"For my employer. He enjoys a change of season." Klaussen smiles. "Think of him as a reverse snowbird."

"Around here we call them vultures." Sid's face is a grim mask. He grew up splitting time between the South End and South Boston, but can't afford to live in either one now.

"If you say so." Klaussen is unmoved. "It's not my role to arbitrate housing issues. My boss sends me because I grew up here and he trusts my eye."

"Fucking real estate," I say aloud, thinking of Charlie with no roof over his head, my overpriced closet on Union Park that I won't be able to afford when the lease is up, of Detective Brill, who had to rescue his childhood home from being foreclosed on, of Darryl sitting and watching the skyline change as he scratches out days on the wall of his cell.

And no doubt, nothing but penthouse views for whoever Karl Klaussen's employer happens to be. Oil, drugs, money laundering, corporate tax breaks and corporate shell games, who the hell can tell the difference anymore? Boston doesn't need to hire more street cops, they need an army of fucking masked accountants.

"Yes, of course, real estate," Karl says with the ugliest smile I've seen all week. "Really, is there any safer bet?"

TWENTY-FIVE

Our open-mike night has shifted to Allston, to a new bar that splurged on a canvas backdrop of printed bricks and a stand-up microphone that looks like the kind those old-time torch singers would belt into. Dark stage. Monocle spotlight.

"We missed you last night." Hank Aroot pulls me aside to show me my spot in the line-up. There's only a few customers at the bar. That's probably a good thing since I haven't sharpened any of my jokes since the firebombing and the only new thing that comes to mind is *A rabbi walks into a bar in Dorchester. . . .* That's it. No punch line. No shortage of punches.

"That's a hell of a shiner there," Hank notes with a wince. "Hazard of the job or something a little extracurricular?"

"Little of both, I guess." Depending on which job I want to claim for the damage. "But I'm here and ready to fail." I smile.

"Half the battle." Hank pats my back. "You're up after Caitlin. And let me just say, I admire your courage. Now go out there and bomb."

I don't let him down, opening with: *I saw a Who cover band the other night. They were called the Whom.* And followed with: *Terrible thing happened to me yesterday. I was arrested while loitering on the Stairway to Heaven.* I should have left it there, but I sang it: *On the Sta-ir-air-air-way to Hev-uun.* And closed with: *I auditioned for this superhero group called the Justice League of America. They said I couldn't join. I asked why not. They said because we're called the Just-Us League of America. Which means Just Us.*

Different club. Same crickets. Caitlin had killed before me. It was time to give that girl her due. She was just plain funny.

And after the show, instead of continuing down Allston Ave. to where it intersects Commonwealth, I cross back into Brookline, stopping in front of my father's house, where the blue wink of the television shines in the living room and I catch a glimpse of a play-off game in progress—green field, outfield wall—my father and Sid side by side on the couch now.

And from an open window on the second floor, I see the Kara Walker outline of two large men behind the shades and hear the Rabbi's deep locomotive of a voice reciting a familiar prayer, followed by moments of silence and then Zero's halting voice delivering an echo of the Rabbi's words, a phonetic retelling:

> *Yit-gadal v'yit-kadash sh'mey raba,*
> *Magnified and sanctified*
> *May His great name be*
> *In the world that He created*

The Mourner's Kaddish. The Hebrew prayer for the dead.

TWENTY-SIX

JJ Foley's is a longtime Boston cop bar on Berkeley Street, one of those magical buckets of blood that used to exist in the shadow of the elevated Orange Line, which ran practically on top of it, blocking any hint of sunlight that might happen to stray down to street level. It was also a vampire bar. While all the surrounding shops were shuttered and closed, the industrial neighborhood on the outer edge of the South End neglected and falling into decay and disrepair, Foley's stayed the same.

A long L-shaped bar was there to greet you as you walked in the door under street signs written in Gaelic. The corners were dark enough to disappear into if the only solace and company you needed was in the form of a shot glass or a pint of Guinness.

Was the proprietor Jerry Foley prescient? A Real Estate Whisperer? Master of the neighborhood reversal? Or did he simply decide that while the world spun outside, he would just keep doing what he did best, offering a warm home away from home for the cops, firemen, and municipal workers who toiled in the surrounding environs?

My father frequented Foley's practically his entire life and had made it into a picture or two on the walls to prove it. It's a wonderful thing to drink where your father once drank. I also happened to be arrested inside of Foley's once, got cuffed at the bar, kept drinking and still almost got laid. Top that if you can.

Foley's was also the place Sam and I had long ago arranged as a drop site in case he ever got jammed up, a likely occurrence had he not sold his fledgling hallucinogenic business and all the recipes to Cedrick Overstreet and Otis Byrd, Darryl's lieutenants, who were holding down his spots until Darryl served his sentence at MCI Concord.

And anyhow, it was always good to see Jerry working, a rare sight now that his sons had taken over and added a restaurant in a second room adjoining the bar; even Foley's wasn't immune to change as the neighborhood morphed into a monied playground.

"Well, if my eyes don't deceive me," Jerry exclaims as I take one of the few remaining open seats at the bar. The place is packed.

"Jerry, how are ya?" I say.

"Grateful as always." Jerry slaps a white rag over his shoulder. "Why has it been so long, Zesty? We've missed you around these parts."

"You're too upscale for me, Jerry. Look at all these people. The only time I've seen your place this crowded there was a wake going on. Somebody die?"

"Not to my knowledge. Blame my boys. The ambition of youth." Jerry shrugs an elaborate apology. "I did all I could to steer them away from working the stick, you know that."

Indeed I did. All four of Jerry's boys went off to college. Three of them came back to work the bar. One went into the priesthood. You don't get much more Irish than that.

"The world was their oyster. And what do they do? *Restaurateurs.*" Jerry enunciates the word with mock disdain. "And you? How's business?"

"Hanging in there."

"And your da?"

"The same." Jerry pours me a Guinness and two shots of Jameson without my having to ask.

"Speaking of change." Jerry directs my attention to a handful of pictures hanging above the ancient key-punch register, in the center a photograph of my father in his youth, drinking with Kevin White and Barney Frank. The last time I'd seen the photo it was yellowing at the borders, the corners curling toward the glass frame. When the restaurant construction was in full swing, the space where the picture once hung was blank and I'd assumed it was gone forever. But instead, it had been reframed and given a spot of prominence. I could now look across the bar into my father's smiling face.

"You do that?" I pretend to have something in my eye, pull at the short sleeve of my shirt to dab at it.

"My boys. Hardheaded, but respectful." Jerry lifts the shots and hands me one and we clink glasses. "To your da. May the road rise to meet him."

"To your sons." We throw the drinks down.

It's about twenty minutes before Jerry pays me any attention again, returning with a small manila envelope with my name on it, which he places in front of me. Not an ounce of curiosity plays on his face.

"How long have you had this?" I ask him.

"Two weeks."

"You could have called."

"I could have also given it to Zero," Jerry replies. "Would you have preferred that?"

"He's been in?"

"Sure. Him and the Rabbi. I have to say, we don't get many rabbis in here. Why do you think that is, Zesty?"

I make an exaggerated show of looking around me, the pictures of cops and priests and ballplayers and firemen and politicians. Gerry Adams and Sinn Féin. Irish street signs. Irish politicians. Shamrock Heaven.

"You got me," I said. "You carry Manischewitz?"

"No."

"Well then, mystery solved." I open the envelope and shake a thumb drive onto the bar. Written on the black plastic casing in Wite-Out are the letters *A.T.*

Anitra Tehran?

If it is, why hadn't Sam just sent it directly to the reporter? I don't have a clue, but if Sam's skipped town, I'm sure he has his reasons and I'm assuming those reasons are probably on this drive. I drink the Guinness. Jerry refills my shot glass and I drink that, too.

Sam's a sly bastard because he knows that if there's one thing I can always be counted on to do it's make the delivery come hell or bong water, and he also knows I consider whatever I might be delivering or why none of my business. I slip the drive back into the envelope and the envelope into my pack and finish my beer as two teams, neither of which is the Red Sox, play some fundamental baseball: the batter dropping a nifty bunt down the third base line, moving the runner to second; the infield playing the wheel, everybody shifting over to cover a base; even the outfielders twitching in case they have to back up an errant throw.

"That's what happens when they don't take steroids anymore," says the guy to my right, fresh off a buzz cut, silver stubble tapered to the back of his neck. He smells like he's been marinating in a vat of Aqua Velva. A detective's badge is pinned to his belt.

"You mean boring baseball?" says his partner, a pretty brunette whom I haven't seen since she was hammered at Foley's on the very night I'd been arrested at the bar. She's changed her hair since then, had it straightened.

"Fundamentals," Aqua Velva replies. "Like their daddies taught them."

I'm pretty sure she doesn't recognize me. I spare her the embarrassment of telling her that her lips had tasted like strawberries.

"I didn't realize Zero was so religious," Jerry says to me as I cup my hand over my glass so he doesn't pour me a third shot.

"The Rabbi works at Zen Moving. Between congregations," I explain, echoing the Rabbi's words.

"Yet still imparting wisdom." Jerry swipes at the bar in front of me even though it's clean enough to lay out a body and perform surgery.

"How's that?"

"The two of them, for hours, nothing but talk and hand signals. Rabbi Eleazar says this and Rabbi Akiva says that. Zero says this, the Rabbi counters with that. Strangest pair to walk through these doors in quite some time. Though to be honest, most of it was depressing."

"Why?"

"Well, I'm not a learned man, Zesty, but if there's one thing we Irish do well, it's death."

"You mean the wake?"

"Indeed. A proper farewell. Eat, drink, share stories, make certain the deceased is deceased." Jerry winks. "Drink some more, celebrate the life that was. If done right, it's a party, laughter, tears, the works." Jerry leans his elbows on the bar. "Did you know that the wake actually came about off the Jewish custom of sitting shiva?"

"I did not know that. So you take a Jew, add whiskey, and you get an Irishman?"

"Precisely! Some of the customs are still shared, the stopping of the clock at the time of death, the covering of the mirrors. But your seven days of sitting shiva last too long, don't you think?"

"You're suggesting the Jews condense to the Irish version?"

Jerry grimaces. "I'm not suggesting anything, just noting the comparison. And the Rabbi informed me your duties don't end there. A year you're supposed to grieve? It sounds exhausting."

"You mean the Kaddish."

"Ah, so you've talked to the Rabbi about this?"

"No. In fact, I just met him for the first time tonight." Jerry contemplates that fact in silence. "I overheard him teaching Zero the prayer at my dad's place."

"Where he's looking after your da, Zero tells me."

"So it seems." Again, I'm out of the loop, last to know. "Is there anything else I should fuckin' know about, Jerry?" I say, the two cops turning their heads to me. I didn't mean to speak so sharply, but it's too late to cram the words back into my face.

"There a problem, Jerry?" the brunette says.

"This is a private conversation, do you mind?" I look her in her eyes.

She ignores me. "Jerry?"

"Your lips taste like strawberries," I say to her.

"Excuse me?"

"I said your—"

"Everything's fine, Officer McKim." Jerry makes like a matador, waving the bar rag in front of my eyes. On the television, the batter lines a single to center, the crowd roaring as the runner cuts sharply around third and slides home on a close play at the plate.

"How's that for boring?" Aqua Velva slaps the bar, challenging his partner.

"That's because the catchers don't block the plate anymore. The whole fuckin' game's gone soft." She throws back the last of her drink. Rifles her shot glass loudly on the bar. "Bunch of fuckin' pussies. And by the way, Zesty, that's your name, right?" McKim gets way up in my face, forcing me to lean away from her hot breath. "It was cherries, smart guy. Cherries. Learn your fuckin' fruits." She winks at me, not a trace of embarrassment in her eyes.

I'm not quick enough to catch her number as she sashays out the door.

TWENTY-SEVEN

The *Boston Globe* offices on Morrissey Boulevard in Dorchester are barely two miles from Foley's, but it's a hard two miles with the cold autumn wind blowing in off the water between the JFK Library and the UMass campus. Talk was that the *Globe* would be moving downtown soon into a new high-rise on State Street, but right now it's still on Morrissey.

Not that it does me any good, Anitra Tehran insisting on meeting me at some bakery on the rounded corner of Dorchester Avenue and Adams Street, the most direct route leading me past the *Globe* offices. The bakery is closed when I chain my bike up outside, but the side door on Adams Street is unlocked as Tehran had said it would be, three bearded, tattooed men working large tables of dough as I walk in, the largest of the trio tilting his head to indicate the door into the shop.

Anitra Tehran sits in darkness behind the counter with her computer, which I'd asked her to bring to the meet. There's only a small puddle of light from a short lamp on the counter, but it barely reaches the reporter, who's wearing dark jeans and a New England Patriots hoodie from the Steve Grogan era, the old one with the Minute Man ready to snap the ball, not the Elvis version.

My dad loved Steve Grogan. But probably for all the wrong reasons: The man could take a beating. And then come back the next week and do it all over again.

The hood on Tehran's sweatshirt is up, her face framed in blue shadow from the computer glare. Wisps of her long hair fall out of the dark recesses of the hood down past her clavicles.

"Nice place." A car's headlights sweep the café and Tehran flinches at the computer. "I'm impressed by the twenty-four-hour access."

"Don't be. They have this plan." Anitra recovers quickly and looks up from whatever she was pecking at. "If you can prove ten percent of your body weight is made up of their pecan sticky buns, you get keys to the kingdom." She double-points down to her thighs, flips her hands into a double thumbs-up. "Mission accomplished."

"I think you need a new mirror," I say. Or a better therapist. Women truly are amazing creatures. I don't doubt for a minute they're smarter than men, but they pick themselves apart like ravenous wolves. Men can be total disasters but rally their souls over one or two redeeming features and then take it to the bank. I'm no different: long thick hair, strong legs.

If Anitra Tehran is smiling at my remark, her face is too far back in the oversize hoodie for me to see it.

"How come we're not meeting at the *Globe* offices?"

"I know, it was a longer ride for you to come here. I'm sorry. How about a sticky bun for nourishment. I smell the first batch out of the oven now."

So could I. It smelled like heaven if heaven was fifteen hundred calories' worth of caramel, pecans, and cinnamon. It also smelled like an evasion.

"How about you answer the question instead?"

The hoodie nods multiple times, but doesn't speak. Dorchester Avenue isn't entirely deserted even at this late hour. Occasionally somebody walks past the shop or the headlights of yet another car swings the corner onto Dorchester Avenue, sending a quick swipe of light into the store so I can read the outrageous prices marked on a giant chalkboard. Dorchester was another neighborhood under siege, the Boston Renaissance spreading its golden touch to every far-reaching corner of its once parochial hoods. Good for some. Bad for others. Not a lot of room in the middle.

The passing light also lets me see the reason Tehran chose a sweatshirt large enough to house the entire New England defensive secondary. She's wearing a Kevlar vest beneath it.

"You're scared," I answer for the reporter when she says nothing. "And hiding. There not a lot of people you can trust, Ms. Tehran?"

"I trust you," Tehran counters.

"Why? You don't know me."

"Because Batista said I could. That you were loyal. Possibly crazy, but loyal."

"Is that all he said?"

"No." She grins perfect teeth. "He also said you were as predictable as a game of pinball played on the deck of the *Titanic*."

"Really? Then he's terrible at similes because that would imply imminent disaster." Or maybe that's *exactly* what he was trying to tell her.

"Why did you call me, Zesty?"

"Why are you wearing a Kevlar vest?"

"Somebody shot at me. Through my apartment window."

"Another warning?"

"No." Tehran scrunches up her face, tilts it to the ceiling to lock in the tears that I heard in her one-word response. "Batista said I was lucky. And he's right. I moved just as the shot came."

So much for the parked Boston Police cruiser as a deterrent. I take the thumb drive out of my bag and lay it on the counter face-up so she can read her initials on it.

"What's that?" Tehran leaves the drive where I placed it.

"It's called a thumb drive and—"

"Zesty, please." Tehran's voice is small.

"I'm just a messenger," I tell her. "Can you push back the hoodie a little so I can see your face?"

Tehran hesitates before doing what I ask, the hoodie essentially propped on the ponytail she'd tied her hair back into. There are bags under her eyes and not a trace of makeup. The small cut she'd sustained on the sidewalk of Nick's Comedy Stop somehow makes her more attractive than when I first saw her.

Some people have all the luck. My facial scars and black eyes just make me look like I'd lost every fight I've ever been in.

"Who gave this to you?"

I tell her, reading her face to see whether the name means anything to her; the real reason I wanted her hoodie pushed back.

"I don't know who that is."

"I know," I say. "But sooner or later you'd have come across his name or Detective Wells would be forced to give it to you."

"Why would Batista *give* me anything? Oh, I get it." Tehran works her tongue angrily over her teeth. "You think I'm fucking him."

"That's your business," I say. "But let's not pretend there's not some kind of reciprocity going on between the two of you. One that neither of you want the powers that be to know about. Isn't that why we're meeting here and not the *Globe* offices? Budoff's just a name on Wells's list that he's trying to cross off for the Rambir Roshan murder, but he can't find him."

"And you did?"

"Not exactly." I give Anitra Tehran the short version of Sam's pharmaceutical past and our long-standing arrangement if things ever went south for him. I also tell her of the connections Wells made between Roshan and Sam, the courses that intersected at MIT and the internship at Kirilenko Labs. I keep the nearly million dollars' worth of poker chips to myself.

"So what's with the drop site if your friend's out of the business?"

"Old habits. I was just playing a hunch." And Sam had played his hand the same way. "You think you know what's on that drive?"

"No. But we'll see in a minute." Tehran plugs the drive into the computer and hits a few keys, her face fully lit by the ghostly blue-green computer screen. "You're right about me and Wells." She continues as we wait for it to load. "Not the fucking part, but as a source. That's why we were at Nick's. You thought it was a date? The dress and heels? I was actually coming from a fundraiser when I called him. I had the sense I was being followed and it scared me because I've learned to trust my instincts. He picked me up and we went to Nick's just because. Pure coincidence you were there." Tehran squints at the screen. "This drive is from Rambir Roshan's computer. Did you know that?"

"No. Did Wells spot anyone following you?"

"He didn't pick anything up."

But then came the Molotov cocktail. Which means whoever Anitra Tehran felt was tailing her must have been pretty adept at it because Wells, though outwardly looking as if all he did was peer into mirrors to check his hair, was as perceptive and tuned-in as anybody I'd ever met.

"You know they identified the body parts they pulled out of the harbor," Tehran tells me. "It's what's left of Oleg Katanya. Batista said you were up to speed on his connection to Rambir Roshan. The poker chips he was carrying?"

"I am. Are you working on anything besides the Roshan killing? Or do you have any reason to think that an old story might be blowing back on you?"

"You mean the real estate series, don't you? Aside from Eastern Europeans everywhere, I don't see a solid connection, just a bunch of loose threads."

I agree with Tehran, who pulls the hoodie back up as a car pulls to the curb. After a moment, a woman dressed in baker's whites gets out and heads toward the side door. Tehran leaves the hoodie up.

"This is all tied in somehow to Rambir Roshan, only I don't know which tree I'm shaking is the one that's causing the problem."

"A problem? Is that what you call being shot at and firebombed?"

"A *big* problem?" Anitra Tehran shrugs bravely. "Anyway, MIT was the logical place for me to start since Roshan's got no family in the States. But the university really just gave me boilerplate, citing student privacy rights, university protocol. MIT wants to have it both ways. They'd prefer the coverage of Rambir Roshan's murder just disappear, but they also want to have it publicly stressed that he was killed off campus."

"By like a quarter of a mile."

"Still, they didn't want the publicity to rub off on them in any negative way."

"Who'd you get to talk to?"

"From MIT? Some PR flack, administrators. Campus police, but they only gave me the numbers."

"What do you mean?"

"Statistics. Student safety, citations, on-campus arrests, break-ins. They'd have you believe the campus was Shangri-La and it probably is. Usually."

"Location, location," I say.

"Endowment, endowment," Tehran counters. "Do you know where MIT ranks on the national endowment list as of this year?"

"Not first," I say, that spot perennially belonging to Harvard, hovering at about thirty billion dollars. But I knew that MIT wasn't that far behind and is easily the largest landowner in Cambridge, a decade's worth of property buying expanding its reach into every neighborhood, which included where the Western Front once stood. The value of that land and everything else MIT's sucked up is worth billions now.

"Right. Harvard's first and MIT is somewhere around fifth with about fifteen billion."

"Okay, so the geeks and the preps have more money than God. What's your point?"

"I'm saying that they have a large interest in protecting what they have and they have a mechanism in place that makes getting a straight answer almost impossible."

"So they don't want an investigative reporter digging around on a murder case. Makes perfect sense to me. Spook the kids. Spook the big-pocket donors who send their kids." I smile. "But you're digging anyway."

"As best I can. It's what I do."

"But not with the blessing of your editorial board."

"I'm not sure how I'd characterize it. Nobody's pulled me off the story, but they've made it clear they want me to stay clear of any MIT angle."

I don't have to ask why. The cities of Boston and Cambridge both feed at the trough of the multiple educational institutions within their borders. These schools, both small and large, attract massive federal government research money, which powers the humming job engines of the city, which in turn attracts businesses who recruit the best and brightest graduates. Even the housing cycle of leases is dominated by the student and school schedules, the bulk of them renewed every September; Zero's crews triple in size for what we call Hell Week at the tail end of August, with trucks leased from as far away as Maryland to accommodate crews running eighteen-hour workdays. If you can handle the strain, there's thousands of dollars to be made, cash on the daily from these moving jobs. And that's just one business among thousands that rely on schools like MIT to prime the cash pumps. So what's one dead Indian kid worth on their ledger?

"And the MIT campus police force is no joke," Tehran continues. "Every time I show up, there's somebody there to escort me around, make sure I have *access*."

Enabling them to keep tabs on what questions Tehran's asking and what she knows. So where has she been? To Rambir Roshan's graduate housing unit. To the campus gym, where he worked out, the dining halls he ate in, the classes he took, the professors who taught him. The sum total being that he was a model student with a knack for coding, highly intelligent and motivated enough to land himself the TA spot in the poker analytics class taught by Yuki Fuji, who according to Tehran was something of a rock star on campus, as far as professors go.

"I'm sure you'd get a kick out of her class." Tehran taps her keyboard momentarily as the light on her screen changes. "Poker being your family thing? So many students sign up for her poker analytics class, they hold a lottery for entry. And the classes are still big enough to warrant Huntington Hall, which seats over a hundred students. Roshan was Fuji's TA for both semesters last year. Usually they rotate another grad student in, but Roshan stayed for a double."

"How unusual is that?"

"Enough for me to talk to her."

"And?"

"She said Roshan was the only one capable of handling the workload the way she needed it done, due to the size of the class. So she kept him on."

"Makes sense. Didn't have to retrain anyone for the job, take extra time to show them the ropes." When I have to train someone I just hand them a walkie-talkie and implore them not to get killed. Mostly because I need the Motorola back.

"Sure," Tehran agrees.

"She must have been pretty upset about Roshan, right? Professionally, personally. They must have spent a fair amount of time together."

"She played it pretty tight, but no judge, everybody copes different, right?" Tehran takes her eyes off the screen and tilts me a long look from deep inside the cover of her hoodie, like she's trying to find something on my face. I'm pretty good at this game, but after a while it makes me uncomfortable.

"What?" I say.

"Nothing." Tehran's eyes move back to her screen. "I was just thinking."

"That Professor Fuji was hiding something?"

"I don't know. I'm just not getting much from MIT. I guess what you're seeing is frustration."

"Okay, so let's say there's nothing there," I propose. "What else have you got that's worth sending a warning via Molotov cocktail and then following up with a sniper's bullet through your window?"

"Therein lies the problem. I don't know. I've also been to Kirilenko Labs. You know, Roshan never actually finished his internship."

"Why's that?"

"He was fired."

"For what?"

"HR said he was unreliable. Either showed up late or not at all. Or didn't complete the work he was assigned. Sometimes his supervisor would find him asleep at his terminal or they'd check on him and he'd be playing online poker. Did you read my last piece?" Tehran asks.

"I did." There had been no mention of MIT getting in the way of an investigation or withholding information. As a matter of fact, there wasn't much to the column at all.

"Were you able to read between the lines?"

"That your editors have you on a tight leash when it comes to MIT?"

"Not exactly, but close enough. Nobody's come out and *told* me to go soft. We do good work and if I can confirm everything I write, I know they'll run it. But at the same time, nobody wants to be responsible for jumping the gun, portraying this city as unsafe for anybody, especially foreigners with all the money international students bring in."

"And has Wells had the same luck you did?" Meaning, did the badge get him into places Anitra Tehran couldn't go?

"I think we're in the same boat. Unless he's holding out on me. All he claimed to get was Roshan's course schedule, interviews with faculty and some kids in the housing unit where he lived. They have their own police force just like every college campus, but these guys are serious and even cop to cop, pretty tight-lipped."

"Like they'd already gotten their marching orders," I say. "You think Wells is telling you everything?"

"Probably not. He held Sam Budoff's name," she points out. "But he did tell me that when the MIT police searched Roshan's room after they IDed the body, something was missing. Let's see how sharp you are: What would be the one indispensable item you figure would be in every kid's room who went to MIT?"

"That's easy," I say. "A bong."

"Very funny."

"I dunno," I try again. "A computer?"

"Right. Two days *before* Roshan was killed, there was an attempted break-in at his place, Ashdown House. Campus police made an arrest on the spot."

"Who reported the break-in, Roshan?"

"Nope. He hadn't been seen for a couple of days at that point."

"He was reported as missing?"

"No. From the people who were willing to talk to me, I heard it wasn't unusual for Roshan to disappear for a few days at a time. Obviously someone was looking for something."

"You get a name on who was arrested?"

"You ready for this? Oleg Katanya."

"And he was busted with Roshan's computer?"

"No. The rooms are tiny; it's not like there's space to effectively hide a laptop."

"Did you find out where Roshan would disappear to when he went ghost?"

"See, there's the interesting thing. Foxwoods, Vegas. Once even to Macau."

"Jesus, that's halfway around the world. You confirm this with anybody else?"

"Some of the other students in his housing unit. But it was like pulling teeth. None of the internationals would talk. Scared of compromising their scholarships, I think. Maybe they've been warned."

"But someone talked. And Wells confirmed it?"

"Yes. He backtracked and spoke to the airlines and Roshan was racking up the frequent flier miles to Vegas. Always paid in cash so it took some doing to track the info down. Also because he used different driver's licenses, never traveled under his name except for the Macau trip."

"Because he needed a passport for that."

"Exactly. Wells got hold of the domestic airline footage and it was him on multiple occasions. He even flew out to Vegas for a day, tracked Roshan's movements and hotels under those names he used."

I wonder what he learned. The casinos were pretty tight-lipped regarding personal data on high rollers and it might take a court order to shake that information out of the money tree. But the poker chips seemed to indicate that Roshan had done well. How else would he acquire them? And then give them to Sam for safekeeping.

"But you're what, holding on to these nuggets until you piece things together for a bigger story? Or is it a little more complex, like sitting on the story about Brill moving the body on the bridge? And in return Wells keeps you in the loop on the investigation."

Anitra Tehran again looks at me for a long time without speaking, but I meet her eyes this time.

"I know, it sounds like blackmail, right?"

"Pretty much," I say. *God, your eyes are beautiful,* I want to say.

"It's not. I was the first reporter on the bridge only because I was doing my morning run on the Charles. I'd just cut up into the Back Bay when I saw all the squad cars and knew this was more than a traffic accident. Brill moved that body *back* to the Boston side. Those Cambridge Homicides, Powers and Mc-Gowan, were the ones who pulled it first."

"You *saw* that?"

"No. But I've seen enough murder scenes to know what it should have looked like. And by the way the blood was streaked, I could tell the body had been dragged. I also saw Brill break Mc-Gowan's nose. If you ask me, both detectives must have lost their minds."

But it's all good, I think to myself, because Tehran gets to play the middle, cashing in with Wells as a source as he works this case.

And she gets to keep that ace up her sleeve with Cambridge PD for whenever she needs it down the line. Makes perfect sense. What I don't get is are things so slow in Cambridge, they'd actually pull a body over the line to get some work in? Did Cambridge Homicide fear for their jobs, have to justify their existence in the world's most liberal city, where property values have driven out every single criminal?

"A girl's gotta eat." Tehran reads part of my mind and scrutinizes the computer, turning it so I can see numbers scrolling across the screen.

"And you think whoever followed you to Nick's and put a bullet through your window is tied to Mass Ave.?"

"I don't know shit except that there's a lot of pressure on Batista to solve this case fast."

"And if he doesn't?"

"Really, Zesty? You need me to answer that question?"

I didn't. The police commissioner will look for a scapegoat, and that would be Brill, whom they'll claim contaminated the crime scene and botched a high-profile murder case. And what would the fallout be for Wells? Possibly the same thing.

And if that happens, MIT would probably prefer Roshan's murder fade from the public's consciousness, not much stink likely to be made all the way from Mumbai, maybe some sort of reparation paid to tamp down the family's grief or outrage. Only Wells isn't the type of cop who would just drop an investigation even if he did get canned. Badged up or not, one way or another, Wells was going to solve the mystery of Rambir Roshan.

"So what am I looking at?" I point to the screen, where the numbers had finally stopped moving.

"If I had to take a guess, I'd say they were some form of transactions. Look at the numbers; if you add them all up, they're in the millions." One hundred and thirty-seven of them, according to the computer count at the bottom. "And then there're these . . .

Holy shit." Tehran's mouth drops open as a number of files appear on-screen. She clicks on a file titled *Albov LLC*.

"That means something to you?" The file doesn't open.

"Yes. I've seen these names before as I researched the real estate series." There are other files on the screen: Odessa Holdings. Baltic LLC. Park Place LLC. Marvin Gardens LLC. Each click yielding nothing.

"They're all shell companies. Each of these LLCs owns property in Boston. Some of them multiple properties. None of these files will open. They seem to be encrypted."

"Why would Rambir Roshan have this information on his computer?"

"I don't know."

"Aside from Katanya and Namestnikov, have you come across more Russians digging into the Roshan thing?"

"No," Tehran says. "Yes," Tehran says. And that right there is probably why I don't have a girlfriend. I hear yes and I hear no and I'm supposed to find the true meaning lying somewhere in between?

"Kirilenko Labs, where your pal Sam Budoff and Roshan interned. Viktor Kirilenko, the founder, is Russian. The firm is a relatively new start-up, but already they've scored some pretty hefty government contracts, private businesses. You ever listen to NPR, Zesty?"

"No, I live in a cave, under a rock," I say. "Kirilenko Labs is a WBUR/NPR underwriter."

"Exactly. And I apologize." Tehran pauses to look at me with that slight tilt to her head again, this time the hoodie falling off her ponytail. "How come you don't have any tattoos, Zesty?"

"I wanted to be different," I say, the swerve in conversation puzzling me. "And I'm Jewish."

"You're religious?"

"I pick and choose from the menu." I shrug. "That's just one thing."

"There are others? Like what?"

"I don't eat pork. I don't drive on the Sabbath."

"Now you're playing with me. Batista told me you don't drive at all, not legally at least. And Zero?"

"What about him?"

"He's all tatted up, works on the Sabbath. . . ."

"I didn't say I didn't work. Can we finish up here, there's someplace I have to be."

"At this hour? It's two in the morning."

"Moonlighting," I say. "Literally. So the pipeline of interns from MIT makes sense, then," I say. "For Kirilenko Labs. Plus, it's MIT, where the kids dream in physics and piss math. Why would they recruit from anywhere else?" Not that the other twenty thousand colleges in Boston were slouches.

It's not really a question I need answered, but I have learned something new. Sam Budoff scored Roshan an internship he squandered. Roshan gave Sam almost a million dollars in chips to hide and hold. When he ends up dead, Sam goes into hiding and sets me up with Roshan's computer drive with encrypted files of shell companies Tehran had exposed though not fully unraveled through her reporting; many of the true ownerships of the properties were still cloaked in secrecy, the whole thing getting more complicated by the hour.

"And Wells has also made the rounds at Kirilenko?" I figure.

"Yes."

"Before or after you felt like you were being followed?"

Tehran squints in thought. "After."

"And before or after you got stonewalled at MIT?"

"After. Right after."

"So someone picked you up at MIT or at Kirilenko. Were you

threatened directly before the firebomb? Phone calls, emails, notes warning you off this story?"

"You mean did someone named Natasha or Boris call me with a heavy Russian accent and a sizzling stick of dynamite?"

"Something like that."

"No." She stops and thinks. "But I did receive an un-marked file at the *Globe*. Sent by messenger. It was a bunch of clippings, photographs and information about some neo-Nazi anti-immigrant groups. A couple of men listed had criminal histories for assaulting immigrants, actually pretty shocking stuff for Boston. This city might look placid but there's definitely some shit bubbling beneath the surface."

"Really?" I say, sarcastically. "You're surprised?"

"What?"

"You act like people being priced out of their neighborhoods somehow shouldn't be resentful of it."

Anitra rears back. "You're justifying their actions?"

"I didn't mean it that way. I'm just saying people are angry. And vulnerable to all sorts of things. Fuck it, I don't really expect you to understand."

"What's that supposed to mean?" She's angry now.

"Different worlds," I say. "Let's just leave it at that. You followed up on what was in the file?"

"Of course. But it was a total dead end."

"Did Wells follow those same leads?"

"Yes."

"Because you fed him the information."

"Yes."

"And it went nowhere for him, too."

"Yes."

And meanwhile, all his other leads grew cold. Tehran and Wells in sync, doing the same dance moves, but to all the wrong songs. Anitra Tehran takes a deep breath and looks to the ceiling, her index and middle fingers on both hands making a running-man motion, probably a habit of deep thought.

"What are you thinking?" I ask her.

"That misinformation is a very Russian way to exploit a situation," she says after a moment.

"The file had no return address, no marking?"

"Just my name and the *Globe* address."

"Delivered by courier," I say. "I know your front desk security procedure is for everything to be signed for, messenger's name and company."

"Yes. So if I have that—"

"You can backtrack where the file was picked up," I finish for her.

"And if it was just on a random street corner? Would you do that type of pickup?"

"Sure. But that tells us something, too."

Tehran nods in agreement. "Why would some kid like Rambir Roshan have all these account numbers, if that's what they are, stored on his computer? And these LLC files to boot?" Tehran starts up with her running-man motion again.

"Wells says that Rambir's bank account had some serious irregularities to it, large wire transfers of cash, but just below the ten-thousand-dollar threshold that would set off the automatic alerts that obligated the bank to notify the IRS. There was a constant cycle of deposits, transfers, and withdrawals. I'm no computer geek but this could be what we're looking at here with these numbers."

"Which tells you what?" The only thing I know about banking is deposits, withdrawals, and overdraft fees. Well, mostly overdraft fees. And mysterious charges that the banks will generally undo if you happen to notice them. Here Tehran and I were trying to solve a crime while Citibank and Wells Fargo keep holding everybody up in plain sight.

"Roshan was obviously into something that caught up to him, only we don't know where it originated from. I know BPD has a cyber unit working on unraveling the transfers and deposits, but it's going to take some time."

"You going to share this drive with Wells?"

"I think I have to. I don't have anybody outside the *Globe* who's got the skills to access those Monopoly plus-one files." And then Tehran turns the question around. "Why do you think Sam wants me to have this and not the police?"

It was the same question I'd asked myself a moment ago and wasn't sure I liked the answer I came up with.

"He's probably involved in some way," Tehran answers for me when I don't say anything. "Maybe hoping there's a way I could use this information but keep his name out of it." Obviously I don't know a lot about women, but what especially stumps me is why they always seem to ask questions that they already know the answers to.

"Can you?" I ask her. "Keep his name out of it?"

"I'm not sure that's possible."

"Why not? You did it for Brill and Wells."

"Because it would have meant the end of Brill's career," Tehran says pointedly. "You think I'm just picking and choosing my ethics at random?"

"It sure feels that way."

"Like your religious menu? I'm sorry, that was a cheap shot. I'm just saying I can't ignore information if it's important or if it might lead others to getting hurt. And I'm certainly not in a position to offer him any kind of immunity or plea deal. That would be Wells's ballpark."

"I wasn't asking you to bury anything," I say. "I'm just trying to protect a friend."

"Even if he's done something illegal? Again."

I had never thought of Sam's psychedelic laboratory as a moral

failing, the stain of the hypocrite not something I wanted to wear
since I'd often been the beneficiary of his pharmaceutical talents.
But Anitra Tehran was of a different world. She was good-looking,
educated, surrounded by others who, whether consciously or subconsciously, believed that success was their birthright or destiny and
if they just followed the path of the straight and narrow, followed
the rules, the world would open its wings and give them flight.

What these people never acknowledge is the safety net that
they operate so high above, that foundational network that's
propped them up—visibly, invisibly—every step of the way. It's a
smugness born of willful ignorance. Most of the people I grew up
with in the South End didn't have that option; when they faltered
and fell, you heard their bones crunching, saw the blood on the
pavement.

"I try not to judge," I say, judging her. "I'm just saying that
sometimes the right thing to do is leave things where they're
buried."

"I don't think Batista would agree with that view."

"No, you're probably right about that. We don't agree on
much, me and Wells. Except maybe on our love of fine coffee.
Speaking of which. You think there's any chance of scaring up a
cup from this joint? I've got another long night ahead of me."

TWENTY-EIGHT

"Well, I'll be damned. This is definitely not something I'd ever
thought I'd see." Detective Batista Wells looks like he's just
stepped out of a spa, his fedora in hand, his hair meticulously
parted to one side with a freshly razored line down the scalp,

his beard neatly trimmed, his eyes glowing with early morning vigor.

Only it's four in the morning. Brill and I are covered in a fine white drywall powder, even his trademark brown cigar looking like a grown-up candy cane, his diagonal fingerprints encircling the smoking baton.

Earlier in the day, or I should say yesterday, Brill had gotten a delivery of Sheetrock lifted through the window, which was now out of its frame. We'd spent the last hour putting the drywall up, my fingers bloodied from reaching into my waist pouch full of sharp screws, my shoulders stiff and tired from holding up the wall and trying to get the screw to stay on the magnet-tipped end of the electric drill.

"You're gonna get your shoes dusty," Brill growls at his partner, maybe still angry at him for sending me around to check up on him.

"Why is it you don't sound happy to see me?" Wells inquires.

"All the usual reasons. Plus I don't see a bag of doughnuts in your hand." Instead a large manila envelope.

"I need you to look at some pictures," Wells says. "Fast."

"I thought you were suspended," I say to Brill.

"I am. Now I just run a charity." Brill leans into his drill, the screw whining as it catches the wood framing behind the drywall. "I do all Detective Wells's work for free and hire unskilled labor that can't put screws in a straight goddamn line."

"Ah, but look at the taping." I point to where I'd started. "Nice and clean."

"When we paint you'll see it's gonna bulge."

"So that's where you'll hang some artwork."

"You got an answer for everything, Zesty."

"Consistency is underrated," I point out. "At least I show up."

"Can't argue with that," Brill says, grudgingly extending a sliver of respect.

"You going to wash up first?" Wells, who's watched our exchange like a tennis match that delivered an unexpected winner, hands the envelope to Brill.

"With what?"

"You don't have running water in this place?"

"Nope." And though the wiring had been finished before we put up the drywall, Brill was still only using the generator to power the construction lights. There was still plumbing to be done, which was well beyond my scope of knowledge; the windows needed new frames, some pane replacement; tiling in the bathrooms needed to be laid; and the hardwood floors all had to be sanded, something I'd be interested in taking a crack at if Brill will let me.

Traditionally in Boston, the Irish do the drywall and electrical, the Vietnamese cornered the floor sanding, the plumbing gets pieced out to all the other minority groups, and the Jews maybe come in and bless the place when it's all finished, hang a mezuzah. Brill's building was operating as a true meritocracy, roles given to whoever shows up on his ungodly nocturnal schedule. Which will either prove prudent or the first time he turns on a light switch, all the toilets will explode.

"And you're *staying* here?" Wells is aghast.

"Yep."

"So how do you . . ." Wells registers the Gatorade bottle in the corner. It looks like lemon lime. The label reads *Orange.* "Never mind." Brill pulls out the photographs and shuffles through them. Recognition, but no real interest shows in his eyes.

"Yikes," I say from the middle rung of the ladder looking down over his shoulder. "These the Russians?"

"Nikita Kucherov," Brill says. Wheat blond hair, icicle blue eyes. It's a name I hadn't heard before. "Oleg Katanya. Also goes by Mikhail Sergachev." Erosion face, almost block-square ears, neck-scrawl tattoos. The next photos are of the parts that

Wells fished out of the bay. "You found any more of him?" Brill looks up.

"No. But it's him."

"Leads?"

"None. But he couldn't have been an easy kill. Plus the dismemberment. Marks of a pro, likely one of his own tribe. Namestnikov, maybe? He's still missing."

"Antti Voracek," Brill continues to shuffle, reciting. "Boston boss. Jakub Namestnikov's boss." Cliff brows, thornbush eyebrows, boulder nose. "Kucherov drives for him. Maybe more. All but Voracek by way of Odessa, not Moscow. Jews for the most part. Brighton Beach to Brighton, Mass. For all I know they have a beachhead in Brighton, UK. Actually, scratch that. All the big-moneyed Russians are in London, but we're talking an entirely different class here." Brill squints hard at a second set of photos. Surveillance pictures. "Where were these taken?"

"Security cameras from MIT."

"All of a sudden they're helpful?"

"I pulled a few strings."

The pictures are of Oleg Katanya on the MIT campus.

Wells says, "Katanya used to be muscle in New York for Namestnikov. When Namestnikov got himself a little franchise here in Allston, he came with. The poker club. Other ventures. Word from New York is everybody was happy to see them leave."

"Why?" I ask.

"Namestnikov was one of the old thinkers, brutality for every problem."

"You mean like burning whores?"

"That. And there are at least a half dozen murders linked to him, but nobody will testify."

"So what's the new way of thinking?"

"Technology. Insurance, mostly Medicare fraud."

"Katanya was arrested trying to break into Rambir Roshan's student housing," I say. "Ashdown House on campus."

"How the fuck you know that?" Brill says and then sees it. "You've been talking to Tehran, too." He turns and points his cigar emphatically at Wells. "That's on you. Like Zesty wasn't enough of a pain in the ass the first time around."

"Since when has the Russian Mob been a player in Boston?" I ignore Brill's compliment and direct my question to Wells, who has taken back the photographs, blowing at the dusty fingerprints Brill left.

"Low level about ten years." The photographs go back into the envelope. "And you can thank the Big Dig for that. The Dig brought opportunity. Construction, paving, steel. And that means unions. A lot of these Russians had experience on large-scale dam operations in the Ukraine, something called the Rogun Dam in Tajikistan. But it's mostly been white-collar crimes like I said, and some gambling, high-end prostitution. We think murder for hire, but not in Boston. Miami mostly. Down south. Atlanta. New Orleans. That's Nikita Kucherov's thing. Along with his driving he provides security for Antti Voracek."

"What Wells is trying to tell you is the Russians are big believers in not shitting where they eat. And they have the ability to blend in if they don't open their mouths to talk. And anyway, in a city with so many people from someplace else, they usually don't get much of a second look."

"That sounds to me like code-speak for *they're white*," I say.

"Sharp." Brill points his cigar at me. "Give Advil a headache, but sharp."

"And Jewish," Wells adds. "These psychopaths. That's a wrinkle most people can't wrap their heads around. But mostly they're just Russian."

"Which means what?"

"You ever seen the babushkas at the market, Zesty? They'll cut you in line, snatch the last apple out of your hand, play bumper car with their carriages and send you flying. They have that mentality still and no reservations about doing it. Even when there's plenty to go around."

"They make up their own rules is what Wells is telling you. Whatever does the job or sends the appropriate message."

"Like shooting a reporter?" I suggest.

Brill and Wells look at each other. Eyebrows up for Brill. Lips turned down for Wells. In their relationship, that's the face of an agreement.

"Zesty, you missed your calling. So what's with Katanya breaking into Roshan's place? Obviously he was looking for something and now both of them are dead. You got any theories on that?"

"Talk to Anitra Tehran," I say.

"I already did," Wells says. "She's got something for me to look at, maybe account numbers, maybe something more that ties Roshan to the real estate deals she covered." Wells runs through the list of Monopoly names on the files that Tehran couldn't penetrate.

Brill shrugs. "What are they? And how'd she get ahold of them?"

"She wouldn't say." Tehran has kept her word she'd leave Sam's name out of this mess for as long as it was possible. "But I'm about to go in and try to find out. There are two geeks arriving at headquarters who are not very happy with me right about now. And speaking of geeks. Sam Budoff?"

"Nada." The lie rolls easily off my tongue. Wells can give me the stank-eye as long as he pleases but I'm to the untruth what a zombie is to the undead. The only thing the detective will catch in my eyes is his own reflection.

"Well then, I'm off." Wells looks about, appraising our work.

The walls will be up by the end of the morning. Brill had salvaged and sanded some molding from a house in Mattapan and we'll be putting it up soon, too. All the exposed brickwork around the windows and above the fireplace mantel have been stripped of paint, the first coat of sealant giving them a shiny reddish coat that stands out beautifully in contrast to the light marble fireplace and the metal barn door on the sliding track.

In a couple of hours dawn will break outside the open windows with a view of the shade trees lining the street and the other turn-of-the-century townhouses that have already been restored to their original beauty.

"Place is coming along." Wells nods approvingly.

"Too bad you can't afford it," Brill replies, his back turned to his partner, getting in the last word. Only, when he wheels back around to see how it landed, Wells is gone, not even his footprints left in the fine snow-white drywall dusting.

TWENTY-NINE

Alianna Solarte pulls up in front of Buttery, where I'm waiting with a couple of coffees and two plain croissants. A familiar-looking blonde who's never given me the time of day actually looks at me from her outside corner seat. Probably because I'm out of my biking gear and dressed in dark Levi's, weathered chocolate brown Doc Martens, and a navy sweater with a black cashmere scarf. Or maybe she's impressed I'm back two days in a row and could afford not one, but two coffees, a sure sign of prosperity if ever there was one.

Solarte is of the same mind. When I sit, she dips her head

below her visor and says, "Wow, you can afford this place? I must be paying you too much."

Actually, Brill had paid me two hundred dollars in cash and had fronted me another three to lock me in for the rest of the week as we had to coordinate the timing with the plumber he'd scheduled.

As I move a manila file aside so I don't crush it, Solarte starts navigating the neighborhood and doesn't need me to guide her as she catches 93 North, against traffic. We make our way to Chelmsford in only twenty-five minutes before entering Billerica, a mostly working-class suburb that's also, inevitably, showing signs of new money: larger-house construction next to modest ranches and colonials, a Starbucks in what was once strictly Dunkin' Donuts Land.

"Remind me again why you wanted me with you on this?" I'm still groggy from only a few hours of sleep and just one cup of coffee. If Solarte doesn't drink hers soon, I'm going to guzzle it, the red lipstick smudge on the lid not scaring me one bit. Solarte is dressed almost identically to me, minus the savoir faire of the scarf.

"I figured I'd get you out of your biking gear, show you the ropes of an investigation." When Solarte smiles, tiny cracks show around her eyes. "Let you watch a master at work."

"You're training me?"

"Opportunity knocks, baby, but it rarely begs. Don't you think it's high time you picked up a couple new skills?"

"Gee, Mom, I don't know."

"Now *that* shit, you better cut out." Solarte jabs at my head but keeps her eyes on the road. "Read what's in the file and tell me what you pick up."

I open the file to a couple of stock photographs of Homicide detectives Peter Polishuk and Eric Nichols and leaf through the pages of Solarte's handwritten notes. There are two addresses written down, one of them in Billerica. "We're going to visit the detective who worked the Camilla Islas case," I say.

Polishuk is retired. His partner, Eric Nichols, deceased. Stint in the military, tail end of the Vietnam war, graduated Holy Cross after he'd already become a cop.

"You put this file together, it's not official." I shuffle papers. "These guys seem to have a pretty good clearance rate, but I don't know. What's a good batting average for a homicide?"

"A thousand. Easy, tiger." Solarte snatches her coffee as I start to reach for it.

"Obviously the Islas case set them back a few digits. Can't solve them all, right?"

"Nope. You can only try."

"Polishuk and Nichols tried?"

"Like you said, the file's not official; this is just what I was able to dig up."

"Well, obviously, the case was never solved. And we know, officially, it doesn't exist. And with BPD, once you're out, you're out?" I say.

Solarte looks at me long enough with her eyes off the road to get her Official Boston Driver Scorecard. "There something you want to say to me, Zesty?"

"Yeah. Brakes!"

Solarte deftly swerves around the mail truck pulled halfway over to the side of the road. "Tell me more." She motions to the open file.

I look at the photographs again. They're pretty standard professional head shots with a BPD blue background, Polishuk with a look on his face that's somewhere between an uncomfortable eighth-grade grin and a mug shot scowl. He's large through the shoulders with no-nonsense eyes and a straight-up crew cut, big ears, and a sunburned nose.

Nichols is a dead ringer for Art Garfunkel if you'd stretched the singer out on a medieval rack and elongated his features—parabola chin, butter popcorn hair.

The back of Polishuk's picture is dated 1996, which would put him probably somewhere in his mid-fifties then. Judging by the lines around his eyes and mouth, it looks like he's forgotten how to smile. Is this the fate of all Homicides? Does Wells realize that all his exfoliating creams and spa treatments will be for naught when the final score is tallied? Or will he be the first to buck the trend, age like George Clooney, and buckle knees well into his seventies?

"Married and divorced. Couple of kids," I drone on. "Must be in their forties now." Simple math. "The file's pretty thin. No offense."

Solarte snorts and turns the wheel sharply. "And I was just about to give you the rest of my coffee. Okay. We're here."

"Here" is a long driveway off the main road, a thick line of pine trees blocking the northern edge, the steep descent bringing us into an unexpected pocket of serenity, marshland and a wave of silky milkweed to the south, a deep woods on the eastern edge. The house itself is modest, vinyl sided, made to seem larger by the attached screened-in porch that looks out over the marsh and tiered variegated shrubbery that had been planted along the walls and stairs fashioned from four-foot-long rectangular granite blocks that must weigh close to five hundred pounds apiece. Large black solar panels are attached to the roof.

There's a grassy yard that rounds to the side of the house ringed by mature elm or something that isn't just pine, a large fenced-in garden to the left of where we parked, a few late tomatoes still coloring the vines. A brick path meanders through a garden somehow still retaining its mix of blue, orange, and white flowers. What's probably an old well is covered by a square of treated pine and held in place by a five-foot cut piece of rusted train track sitting diagonally across the wood to keep it in place.

Metal sculptures fashioned from discarded appliance parts hang like mobiles in the trees. Pottery overflows with cuttings from other plants I don't see growing in the garden out front. A sign to the left of the front door reads 1876 and it takes me a moment to realize it's referencing the date of the house's construction, not the address.

"Do you hear that?" My question stops Solarte's cocked fist at the door. She's already stabbed the doorbell twice to no avail.

"What?"

I look around the property. There's not another house within view. If there's traffic above on the road, I can't hear it. A squirrel dashing through the trees snaps a twig, which pops like a fire-cracker. A soft breeze brings the smell of lavender and the hollow knocking of wooden wind chimes somewhere close but out of view.

"Nothing," I say. "I just haven't heard this kind of quiet in a long time. It's nice, right? Even the air feels different. Those flowers," I point to the garden, "shouldn't still be in bloom."

"If you say so. I'd go crazy here. What the fuck . . ." Solarte nearly falls through the doorway as a man opens the door wide and reaches for her at the elbow to keep her upright.

"It doesn't work," he says, releasing her. "Or to be more specific, I'd detached it because I can hear whenever anyone pulls into the drive. Please, come in. And I'm sorry, I don't mean to rush you, but I forgot when you called earlier that I had something else scheduled for this time. I can only give you a few minutes."

Polishuk looks nothing like his photograph. In fact, he looks like Ansel Adams, the famous Yosemite photographer, if Adams also went to a lot of Grateful Dead shows and favored rounded John Lennon eyeglasses. He's balding in front but his hair is long and tied in a gray ponytail behind him. A tangle of white beard covers most of his face and his eyes seem lighter through the glasses; not in that milky cataract sort of way, but as if there's something that's been lifted out of the dead-pool darkness that had shown in the stock photographs. Solarte sees this change, too, and makes a gesture with her hands that's halfway between a question and an open invitation for a hug.

"I know what you're thinking." Polishuk leads us into the living room. "I get some version of this whenever someone who I haven't seen in a while from back in the day stops by. Which isn't often."

"You have to admit, it's quite a change." Solarte looks around. The room is filled with plants, built-in bookcases crammed with novels and ornithology guides and books of bird photography, a wood-burning stove in good working condition with a glass door on blackened hinges. Wide plank glossy floors reflect a vaulted dark cedar ceiling about twenty feet high at its apex, two domed skylights bringing in twin columns of natural light that cross in a giant X in the center of the great room. Percussion instruments are hung in a row on a crossbeam—maracas, tambourines, triangles. On the surface of a cherry antique roll-top desk are two color photographs in matching frames. Most likely his grandkids; they look too new to be his own children. Sliding glass doors offer a view of the grassy backyard and a small pond with lily pads and pink lotus flowers floating on the surface. "What can I tell you," Polishuk responds after a measured moment. "When I left the force, I just decided to be me; let the freak flag fly."

"You'd been holding it in?" Solarte is genuinely puzzled but I totally get it. Sometimes people put themselves in a box and that's where they stay forever, defined by what they do for work or the familial responsibilities that bind them to others—spouse, children, parents. Genuine metamorphosis, a true shedding of that first skin, is a rarity, at least in my experience, likely because it doesn't come easily; only to those who dare to take that risk and walk through that fire, navigating the ultra-thin tightrope between narcissistic selfishness and outright courage. Or maybe it's not that complicated; if you can lay your head on a pillow and sleep at night, that's all there is to it, fuck everybody else.

Whatever the case happens to be with Polishuk, it looks genuine and it's a good reminder, for me anyway, that we only stop evolving when we allow others to define us. Now stick that in your pipe and smoke it.

"I can't say it was that conscious a decision, Ms. Solarte. It's just something didn't feel a hundred percent right with me, like I was constantly keeping something at bay. Throughout my entire career."

"Huh." Solarte grunts.

"I didn't know what it was at the time. Now I do. Ms. Solarte—"

"Alianna."

"Alianna. As you know, I can tell you'd been a cop once, so you know what I'm talking about. It's not just a job, is it?"

"No."

"It's a way of being."

"Yes."

"And if you've never been a cop, say like this young man . . ."

"Zesty Meyers," I introduce myself and we shake hands, Polishuk with a slight tilt of his head indicating the name is ringing a bell to him.

"Like Zesty," Polishuk continues. "Then you never fully realize how the job doesn't just define you, but becomes a part of everything you do, from where you decide to sit when you're in a restaurant, to how you look at people, question their motives. You don't look like a private investigator, Zesty. Where'd you get that shiner?"

"I'm a bike messenger." I kill two inquiries with one answer.

"Ah, interesting." Polishuk looks like he's trying to conjure something up from the back of his mind, but then gives up. "What can I do for you, Alianna? Like I said, I only have a few minutes."

"Then I'll get right to the point. I'm looking into the disappearance of Camilla Islas."

"You mean her murder." Polishuk's smile fades. "She was declared dead in 1983. That's a long time ago."

"Yes," Solarte says.

"And if I remember right, I heard her father died in a car crash in eighty-six and her mom of cancer in ninety-three, a few years before I retired."

"That's correct."

"And she had no other relatives in the country, her parents were Mexican immigrants. Illegal, in fact, not that it had any bearing on the case. We let them be. They'd suffered enough. We live in less welcome times now, don't we?"

"Unfortunately, yes."

"So it's thirty-plus years later and you're looking into her murder. Why?"

"You mean who hired me?"

"That would be a start."

"I'm afraid I can't tell you that."

"Really? Well then, I'm afraid that's just as well because now I have to go." Polishuk gestures to the door like a practiced maître d'. "If you'll excuse me."

Solarte doesn't budge. "Your memory can't be that good."

"Excuse me?"

"To remember when Camilla Islas's parents died. I doubt that information was ever added to the cold case file." Solarte smiles painfully, like a tooth is bothering her. She takes a deep breath. "What I'm saying is, for all your Trappist monk appearance, your beautiful and secluded home, you never let go of the Islas case. How could you? She haunted you, didn't she?"

Polishuk looks at Solarte for what seems like a long time before nodding to himself. "Why don't you have a seat, Alianna, Zesty. Can I offer you some tea?"

Solarte and I decline the tea but take a seat on the couch as Polishuk putters around in the kitchen before pulling over an old platform rocker with new upholstery. He sets the tea down on a small table and I notice tiny waves starting to move inside the mug as he's about to speak, followed by the ceramic rattle of the cup on saucer, the entire house starting to tremble lightly, a few of the percussion instruments—maracas, tambourines—coming to life on their own and then, as if guided by an invisible conductor, joined by the tinkling of glasses in the kitchen, faint at first, and then the entire orchestra drowned out by the thundering passing of a train just beyond where we'd parked the car.

"Holy shit." Alianna white-knuckles her fists by her sides, looking poised to spring off the couch and sprint outside to safety as if it had been an earthquake.

"It's the Chelmsford Line commuter rail. This house was the former stationmaster's depot, which is why it's so close to the tracks," Polishuk explains, preempting the question as the echo of the train fades. "At one point in its illustrious history it was also home to a chapter of the Hell's Angels." He shrugs elaborately, as if to say even a house can lead multiple lives. "You're right and wrong about me and the Islas cold case, Alianna. Camilla did haunt me like every other case I didn't solve. But to some degree Camilla more than most."

"Why her?" I figure if I'm actually in training, I might as well get a question in.

"Because the whole case was screwy from the get-go. Though we never found Camilla's body we had solid suspects, circumstantial evidence, not necessarily a definitive motive, but enough to get a prosecutor involved, bring charges before a grand jury."

Suspects. More than one. My heart starts hammering in my chest, a heat rising up in me. Is this really why Solarte brought me along, to expose me to the truth of my father? To confirm Brill's and Karl Klaussen's version of events, as if I needed to hear my father's misdeeds from the horse's mouth to believe them?

"So what happened?" I say, my voice shaky to my ear, but not enough for Polishuk to pick up. Or maybe he was just that far out of practice.

"Well, Karl Klaussen you must know about. He just disappeared. Either took a runner or maybe he was killed himself. I never got a chance to find out."

"Why?" Solarte and I speak as one, look at each other. I'm tempted to follow up with *one, two, three, jinx! you owe me a Sprite,* but the moment seems too fraught for that.

"Because as me and Nichols, my partner at the time, started to piece things together, we got called in to the chief of detectives' office and that," Polishuk makes a washing motion with his hands, "was the end of that."

"You were pulled off the case?" I needed to hear the words again. "Why?"

Polishuk just shakes his head.

"Okay then." Solarte picks up my line. "How about by who? Chief of detectives isn't high enough on the food chain to make that kind of call."

"We were never told. But it didn't take a genius to figure it came from the Boston field office of the FBI. I knew some standup people in the Bureau then, and they told me to let it go, that we were wading into some shit that was over our head and to leave things alone."

"You mean leave William Meyers alone?" I say.

"Now how the hell would you know that?" Polishuk rears back in astonishment. "I know for a fact that's not in any file you could get your hands on. Matter of fact, you can't even get your hands on the cold case file or you wouldn't be here in the first place."

"Will Meyers is my father," I say.

"Like hell he is."

"And he's got Alzheimer's," I say. "Bad. I can't really trust that anything he says is real." Not that he's talking at all anymore, but Polishuk doesn't need to know that.

"So fuck him," Polishuk spits. "He deserves it." His eyes are wild, the darkness that had shown in his file photograph pooling and then draining just as quickly as he looks beyond me, to the pond outside and the reeds swaying gently in the breeze. "I'm sorry. I didn't mean that," he says softly, meeting my eyes. "The sins of our fathers."

I accept his apology with a nod. "You're convinced my dad was a suspect in her killing? How? I mean, I'd heard the motive ascribed to him, protecting Klaussen and Mass's album release. But Camilla Islas was a junkie, I'm sure you knew that, her and Klaussen. Maybe she ODed. Or maybe they'd planned on disappearing together. She'd gone first and then Klaussen met her and they walked off happily ever after into the sunset."

Though of course I knew that scenario wasn't true. Because it was Klaussen who had hired Alianna Solarte to reignite the investigation, though not for the same reason Polishuk would want it resumed. Aside from Klaussen's assertion that he just wanted to give Camilla Islas a proper burial in time for Día, was there something else he might be after that Solarte and I just weren't seeing?

"What did my father have to gain by getting rid of Islas?" I move on, Solarte just content to sit back and watch me now, maybe filling out some trainee evaluation form in her head.

"It's not so much gain as it was to lose," Polishuk says. "Your father had too much on the line, too much invested in Mass. It was Camilla who got Klaussen hooked on smack. I mean, he was no choir boy, it was Boston rock and roll in the 1970s, but prior to Camilla there was no indication he was a drug addict. After? They were Boston's Sid and Nancy. Courtney and Kurt. Pick your era. Mass had just come out with their album, just landed that gig to open for Led Zeppelin, right? They were going to be bigger than fucking Aerosmith. Bigger than The Cars. But your dad knew none of it would happen if Klaussen kept on the path he was on, a full-blown junkie. So he gets rid of Camilla. Maybe with Klaussen. And that would have been his mistake. Klaussen was losing his shit, probably getting weak, maybe even wanted to confess. Every time Nichols or I went to interview him, your father was there, or had Klaussen lawyered up. I remember going to a show at the Channel to keep an eye on him and people were throwing shit at the stage, booing him through the entire set. I'll give him his due, Klaussen was no pussy. He waded right into that crowd and took on a whole pack of meatheads. Got his ass kicked and the bouncers were slow to break it up, too. If I was a betting man, I'd wager the house your father decided to cut his losses and get rid of Klaussen, too."

"No," I say. "That's not what happened."

"How do you know?"

I look at Solarte before I answer. *Your call,* her silence says.

"Because I know my father," I say, but the words sound trite as soon as I utter them. How much do any of us really know anybody, especially our parents, whether they disappear all at once like my mother or one piece, one memory at a time like my father, that Alzheimer's boulder rolling downhill and picking up speed every day? And of course, also because Klaussen was still alive and strumming, though I wasn't about to tell Polishuk that, at least not yet.

"Truly, Zesty." Polishuk regards me like a wounded bird that's fallen out of his nest. "What I said about your dad and his Alzheimer's . . . I'm sorry, I've lost my train of thought. . . ."

"The FBI." Solarte stirs from her corner.

"Yes. Thank you. Klaussen was gone and as I said, the focus moved to your father and that's when the FBI warned me and

Nichols off through the chief. And I'm pretty sure I don't have to remind you of the FBI and their entanglements with McKenna and the Boston Mob of those days." Polishuk snaps his fingers and points at me. "I read about you in the papers, not that long ago? You were somehow involved in the McKenna hunt."

"I was," I say. But if all he knew came from the papers, then he didn't know much. But he did seem to intuit that was the extent of what I was willing to say about it.

"That's some heavy burden for any young man to carry around."

"Family is family" is all I say to that, leaving the metaphorical messenger allusions alone.

"Understood. Well, aside from Klaussen and your dad, there were really no other leads. Camilla worked at Spit, which was a dance bar on Lansdowne Street. We pretty much checked everybody out there. She was also dealing some coke to support her habit, no surprise, but it was small-time. She wasn't connected. But you didn't just come for stories and conjecture from an old man. So what can I do for you, Ms. Solarte? Alianna."

"I was hoping to look at the cold case file." Solarte locks Polishuk in the tractor beam of her vision.

"You know it's against departmental regulations to make copies of files," Polishuk says.

"Okay," Solarte says. "I still want to see it."

"I'm afraid you can't."

"You mean you won't let me."

"I know who you are, Ms. Solarte. But you don't work for IAD anymore. When I say you can't, I mean that you can't, in the literal sense. Ten years ago I was living in Arlington, in the house I grew up in, actually. My mom had recently passed and I was sorting through her things. I'd moved in to take care of her during her last years. There was an electrical issue and the house burned down. With all the files in it. Everything."

Which explains the lack of pictures anywhere in Polishuk's house except for those two on his desk.

"That's really what it took for me to be here. To be this." Polishuk tugs on his wild man beard, flips his silver ponytail.

"You lost everything," Solarte says.

"That's right. All the files, the badges, the old uniform . . ."

"And started clean. No dead girls, no past failures and re-grets."

"It was the best"—the house begins to shake again, the rattle of glass—"thing that ever happened to me and when . . ." Poli-shuk's lips continue to move, but everything he says is drowned out in the long rumbling of the train as it thunders by and we sit and look at each other waiting for it to pass, for the tranquility and calm and quiet to return to the room. But whatever it was that Polishuk had spoken, he must have decided it wasn't important enough to repeat and so we just continue to sit there in the si-lence, in the thick warm crossbeams of light from the skylights as a galaxy of dust gently undulates in the air. I swear, if I closed my eyes for ten seconds, I could fall asleep right here sitting up, it's that peaceful.

Instead, we all rise and shake hands and Solarte says, "I'm happy you've found this place, Peter, it is beautiful here. I just don't know how you live with that noise."

"What noise?" Polishuk creases his face with a modest smile and winks at her. "Give it time, Alianna," he adds. "That's all it is. Time. You'd be surprised at what fades away. I actually don't even hear it anymore. Any of it. Any of them."

THIRTY

Yuki Fuji's Poker Analytics and Theory graduate-level course is still popular enough to be held in Huntington Hall, which offers stadium seating, the security attendant giving only a perfunctory once-over to the students entering the classroom and not picking me out of the crowd even though I wasn't carrying a laptop or a trillion dollars in student debt. Or maybe I'm not giving myself enough credit. For all I know the guy at the desk was the next Spenser for Hire and I just looked *that* smart out of my biking gear.

It was nice to pretend, though. As kids, Zero and I would often skip school and meander through college campuses, marveling at the tidy and organized otherworld maintained for a class of young people who appeared to know what they wanted from life and had the means and good fortune to incubate their dreams in a place that shielded them like a force field.

Zero and I would speak of this as we leaned in shoulder to shoulder to share a clove cigarette or the last of a roach, and though we were seeing the same things, we had completely different takes on it.

While I maintained an idealist's view of college campuses—an occasional pause of study among Ultimate Frisbee, keg parties, and coffee shops—I also had legit respect for the steady grind it must have taken some of the kids to be there. They couldn't have *all* waltzed in on the backs of tutors, essay mills, test-prep factories, and their parents' legacy status.

Zero, in contrast, saw nothing but a zoo of privilege. To him, the ivy-covered walls, the hovering security, was nothing but evidence of a machine that feigned meritocracy but was as insular and guarded as any criminal organization. Zero's young anarchist's brain seethed at the seeming ease with which these young people glided through life blissfully unaware of the bumpers set up in their lanes to make sure that they knocked over the pins lined up before them.

At this point in our lives, our mother was long gone, her once sporadic and unpredictable communiqués dwindled to nothing, the vanishing point arriving as a silent pinprick of pain that we never discussed. Did my father speak to Zero of our mother in those days? I had no way of knowing. We each occupied a different space regarding our relationship with him, though Zero shared more of his outlook on life, his distrust of the system, his cynicism.

My father's silence after our mother disappeared must have frustrated the FBI as they bugged our phones, and then showed up periodically as another political contemporary of hers was either freed from prison or published a book, the public infatuation regarding her actions and disappearance always resurrected on the anniversary of the Bank of Boston heist.

The vanishing point was so much closer at home, our father's nocturnal poker schedule, games that we no longer attended as we grew older, creating a distance between us; we were basically on our own and left free to play our own hands. We often played them wildly, Zero relishing his barroom brawls, our father's connections effortlessly getting us into bars and clubs even though we were underage and looked it.

When Zero started his moving company, the bulk of his early jobs were student moves, the two men and a truck variety. They were quick, relatively small hauls in or out of campus housing, or first apartments, generally speaking a step up for these young customers who rarely tipped and who confirmed Zero's early beliefs regarding the incubation of wealth and privilege. These customers treated Zero as he suspected they would. As if he were barely there at all and at most a curiosity, their rare brush with an authentic blue-collar world.

It must have stung Zero in those early days, though he would never admit it; every few months another tattoo was added, an armor of color going up on his skin and something harder settling in. Or maybe that's just my way of looking at him, trying to read his down cards. Even preparing for our father's death without me was another layer between us; not a word spoken, only the prayer for the dead filtering past his lips and giving him away.

"Why does MIT offer a course on poker?" Yuki Fuji must be wearing a small microphone that blends into her long black dress because I can't see it, her confident voice flooding out of the speakers filling the hall while her graduate teaching assistant, a short kid in an MIT hoodie with the starched button-down collar peeking out at the neck, works the PowerPoint, eager as a DJ spinning records. A few of the students had actually applauded her entrance as she appeared through a side door, stage right.

"Well, for starters, nobody wants to be a donkey," she says and a couple of predictable *eey-yaws* filter out of the crowd.

A donkey in poker parlance is somebody who thinks they know the game because they've played in house games and won some money, maybe even been anointed king or queen of their small poker world, but would get eaten alive by experienced professionals.

"And because you're sitting here, because this grand institution of learning has invited you to pursue your passion, you chose this class because you thought it would be fun. And it will be." Yuki Fuji smiles slyly. "But when we talk poker, what we are really talking is risk assessment as the type practiced in the business and finance world, where most of you will undoubtedly end up. We're talking a basic stoicism which many of you will probably never actually master, and by which I mean poker face. Why won't you master it? Because your alumni predecessors have shattered your attention spans by making you screen addicts." At this, Fuji's TA clicks a button, the screen projecting a mathematical formula I'm likely the only one in the audience who doesn't have a clue what it means. "Expected value is identical in poker as it is in math," Fuji says as students squirrel their fingers over their keyboards, taking notes. Or order shit off Amazon.

"And this," Fuji says, as a slide with a curved line graph appears behind her, "is where calculus comes in."

And here I totally lose her, though a number of young men start shifting in their seats like she's gotten to the gospel, their dicks gone rock hard at the mention of calculus.

I try to picture Sam in this class. Undoubtedly he would have understood the math, but I'd never seen him play poker and not once had we ever talked about the game.

"Any questions thus far?"

There were, mostly mathematical in nature; they could have been talking another language. I wait my turn then raise my hand.

"Yes?" Fuji points at me.

"This is all pretty interesting but I have to note you didn't say anything about the human element. I'm wondering how you think all these sexy math formulas will work when they're thrown off by what you haven't mentioned, which is bluffing."

"I'm sorry, I don't mean to castigate you, but you need to pay closer attention . . . your name?"

"Zesty."

"Zesty," she repeats, as most people do initially. Which you'd think would annoy me but doesn't as I'm always curious to see what condiment they'll relate my name to. "Bluffing is *exactly* what I've been talking about for the last ten minutes." She winks at me and the curved line graph goes up again, followed by what could be Einstein's theory of relativity, followed by who the fuck knows; it might be the magic formula for getting into a coed's pants, in which case I really should be taking notes. The graduate assistant is practically dancing now. Maybe he's seen this impending dressing-down before and it's about to get hot in here.

"It just looks like game theory to me," I say. "Not real life."

"No? You're qualified to argue with"—she laser points to the screen behind her—"$R*T/k=T/E/t=1*ut*(Qk)-ut(0^t)$? You don't consider this real life?"

"People are emotional," I say. "I don't need to understand the math to understand the play on a particular hand if I can play the person."

A small murmur ripples through the auditorium, bringing a frown to Fuji's face. I'm assuming that when she plays poker, she manages to hide her annoyance better.

"You're saying that it's easier to play the complexities of a person than absorb and utilize these formulas?"

"Exactly."

"Which have been run through more hands than you're likely to play in a lifetime?" Fuji arches her well-defined eyebrows.

"I'm saying—"

"This formula, in case you didn't catch this the first time I said it," Fuji's voice has risen to bully volume out of the speakers, jarring everyone whose attention was still on their computer screens like a flock of birds startled to the same danger, the graduate assistant's eyes wide with glee, "*has* a very human component, which you're so enamored with. Built into it. Its very name, regret minimization, addresses how your opponents at the table are playing and therefore addresses how you should approach your hand."

"It's a great name," I concede. "It doesn't factor fear. Or history. Or greed. Or lust."

"Lust?" Fuji rears back like I've just thrown a fastball under her chin.

"The mind wanders, is my point. Even with all that cash in the pot. You might already be spending the money in your head or formulating lies to explain where the money went, already making up bad beat excuses. What I'm saying is people carry baggage into games. Eventually it shows if you're paying attention and you're skilled enough to catch it."

"And you're skilled enough to catch it, Zesty?" Fuji had regained her composure, maybe even lowered the volume on her microphone, her TA registering his disappointment at a lack of fireworks and moving on to the next slide, an unspoken signal passed between them to continue.

"I'm one step ahead of that," I respond. "I know better than to get into a game that I can't afford to lose."

Fuji blinks as if I've struck her.

THIRTY-ONE

They surround me as soon as I'm out of the lecture hall. I'd noticed them perking up during my exchange with Fuji; four of them sat together, though there were plenty of empty seats in their row, and from the heat in their eyes it doesn't look like they just want an autograph. Three days ago it was a Mexican gang tasked with protecting Karl Klaussen, who had ignored what makes a legend most—dying young or disappearing forever—and returned to Boston to find the girl whom he and my father had disposed of like garbage.

According to Polishuk this makes my father either a murderer or an enabler, my dad acting in his own callous self-interest in a last-ditch effort to cash in on Mass making it big before the Zep-

pelin fiasco wiped it all away, the karmic bitch, sister to Lady
Luck, child of Mother Nature, making sure she's heard. He should
have known better than to piss off a troika of such powerful and
unpredictable women.

Today's threat comes from a more diverse group of Southeast
Asians, but all they want is my money.

The rec room in Ashdown House has a wide-open floor plan,
plenty of light, and couches and tables spread throughout. In a
smaller side room there's a giant flat-screen TV mounted to the
wall, tangles of gaming gear, and an octagonal poker table covered in MIT red felt in the center with chairs already set up around
it. There's only one small window. Next to it hangs a sign that
reads NO GAMBLING, which like most stop signs in Boston seems
to be thoroughly ignored.

"This is where we do our homework." Everybody chuckles
like it's the first time they've heard the joke. A friendly bunch.
Sunil to my left, Bill to my right, Ameer and Sanjay, and I don't
bother trying to remember the rest, more focused, even before the
cards are on the table, on the subtle communications they send each
other, the limbering of fingers and necks like they're about to enter
a boxing ring or exert themselves in a sprint around the block.

I don't expect them to cheat, they're too smart for that. And
like most seasoned players, they enter with a certain amount of
confidence, everybody in the game initially thinking they're a
shark, even if they've only got their baby teeth and a tiny dorsal
fin. "As long as there's no *actual* money on the table we are allowed
to play." Sunil winks playfully.

"The magic of poker chips," I say. "Buy-in's what?"

"Normally, house rules, five hundred dollars. We also take
cards."

"You're kidding."

"PayPal. Western Union."

"Cash?" I smile.

They all laugh heartily. Where are these guys when I'm bombing behind a microphone? Everybody has cash. I make sure they see I'm loaded, plenty more where that came from. Smiles all around.

"We do a couple of hours of pot-limit Omaha Hi-Lo and then switch to no-limit Hold 'Em tournament style, blinds rising on the half hour," Sunil informs me. "You can buy back in at any time for the full five hundred. Sound good?"

"Sounds great. Be even better if Professor Fuji were here."

They like that one. "I wouldn't mess with her, dude. She's a player."

The chips are heavy clay, value numbered, the MIT logo emblazoned in the center. Not Paulson chips, but still high grade. The deal rotates among the players. I choose to play loose-aggressive, betting often and in most pots, but not allowing myself to be pushed around. I lose more than I win, the winning pots smaller than the losses, a steady decline.

"Take *that,* regret minimization formula!" Sanjay says with a small grin as I rake a small pot into my well. Supportive.

"True, true. Take a picture and send it to Professor Fuji," Sunil says in a singsong voice. "The true reason we sought you out, Zesty. Not many people challenge the Queen. Though your grades will suffer, I'm afraid."

"I'm just auditing," I tell him. "No worries. Actually, I've been looking for this game for a while. Rambir invited me a month ago and then . . ." I open my hands in resignation, purposely flashing the cards I hold. Careless. And sad.

"Terrible," Sanjay says, pretending not to have seen my pocket spades ace and eight. Dead man's hand.

"Awful," Veejay chimes in and lays his cards down. "Scary. Where is safe anymore?"

Everybody folds and I rake another small pot.

"Teacher's pet." Bill smirks. "He never would have done what you did in class."

"Why's that?"

"Well, for one, being her graduate assistant. You might as well slit your own throat if you challenge your dissertation mentor."

"She was Rambir's mentor?"

"Dude, she was more than that. He was boning her."

"No fucking way," I say. "I think I saw that movie."

"Why aren't you dealing?" Sunil complains.

"It's your deal." I point out the cards in his hands. His face flushes. "You guys knew Rambir that well he'd tell you he was sleeping with his professor? Couldn't that get them both in trouble?"

"Not Ramb—"

"Sure," Bill says. "Rambir basically founded this game. The only time he wasn't playing is when he'd go to Vegas and Fox-woods with Fuji."

"No shit? But you guys would play without him? Or did he take you to that Russian/Ukrainian place in Allston?"

"There are many games around campus," Veejay says non-chalantly, dealing the cards deftly around the table. "Last hand before no-limit Hold 'Em."

"Small-time," Bill says. "This is the big money game." The other players start to cut their eyes at one another.

"He win or lose?" I say.

"What, here or in the casinos?" Bill asks.

"With the Russians."

"How did you know him again?" Sunil stares hard at Bill, who's too immersed in his cards to notice.

"I actually owed him money." I frown.

"You, too?" Bill mucks his cards.

"Shut *up,* Bill."

"What, don't pretend I was the only one. It's not like we'll have to pay him now anyway."

"I got interviewed by a homicide detective from Boston." I mix in a little truth with the bigger lie forthcoming, which is the secret to all good lying. "I don't even know how he got my name. He ever find you guys?"

"He was very thorough," Veejay says admiringly. "But of course, how could we help?"

"Did you tell him that you owed Rambir money?"

"Did you?" Bill shoots back, showing some teeth now after catching Sunil's vibe.

"No." I laugh. "Because I sure as hell didn't kill him, but the last thing I needed was to be a suspect in a homicide investigation, I got enough worries as it is."

"Thank you!" Bill pounds the table and looks at the players, who nod in grudging agreement. Obviously this was something that had already been discussed among them. "Did that reporter track you down?" Bill looks at me with what must be his truth serum stare, already thinking he's pushed me around the table all afternoon, he's got my number for everything.

"No," I lie easily. "No reporter."

"Yeah, well, this lady reporter came next with some of the same questions the Homicide guy asked. Only she was cut short by campus police."

Sanjay buries his face in his hands and rubs hard. "Play. The. Fucking. Game," he says through gritted teeth.

"It's upsetting," Veejay says. "Don't pretend it's not. He was a friend."

"Friend? He fucking fleeced us and then—" Sunil stops himself short.

"Why wouldn't campus police let you talk to a reporter?" Or more important, how could they stop them from talking? "You think they knew about the affair and were covering up?"

"Well, not on campus, they wouldn't allow. She gave out her card, but if campus police say not to talk, I'm not about to put my scholarship in jeopardy. None of us can afford to do that. Except for Bill. I don't know if you noticed, but every time he gets good cards, the silver spoon stuck up his ass begins to vibrate."

"Fuck you," Bill says, but he's smiling. That was the beauty of playing poker with people on a regular basis: You get to abuse each other, tell bold-faced lies in an attempt to take each other's money, and then come back and do it all over again.

In the majority of house games, the winning generally gets spread around, creating its own little microeconomy of debits and credits, the injury usually more to the ego than the wallet. And at most house games you don't wager more than you can afford to lose. There's a spirit of *we're all in this together* and you can dust yourself off after a beating, tell yourself all the lies you need to hear to make yourself whole again, knowing that there'll be another game tomorrow, or next week, or whatever the cycle may be. Only I was getting the vibe that Rambir was the only big winner here, maybe mastering Yuki Fuji's formulas to the max.

"Anyhow, we all talked to the police. We've done our duties as citizens, but if the university doesn't want us talking to a reporter, it's not for me to wonder why."

"I hear you. Listen, one last question only because I'm curious and then I won't ask you anything else. I owed Rambir, like, five thousand dollars. Did you guys owe him less or more than that?"

"Oh no, much less than that. Up until Rambir's death we had a strict table rule that there was no credit allowed. Five hundred dollars to buy in, rebuy if you had the money, but nothing owed."

"And you had that kind of money?"

Again, everybody starts looking at each other, an electrical current of warning flowing among them.

"I thought you said that was your last question," Sunil says. "Are we going to play or not?"

We play in silence, which suits me. The friendly mask has fallen off; there's no point in pretending anymore. Rambir Roshan was the big shark on the MIT poker circuit, founder of the biggest cash game in this insular academic world. Probably enough brain power in this room to build a nuclear reactor on the moon, but not enough to master the table when emotions and the personal history I'd challenged Yuki Fuji with come into play.

Except, it seems with the exception of Bill, all these guys had some form of scholarship that allowed them to afford what was one of the most expensive universities on the planet in one of the most expensive cities in the world. By all rights, they should be on a meal-plan diet and stuffing their pockets with hors d'oeuvres from faculty receptions, and yet they could consistently lose thousands of dollars to Rambir. So how did they pay him? Where did this flow of money come from?

I keep losing, but my losses are smaller, my forays into pots less frequent. Sunil is sweating even as he wins. Nervous. It has nothing to do with cards. Sanjay is losing, his fingers drumming on his chest, and after a while he places them under his thighs to quiet them.

Does Wells know that Rambir was a poker shark? Does it matter? Does it matter that most if not all these geniuses owed Rambir money he'd never be able to collect and they'd never have to pay? Could they have owed Rambir enough money to kill him? Regret minimization theory: not a fucking chance in the world. So why were they all so wary of talking about him? What were they holding back?

I was down to my last four hundred dollars, having already dropped six, the blinds alone threatening to drain me in just a few hands; it was now or never to make a play. Only I didn't control the cards and the hands I was getting deserved the mucking they received.

But I catch a pair of deuces and push half my chips in the middle, not because it's the statistical play, but because it's the only play I have, and all the others except for Bill are in the hand to see the flop, nobody scared of me at this point. The turn brings my third two, a deuce of spades. We all check. The river brings a second seven and a full house. Sunil raises. Rajeev calls. Everybody else folds. I don't hesitate and re-raise all in. Rajeev folds out of turn. Sunil takes his time to run the mathematical equations through the computer in his head. One day soon he'll make Google another trillion dollars for their war chest.

I can see in his eyes that he realizes that I have him beat. He even says it aloud. "Turn trips. River boat on pairing the seven." He flicks his cards loudly with his index finger, shakes his head, and then does something that would get him a failing grade in Yuki Fuji's class.

"Call." He pushes his chips into the pot.

I turn my cards over to show him the hand he knew was coming but couldn't control his emotions enough to take the practical loss as opposed to the crippling one. His two-pairs, kings over sevens, are losers. The chips make a satisfying clatter as I drag them into my well. The handcuffs make a more metallic *snick* as they're removed from the campus policeman's belt.

"Stand up and put your hands behind your back." The MIT cop points at me only. The MIT uniforms are almost identical to those worn by the Massachusetts State Police, from the blue hard-cloth caps and low visors to the shiny high-gloss riding boots outside the flared blue pants.

I do as I'm told. The cuffs have a familiar feel to them, but I forget the girl's name, only that she was super-freaky. The officer tightens them too much, forcing me to my tiptoes. Now it has a totally different but still familiar feel to it. He turns me around and marches me to the door.

"Continue with your homework, gentlemen," he says over his shoulder with a smirk.

THIRTY-TWO

The MIT chief of police has a large light-filled corner office on the second floor of the two-story police headquarters, a small building with a small waiting area on the first floor, where five cops sit behind a wall of glass in ergonomic chairs monitoring live video feeds from around the campus.

There's only one computer monitor in the chief's office and it's not so large. But then again neither is the chief, who for some inexplicable reason, when I see her, makes me think she'd be happier living on a farm, taking care of animals and growing vegetables. She's also got a military bearing about her, shoulders back, and a wry welcoming smile that tells me she doesn't need to impress anyone, not even FBI Agent Wellington Lee, who's seated in one of two hard chairs arranged in front of her desk.

"Why is it you don't look surprised to see me, Zesty?" Lee flashes me a quick finger before I can respond. "And don't tell me poker face." He approximates a smile, but there's nothing in it. He might even be following some new departmental playbook, now that he's climbed the ladder on the back of our shared ordeal with Devlin McKenna. Step one: Smile. Step two: Nod with chief to remove handcuffs. Step three: Let suspect know you can read his mind.

I have my own playbook. It starts like this: "Oleg Katyana," I say.

"Who's Oleg Katyana?" the MIT chief asks, scribbling something on a pad of legal paper. She doesn't introduce herself and Lee doesn't do the honors, but it's on a couple of shiny plaques hung on the walls. Rosalinda Worth. "That's not the guy we busted breaking into Ashdown House?"

"Actually, it is," Lee says. "Which is why I'd asked to meet with you again."

"He also goes by the name of Mikhail Sergachev," I volunteer with a smile, and the chief again scribbles something on the pad and addresses Lee.

"So you're telling me that Doc Martens, Levi's, navy sweater, long hair, big eye shiner knows more about what's happening on my campus than I do?"

Before Lee can respond, Rosalinda Worth swivels to me sharply and says, "No offense, you look great, in a beat-up kind of way. It's just I've developed this mental block with names. . . ." She waves the pad and then points at me.

"Zesty," I say.

"Zesty." Worth winces, snaps her fingers. "So I play this little mental details game with myself; for some reason they stick. I'm seeing a shrink for it, of course. Want to know what she says?"

"I can't even imagine," I admit.

She turns to Lee. Stares at him. Lee stares back, says nothing. Does nothing, wearing well the disguise of the caricature bureaucrat. Somewhere in Lee's office sits a first place trophy for the Mannequin Challenge.

"Lee," I say to Worth.

"Fuck. Me." Worth taps the side of her head with two fingers. For as long as I've known him, Lee's always presented himself as a dispassionate minimalist. One suit. One look. One emotion. The secret he's hiding? Probably as exciting as a messy closet. The corners of his lips might have momentarily curled up for a millimeter of a smile, but as I look at them now, they've resumed their flat-lined inscrutability.

"My therapist says, get this, that not being able to remember . . ." Worth pauses, shakes her head. "Scratch that. That *failing* to absorb people's names but retaining all the impersonal attendant details is a sign of a self-centered egotist of the highest order. A borderline egomaniac-narcissist. *Moi*." She spiders her fingers just above her ample bosom. "Thoughts, gentlemen?"

"Pretty harsh, shiny boots, blue suit, straw blond hair in a bun," I say.

"Very funny. What the hell are you doing on my campus? According to this guy," Worth doesn't even try to recall Lee's name, employing her thumb instead, "everywhere you step things tend to get way worse before they get better. *If* they get better. And he'd used curse words to express these sentiments."

Finally I've found something Lee and Zero could bond over. The Zesty Path: where angels tread in shit.

"I was just trying to make a few dollars," I say. "Any chance of cashing out those chips I won?"

But the real question is, what is Lee doing on campus? Oleg Katanya aka Mikhail Sergachev was a burglary that resulted in an on-campus arrest. The Rambir Roshan murder was Boston Robbery Homicide, give or take a couple of inches. What happens when you're arrested on the MIT campus? Probably one of two things. Either you get atomized in an experiment and are never heard from again or you're handed over to Cambridge PD.

My chip query is greeted by twin blank stares even though for two agents of law enforcement, these two couldn't be more different. Lee could trip into a seismograph needle and not make it move, all his machinations hidden behind dark eyes shaded by twin caterpillar eyebrows, though under his crisp suit is a horrific scar across his abdomen from the stabbing that had almost killed him and an aggrieved sense of justice incomplete. But on the surface he gives off the flat expression of the jack on a playing card, neither here nor there as a hand, but just enough to justify staying in the game.

Worth, I'm convinced, carries a military past, the rounded shoulders kept back possibly as much a habit from carrying a seventy-pound rucksack as from discipline. She has a pugnacious-ness that makes her seem much larger than her height, candy apple cheekbones that have probably braced hard suns, intelligent satellite eyes that miss nothing. Worth rolls those eyes and shakes her head.

"Let's stick to the facts. At 1:17 P.M. you tried to access Ash-down House but were stopped by security, who you gave some cockamamie visiting story to. You went around back and found the door locked and moved on." Worth pauses to glance at the paper on her desk. "At 1:55 P.M. you crested your way into Hun-tington Hall for Professor Yuki Fuji's poker analytics class, where you caused quite a stir. Judging by the Internet traffic, most nota-bly Facebook, you must have—"

"Whoa, you monitor students' social media?" I'm aghast. And by aghast, I mean I'm only acting.

"Who needs to monitor? These kids post everything. Just wait until their Goldman Sachs interview; there's going to be some se-rious reckoning for those party pics. They ought to know noth-ing disappears forever."

Worth is right about that. Devlin McKenna came back. Karl Klaussen came back. It's only poor Camilla Islas and my mother who are gone forever, Solarte and I no closer to finding Camilla's body than when we started looking.

"These students only post to their friends," I point out. "You're invading their right to privacy."

"I friend every student in this school." Worth grins wide. "They're all my babies." She points to a framed *New Yorker* cartoon behind her. Two dogs seated at a computer. One dog says, "Nobody on the Internet knows you're a dog."

"You maintain fake accounts?"

"And a million excuses why I can't meet. I have people tapped in to the busy lives of our students, let's leave it at that. Stop trying to deflect, this isn't about me. By 3:11 P.M. you've made new friends and started playing poker. I want to know what you're up to."

"Zesty has a proven track record of insinuating himself into situations, making things more complicated than they ought to be," Lee interjects.

"You should talk," I say.

"He also," Lee is undeterred by my aside, "has a history of misdirection, a shirking of responsibility, but that perhaps is an inherited trait." Lee lifts his eyebrows. "Where there is poker involved, also, I'm not particularly surprised to find him; he's got a nose for the game. Another genetic gift, perhaps, but more likely a learned and studied trait. I'm here on campus not because you're here, Zesty, though that's a happy coincidence. What I am about to show you has been edited for efficiency's sake, but I'd like to have your interpretation of them."

Rosalinda Worth turns her monitor so we can all see the screen and I watch Oleg Katanya at the front door of Roshan's campus house; cut to Sam Budoff walking across campus with a silver poker case; cut to Yuki Fuji smoking cigarettes outside with Jakub Namestnikov; cut to Rambir Roshan with Namestnikov and Oleg Katanya together.

"Lot of Eastern Europeans," I say. "I'm taking it you know who these people are?"

"Of course," Worth says. "These pictures are not the sum total of how often they have been on campus."

"So what?" I say. "I bet there are a lot of Russians on your campus."

"That's true. There's something about the Eastern European mind and Internet technology."

"Only Oleg Katyana had an entirely different skill set, didn't he?" I say.

Lee nods and reaches into his inside breast pocket. "I'm going to warn you, Zesty, these pictures are not easy to look at."

"Don't bother. I've seen them." Lee and Worth stare at each other and I look anyway. There's a picture here that Wells didn't have or decided not to show me. A heavily tattooed complete arm cut crudely just below the shoulder, the hand holding a severed penis.

"You ID Katanya based on the tattoos? I mean, if it's based on what he's holding, that's your business."

"Really, Zesty?" Lee displays genuine disappointment. "Even in moments like these?"

"It's a coping mechanism, what can I tell you?"

"A little filter wouldn't hurt, though," Worth suggests.

"Noted." I look more closely at the photo and Lee points out the individual tattoos like a roadmap through the Russian prison system. "The red star, Zamkova prison, Ukraine. Assault with intent. The devil and pitchfork, Lefortovo, Moscow. This time, successful. Murder. That Russian lettering on his penis, basically 'fuck the system.' Original, right? In the old days, the prison administration would have burned the ink with acid to smudge it." There's more. "The naked girls? Pimping. Naked girl in a burning martini glass, gasoline-drowned whore. A warning to the others. We don't see this level of brutality often."

"And yet here we are." Worth's face a dark cloud.

"I take it the cock in hand is some kind of message?"

"It's a taunt. Like, a combination 'fuck you' and 'here's what you're left with.'"

Nothing but dick.

"Clever." I frown. "Who's doing the taunting?"

Instead of answering, Lee takes out another photo and lays it on the desk for me to see.

"Antti Voracek," I say, maybe showing off a little in front of Worth, who has to consult her cheat sheet but doesn't write anything down, meaning she's already seen the photos and recorded the names. "Namestnikov's boss."

Lee, if he's surprised I've identified the picture, squelches it.

"Let me guess. You've also got film of Antti Voracek."

"I don't believe this." Worth squints at me angrily. "What did you say you do for a living?"

"I'm not even sure anymore." How many jobs was I shouldering now? Messenger. Construction. PI in training. Failing stand-up comedian. I'd add poker pro, if they'd let me cash my chips.

"Katanya we have meeting with Rambir on numerous occasions. Namestnikov once with the two of them. Voracek we only have on campus at a university gala for a visiting dignitary. He runs in more diplomatic circles."

"Was Professor Yuki Fuji there?"

"Yes."

"Is that the only time you have them in the same place?"

"No. We have them in Las Vegas. Foxwoods in Connecticut."

"Private poker coach?" I say, knowing full well that wasn't the deal. More likely using the casinos to launder money. But money from what? From where? And ending up where? The real estate? The chips Zero now had stashed somewhere?

"When Katanya was arrested on campus, who was he turned over to?" I ask.

"Ah, very good, Zesty. I can see you're focused now," Lee says. "Katanya was turned over to Detectives Powers and McGowan. Cambridge Homicide."

"Why them?"

"Because that's who showed up." Worth sounds disgusted. "We knew it stunk, but they've got their story that Katanya was under their watch. They wouldn't specify why or how, but they had clearance to pick him up and I had orders to hand him over."

And then he ends up in pieces.

"Katanya wasn't successful in getting hold of Rambir Roshan's computer, the one he broke in for, because we already had it." Worth holds the cheat sheet of names as she speaks. Even if she didn't have her memory issues, this whole mess was getting to be more confusing than *Crime and Punishment*. I glimpse my name on the pad underlined multiple times. "Rambir's computer had been wiped clean, but we already knew what he'd been up to."

"And you're holding out on Boston Homicide. What kind of fucked-up shit is that?"

"It's a convoluted situation," Lee states the obvious.

"You mean more convoluted than running multiple accounts, depositing and transferring money just below the ten grand mark that would require the banks to flag it?"

Worth levels a cold eye at Lee. Lee says, "I believe we went over this already. And as for Zesty, it's a family trait. The Meyerses are always looking for angles and when they find one, be prepared to take cover. Proceed. It's impossible to know how much of what you are about to share that Zesty already knows."

"Fine. But I still don't understand why you insist on including him. No offense . . . Zesty, but you don't really seem qualified for this."

"Offense taken," I say. But I see Worth's point. Did I know some things that Lee didn't? Possibly. Was I in any kind of danger personally? Not that I could tell. Anitra Tehran was the target and has the files, which she's right now sharing with Wells, the two of them huddling at headquarters trying to de-encrypt what Tehran didn't even trust her own people to decode.

It's enough to bring on a headache, but my head fills with static instead, putting an end to the longest beat-break my internal DJ's taken since he's taken up residency. A sonic bolt of lightning is followed by the familiar electric strumming of "When Things Go Wrong" by Robin Lane & The Chartbusters:

When things go wrong
Don't walk away
That will only make it harder
Why you want to run away
That won't get you any farther

"Rambir was running at once a complicated but simple scheme," Worth's voice cuts through the music. "Where he would hack into people's personal bank accounts and steal the log-in credentials. He'd then set up fraudulent automated clearinghouse links, or ACH links, between the victims' accounts and prepaid debit card accounts he controlled."

"You mean, like he'd go to a CVS store, buy ten fifty-dollar prepaid cards, and then transfer money from his hacking victims' accounts to these cards?"

"Exactly. Only he wouldn't buy the cards himself."

"Let me guess. He'd pay his poker buddies to do that."

"Yes."

"Because he'd fleece them at the table and they wanted to keep playing, hone their game that Professor Fuji convinced them they could master."

"And why not?" Lee chimes in. "It was all house money to them. Remember, the majority of these Ashdown House players are on scholarships and have no money of their own. And here comes Rambir with a cash spigot, running a big money poker game. He couldn't have won all the time, correct?"

Correct. The margin of error was too fine, the cards sometimes running against you; most likely Rambir's poker buddies took turns walking around the campus with fat dollars in their pockets.

"You notice all the trappings of retarded youth, the large-screen TV, the gaming tech? It was like they were living out their fantasies. And that's where Oleg Katanya came in. Expensive whores, a little cocaine. He met Roshan when Roshan had gone looking for bigger stakes, ended up at his club. Katanya procured the girls and the drugs and he recognized that something was amiss. That these guys shouldn't have had so much money. So like a good soldier, he reports to his boss, Namestnikov, and they figure out what's going on."

So it's not the Kirilenko Labs connection that involves the Russians; they come in through an entirely different side door.

"So what happens once the money is transferred to the pre-paid debit cards?"

"Rambir used his buddies again." Worth uses her cheat sheet and rattles off a list of names much longer than just the guys I'd been playing with. Too many guys, obviously.

"Our fine students. Almost every single one from Southeast Asia, chosen specifically because they were vulnerable and all taking the same class taught by Yuki Fuji. They would fan themselves out around the city, purchase money orders from Money-Gram and the U.S. Postal Service, which they'd then give to Rambir, who would deposit them into multiple accounts—"

"In amounts just below the ten thousand mark."

"Yes. And then he'd pull the cash from the accounts, pay his army of poker buddies, replenishing their poker war chests, and the game went on. The whores kept coming. The drugs. He basically corrupted two dozen nerds, not one, who we could tell, sent any significant money home overseas."

"You were watching them. The Facebook and email accounts." And probably other ways, other eyes in the skies, though none Worth is likely to admit to. "And you didn't stop it."

"I tried." Worth pauses and a pained look begins to dawn on her face.

"But you were overruled," I say. "By people above you."

"If we dismantled the game and expelled the students, there'd be too much noise, bad publicity. After the whole blackjack thing years ago, this institution didn't want the spotlight for another gambling scandal, much less one that involved drugs, prostitutes, stolen bank accounts, and Russian gangsters."

"So your solution was what?"

"A joint university and FBI operation," Lee says. "To contain the fallout."

"You mean to cover up the truth."

"I sense a judgmental tone, Zesty. Do I need to remind you that your family has benefitted from such an arrangement in the past?"

Benefitted and suffered, I could argue, but this wasn't the time or place for it. "So you're not interested in implicating the students," I say to Lee. "You're looking at the Russian angle, trying to keep them contained, because the last thing Boston needs is the Russian Mob getting a solid toehold and start flexing their muscles around this shiny and rebuilt city."

"Precisely."

"And then Rambir gets killed, throwing everything in disarray."

"Yes. Followed by Katanya fished out of Boston Harbor and then Namestnikov disappearing and his enterprises abandoned."

"You think he's dead?"

"I do."

But who would want to rub out Namestnikov? And who had the juice to do it? He was the one who was practically printing money. And speaking of the money, if Rambir had been pulling in the range of eight or nine thousand dollars per account after paying off his buddies and there were 137 accounts on that drive Anitra Tehran and I had looked at, we were talking roughly in the range of the value of the poker chips Zero now held.

Also, who's to say there weren't other accounts out there, security breaches in places like Home Depot and Target and who knows where else, yielding reams of personal and financial information. With every passing day my mattress was looking like a greater and safer place to stash money if it weren't for the cat.

"What was Rambir paying his buddies for their role in all this? I mean besides the coke and whores."

"Ten percent of every deposit. Basically a thousand bucks a pop. Hit five post offices in a day and our little Sunils, Vishnays, Adars, and Zamirs were walking around with serious pocket money," Worth says.

And there was nothing she was allowed to do about it, higher powers giving her some sour marching orders, which I could tell ate her up inside, maybe her name-recognition issues even coinciding with this cluster-fuck.

Until Rambir hit the pavement and the proverbial shit hit the fan. And then there was the added complication of Powers and McGowan trying to wrest control of the homicide scene, doing what they could to grab the case. Why so hot for the Rambir catch? I'd have to remember to ask Wells. Also, could there be more money around besides the poker chips, assuming they belonged to Rambir? I pose that query to Lee and Worth.

"That's the literal million-dollar question," Lee answers. "Or more. Not in a bank account, as far as we can tell."

"And not under his mattress," Worth adds. "We checked."

"Did you check Yuki Fuji's accounts?" Aside from Kirilenko Labs, Professor Yuki Fuji seemed to be the star everybody had been orbiting around. All the MIT poker players had taken her poker analytics class. Rambir had served two semesters as her TA. Fuji probably wrote letters of recommendation for the internships at Kirilenko Labs, and she'd been photographed with Jakub Namestnikov, whom Oleg Katyana worked for. Rambir's dead. Oleg Katanya's dead. Lee thinks Namestnikov is dead.

All pretty lucky for Yuki Fuji if she's somehow a bigger part of this than what Lee and Worth surmise. Every power player with a direct link to these schemes is now either dead or missing.

Do I think Yuki Fuji is capable of killing Rambir, slaughtering a psychopath Russian gangster like Oleg Katanya, and chopping up his body and then disappearing his boss Namestnikov, a Russian Mafia strongman? Not a chance. Still doesn't mean she's not worth talking to, though I doubt she'd be happy to see me again so soon. We all come to an agreement on this point.

Worth hangs up the phone after confirming with Fuji. "Thirty minutes," she says and excuses herself, leaving Lee and me alone to practice our tough-guy stares at each other. When Worth returns she's holding a thick white envelope, which she drops in my lap.

I open it and look inside, thumb through nineteen one-hundred-dollar bills, give or take the pot I'd raked into my well.

"Somebody should come out of this with a winning hand." Worth winks at me. "Why not you . . . whatever your name is."

The door to Yuki Fuji's office is unlocked and open when we get there. Framed degrees adorn the walls—Berkeley, Yale, MIT—sharing space with varsity swimming trophies, medals, photographs of deep water swims. When Worth redials Fuji's phone from her cell, something vibrates in the desk drawer.

"She's running," Lee says.

THIRTY-THREE

Mary Chung seems the logical place for an early dinner. Not only because Lee is Chinese, but because the food is awesome, reasonably priced, and it's within easy walking distance of Yuki Fuji's office.

"Where do you think Fuji's going?" We've arrived during the staff dinner, two round tables pushed together forming an 8, twice as many workers sharing their pre-shift meal off of a dozen large steaming plates of amazing-looking dishes I can't identify and wouldn't know how to order.

"Running or buying time." Lee shrugs himself into a booth. "Who knows. Why do you look so excited?"

"This is the first time I've been to a Chinese restaurant with someone who's legit Chinese." I motion to the tables of workers. "Hook me up, I always get the General Tso's chicken."

A middle-aged waitress comes to the table with menus and Lee addresses her in Chinese. She laughs, holds on to the menus, and hollers something to her coworkers, who all raise their hands without turning in their seats and also respond with a variety of guttural greetings.

"They know you," I say.

"Thanks to you." Meaning Lee is the Chinese equivalent of David Ortiz in these parts. Acts of heroism. Keys to the city.

"You're welcome," I say.

"Let's see if we can avoid a repeat this time." Somehow, Lee frowns without his lips. "Why do you think I asked you to dinner—No, don't respond, I already see the joke forming behind your eyes."

Which reminds me. Tonight's the last night of stand-up, the class moving upstairs at the Hong Kong restaurant at the edge of Harvard Square. It's the late showcase, after the paid performers go on for their regular sets, which means the audience will consist of my classmates and whoever's fallen into their Scorpion Bowls and can't find their legs to walk out the door.

"I have to admit, Zesty, I'm at once amazed to see you in the thick of this and yet not surprised at all considering Sam

Budoff's involvement and the lengths you'll go to protect your friends."

"Boston loyal," I say, flashing nonsensical gang signs across my heart.

"Save your slogans for the T-shirt. Do I have to remind you what became of your friend Gus Molten?"

"That's a fuckin' cheap shot, Lee, and you know it."

"Yes. But it seems I've struck a nerve." Lee lifts his eyebrows, but doesn't apologize.

Should he? Gus had pulled me into what got him killed, his last moments, or the way I envision them in my dreams, still haunting me. Now Sam's pulled me into something that feels just as dangerous. Maybe I just need better friends.

"How much trouble is Sam in?"

"Assuming he gets out of this alive? It depends. It could be no more than the young men you were playing poker with. The only difference being that he no longer falls under Ms. Worth's university-sanctioned protection."

"He graduated?" I say.

"Welcome to the real world. Where you're actually held accountable for your crimes."

"You mean unless you can write a check when you're caught and come up with a new catchy slogan?"

Lee actually smiles, which is a rarity. "You know, you've got a lot of your mother in you, Zesty."

"You mean *fight the power*?" I hold up a Black Panther fist.

"I know it's a painful subject, so you're apt to joke. But you've read your mother's file and I'm sure your father spoke of her often before his Alzheimer's set in. What I mean is your mother was a woman of conviction. As misguided as her expression of those convictions might have been she—"

"Was on the right side of history if you really want to look at it straight. Every goddamn thing she ever stood up for was right.

Her only mistake, my dad's only mistake, was getting into bed with people already compromised by your people. Before your time, granted, but don't you tell me how much I'm like my mother, not by reading some fucking file." Lee and I stare at each other for a long minute over our cups, the tea cooling down quicker than we seem capable of.

"Really, that's where we are, Zesty?" Lee blinks first, breaking the silence.

"Yeah, that's where we are."

"So then, to the heart of it: Unlike most Asians, and this you already know, I'm not much of a gambler, though each time we cross paths I feel as if everything I'm working toward relies on the turn of a card, some variable I can't control." Lee points at me emphatically. "I'm talking about you."

"I got that," I say.

"The Joker," Lee says.

"The Joker's a throwaway card," I say. "We don't use it."

"Ironic."

"Although some people use it as a wild card," I point out. "Though not in poker."

"Doubly ironic then. I don't have much time to spare here so let me tell you my thoughts, and you do your best not to interrupt. I think once again you're neck deep in something that you don't fully understand and in your misguided effort to help a friend, again, you've made matters worse and compromised something that had been up to this point contained—"

"You mean covered up."

"I asked you not to interrupt." Lee looks serious.

"The scope of this investigation is beyond your understanding and more important than your friend who has graduated from pharmaceutical hobbyist to aiding and abetting a wannabe cyber-crime kingpin and now, rightfully, fears for his life. Where is Sam Budoff?"

"I don't know."

"How did you know to infiltrate the MIT poker game?"

"Detective Wells."

"Why is Wells sharing information with you?"

"It's a two-way street," I say.

"What is it that you're sharing with him?"

The workers at Mary Chung have cleaned up their plates and spun the tables back to their original positions. I look at Lee, who has a familiar look on his face, a barely contained smoldering patience that's about to break. But I have problems and duties of my own to deal with, an ailing father, who the more I learn about, the more layers that are peeled back, the more disappointed I am in him. And there's absolutely nothing that I can do about that anymore.

"Nothing you don't already know," I finally say. "All that stolen account information."

"Meaning you've had contact with Budoff."

"Indirectly." I explain what Budoff had dropped on me via JJ Foley's. And I admit to having the poker chips that Sam had placed in the storage unit, but don't tell him Zero's taken possession of them.

"I think Roshan gave Sam the chips that Katanya was looking for when he broke into Roshan's place. The chips and Roshan's computer that Ms. Worth already had. I don't know who the chips actually belong to. Him, maybe. Possibly Professor Fuji."

"Where are the chips now?"

"I stashed them. You're the only one I've told. Wells says Fuji and Roshan traveled to Vegas together. Foxwoods. Did you know that?"

"Yes."

"They were lovers," I say, opting for the more romantic version of "he was boning her" that I'd been given. Classy is what I am. Refined.

"She was using him," Lee says flatly. There's no "maybe" in his tone.

To run point on taking the cash from the hacked accounts and building up a war chest of chips to play with. If they won. If *she* won, cashed out, essentially laundering the money and burnishing her reputation at the same time. Teach. Don't teach. She could do whatever she wanted.

"You think Fuji could have killed Roshan?"

"That is a question for Wells," Lee says. "My focus is on a larger picture."

"Why were those Cambridge Homicides so hot to catch the Roshan case that they'd salt the murder scene?"

"You can't answer that question yourself?"

I can. I do: "Powers and McGowan picked up Katanya and then he turned up as fish chum. Maybe he was a liability of some sort either to them or his boss. Only his boss is now missing and you've already said you expect he'll turn up like Katanya."

"Not like Katanya. Katanya was the message. In a common language everybody could understand. We'll probably never find Namestnikov."

"Who's everybody?" And more important, who's sending the message?

The food comes on a tray, steaming plates of General Tso's chicken, and beef and broccoli, rice, and scallion pancakes.

"What the fuck?" I complain when the waitress is gone.

"I like the General Tso's. What can I tell you?" Lee starts spooning the plate with food and exchanges his ninja chopsticks for a fork.

"FBI Special Agent Wellington Lee," I announce. "The Great Assimilator."

"Powers and McGowan are crooked." Lee speaks with his mouth full. "Into the Russians for something. But that is for Cambridge Internal Affairs to contend with. I assume the detectives wanted to catch the Rambir case to choke off all leads, hunt down your friend Sam. Of course, their story will be along the lines of what Ms. Worth suggested, that Katanya was a confidential informant. Whether or not there's any paperwork to back up that claim remains to be seen; it's doubtful Katanya's murder will be attributed to them. Perhaps Cambridge IA will come up with something else."

"You think Powers and McGowan are capable of doing Katanya like that or they handed him off?"

"I think they are capable of anything at this point, even Namestnikov. But the real reason I asked you to dinner has nothing to do with any of this. I need your brother to stop."

"Stop what?" I have no idea what Lee's talking about.

Lee gives me his hard stare again, but then remembers I just beat him at that game and pulls out a cell instead. *Another* cell phone. Lee's phone has been on the table during our entire conversation, but he's reached into his coat to pull this one out. He slides it across the table to me. "Scroll right. . . . Your *other* right."

I shrug and reverse directions, dark but clear pictures of the Summer Street Bridge at night. Pictures of the path that runs under the bridge along the Fort Point Channel waters where the Channel nightclub used to be. I scroll and look at pictures of Sid and Zero launching an inflatable skiff off of Pier 1 beside Old Ironsides, Zero wearing the neoprene diving suit but with the helmet off and holding what looks like a rack of lights. Last, a picture of Zero tilting backward off the inflatable boat into the coal black channel waters.

"You took these?"

"Yes."

"This isn't an FBI phone?"

"No."

"So this is personal," I say.

"It seems Zero has made it so. You do know what he is look-ing for."

I do. Lee's service-issue Glock 23 that the Boston Police div-ers were unable to find a couple years ago. The gun sunken and lost somewhere among the estimated billion rusted razor blades Gillette had dumped in what had once been a cesspool of Fort Point waters. A gun that, if recovered, would counter the narra-tive fed to the Boston public through the FBI and the brass at Bos-ton Police headquarters that painted Lee as a hero in the wake of Devlin McKenna's return. Lee studies me studying the pictures, shaking my head.

"You didn't know," he says.

I think back to the wet seaweed I'd picked off my sneaker, Jhochelle's story about the diving suit and tanks, the safe Zero had changed the combination to. Jhochelle must have known what Zero was looking for, the safe locked for her legal protection. But like my father, Jhochelle is also fluent in silence.

As to why Zero was looking for Lee's gun is not so difficult for me to fathom; it's the way Zero operates, his mind always searching for that slim margin that separates the house advan-tage from the player's. The fact that the combination's been changed tells me that he's already recovered what he'd been looking for.

Having Lee's gun would provide Zero with an ace up his sleeve any time that he felt he needed to play it, a form of insur-ance if his luck or machinations ever ran bad. Screw Yuki Fuji, Zero should be the one teaching at MIT. You get a failing grade, you get punched in the mouth.

I could tell Lee that it's too late, that Zero already has his Glock, as barnacle encrusted as it might be. I could tell him that I'd given those same account numbers he and Rosalinda Worth had to Anitra Tehran at the *Globe* in the form of the thumb drive.

And that in addition to those accounts there were files that Detective Wells was huddling to open with his BPD Geek Squad; that if all four of them would get together and share the information they had instead of just protecting their turfs and allowing their political bosses to control the narrative, they could probably solve this whole case over drinks at Cheers. But of course that's not what I do.

"I'll make you a deal" is what I say.

THIRTY-FOUR

The Citgo sign is on, doing its thing across Kenmore Square, as I walk into Solarte's office, and it's a good thing I'm not high because if I were, I'd just stare out the window, pencil lame jokes on scrap paper, and scarf down an entire pizza. Instead I lay a file on Solarte's desk before taking a seat.

"Is that what I think it is?" Solarte looks impressed.

"Probably not," I say. "It's from the FBI."

"Say what?"

"Zesty Meyers, PI," I say. "Put me on salary, boss."

"I just might. But before I look at this and you tell me how you were able to get ahold of it, I'll see your file and raise you . . ." Solarte opens the top desk drawer and gently lays Charlie's gun on the table, the barrel facing away from us toward the window.

It's my turn to be impressed, but I don't touch the gun.

"You don't want it," she says.

"No. And I found out it doesn't belong to Charlie." I explain how he came to hold it in the first place.

"So." Solarte slides the gun off the desk and back into her

drawer. "You've been busy, I've been busy, too. I got the grand tour with Klaussen today after I dropped you off. Up and around Allston, Cambridge, Somerville, all the places he and Camilla Islas used to hang out or scored. Of course, most everything's changed; I just wanted to see if anything shook loose out of him. I offered to have him sit with someone I know who could hypnotize him, but he wasn't having any part of it."

"I don't blame him," I say.

"Why's that?"

"Control, mostly. I wouldn't want somebody to have that kind of access to the things I know."

"You mean the secrets you keep?"

"I thought we were talking about Klaussen," I say.

"We were. Now we're talking about you. I know this can't be easy for you, Zesty, to learn these things about your father so late in the game when he can't explain himself." Solarte's voice goes dry. "It's not what I intended when I brought you in on this."

"No?"

"You give me too much credit. I rarely see that far ahead. I just go where the leads take me. Anyhow, we weren't about to go shoveling in Tenean or Wollaston since they'd bulldozed and cadaver-sniffed those spots years ago. You know the story."

I did, of course. Just about everyone in Boston knows the story now. I only wonder how *much* Solarte knows that I know. It's hard to tell. Everywhere I've careened this last week I've stumbled into women who are kicking ass, taking names, and playing their game tight. Conversely, the men are all running around like chickens with their heads cut off, making up shit as they go along and cutting corners at every opportunity. Something I'm sure Jhochelle would characterize thusly: *business as usual.*

"Klaussen thought it could have been around the Revere shoreline, any one of those places, really, but he doesn't remember shit. The only rise I got out of him was in Islas's old hood near

Davis Square. He couldn't believe how nice the neighborhood is now. It was never a shithole, but it was always working class, pretty mixed by Boston standards. You know, I never realized Somerville back-ended into Charlestown, but now it makes sense McKenna's crew were all Irish with Charlestown roots, Southie. Everybody knows Charlestown used to be the bank robbery capital of the world, but did you know—"

"Somerville was the car theft capital during the same time period?"

"I guess you do. Makes perfect sense, right? They're not driving their own *cahs* to hit the banks," Solarte purposely butchering the word. "Anyhow, Klaussen says he's pretty good with names so we went mailbox reading, rang a few doorbells. Most everybody in the neighborhood, at least the people we met, hadn't been there more than ten, fifteen years tops."

"Did Klaussen recognize Camilla's place?"

"You mean her parents'? Barely. It had been fixed up, pretty much like every other house on the block. I'd live there in a heartbeat if I could afford it. We checked the mailboxes. The Islases, as you know, are deceased. Nobody answered when we rang. We asked whoever answered the door in the houses closest to Camilla's if they knew the family back in the day."

"Did anybody?"

"One old lady, who must have been confused, said the daughter had moved back a long time ago. Poor thing. It looked like she lived alone and I could smell the cats from the porch. Hers might have been the only house on the block that hadn't been renovated. Honestly, I'm surprised she answered."

"Why's that?"

"There must have been a half dozen fliers in her mailbox, those cash-for-your-house deals, reverse mortgage, all that bullshit. I'm sure there are vultures who go by that house every day just waiting for her to kick."

"How long ago did Polishuk say Camilla's parents died?"

"Eighty-six? The dad died in a car crash. The missus a few years later? Cancer, I think it was."

"You ran the deed? Record of sale?"

"Sure." Solarte had picked up a pencil off her desk and begins to tap it on the side of her head like it might jar a thought loose.

"What?" I open my hands at my sides.

"I didn't really think anything of it when I looked, but now that you mention it, that might be the only thing that was strange. . . ."

"What's that?"

"There wasn't a record of sale, per se. It was a transfer. Like in a will."

"To who?"

"Nobody named Islas, I remember that. I just assumed it must have been somebody else in the family. Didn't think it was important."

"Do you now?"

"Not particularly. But I'll follow up anyway. At this point it's all I have unless that file tells us something new."

We open it. It doesn't. Except for what's not there: my father's name missing or redacted from any of the paperwork that makes up the FBI file and any connection to Camilla Islas's murder. Confirming what Polishuk said about being warned off by the FBI and his superiors: one of his two leading suspects was declared off-limits and Karl Klaussen vanished, whereabouts unknown to everybody except my father, safely across the Mexican border with a new name and identity. Only to resurface thirty-some-odd years later, hoping loss would be his guide to exhume Camilla's bones and usher her soul to heaven in time for Día de los Muertos.

Is Klaussen a religious man? He doesn't strike me as one. But death has a way of forcing that conversation. At least it has with me. Maybe not religion in the organized sense, but the start of a relationship with what lies beyond, the living's responsibility to the dead. And it also dawns on me at that moment that I know next to nothing about my responsibilities to my father when his time comes to pass. Nothing about his wishes for his burial or what to do with his remains, or the ceremony he'd like to mark his passing, the words he'd prefer were spoken over his mortal coil.

His end is nearing. Why can't I face that? Even Zero seems to have come to some form of acceptance of this inevitability. No. It's more than acceptance. He's preparing himself. Without me. Because I haven't been strong enough to face the truth.

I close my eyes and think of my father and the choices he's made over the years, not a single meaningful decision that hadn't drawn blood or pain. It would be comforting to think that Lee was right, that I'm more like my mother than I know, at least trying to do the right thing, to swerve hard to the choices that don't burn anyone else, or make matters worse than they are. But Lee only knew my mother like I did, through newspaper clippings and files and stories. Meaning, through other people's eyes.

"What's wrong, Zesty?"

"What?" Solarte startles me out of my thoughts.

"You're crying."

"I am?" I reach to my eyes, touch the wetness that I hadn't felt streaming over my cheeks, and look down to see the accumulation forming almost an arrow of a stain on my sweatshirt. I open my mouth to say something, but nothing comes out, so we sit there together in silence, until the motion-sensor lights in Solarte's office click the room into darkness and I come to realize that the bitterest thing I've ever tasted are my own tears, which just won't seem to stop falling.

THIRTY-FIVE

I make it clear to Anitra Tehran that she has to meet me on my turf this time, my insistence delivered with a guarantee for her safety that only a cop bar like JJ Foley's affords.

I'd stopped back home, changed into my messenger gear, and when I arrived at the bar, stashed my bike next to the side door that opens off the alley. Jerry's not working tonight, but his youngest son, Jeremiah, fills in capably for him, a third generation of Foley behind the stick, as professional a bartender as you'll find anywhere in this city. Shirt. Tie. Apron. Bar rag.

Anitra Tehran looks amused. And alluring. She's ditched her Pats hoodie and Kevlar for dark jeans and a black sweater, her hair loose around her shoulders. Patent leather unlaced Doc Martens rest on the rail below our high chairs at the bar.

"What is it?" I say to her after introducing Tehran to Jeremiah, who before serving our drinks and making himself scarce had shifted into wingman mode and talked me up like I was the second coming of Ryan Gosling.

"You must be a big tipper." Tehran holds up her shot of Jameson and we clink glasses and throw them back with a chaser of Guinness. "And he didn't even ask you what you wanted. This is your place, huh?"

"Continuity," I say. "It's an underrated quality."

"I've got a lot to learn." Tehran looks around again, though when she'd first come in, she'd made a circuit around the bar looking at all the pictures, jerseys, and clippings as if she were at a museum. "I didn't even know this kind of place existed anymore. It's the real deal. And if I was to listen to Jeremiah, so are you."

"Take it with a grain of salt," I say. "He hasn't seen my bank statements and he probably thinks this is a date."

"Common mistake lately," Tehran complains lightly, a shade of mischief in her eyes that I haven't seen before, maybe the Jameson going straight to her head. "Should we pretend?"

"You haven't seen my bank statements, either."

"What makes you think that matters to me?" The twinkle is gone, replaced by something else.

"I dunno, I'm sorry."

"No, really, I want to know. What are you trying to say?"

"We're just different is all. You're an accomplished professional, educated. . . ." My words drift off and I let my open hands say the rest.

"Oh, I get it." Tehran downs half her beer in one pull, wipes her ringless fingers across her lips. "We're divided by what, class, is that it? Upbringing? You were raised by wolves?"

"Practically. Where did you go to school?" I ask.

"Harvard. What difference does that make?"

"I did two years at UMass-Boston. Barely. Tell me the last three dates you've been on, what did those guys do for a living?"

"Are you serious?"

"Yeah. Stop buying time trying to come up with something to say. What did they do?"

"Bond trader, lawyer . . ." Anitra Tehran bites her lip and squints in thought. "High-tech start-up."

"Thank you," I say.

"What's that prove? I'm not dating them now. And I didn't go out with them because they flashed me their bank statements." Anitra turns the question around like any good reporter would. "Give me *your* last three dates."

"They weren't exactly dates," I say.

"No? So what are you telling me, they were hookups? Internet flings?"

"No. No Internet. I'm just saying it was more . . ." I stall to find the right word. "Organic," I choose poorly, regretting the sound of it the second it comes out of my mouth.

But Anitra Tehran only laughs. "You mean there was alcohol involved?"

"Exactly." I point at her.

"What do you think this is?" Anitra rattles her empty shot glass on the bar.

"Okay," I say. "You win."

"Win what?"

"I dunno, whatever point you're trying to make, debunking whatever the hell I was trying to tell you."

"Which was what, remind me." Tehran angles her head a little, looking up into my eyes with a neutral smile on her lips, still with a dab of Guinness foam that she'd missed.

I shake my head. "I'm sorry, I'm bad at this." I look down the bar where Jeremiah is tending to a couple of Gang Crime officers with shaved domes and matching BDP windbreakers.

"Your friend can't save you, Zesty. You're on your own with this. Come on, you can do it."

"All right," I say, giving up on Jeremiah. "After all this is over, I mean the Rambir Roshan thing, the Russians, can I maybe, like, ask you out?"

"Out where?" Tehran's not going to make this easy.

"On a date?"

"Aw, aren't you cute. That was really hard for you, wasn't it?"

"Yeah," I admit. "Usually I just go with 'baby, let me be your bad-boy mistake.'"

"That's pretty terrible." Tehran laughs. "So let's see just how bad you are. What's that phone you got there, you've been treating it like a hot potato since we got here. There something you want to show me?"

There is. I do.

"I don't understand," she says. "Whose phone is that?"

I tell her and watch Anitra trying to piece things together, but coming up empty except for, "It's about timing, isn't it?"

"In comedy and in life," I say, and explain the significance of the picture's locations in case she doesn't recognize them.

"Your brother's got something on FBI Agent Lee?" Tehran connects a few of the dots on her own. "And we can assume he gave you the phone because he's got those pictures saved elsewhere."

"I figure."

"Have you considered . . ." Tehran slides off her stool and whispers in my ear, so close that I can smell the Jameson on her warm breath. ". . . that maybe he's listening to our conversation with that thing right now, or at the least tracking you with the signal?"

No, I shake my head, I hadn't considered that at all. Except now it was my turn to slide off my chair and whisper in Tehran's ear.

"No," Tehran says, "not paranoid. Cautious." She waves Jeremiah over and asks him to stash the phone somewhere next door for a few minutes, which he does without question. Like I said, Boston's most professional bartender.

"So tell me about your deal with Lee." Tehran is satisfied enough now to speak in her normal voice, sliding back up onto her chair. I want to tell her I preferred the whisper and the warmth, but I'm not nearly that confident. She'd sidestepped my asking her out like a pro. Gentle. No hurt feelings. Then again, she hadn't said no.

Zesty Meyers, optimist in training.

I tell her everything I'd learned at MIT and through Lee, some of it cross-referenced with what she already knew, having talked to many of the same people before being escorted off campus by Rosalinda Worth's ever-present force.

"Wow, some reporter I am." Tehran's clearly impressed with what I'd garnered, though she shouldn't be. My father had always maintained that an emblem of authority—badge, license, press card—automatically makes people wary, especially people who have something to hide. And most everyone on the MIT campus had something to hide. What held Tehran back was the reporter's rulebook and the lanes in which she operated, but to me, a messenger at heart, every street runs both ways, regardless what the signs say. But Tehran is smart and she'd been busy, too. And as I already knew, in touch with Detective Wells. Share and share alike.

"First of all, it looks like I'm in the clear, safety-wise. Batista's put out the word that whatever someone thought only I knew is now shared knowledge. Getting rid of me won't stop anything. I'll start with the account numbers, just for the sake of sequence, to keep everything straight in my own head, though you know about the ATM and account hack scam already through Lee and Worth. By the way, Worth is no joke. That lady was straight-up CIA, posted in Libya for a stint, Turkey, Poland. She's covered some ground."

"Should I be surprised?"

"No. MIT, beyond hosting heads of state and presidents, which requires some serious knowledge of security measures, has a pipeline of engineers and government contracts for defense, weapons, cyber-warfare; anything you can think of, they're pretty much spearheading it. These contracts are worth billions of dollars and billions more if we start talking endowment money from big-ticket donors. It's no surprise they'd cover up this hacking scheme Rambir thought up, maybe with Professor Fuji, using those idiots at the card game. There's your Russian connection, coke and whores. It didn't take a genius for Katanya to realize there was way more money being thrown around than there should be and to work it back to Rambir and Fuji to cut him and his boss, Namestnikov, a slice. And I've been told Namestnikov is probably dead?"

"That's what I heard."

"So who could kill a Russian crime boss and his right-hand man and think he can get away with it without retaliation?"

I don't have an answer to that, but I say, "Left-hand man. They only found his left."

"Ugh, Zesty, that's terrible. You do that a lot?"

"What's that?"

"Put shit out there to see what sticks, gets a rise out of people?"

"Beats small talk," I say.

"Who told you that?"

"I know, 'you love me, I'm perfect, now change.'" I finish my beer and smile at Tehran with a foam mustache.

"God, Zesty. You really are a piece of work." Anitra Tehran shakes her head with a bemused frown on her face. Or is it disgusted? "Worse even than Batista told me."

"You asked?" A glimmer of hope.

"Try to focus, please. Katanya dead. Namestnikov gone. Who could make this happen?"

"And don't forget Powers and McGowan trying to catch the Roshan case so bad they'd drag his body across to their side of town."

"Right. Excuse my shitty Shakespeare, but methinks something stinks in Cambridge."

"Amen to that." I wave Jeremiah away as he gestures to our glasses. I've got about two hours before my set at the Hong Kong and tipsy won't work well for me, though I'd probably burn off the alcohol by the time I bike it up Mass Ave.

"Well, here's what I got." Tehran produces a small leather-bound reporter's notepad, flips it open. "It seems like those one hundred and thirty-seven account numbers were months old and unless there are other files with other accounts on them, it looks like Rambir hit the brakes on the money train a while ago."

"Why would he do that?" Did Worth warn him off? Cut a deal that everything could go back to normal if he just ceased and desisted, could even keep his windfall from the scam? That kind of deal would have had to involve Worth's overseers at MIT and Lee's handlers at the highest levels of the FBI, too. Those were federal crimes. Money laundering. Mail fraud. Old hat for the Boston branch of the FBI. Nothing they hadn't done before with a lot more bodies to bury.

Tehran's answer is not something I expected: "Those files that Rambir had on there? The Monopoly names? He'd moved on to another scam, something he didn't need to share to get the money out."

"Which was what?"

"Ransomware." Tehran's juiced now, having caught the missing pieces I provided, fitting everything together. "Do you know what that is, Zesty?"

"I'm assuming it still involves hacking into somebody's computer," I say. "Beyond that . . ."

"It's actually pretty old-school in nature, but yes, it starts with a hack. Rambir could target a computer, pretty much any computer he wanted, and send the user something they'd click on, which would then download a compromised file onto their hard drive. Anything, really, it could be a PDF, a picture. Or he could entice them to join an infected file-sharing network, like a pirated music- or video-streaming service. Let the algorithm figure out what the user was interested in and send them something to click on. Once it's embedded, the ransomware actually searches and filters files that are likely to be valuable to the owner of the computer, like old photos, compromising or just sentimental, tax filings, investment data—"

"Files with Monopoly names. Shell companies. LLCs."

"Exactly."

"Okay, so the computers are infiltrated. What then?"

"The files get compromised. Rambir encrypts the data and then offers to unencrypt it, basically sell back the data to the owner. Literally ransoming the information, just like kidnappers sending a ransom note demanding payment."

"Except now instead of a live body it's information they're holding."

But the issue with kidnapping is always about getting paid. Kidnapping generally fails because the kidnappers have to collect their money at some point. And that's when they either get smoked or arrested. So how did Rambir get paid? Or is that when he was killed, when he went to pick up his payment?

"Do you know what Bitcoin is, Zesty?"

"Some new Internet currency?"

"Exactly. Rambir takes his payments in Bitcoin and it's basically untraceable. At a later date he can sell off his collection of Bitcoins on a private exchange, which is pretty murky to begin with, and walk away with cold hard currency."

"That's fucking insane," I say. "There's no guarantee Bitcoin is going to be worth anything in two days, let alone two years. It's not regulated, right? It's not recognized by any country. It's a fucking scam. Those Monopoly names? He might as well be paid in Monopoly money. It's not real cash, it's a fucking computer program!"

"It's real if people think it's real and are willing to pay for it," Tehran counters. "Wire transfers, direct deposits, bank cards, microchips. Fifteen years ago it wasn't conceivable to the average citizen that they'd hardly ever see the money they earned, paper money, but that's where we're heading."

"It's lunacy," I say. "But okay. So this is Rambir's latest scheme. I still don't get how it ties in to him getting killed. Katanya and Namestnikov came into play through the poker games. And do we know for sure that Rambir was actually pulling off these ransoms, like getting paid?"

"We do. You ready for this? When Wells's techno-geeks cracked the files, they found one belonging to Newton-Wellesley Hospital. He hightailed it there and pressed them, played the murder investigation card, obstruction, until they admitted they'd paid to have their files unencrypted."

"What?"

"Think about it, Zesty. Patient financial data, private medical information, even vital patient chart data, drug allergies, things like that, are all on computers. The hospital paid the ransom right away, I mean as soon as their IT people told them to. In a matter of *hours*."

"For how much?"

"It was pretty cheap. Twenty-five thousand dollars."

"You mean cheap in comparison to the lawsuits if something went wrong with a patient because their charts were tied up."

"Exactly. There were other places, too, including some small suburban police departments. Hingham. Concord. They all paid. And kept their mouths shut out of embarrassment. It's the perfect crime."

"I still don't—"

"You remember the package that was messenger delivered to me? The one with the false leads that had me and Wells chasing our own tails for a couple of days? Here's where they screwed up. Whoever 'they' is, we still don't have a clue about that. But I tracked down the messenger who'd made the drop at the *Globe* offices. Through his dispatch. And sure enough it was a street corner pickup."

Which wasn't that unusual; sometimes people meet us on the

run, picking up ball game or theater tickets on-site, or doing business out of a coffee shop or restaurant without faxes and copy machines, a live signature still required on some paperwork. The question is, where did the messenger make the pickup?

"Innovation Row." Tehran uses the name given to part of the new South Boston waterfront, where a large number of start-ups and tech companies have set up shop.

Back in the day, the Southie waterfront was an industrial wasteland—storage facilities and truck depots—about as private a place as any to shoot somebody in the head and leave the body for the wharf rats to feast on.

"Please don't call it that," I say. "It fuckin' depresses me."

"Okay. You want to take a guess who just set up a new branch, has their headquarters right there around the corner?"

"I don't have to guess, I'm a messenger, remember?" I point toward tonight's outfit, a black crew-neck Adidas sweatshirt with the white Trefoil logo, and black Lycra tights under black Adidas basketball shorts. Impossible to see at night on my bike. Less of a target for Boston drivers. "Kirilenko Labs," I say.

"The MIT internship capital. Where Sam Budoff and Rambir both worked."

"You think Kirilenko is tied into the Russian Mob? They're, like, one of the biggest cyber-security firms in Boston. They probably even have government contracts. Nah, I don't buy that."

"Okay," Tehran concedes. "We don't know how deep this goes, but what we do know is that Newton-Wellesley Hospital and all the police departments had contracts with Kirilenko Labs to secure and prevent things like ransomware from happening to them. Another firm that had a contract with Kirilenko, the one that had the Monopoly names, belongs to Visners & Miraglia, a title holding company and real estate escrow firm who also have their offices in South Boston."

"Slow down for me, we're back in your boyfriend tax bracket again," I say. "What's a title company do?"

Tehran ignores my boyfriend comment and explains, "What we think is that when Rambir wasn't playing online poker or falling asleep at his terminal, he was trolling contracts that Kirilenko had. Newton-Wellesley and the police departments were all clients. Visners & Miraglia. Rambir essentially downgraded their defenses and inserted the malware, then brought them back up to speed. If anybody noted the disruption, it was only temporary and nothing was disturbed or stolen. He waited a bit and then struck, pretty much testing his methods."

"And they worked," I say.

"Perfectly."

"And at this point he's no longer hacking personal accounts for his ATM scam that MIT and the FBI were covering up, or at least not prosecuting."

"Not prosecuting yet." Anitra buying Lee's claim that the FBI was holding off because they were trolling for bigger fish.

"So where did he screw up enough to get himself killed?"

"Well, let's get back to the title company. Basically, what a title company does is act as a middleman between a property buyer and seller when there's a formal purchase agreement. They're involved in the transfer of titles and help the buyers take possession of titles, and they play a large role in the formal sales closing."

"I don't get it. This all sounds like traditional paperwork."

"I'm not done. The title company also maintains escrow accounts for both the buyer and the seller. If it's a big company with a large client base, those accounts could be in the tens of millions."

"So Rambir hit the title company and got those millions?"

"No." Tehran shakes her head. "He didn't get a chance to. Because somebody killed him before he made the demand."

"And you know who that is?"

"No. But I think I know they killed him because they wanted those files back."

Only Rambir didn't have them anymore, they were in Wells's hands now. And the title holding company was the missing link to all those shell companies Tehran had initially reported on. The only real questions remaining were who owned Visners & Miraglia and were they worried enough about being exposed to do something more about it?

THIRTY-SIX

I open my Hong Kong set with a joke about marriage and death, which gets a pretty good laugh. It goes a little something like this: *Half of all marriages end in divorce. The other half, it means, end in death. So if I was a divorce attorney, my tag line would be: Hire me, I'm the only way you get out of this deal alive.*

It's all downhill from there. And as I head back to the South End it only gets worse, a black town car with midnight windows revving behind me as I cruise down Bow Street and then scraping me into the row of parked cars. I take out four sideview mirrors like an alpine skier, the impact crumpling the front wheel of my bike and bouncing me hard to the pavement. I'm not really hurt, only a bit stunned, as the town car screeches to a stop; maybe all the poker winnings and hard-earned cash in my bag cushioned the blow.

It doesn't do anything to cushion the straight punch to my face from the driver who'd gotten out of the car and follows up with "*Zdravstvuj,* asshole" before throwing me into the back of the limo and shutting the door.

It takes me a second to realize I'm not alone, my eyes watering uncontrollably from the punch, tears mixing with the blood gushing from my nose onto the front of my sweatshirt.

"Hello, Zesty Meyers." Antti Voracek's accent is heavy with the guttural roll of the Soviet Bloc, the verbal equivalent of the car's garish interior: upholstered blue velvet ceiling with corded maroon piping, the windows heavily tinted and curtained, the view to the outside shaded almost to black. But I can see the smudge of the driver tossing my bike against a fire hydrant and get a little bit of karmic retribution moments later as something thumps from the front with a bilingual curse, the driver maybe hitting his head as he gets back in. There's a highly polished thick wooden partition between the front seat and the back, for maximum privacy. It smells like cigarettes and boiled cabbage.

Voracek is one of those rare people who looks the same in person as he does in photographs; in his case, like a gorilla haphazardly stuffed into a suit cut from silver shadows, a black toupee malingering on a granite-block head. He doesn't have a gun or any weapon that I can tell, but the door locks had engaged loudly when the driver returned and I'd been too dazed to make a break for it. I should have taken back Charlie's gun when I had the chance. Too late now.

Voracek studies me for a moment and shakes his head like he's already come to the conclusion that this endeavor will be a waste of his time. I've seen this expression before, usually on blind dates.

"Here's how this is going to go, Zesty," he says. "The first question I'm going to ask you requires an answer I can verify and if you hesitate, Nikita there in the front seat is going to chop off your thumb with a gardener's clip. He's good with tools, yes? It comes from practice. Do you understand?"

"Yes," I say.

"Yes, what?"

"I understand," I say, using the sweatshirt to sop the blood from my nose.

"Good." Voracek knocks angrily on the separating panel, beyond which I hear Nikita the Gardener rummaging loudly in the glove box. "Where are my files?"

"Fuck you," I answer. "And by 'fuck you' I mean it's too late. Other people have them. Boston Police."

"That's a shame." Voracek sighs heavily.

Again he knocks a heavy simian knuckle on the wood partition, which slides down to reveal Nikita brandishing his garden tool, a small sharp snipper with green rubber grips, and a resplendent Wells leaning over him, his fedora crushed low on his head, almost shading his eyes. Wells has his pistol screwed so far into Nikita's ear it looks like he'd cut the barrel off at the base.

"Let me tell you how this is going to go." Wells, with his free hand, pops the automatic locks on the doors while continuing to apply pressure into Nikita's ear, forcing him to lean his head all the way to the black window glass. Nikita drops the snipper. There's blood on his blond hair. Wells's eyes are feverish.

"Zesty here is going to get out of this car with all his fingers attached and you, Mr. Voracek, are going to go to your bosses and tell them that their troubles are over, Sam Budoff, no Sam Budoff, it doesn't matter. Your files from Visners & Miraglia, where you're a silent partner. It ends here. Am I making myself clear?"

"Bosses?" Voracek chuckles, his small eyes black as coals. "I have no bosses. Only clients."

Wells is sweating under the hat, the band darkening with moisture. I've never seen Wells sweat before. He doesn't seem used to it, his eyes twitching wildly. His fine cologne smells like it's soured on his body. Like it's expired. He says, "You know you're going to have to shoot him, Zesty."

"Nyet." Nikita grunts and says something to Voracek in Russian as Wells leans harder into his ear, almost sitting on top of him.

"What?" I say, shaking my head. "I'm not shooting anybody. What are you talking about?" There's something in Wells's eyes I've never seen before, emotion without calculation. Something messy.

Wells shoves the hand not holding his gun inside Nikita's suit jacket and comes out with another gun before putting it down beside him and rummaging through his own suit jacket. It only takes him a second to find what he's looking for, a handkerchief, which he deftly wraps around the grip, his face across the partition dividing line just inches from mine as he offers it to me.

"Do you hear me? Take it." Wells's eyes are hard, but his voice is pleading.

"You are out of your jurisdiction, I believe, Detective Wells." Voracek shrugs dismissively, missing what I'm seeing.

"Shut up!" Wells screams at him.

"Even if my clients were assured Anitra Tehran would not report the true owners of the buildings, the source of their money, they would not be comfortable. I have to keep my clients happy, you see. Namestnikov, Katanya, they were too noisy. They stirred up too much trouble. And over what? Peanuts. I think it's time you made a call, Detective. Who would you like to come pick us up? McGowan and Powers, perhaps?"

"There's no other way," Wells says to me.

"This is beyond amusing." Voracek smiles.

"Don't." I'm not sure who I'm addressing, Voracek or Wells, but all the oxygen seems to have been sucked out of the car and I feel like I'm about to throw up or hyperventilate. Nikita feels it, too. Probably because he's seen it from the other side. When he chopped off Oleg Katanya's dick. Maybe when he shot Rambir Roshan.

"No," I choke, but Wells's eyes are on full tilt now, exploding cherry bombs of slot machine jackpots.

Voracek laughs and casually lights a cigarette. "Ah, what theater!" he says. "Bravo!"

"Take it!" Wells shoves the gun into my chest. "Wrap that into the trigger guard. Yes, like that. Point it at his head."

"Wells," I say.

"Do it!" he screams.

I do it, but Voracek's smile only grows. "You are out of your jurisdiction, Detective. Out of your league." He blows smoke in my face. "A stupid cow reporter and this idiot. How do you see this ending for you, Detective? Not well, I imagine."

"Shut up, Voracek!"

"Or you'll arrest me? Yes, let's do that. Your legal system is second to none. Let us engage."

"No. I can't arrest you," Wells says in a calm and soothing voice that doesn't calm me at all. "You want to know why that is, Antti?"

Voracek's face goes hard and ugly at the use of his first name, Wells having just found the Russian Mob boss's tell.

"Because I'm still home, Antti." Wells, recognizing the change, too, uses the name again. "Ordered a movie online and tucked myself into bed. And the lobby cameras in my building will confirm it."

"So?" Voracek says, but something moves in his throat, something new in his eyes that I recognize as the look of someone who realizes that his hand might not hold up, that the cards he'd thought would carry the day, have always carried the day, have betrayed him. Fear is what it is. Straight-up piss-inducing fear. But Voracek isn't looking at Wells, he's looking at me. What could he possibly be seeing?

"The problem is, you people never listen," Wells says, his words coming in cold but not cooling anything. "You'll kill Anitra

Tehran and Sam Budoff when he shows up, and Zesty. And maybe even me and Brill eventually because you know we won't let it stand, we'll keep coming after you."

"Of course." Voracek shrugs like there's no other alternative but his eyes keep growing wider, staring at my face. What does he see?

"Even though I've told you that you're in no danger from these files, that we'll take this no further than Rambir."

"Rambir is nothing. And had we been the ones to find him it would not have been so quick. But it's just your word, Detective, you must see that. And there's too much money involved. Your assurances are worthless. Perhaps if it was only you . . ." Voracek turns his face from me to Wells. "You don't look so well, Detective. But let's be reasonable. This is only a business deal. You and your partner will survive this and grow rich. Of that, you have my word. The others, no. We warned the reporter. She chose to ignore it. So go back to your Boston home, Detective, across the river to your movie, to the comfort and assurances of your life. We'll find Budoff on our own. You know we will. And after we do, Nikita will visit the reporter and rape—"

The roar of our guns begin without words between us, without warning, without thought. Twin flashes of spark lightning illuminating a menagerie of haunted house images, blood splatter and brains painted on the windows and ceiling, the cramped interior exploding with as deafening a sound as I've ever heard, until our guns click on empty, the cordite and gunpowder sting our eyes, and the only sound that remains is me and Wells screaming our rage into a bottomless midnight abyss.

THIRTY-SEVEN

The Rabbi answers the door at my father's home, takes one look at the blood all over my sweatshirt and shorts, and ushers me past my father, who sits at the poker table listening to Karl Klaussen singing on Mass's only album, no telling how many times the record has been replayed behind my father's empty eyes.

I strip and step into the shower and stay there a long time, scrubbing myself raw under the scalding water, before stepping out and parting the curtain to watch the Rabbi methodically burning my clothes in the backyard barbecue pit, stirring it every once in a while with a stick to make sure everything is destroyed, including my sneakers, melted down to slag; the smell of burning rubber reaches all the way up through the window.

I half expect the Brookline Police to show, solve a double homicide on the spot, due to a complaint about the foul odor of burning rubber, gold detective shields handed out all around, a lifetime of prison bars in front of my eyes. I find a change of clothes that I always keep in case of unexpected overnights, get dressed, and come downstairs to sit with my father at the poker table after turning the record over to side two, Klaussen belting out:

> When the door shuts
> It shuts forever
> When the moon is out
> It's black as leather

My father doesn't reach for the cards in front of him. He doesn't hold the chips stacked in his well. Doesn't mouth the lyrics to the song that he once knew so well, doesn't recognize me when he turns his head, finally acknowledging my presence. But something new registers in his eyes.

My father, I realize, *knows*. Somehow that gift, that curse, is still alive in there. The Rabbi can burn the evidence and I can scrub my skin and put on the poker face that he taught me so diligently during my lifetime, but from him, I can't hide what I've done. *Those were your cards,* my father's eyes tell me. *Too deep to fold, only one way to play them.*

This is what happens when you swim with sharks, my father's eyes tell me. *There's always blood in the water. The real trick is making sure it's not yours.*

At least that's the way I interpret them as the Rabbi joins us silently at the table. Whether I'm right or wrong, who can tell? But I understand my father differently now that I've made the same kind of decision he must have made in his past. I've been freed from the burden of judging him. Isn't that a gift of sorts?

"The scholar Nachmanides," the Rabbi's voice startles me, "refers to Jehu, the son of Jehoshaphat, as someone who lived his life like a maniac, the Bible even reporting that Jehu was known for driving his chariot wildly, in a disordered state."

"Huh? What?"

"Though Jehu is generally known more for slaughtering Judah and overthrowing the evil kings of Israel in an orgy of blood in the ninth century B.C.E. And, it must be noted, for personally trampling Jezebel to death. He was an unpredictable and disorganized man. But he did the Lord's work even while he was the prince of instability. Is that where you are now, Zesty? Have you turned that corner?"

"I don't know," I say. "I—"

"Then consider this: You're a messenger by trade, by temperament. Speed and efficiency are essential as you move towards your destination. Sometimes it is the same concept with spirituality. There is something to be said regarding spiritual efficiency. Do you understand what I'm telling you?"

"No."

"Simplified, then: Sometimes, perhaps, the most efficient route to spirituality is through fire."

"How would you know?" I say sharply. I know they're unkind words, but I say them anyway.

"I served in the Israeli Army." The Rabbi grunts a silent laugh and rubs his bandaged knuckles. "Before being ordained. In Lebanon. You know of this?"

"No."

"There, so now you do. And if I might have the last word: You know what I think your problem is, Zesty? You thrive in confusion. The more convoluted the situation, the more threads coming undone, the better you become. This is not an insult. Unpredictability focuses you and you convert it into formulas of probability as best you can. That is why poker runs in your family blood. Chaos becomes you. Chaos as tradition. There's no need to close your heart around whatever it is you've done. It will be harder to serve your father if you do. You and Zero still have duties to fulfill. Obligations. Your father's soul will soon be in your hands. It's too soon for you to have a broken heart. You have a job to do."

When dawn breaks, my father has moved to the couch and rests with a blanket that I'd covered him with. The Rabbi sleeps nearby in the platform rocker. My father seems more withered under the thin covers, slighter than he's ever been, older. I hear the early birds outside starting to sing for their meal money. They don't seem to care what I've done, either. *Life goes on if you let it,* they sing. Sometimes maybe it really is just a choice.

"I forgive you," I whisper to my sleeping father. "I forgive you. And I'll do what you couldn't do, Dad. I'll forgive myself, okay? You hear me? I won't let it bury me. I know you can hear me."

I wake the sleeping rabbi with my foot. "I'm ready," I tell him as he rubs his eyes and stretches himself out of the chair.

"Ready for what, Zesty?"

"To listen. To learn. Just tell me what I'm supposed to do, Rabbi. Teach me the words you've been teaching Zero," I say.

And he does.

THIRTY-EIGHT

"You're late." Brill's smoldering cigar jumps as he speaks. He's in his overalls again, this time with large kneepads worn over the outside of the pants. If a volleyball game breaks out, he's ready. There's no door hanging yet on the bathroom, and I can see the plumbing has been installed and the floor tiles laid down, a nice pale blue-turquoise mix that reflects the late morning light on the white walls. It has the feel of a tranquil aquarium tank.

Only the room smells of smoke. Badly. Not entirely cigar smoke.

"You should get the flue checked," I say.

"Flue's fine. You here to consult or work?"

"Wells—"

"Won't even pick up a damn screwdriver unless it's got a napkin wrapped around it and an orange slice sticking out the top." Brill takes the cigar from his mouth and leans in close enough to my face to kiss me, searching my eyes for something that won't be there.

"Huh." He leans back, satisfied. "Foxhole buddies forever. I'll be damned."

"I'm here to work," I say. "I already took your money, I'm just trying to earn it now."

"Well, all right then." Brill returns me my space.

"But you're gonna have to show me, though. You realize that, right? This is all new territory to me."

"We'll work on it together, then. It's not like we got to build the foundation or anything. We're at the point now where we're just covering up and making shit pretty, smoothing over the rough edges. I was right about your taping job, though." Brill points to the living room wall, small bulges running down the length of the Sheetrock panels where I'd worked with my unskilled hands.

"We gonna redo it?"

"Fuck no. Like you said, just cover it with some artwork or something. Anyhow, didn't you say you were looking for a new place?"

THIRTY-NINE

Lee meets me in Zero's office. There was no need to give him directions, he's been here before.

I take out Lee's phone and place it on Zero's desk as Zero drives his thumb below his eyebrow to dissipate the headache I'm causing him. Lee looks starched. Straight-up stiff in a suit.

"I'm surprised you didn't get rid of it." Lee looks at the phone, but doesn't touch it.

"What's the point, right? You can ping my locations anyhow,

figure out where I've been. Is there anything else that phone can do?"

"No," Lee says. "It's just a phone."

"A phone that doesn't fucking exist." Zero gives up on his self-healing touch, opting as he usually does to embrace the pain. Or at least the annoyance, the prophecy of the other shoe falling coming to immediate fruition.

"That's correct," Lee confirms. "A phone that doesn't exist and doesn't have Zesty at the site of a double homicide, though nearby, which can be explained by his appearance onstage at the Hong Kong. By the way, how did your set go?"

"Were you there?" I ask.

"No."

"I killed," I say.

"Jesus Christ!" Zero exclaims.

"No, it's a good thing, I think," Lee addresses my brother. "Hasn't this always been the way he has coped?"

Partners in suffering, Zero and Lee finally find something to agree on. It's enough for Zero to swivel in his chair and spin the dial on the safe a few times before opening the heavy door. He sets a small wrapped bundle down next to the phone and uncovers it for Lee to see.

"You ever go scuba diving, Lee? Florida? The Caymans?" Zero tilts his head toward the scuba gear in the corner. "I could give you a good deal on the suit."

"No, thank you."

"I don't blame you. After seeing all the shit that was still down there in the channel . . ." Zero shakes his head. "It's practically an entire neighborhood, parked cars, half a building, I swear. If Atlantis had a ghetto, I just found it. And fuckin' Gillette oughta be tarred and feathered for what they done."

"You strike me as an unlikely environmentalist," Lee says.

"What are you talking about? My boxes are made from re-cycled cardboard. Those giant rubber bands? Cut from old tire tubes. And my trucks, I'm having them converted to biodiesel."

"Interesting." Something recalibrates in Lee's eyes. A momentary pause like a GPS that's just steered itself into a dead end.

"Well, I got a kid now," Zero explains. "It makes you see shit differently. We good?"

"We are." Lee rewraps the rusted Glock and places it in the briefcase by his feet. "Don't be surprised if Cambridge Homicide shows up to ask you a few questions. It's just due diligence. They know nothing, will learn nothing, from the Bureau, from me."

"Powers and McGowan?" I ask.

"Possibly. Depending on what Cambridge Internal Affairs already has on them or whether they want to own the stain of two corrupted Homicides. Anyhow, even if it is McGowan and Powers riding shotgun, it would not seem to be in their own best interest to solve this case, seeing how they are off their master's chain now."

"That's a good thing?" Zero looking at it from every conceivable angle, not entirely convinced. I want him to be convinced. Like both my parents, I made a choice that I thought was right, that was just. And in the heat of the moment.

Zero really was more like my father, more calculating. Would he take out two dirty cops if he thought that was the play? I don't doubt it for a second. I even believe Jhochelle would do it, trained Israeli sniper as she is. Who knows, maybe even the Rabbi would assist. Powers and McGowan wouldn't even know they were dead.

"I don't believe they are smart enough to put all the pieces together, if that's what you're asking. But I do think that they're intelligent enough in a self-serving manner to not look so hard. The same applies to the Russian Mob, what is left of it. We've picked up talk that perhaps Boston is not such a hospitable place to set up shop. The cost of everything is too high. Zesty is safe.

Cambridge will make a big deal of the Nikita Kucherov and Antti Voracek killings, the papers as well. But wait for a little time to pass; Harvard will lend their considerable weight to convincing CPD to move on quietly since it was so close to their campus. After all, there are no mourners clamoring for justice in this case and remember, as far as statistics are concerned, Rambir falls under unsolved for Boston Homicide, not Cambridge."

"And what if Rambir does get solved?" I say. Knowing Wells, I could have said *when* Rambir gets solved.

Lee is quiet for a long time as he plays the scenario out in his head. "That is entirely up to Detective Wells, I imagine." Lee stares hard at me, letting me know that he knows I wasn't alone on Bow Street. After all, there were two different guns used in the killing of Voracek and Kucherov, two different caliber bullets, which points to two shooters. "If he solves the Rambir murder, I suspect that he will control the narrative as best he can."

"You're talking about Anitra Tehran," I say.

"Yes."

"I think she'll cooperate," I say. "Though I doubt she'll let him write the story himself." By which I mean, she'll have the inside track on her scoop and write her piece and collect her accolades and never really learn what Wells and I did for her. For Sam Budoff. For all of us.

MIT won't like it, whatever *it* turns out to be. But they have the machinery in place to limit the damage and someone more than capable of doing it in Rosalinda Worth. At least until she figures out it might be her conscience that's bothering her, her name-memory issues maybe manifesting themselves out of guilt. But what the fuck do I know? Worth didn't say she was losing sleep and we can justify just about anything when our backs are to the wall.

"And what about you?" Zero looks to close the loop. "Your people?"

"We will follow up on the files and see where they lead, but these are financial crimes we're looking at, movement of money, wire fraud, perhaps money laundering. Essentially work for lawyers over expensive lunches and riverfront views."

"Tawdry," I say, because it is tawdry and because it's a classic word to be spoken in a heavy Boston accent, like *cahs,* and *buhrds,* and no holds *bahhed*.

"Yes," Lee agrees. "Tawdry to the extreme. Boston is awash in money. Real estate money. High-tech money. Though there is very little out there on the streets."

"Except for the nearly million in poker chips Sam has," I remind Lee. "Rambir's chips. Maybe Yuki Fuji's chips."

"Like I said before, Zesty. That is Detective Wells's call. As far as I know there were only two poker chips from Mr. Roshan's socks and they are worthless. And that is all that I am putting in my report on the matter."

Which actually causes Zero to smile. "It's a pleasure doing business with you, Agent Lee." Zero brings the meeting to a close. "Don't take this the wrong way, but unless you need someone to move you out of town I hope I never run into you again."

"Likewise." They shake hands and look at me like a stain on the carpet they can't get out.

FORTY

Wells and I share a table at Flour on Washington Street, the restaurant filled with green-and-blue-scrub-clad nurses and doctors from Mass General nearby. Or maybe we've stumbled into the casting call for the Boston version of *ER*.

Wells looks the same. By which I mean he shows the aftereffects of copious manscaping, his green eyes radiant and alert, his fine pinstripe suit and solid blue tie making him look taller than he is, his shoes making him seem richer than he must be. A lot of coffees get spilled around us, both men and women distracted by his star quality and graceful bearing. He'd be the perfect wingman if he could just tone it down a little, not attract all the attention.

Only, I can tell he's changed. It's the perfection that gives it away. It's calculated now, where before it just seemed to come naturally. His hair is gelled to a shellacked finish, hard like black ice camouflaging a rough road.

"We'll talk about this one time, Zesty, and then never again." Wells peers over my shoulder, feigning interest in a stunning brunet physician who wears her surgical scrubs like runway fashion.

"We don't have to talk about it at all." I don't feign interest in anyone. There's no point with Wells beaming Day-Glo heartthrob.

"No?" His eyes shift to mine. "There's still unfinished business."

"I know," I say. "You sure you want to do it here? Pretty public spot."

"It's perfect." Meaning it's loud with twenty conversations over the din of ordering, the percussion of plates, silverware, and loose change. Put it all together, it sounds like Iron Man falling down a flight of stairs.

"We did what we had to." Wells gives me the full measure of his eyes.

"I don't need convincing," I say.

"I see that. But still, I'm sorry. Really, that's why we're here. I needed to tell you that."

"Why? What are you apologizing for?"

"I could have done it myself. Should have."

"You mean like one, two, what's the difference once you cross that line . . . ?"

"Yes. There was no need for you to cross it."

"Are you religious, Batista? You don't really strike me as religious, but if you are, Cathedral's right down the street, we could go together and square this away for you."

"You mean confession?"

"No. I mean to get the weight of the angels off your shoulders. I think what's bothering you isn't that you shared the burden, responsibility, whatever you want to call it. It's that you're convinced it was the only way, that there wasn't any other option. And that conclusion runs counter to your . . ." I can't find the word. "It turns everything upside down for you" is what I manage.

"Maybe. It doesn't make it right."

"Yes, it does. It makes it exactly right. At least for me."

"And what does the Jewish faith have to say about this?"

"I'm not religious, either." I shrug.

"Really?" Wells sips his coffee. "You've been spending a lot of time with the Rabbi lately."

I sit back and smile. "You've been watching me."

"Like I said, we had unfinished business."

"So you've seen me in Somerville, too, on Hall Avenue?"

"Watching the blue house. Yes."

"Do you know why?"

"Sure. I talked to Solarte."

"Wow, all up in my business," I say calmly.

"A business I'm told you're pretty good at. Maybe you *should* think about it. You stack up apprentice hours with Solarte, get yourself a license, hang your own shingle after a while. Don't tell me Martha wouldn't join you in a heartbeat, trade quips with all the hot dames in furs that would come waltzing through your door."

"You mean live off all the cases you don't solve? Pretty slim living." I send Wells a rare compliment.

"There are other types of cases, no?"

"I'll give it some thought," I say. "Hell, I got a head start. I already drink Jameson."

"Exactly." Wells reaches into his suit jacket, pulls out nothing, and then pantomimes placing it on the table between our coffee cups. He looks at me with the old sparkle in his eye.

"What's that?" I play along.

"That," Wells says, "is the cold case file on Camilla Islas. Go ahead, open it."

"What are you getting at?"

Wells opens his hands to the imaginary file. "Just that."

"That there really is no file?"

"Precisely."

"I'm not following you," I say.

"Yes, you are, Zesty. Or you wouldn't be watching the house. Or hitting the restaurants and bars around Camilla Islas's old Davis Square neighborhood. You've already figured it out. You're just not sure how to play the hand."

"Thanks for the poker allusion," I say.

"You're welcome. I know it helps you see things for what they are."

"There used to be a cold case file," I say.

"Of course. Camilla Islas was declared dead in 1983, but the murder was never solved."

"So what happened to the file?"

"Stolen, probably. Misplaced? I'd go with stolen."

"By retired detective Peter Polishuk."

"Who else is there?"

"Who lost everything in a fire."

"Tragic and true."

"Before BPD moved from Berkeley Street to Ruggles and digitized all the files."

"Poof," Wells says with a flourish.

Dr. Love discreetly drops her card on our table as she makes her way out the door. Wells ignores it. So do I because what are my chances? And anyhow, lately, there's been a sea change in me; only one woman has been on my mind. It takes a lot of getting used to, especially because I haven't done anything about it yet and I'm not sure I will. Or can.

"I like men." Wells winks at me and flips his brand-new fedora onto his head.

FORTY-ONE

"So this is a real date?" Anitra Tehran smiles at me across the candlelit table at the Franklin Cafe, the place usually out of my price range only Sam had resurfaced and given Zero the go-ahead to turn the casino poker chips over to Darryl's men for forty cents on the dollar. Who then sold them for sixty cents on the dollar, flights to Vegas filling up fast with fools who think they can beat the house armed with house money.

Zero took a cut. Sam took a cut and donated a third of it to a harbor cleanup fund; I'm not quite sure if Zero had a hand in that decision, but it sure points that way. Sam has never cared much about money. He's an MIT grad with a goddamn doctorate, he can do whatever the hell he wants. The other thirds he split between an organization that assists homeless veterans and to directly secure an apartment for Charlie, back among his people in Medford.

With my share I paid Brill for two years' rent up front and figure I can get that up to three years with the sweat equity I've been putting in. The rest I donated to Alzheimer's research.

"I've been playing hard to get," I say. "Had to give myself time to heal up." I point to my face.

"A *month*?" Anitra says.

"I'm a slow healer. At least my face is."

"Which you busted up crashing your bike."

"That's right."

"Even though you're a pro."

"Boston," I remind her. "We live in Boston."

"And how exactly does Boston pavement taste?" Anitra's smile is there, but it's a reporter's smile, not a date's. Though she's wearing something fancier than jeans and a sweater tonight: a pencil tweed skirt and black sleeveless shirt. "Nowhere near as good as this meal," I say. "But maybe it's just the company."

"Hey, that's pretty slick." Anitra points her knife at me. "Definitely a step up from your 'bad boy' line." Her hair is downright silly: twin ponytails that are more punk rock than anything else, a shiny part straight down the middle.

"It's not a line," I say. "But enough about me, tell me about the files Sam unencrypted for you. I've been watching for your byline but you haven't written anything lately. You still have a job?"

"I do." Her date smile returns. Brown eyes flicker in the candle flames. Something inside my chest hurts. A lot. I try to ignore it.

"It basically comes down to this: Rambir was using the ransomware like we'd figured out before. He just had the dumb luck to encrypt and ransom the files of Visners & Miraglia, which Antti Voracek was a silent partner in. Files which included the holdings and titles of a half dozen Russian escrow accounts, all this big foreign money buying up Boston condominiums with price tags in the millions."

"Why?"

"Why what? Why buy property or why buy Boston property? It's really the same answer for both. It's a safe investment, especially in this new city. The values of these properties will only go up over time, barring a nuclear war. And the current laws still allow ownership to be cloaked in secrecy, layers and layers of LLCs and holding companies that don't have to report massive cash infusions like the banks do. It's essentially the perfect way to launder money. Big money. This story is fucking huge and it's not just a Boston story. It's the same in New York, Los Angeles, San Francisco, all the super-expensive towns."

"How much money are we talking about?"

"Do you know what deoffshorization is, Zesty?"

"Yeah, I think I tested negative for it last year."

"Very funny." She points the knife again.

"Everything else came up negative, too, I'm just saying."

"TMI," Tehran says, the knife still employed, this time with an extended arm, prompting me to back off. "And stay focused. I'm trying to teach you something here. Since Putin came to power, Russians have squirreled away hundreds of billions of dollars overseas. Even as the Kremlin was pushing a deoffshorization campaign, which is basically aimed at repatriating Russian capital. Just last year over a hundred billion dollars left the country and more is headed this way if the Russian economy continues to flop around like a dying fish. For wealthy Russians, these new Boston waterfront high-rises and condos, some of them selling for upwards of twenty, thirty million dollars, serve as a double parachute, a safe-deposit box of sorts, and a nice cushy landing spot in case the political climate back home forces them to run. You following me here?"

"You have pretty eyes," I say. "You don't even wear any makeup, do you?"

"Shut up. Even if these condos are empty, it doesn't matter. It's not like you'll notice a huge influx of Russians around town or anything. At least not like in some hot spots in London where you can't walk down the street and *not* hear Russian being spoken."

"Where did all this money come from?"

"Great question. A lot of people got rich when Yeltsin privatized Russia's massive state companies. The timing was perfect. Technology made it easier for vast sums of cash to flow unchecked across borders, shell companies were created in a day, whole colonies of the super-rich buying up property without ever having to put their own names on leases. Purchasers could legally register these companies in the names of accountants or lawyers, or relatives, or their fucking poodle, it almost seems. And these purchases at thirty, sixty million dollars at a pop can also be made by a group of investors, further obscuring the source of the money. And what's more, get this: Ownership of shell companies can be shifted at any time with absolutely no indication in property records. And all this continued in the first years under Putin."

"The makings of the oligarchs," I say.

"Exactly. You're pretty smart for a messenger."

"Ouch."

Anitra Tehran looks at me for a long time, starts to say something, but then pulls back.

"What?" I say.

"You were right, Zesty."

"About . . . ?"

"What you said about me and the men I dated. Pretty much all of them."

"There were a lot?" I wrinkle my face.

"Shut up. And the women who I work with, too. *And* my former classmates. Almost everyone had something cruel or snarky to say when I told them I was going on a date with you."

"Oh." I sigh. "Them, too, huh?"

"Yeah. There really is a class divide in this city, in the neighborhoods. I didn't look at it that way before I met you, but it runs deep. I see it now. It hurts you, doesn't it?"

"I just don't know exactly where I fit in anymore," I say. "Or if I want to if the city keeps turning like it is. I fucking love Boston, but I think I love it more for its scars and imperfections. Its rough spots. And all of that just seems to be getting smoothed over now. I dunno, maybe I'm just nostalgic. Anyhow." I shrug. "What did your coworkers say? That I'd take you to Wendy's, try to grope you in the alley behind JJ Foley's?"

"Pretty much. But actually, I like Wendy's and JJ Foley's is awesome."

"True, but you've never been in the alley. *No bueno.* Anyhow, I think we ought to finish up." Without our noticing, we were the last table seated, the waitstaff going about their preps, folding napkins, making up tables. I signal our waiter.

"Take your time," he says.

"That's sweet of him," Anitra says. "But I'll give you the condensed version. The files that Rambir encrypted and tried to ransom, as you know, belonged to Antti Voracek. Not directly, of course, but he had a substantial stake in Visners & Miraglia LLP. It was a legit business. Voracek could have just paid Rambir off in Bitcoin and be done with it, but he was afraid that Rambir might recognize all the LLCs, the names of some of these oligarchs, and then try to extort them directly or at the very least bring attention to them. The fact is he couldn't be more wrong. There's absolutely no incentive, in Boston at least, to identify the sources of this money tsunami. Hell, there's not even a legal obligation."

"On who?"

"Everybody who's getting rich off this cash and driving up the prices of your more modest places around here." Anitra switches to her fork this time, swirling around to indicate the surrounding South End neighborhood.

"And by modest, you're now talking only in that one-, two-million-dollar range."

"Exactly. Think about all the players involved: real estate agents, lawyers, accountants, escrow agents, title brokers, condo boards, contractors, building workers, construction companies—"

"Politicians. Campaign donations. Increased tax revenue."

"It's a perfect storm for those at the top," Tehran notes, attached to weather metaphors, which will probably get edited out when the final version of the story comes to print.

And Antti Voracek, as high in the Russian Mob as he was, still had the gutter's view and dealt in violence and death. Karma, if you believe in such things, as I do, though that doesn't really bode well for me in the long run.

"So you're no longer writing about Rambir's murder?"

"No."

"You don't look particularly upset about it," I say, the words not coming out like I'd meant them.

"There goes your groping in an alley," Tehran deadpans.

"Is *anybody* on it?"

"Not directly. But if Batista solves it, we'll cover it. To a degree."

To the degree that MIT and the Boston Police Department and the FBI all put their stamp of approval on it. Call me cynical, but I've seen this show before. It will be radio silence followed by a brief news conference, a story, and maybe a sidebar on page fourteen next to an ad for Bertucci's.

"Wells will solve it," I say. "Plus, Brill's been reinstated."

"I heard. Should we have a drink in his honor?"

"Let's do it at Foley's," I say. "It's practically around the corner."

Jeremiah is back working the bar when we get in and he pours us a couple of shots of Jameson, no beer chaser this time.

"To Brill." We clink glasses, throw the shots back.

"May he be a benevolent and responsive landlord."

The side door to the alley is propped open, a trio of cigarettes flaring as we step outside into the darkness.

"This here is—"

"When you should stop talking."

Anitra Tehran pins me to the brick wall and beats me to the grope.

FORTY-TWO

Dinner at Brill's means takeout from The Smoke Shop BBQ in Southie, plenty of napkins, and an outfit you don't mind getting sauce on. Wells eats standing up because he doesn't own anything he wouldn't mind getting stained. If you didn't know the four of us, you'd probably guess the apartment belonged to him since he was the only one who looked rich enough to afford it, restored as it was to its Victorian beauty: re-sanded hardwood floors by yours truly, repurposed window frames, the salvaged molding up and painted, built-in floor-to-ceiling bookcase, and an open kitchen divided by a pale granite slab countertop where the rest of us sit.

Wells looks around admiringly and says, "It's hard to believe this is the same place of a month ago. You guys went at it pretty hard the last few weeks, huh?"

"I told you," Brill says grumpily, back on the sharp ground of his partnership with Wells. "I used the money Zesty fronted me to hire a real work crew. With skills."

"For *your* floor, at least," Anitra points out. "I still get to wake up with plaster dust in my hair."

"That's your choice," Brill responds gruffly. "Deal with it."

"He's so sweet," Anitra says. She means it.

"Hope your insulation's tight. It's getting cold out there." Christmas lights had started to go up and I can see a neighbor across the way dragging through his door a tree like an open green umbrella.

"Those windows might look old, but they're new," Brill says. "Unless you're talking about noise." He points a thumb upstairs to my place.

"Puh-lease," Anitra says. "You don't hear a thing from us."

"I better not." He points a warning finger at Anitra, who doesn't blush at all.

"Quiet as a mouse," she says. "Anyhow, it's not like he's getting any. I've still got my own place and I've been busy."

Still working on the money trail and condo boom story, though the paper had reversed itself, tasking her with the Rambir story again because it's so juicy. After a few weeks Professor Yuki Fuji surfaced in Macau, the Las Vegas of Asia, which has no extradition treaty with the United States. Obviously, she had planned for the long game, her prior visits there to set herself up if she ever had to run. And run she had to.

Fuji was implicated in the murder of Rambir Roshan and it was a sensational story but one that ended abruptly because there would be no trial unless she set foot back into the country, which was highly unlikely.

Boston Police divers found the gun Fuji shot Rambir with as she tried to get ahold of the chips that Rambir had given to Sam for safekeeping.

Rambir had told Sam that he was meeting someone, though he wouldn't say who, and to bring the chips only when he called, the cautious approach of a poker player getting the sense something wasn't right, that a bad beat was coming his way.

He never called.

That was the theory anyway. Fuji had planned the meeting meticulously, worn a long man's coat sprayed with a heavy cologne, over a thigh-cut neoprene wet suit. The coat lacked any DNA evidence except the blood splatter, which was from Rambir, and the fabric from the coat that ended up on Roshan when Fuji shot him at close range without ever pulling out the gun.

Rambir probably never even knew what was happening to him, the shot muffled enough that nobody nearby remembered hearing any loud noise or seeing flashes from the barrel. Fuji ditched the coat, dove into the still relatively warm waters of the Charles River, and using whatever strokes had garnered her all those swimming medals left in her office, swam in darkness to the other side, the flashing blues of the converging Boston and Cambridge cruisers probably already visible by the time she pulled herself out, laced up a pair of sneakers she'd stashed, and jogged her way to her rented home near the MIT campus, her reentry caught on university cameras.

Cold. Calculated. Regret minimization theory to the *nth* degree. That's about as far as the story went, MIT throwing in a little misdirection with some inane dissertation dispute gone wrong, never mind Fuji's relatively large bank account cleaned out while Agent Lee, Rosalinda Worth, and I twiddled our thumbs in her campus office.

Life goes on. Until it doesn't.

FORTY-THREE

My father dies with Sid by his side. Unexpected, but expected. Which doesn't make it any easier. Zero handles all the arrangements; he'd been preparing longer than I had. He'd rehearsed his role, studied and prepared. Steeled himself. And crumbled. And I crumbled with him.

Memorial services are held at Temple Emanuel around the corner. It's packed. I don't know most of the people, but I know many, blurred as they are through tears that won't stop. Martha, Wells, Brill, Anitra, Charlie, Otis, Cedrick, a massive Star of David bouquet in blue and white carnations with a card from Darryl, retired detective Peter Polishuk, Jerry and Jeremiah Foley, Sid, Van Gogh Capizo, and the other men who looked after my father, too many movers and messengers to name, and I guess the usual congregants that frequent the temple. And family. Zero, Jhochelle, and Eli, who will have no recollection of this event at all, only stories that will one day take on the guise of memory.

Rabbi Day officiates. I assume he left his crowbar at home. He speaks eloquently and fondly of my father and the words pass through me and I can't remember a thing he says the second it's spoken though he told me earlier he wrote it all down and I'll read it when I'm ready. If I'm ever ready.

We sit shiva, cover the mirrors, greet long-lost friends and acquaintances, meet new faces, share memories and stories and food and booze and bong hits and music, lots and lots of music—Etta James, George Jones, Aretha, Marcus Roberts, Miles

Davis, Bonnie Raitt, Stan Getz, Charlie Parker—his entire vinyl collection of local Boston rock and roll—the Nervous Eaters, The Neighborhoods, the Cavedogs, Treat Her Right, the Lyres, Human Sexual Response—and poker. Endless rounds of poker for real, but not brutal stakes, chips stacked and then drained from wells, Lady Luck making the rounds; nobody getting hurt, losing more than they can afford to lose. That time has already passed.

"There is no commandment to be consoled," the Rabbi tells me after the seven days of shiva are over. "Or sober." He notes all the empty bottles around me.

"Those aren't mine," I say.

"I know." The Rabbi smiles. "I was seeing if you're ready."

"He's fuckin' ready," Zero says, coming in behind the Rabbi. He wears a crisp white shirt and a colorful yarmulke on his head.

I wasn't ready at my father's gravesite, at the private ceremony we held on a small Berkshire farm that I hadn't known Zero owned. We kept it small and private because the land wasn't zoned for a burial, but it's what our father wanted. We dug the grave ourselves, Sid, Zero, the Rabbi, Van Gogh, Jhochelle, and Karl Klaussen, who alternates between narcocorrido songs and those from his one and only album until Van Gogh complains that he'd like to "fuckin' hear something I know, you know, somethin' I can sing to."

We lit a fire nearby and shared hits off a massive joint while sitting on the plain pine coffin Zero made himself and stored out of sight behind the giant bins in his garage. The ground was cold and hard and we worked it with pickaxes and shovels, ignoring the tractor in the barn nearby. We worked into darkness, the western hills outlined in a sky of pink during the final moments of light. The digging and hacking brought on blisters and blood. It felt like penance. It felt right. When we were done, we planted a small maple above him. The Rabbi said the Mourner's Kaddish because for all our preparation, we weren't ready then.

According to Zero, we're ready now. We make the short walk to the temple together. When the time in the service comes, we fulfill our obligations as sons, bow our heads, and say the words.

FORTY-FOUR

I ring the doorbell at 34 Hall Avenue on a cold day in February, the sun shining bright and hard, causing the accumulated snow to melt off the rooftop and drip into clear sharp icicles that hang off the front porch like a predator's glass teeth.

I didn't ride my bike. Too cold for that. I don't think I'll ride again in winter if I can avoid it. Charlie can take the frigid shifts. Actually, he can take whatever shifts he decides since he's now a vested part-owner of Mercury Couriers. He'll have to get himself a new dispatcher, though. Solarte, who'd driven me and chooses to wait in the car, has installed Martha at her front desk, business picking up with recommendations that must be coming from Wells and Brill, though neither one has said a word about it.

Camilla Islas answers the door stepping directly out of a time machine. By all rights she should be nearly sixty years old but looks somewhere in her late twenties or early thirties.

"Zesty?" she says and notes my confusion. "I'll go get my mom. Come in. Have a seat."

Of course. Camilla Islas was pregnant when she disappeared.

"So," Camilla Islas says, sitting before me on a chair across from the couch. "What can I tell you that you don't already know?" The real Camilla Islas looks her age, gone thin, not soft the way some women do, but without the ravages I'd expected of a former heroin addict and alcoholic. Her hair is thin but dark where gray hasn't settled in, Islas not vain enough to color it. Or maybe she's just accepted what comes with age, wearing her hair as she's worn her new name and new life all these years.

"You can tell me what to call you," I say. "I still think of you as Camilla."

"So then call me Carrie, please. Camilla's been gone a long time."

"Okay. This visit's kind of more for my own closure than anything else, Carrie. You don't have anything to fear from me. I really just want to know about my father. Can you start with my father?"

She does. "Your father was a great guy. I'm sorry to hear of his passing, about the Alzheimer's. God, he lived, though, in those early days. Those were such crazy times, Zesty. In so many ways. Boston was a rock and roll hotbox, dangerous, thrilling, the city so different than it is now. I don't know why I'm so nostalgic about it, really. Boston would have killed me if it wasn't for your dad. Your dad sacrificed for me. Everything."

"How?"

"I was a full-blown junkie when Mass's album dropped. You could always find me at the Rat or the Channel, working at Spit, wherever there was music and cocaine and then finally heroin. All of a sudden it was heroin everywhere, and me and Karl we were hooked on it and on top of the world. My boyfriend was going to be the next . . ." Carrie looks off into the distance, maybe into the past, a small pool gathering in her eyes but not dropping.

"William, your dad, managed Mass, as I'm sure you know, and he'd done everything right with them, kept them humming even as the band began to fight among themselves as soon as they started headlining and the girls came and the drugs. It was a scene. Your dad kept them tight, cut that album that Zeppelin

heard and loved. It was all right there in front of them. Even with
the backlash over the whole Zeppelin ban, your dad understood
it was just a local rumble and as soon as they got out on the road,
as soon as the rest of the country heard them, they'd still break it
big. Karl was that good. The Dark Angel of Boston, they called
him. The Quantum Mechanic of Cool."

"And you were pregnant with his baby."

"I was. A strung-out junkie with a child growing inside her.
I knew I had to get out, but I didn't have the strength and Karl
was heading in the opposite direction. And losing control. Your
dad was the one who figured a way to get me out, but he knew
it had to be a forever plan. I don't know how he came up with
the paperwork, the new passport, and Carrie Chalmers's birth
certificate, but he did."

I knew how. His city hall, law enforcement, and FBI connections ran deep, my father possibly already a conduit of information for the Feds, working both sides of the street while
dodging traffic in the middle.

"And he faked your death."

"We'd planned it for the night of that show on the Cape. It
wasn't hard. We shot up after the show in the van but mine was
diluted next to nothing. And Karl had more than usual, your dad
saw to that. He risked giving him a hotshot, too much, but Karl
was a horse. The rest was easy. Your dad drove us into the marshes
off of East Boston, near Logan Airport. I can still hear the planes
in my head so close above us, their great white bellies with the
blinking red lights. It was very cinematic, I suppose. I was wrapped
in a sheet with a needle in my arm and Karl was in a stupor,
thrashing around in the reeds, throwing up. I just got up and
walked away to the car your dad had left earlier with keys in the
tire well. I got behind the wheel and drove off into a new life. Your
dad put the sheet in the hole, covered it as Karl puked up his guts,
and that was that."

Only it wasn't. Karl Klaussen and my father came under investigation as my father had suspected they would and he had planned for. He convinced Klaussen he was going to go down for Camilla's murder and spirited him away to Mexico and relied on his FBI contacts to protect him from Homicide Detectives Peter Polishuk and Eric Nichols.

"Your father sacrificed the record deal he could have signed with Mass, the name he could have made for himself in the music business. Your father loved music!" Carrie laughs and shakes her head. "And what a dancer! God, he was a crazy man!"

"But you broke the deal you had with him," I say. "You came back."

"That was his doing, too. The first time."

"The first time?" I'm confused. But then I'm not. "Hold on, what year did you come back the first time?"

"Nineteen eighty-six."

The year of her father's funeral.

"And then my mother got sick."

In 1993, the year the file went missing from Boston Police headquarters. Stolen by Peter Polishuk. Because my father brought Polishuk and Carrie together to show him that she was still alive. To explain to him what he'd done and why. So in turn, Polishuk stole the cold case file, either disposed of it himself or it really did burn in his house fire. He took his own public hit for not solving Camilla's "murder" and eventually retired. No wonder Polishuk was a happy man. He actually got a corpse back. As a homicide detective, I imagine it can't get any better than that.

"And when your mother got ill in ninety-three you and your daughter came back to town and you took care of her until she passed. But kept your new name and identity."

"It was so easy, Zesty, it was crazy. The whole neighborhood had flipped and there were practically no neighbors left who knew me, who knew my story." Except for the old lady across the way who Solarte and Klaussen initially dismissed as confused.

"As long as I kept out of the club scene and away from the bars, nobody knew who I was. And anyhow, even the clubs changed, a whole new generation came in. And now I'm just an old and forgotten rock and roller. I get a kick out of it, actually. I'll go out to eat and my waitress will have a sleeve of tattoos, a nose stud, thinking she's living that rock and roll life, and she's like 'More tea, dear?' like I'm just some old hag who's probably never even smoked a joint. Never lived. She has no idea. None at all." Camilla Islas brightens. "But how many people can say they visit their own grave every once in a while, Zesty? Not many, I'm sure. Really, no idea. Nobody has any idea at all."

And the same goes for Karl Klaussen, who finished up his real estate chores for his petrol-siphoning boss, maybe even buying up a few condos in the same buildings that the Russian billionaires were purchasing, those vacant dark apartments looking out over the New Boston like dark unblinking eyes, while everybody scurries around below just trying to carve out a living.

Alianna Solarte took Klaussen's money and declared it the cleanest cash she'd ever earned. If Carrie Chalmers wanted to let Karl know he had a daughter and hadn't played a role in killing her, it was up to her to decide where and when to deliver that news.

My job was done.

Unless you count spinning records for Anitra Tehran as work, which I sometimes do, her lack of knowledge of the Bosstown Sound always astounding me, and a reporter yet. But in the dark, in the night, the needle hissing on its final groove, forgotten and ignored, Anitra whispers to me as I hover above her on my forearms, our hips pressed together, her hair fanned out in a halo around her head; bright gold-flecked eyes piercing the cover of night, she whispers, "I know what you did for me."

And rises to my lips like smoke.

ACKNOWLEDGMENTS

With sincere gratitude for my children, Sam and Antonia, for showing great patience with Zesty, who dominated too many conversations and took up more than his fair share of space inside my head. Two more engaging, funny, insightful, tolerant, and open teenagers could not possibly exist on this planet.

To my mother, Devora Abramowitz, always the first reader and my go-to for wisdom and perspective.

To my father, Martin Abramowitz, for his humor and positivity in tough times.

To Rhoda Grill, warrior for justice.

To Blake Voss, dad number two, always there.

To Yosef and Susan, because they're the people who make this world a better place for others.

To Uncle Carl and Aunt Margie Abramowitz, who set the gold standard for love and devotion.

To Samantha Zukergood and Karen Richardson, for their keen editing eye, attention to detail, and patience with a writer who stretches deadlines.

To Tom Foley, family via friendship, always there when I need him.

To John Lockwood, last of the true renaissance men.

To Debra Stern, Bruce Tanner, Jamel and Terri Scott, Jerry Lester, Lorice Townsend, Harvey Zuckerman, Mailyn Irizarry, and the rest of my Amani family.

To Chris Remediani, who knows what it takes.

To Martha Pitts, way smarter than me.

To Meg Ruley and Rebecca Scherer of the Jane Rotrosen Agency, who make things happen.

In loving memory of my grandparents, Jerome and Lillian Gleich and Israel and Rose Abramowitz.

To the Monday-night poker crew: Eddie Brill, J. R. Havlan, Hank Gallo, Pat Dixon, Costaki Economopoulos, Dave Freed, Jacob Grill-Abramowitz, et al.; still no better place to hold a losing hand.